www.MinotaurBooks.com

The premier website for

the best in crime fiction:

Log on and learn more about:

The Labyrinth: Sign up for this monthly newsletter and get your crime fiction fix. Commentary author Q&A, hot new titles, and giveaways.

MomentsInCrime: It's no mystery what our authors are thinking. Each week, a new author blogs about their upcoming projects, special events, and more. Log on today to talk to your favorite authors. **www.MomentsInCrime.com**

GetCozy: The ultimate cozy connection. Find your favorite cozy mystery, grab a reading group guide, sign up for monthly giveaways, and more. ww.GetCozyOnline.com

www.minotaurbooks.com

ALSO BY CAROLYN HAINES

SARAH BOOTH DELANEY MYSTERIES

Bones of a Feather

Bone Appétit

Wishbones

Greedy Bones

Ham Bones

Bones to Pick

Hallowed Bones

Crossed Bones

Splintered Bones

Buried Bones

Them Bones

NOVELS

Revenant

Fever Moon

Penumbra

Judas Burning

Touched

Summer of the Redeemers

Summer of Fear

NONFICTION

My Mother's Witness: The Peggy Morgan Story

WIS⅄BONES

Carolyn Haines

St. Martin's Paperbacks

This is a work of fiction. All of the characters, organizations, and events portrayed in this novel are either products of the author's imagination or are used fictitiously.

WISHBONES

Copyright © 2008 by Carolyn Haines.
Excerpt from *Greedy Bones* copyright © 2009 by Carolyn Haines.

For information address St. Martin's Press, 175 Fifth Avenue, New York, NY 10010.

Library of Congress Catalog Card Number: 2008013402

ISBN: 0-312-37709-6
EAN: 978-0-312-37709-0

Printed in the United States of America

St. Martin's Press hardcover edition / July 2008
St. Martin's Paperbacks edition / June 2009

St. Martin's Paperbacks are published by St. Martin's Press, 175 Fifth Avenue, New York, NY 10010.

10 9 8 7 6 5 4

For John and Judy Adams—my talented friends

ACKNOWLEDGMENTS

Growing up in Lucedale, Mississippi, I had several advantages, but one of the biggest is that my family told stories. My mother, father, and grandmother were all accomplished creators of tall tales, spun out with pace and drama. The fact that we all leaned a bit toward ghost stories was also helpful—except on those dark nights when the old house I grew up in began to creak and talk to me.

My love for "the possible" in each story and in life comes from these people, who enriched my imagination every night with a bedtime story. Good or bad, I am a product of the things they instilled in me.

I also have to thank my agent, Marian Young, who shares my love of dogs, cats, horses, and a good yarn. And Kelley Ragland, my editor, who has followed me from the dark side to the more humorous stories of the Mississippi Delta mysteries. Her instincts are right on target and because of her, I end up with a better book.

The entire St. Martin's team has been terrific. Matt Martz makes the day-to-day business of being a writer easier to bear. Lauren Manzella in the PR office, the entire art department, and the library team—thank you all. This has been a great publishing experience, and I'm looking forward to the next book.

I also have to thank Aleta Boudreaux, Alice Jackson, Renee Paul, Stephanie Chisholm, Susan Tanner, and Gary and Shannon Walker. These members of the Deep South Writers Salon have been great readers. And good friends. Talented in their own rights, they've shared their time to read my manuscript.

A special thanks goes to Suzy Dutton, who won the Bones naming contest. She was the first person to suggest *Wishbones* as a title. And for all of her hard work, she ends up a glamorous movie star who . . . well, you have to read the book to find out.

In the past few years, I've lost several of my wonderful family of four-legged friends. Sweetie Pie, my valiant hound who fought diabetes and other illnesses, and the beautiful and fabulous Maybelline, who stood in for Sweetie at book signings and photo shoots wearing sunglasses and a scarf, have both died. Sweetie was twelve, and she lived far longer than anyone expected. Maybelline was seventeen. Both leave a hole in the fabric of my day.

Younger dogs and cats, many of them abandoned after Hurricane Katrina, have found their way to my home. Down here in the South, there are no laws requiring neutering of pets. But I urge you to please spay and neuter, and to adopt from your local shelter. You never know when you'll find your own canine or feline star.

If you wish to write me, please do so at cehaines@mind spring.com. And visit my Web site at www.carolynhaines .com. There's no telling what shenanigans we'll be up to there.

WIS✦BONES

CHAPTER ONE

Spring is not the time to leave the South. This is the season when Mississippi is truly the belle of the ball, dressed in vibrant azalea frills, white lace dogwoods, and bridal wreath. The promise of money drifts on the dirt-scented breeze that blows across freshly planted soil. For those of us with Irish blood and the heritage of farming, this is the beginning of the gambling season, when futures will rest on the unpredictable weather and the possibility of a good crop.

My great-great-grandmother Alice planted and farmed the land around Dahlia House. She stood each spring, hands on her hips, determining what to plant, where, how much. One wrong decision could mean the loss of the land—which to a Delaney is equal to the loss of our soul. Year after year she bet and won, hanging on to the plantation against all odds. I won't be planting this year. Like Alice, I'm taking a gamble. Not on crops, but on my own talent.

Sitting on the front porch of Dahlia House with my mother's battered red "good-luck" suitcase at my feet, I'm going to my new life.

Whenever I think of the future, my stomach jigs and lurches. As hard as that is, it's better than thinking of the past and all that is gone and can never be again. Somewhere between the two is the lost dream of Sheriff Coleman Peters and a family of our own, living here in my ancestral home, raising our children, and continuing on with a life that once sounded near perfect.

"He was never less than married." The voice drifts to me from inside the open front door.

Jitty, the resident haint at Dahlia House, has come, at last, to tell me farewell. I was afraid I'd have to go without saying good-bye.

"Now that I'm leaving, do you think Coleman will divorce Connie?" I asked her. In the year I've been home, I gave my heart to Coleman but never my body.

"Did you really want him to leave his wife to be with you?"

I drummed my fingernails on the gray floorboards of the porch and wished for a cigarette. Instead, I pulled out a stick of gum. Jitty stabbed too close to home. I didn't want him if I had to take him from someone else. I didn't want him if I had to "take" him at all. Love has to be a willing surrender.

If I'd insisted on action, if I'd seduced or demanded that we consummate our love, I could have snared him. Instead, we'd both played by honor rules and tempted fate to snatch away the offered gift of our relationship. We'd hesitated, and he who hesitates is lost.

"I guess what I wanted was for Coleman to leave Connie and then find me."

"Your life got out of order, Sarah Booth. Sometimes it happens that way."

I turned to see if Jitty was being consoling or annoying, and I almost swallowed the gum I was chewing. Jitty came swooping toward me, her eyes wide and glazed with madness framed by lashes at least two inches long. She wore a dress with shoulder pads and her hair was smoothed into perfection.

"Camera! Lights! Action! I'm ready for my close-up, Mr.

DeMille," she said as she came down the front steps of Dahlia House. She swiveled and gave a low bow. "How was that, Sarah Booth?"

"An excellent imitation of Gloria Swanson." I applauded. "Come out to Hollywood with me, Jitty." I'd been trying to work on her to make the trip with me, but she wouldn't commit. In fact, she ignored my request and generally took a powder. Now, at least, she was listening.

She sauntered back to the steps and dropped down beside me on the wooden porch. "I don't think so."

"Then you'll stay here and keep the home front safe while I'm gone, right?" I was taking Sweetie Pie with me, and Reveler, my horse, was already grazing peacefully in the lush pastures at my friend Lee's. This trip to Tinseltown wasn't permanent, but it was my shot at being a movie star.

Jitty lifted an arm and the silver bracelets she'd worn since the first day I met her jingled merrily down her wrist. In contrast, her voice was low and sad. "Sarah Booth, we need to talk."

Her words sent an Arctic chill down my entire body, and suddenly I realized that since I'd been cleared of Renata Trovaioli's murder only a few weeks ago, Jitty and I hadn't really talked. My life had whirl-winded from clearing my name to going to Hollywood to star in a movie with Graf Milieu. Everything was moving way too fast for me.

"What is it? You will stay here, in Dahlia House, and watch over everything, won't you?"

Jitty stared straight ahead, sighting on the driveway and whatever memory that held her undivided attention. "I'm not sure that's the right thing to do."

She was freaking me out. "What do you mean?"

She turned to me, and her smile made tears spring to my eyes. I'd never seen anything so lovely or so sad. "Remember the first time we met?" she asked.

How could I forget that? She'd nearly scared me out of

my shoes. But she wasn't interested in funny stories of the past, she was making a point. "Go on," I requested.

"I came to you because you needed me. When you first came home, after all the loss you'd suffered and after things didn't work out in New York, I came because you were alone, without the guidance of family. Dahlia House was a big responsibility, and potentially a huge burden."

"It's still big. It's a really big house, and I still need you." I talked so fast my words were almost incoherent. I had this horrible idea that she was going to say it was time for her to leave, to go on to that Ghostly Reward in the Sky. She was already dead, but a little thing like that wouldn't stop Jitty once she made up her mind.

"Dahlia House hasn't shrunk, Sarah Booth, but you've grown."

Jitty wasn't one to hand out a compliment, and I didn't want to hear this. "Not that much. I haven't grown hardly at all. I'm still scared and alone and—"

"You're taking a shot at your dream, Sarah Booth. Now that's something." The curve of her cheek lifted as she smiled. "Your mama would be proud of you. She is proud of you. And your daddy and Aunt Loulane, too."

My throat closed with emotion, and I swallowed and fought for control of my tears. If I started crying now, I might not quit. "Mama would want you to go to Hollywood and look out for me. Mama will be mad if you leave me now."

Her laughter was clear and sparkling, and for a moment I thought I'd won her over.

"You sure are the devil to play that card, but it won't work. Guilt never worked very well on me."

"What would you do if you didn't stay in Dahlia House? Where would you go?" There were so many things about the Great Beyond that I didn't understand. Normally, Jitty refused to discuss it. I'd asked her once if she could cross over, why my parents couldn't visit me. They'd died when I was twelve, and I'd never truly overcome that sense of abandonment. When I wasn't haunted by Jitty, I was haunted by that.

"I don't know, Sarah Booth. Being dead is . . . a bit vague sometimes. I'm here with you right now. After that, maybe it's just a long sleep."

"You don't sleep! You're always rambling around at night. That's when you do your best haunting." I stood up and began to pace. "I do need you, Jitty. You can't just disappear."

"I love you, Sarah Booth. Remember that, no matter what."

I felt the feathery tickle of what might have been a kiss on my cheek. I reached for her, grasping only air.

"Jitty, promise me that you'll be here when I come home." The words choked me. "Jitty!" I lost all efforts to control my emotions. "Jitty!"

"Be strong, like your parents taught you." Her chuckle was hollow, merely an echo. "And break a leg."

The last bit of her shimmered away, and I was left on the front porch drowning in the sweet smell of wisteria that blew up on the wind.

Down the driveway I saw Graf Milieu's car headed my way. He was picking me up for our flight to Los Angeles. I stood, wiping the tears from my face, walked to the front door, and closed it. The sound of the lock tumbling into place was empty and final.

Picking up my suitcase, I turned to meet my future while my past, once again, broke my heart. What would my life be like without Jitty? I couldn't bear to think about it.

On the plane, Graf did his best to entertain me, but he was no competition for my companion riding shotgun—self-doubt. Through some of his movie connections, we'd managed to buy a first-class seat for Sweetie Pie, who took to the skies with the aplomb of a seasoned traveler. Her gentle howl brought immediate attention from the efficient stewardess, Moesha, assigned to take care of us.

"Are you three movie stars?" Moesha asked.

"Only the dog," Graf answered. "We're taking her out for a starring role in *Lassie and the Hound*."

"I can see where she'll be big box office." Moesha gave Sweetie's ears a gentle caress. "You can bet I'll be in line for a ticket as soon as the movie comes out."

When she walked away, I punched Graf in the ribs, hard. "Liar."

"Maybe not," he said, grinning. "Along with your screen test, I've booked one for Sweetie. We might as well employ the entire family. Just think, Sarah Booth, we can work four or six months and the rest of the year we can do what we want."

For the first time that morning, I felt the dark cloud of despair lift. I'd left behind a life I loved, but it wasn't gone. It hadn't evaporated. And neither had Jitty. Or Tinkie. Or any of my friends. They would be in Zinnia when I returned.

Graf gave me a hug and signaled Moesha. "Bring my lady a spicy Bloody Mary. I think she just decided to enjoy the life of a movie star."

"Coming right up." Moesha leaned down to whisper. "I'll bring a bone for Sweetie Pie. On this plane, you all get the star treatment."

"What do you think?" Graf held me against his side as we stood in the driveway of the most incredible house I'd ever seen. Hanging off the side of Lettohatchie Canyon, the house was clean, modern stucco and steel with a wraparound porch. The view was incredible—mountains highlighted in glowing pinks and oranges to the east and visible to the west, the Pacific Ocean, where a cresting moon hung over the dark waters. We'd spent the entire day traveling to California and arrived just in time for a spectacular sunset.

"I've never seen anything like this," I told him.

"I thought about a beach house in Malibu, but I thought this would be better, and then Bobby Joe Taylor said we could have his place for a few months, until we decided where we wanted to settle."

Stepping away from his side, I entered the house. I hadn't committed, in my heart, to settling anywhere in California. Zinnia was my home, and even though I'd only been gone for twelve hours, I missed it.

"Why don't you call Tinkie?" Graf asked. "I'll take Sweetie for a walk and then open a bottle of wine. I had some salmon steaks and a spinach and artichoke salad delivered, so dinner is ready whenever we are."

I faced him, taking in the leading-man good looks. I'd been very much in love with him when I lived in New York. Now the shoe was on the other foot, and I wasn't certain what I felt for him. Sharing a house might be tricky, but he'd already put my suitcase in my bedroom. He'd promised no pressure. "Thank you, Graf."

"Your screen test is tomorrow at eleven. I'll drive you, and you're going to do great." He stepped forward and kissed my forehead. "Call your girlfriend. Sweetie and I'll be back in half an hour."

I watched the two of them head down the winding driveway as I pulled my cell phone from my purse. Tinkie might be the perfect medicine for what ailed me.

Her phone didn't even ring once before she snatched it up. "Sarah Booth," she said, her voice breathy, "are you okay?"

"I'm fine." It was only half a lie. "I'm sorry I asked you all to stay away when I left. I simply couldn't have stood it to say good-bye to you and Cece and Millie."

"We understand. And as soon as you're settled in and working, we want to fly out and watch. Millie bought a copy of *The Hollywood Snoop* today and there was a big story about you and Graf and how you two are the leading candidates to play Matty and Ned in the remake of *Body Heat*. They had a great photo of you."

"I'll bet."

"How are things with Graf?" she asked.

"He's being a real gentleman. No pressure." I laughed. "He's taking care of everything."

"Everything?" There was a note of mischief in her voice.

"Not that." I tried to match her foolishness, but she must have heard the sadness.

"I saw Coleman this morning. I told him you were gone."

"And?"

"He said he was happy for you. He said that he saw your talent in *Cat on a Hot Tin Roof* and knew you'd leave Zinnia again."

The anger that touched me was pure and hot. "What a bastard! So I've chosen career over him. That lets him off the hook, doesn't it? He couldn't manage to get himself disentangled from a crazy woman who pretended to be pregnant *and* produce a brain tumor just to manipulate him, but I left to follow my career."

"Whoa, there!" Tinkie pulled me up short.

"Sorry. It's just so unfair."

"Sarah Booth, you do have an amazing talent. Whatever you decide to do with it is up to you. Remember, you can only paddle your own canoe. Coleman has to paddle his."

And that was the perfect answer. "Thank you. I am now paddling mine. My screen test is at eleven tomorrow."

"That'll be one o'clock here in Zinnia. I'll rally the troops and we'll light a candle for you in Millie's while we're eating burgers and fries."

My mouth watered at the thought of one of Millie's burgers. Now that I was in Hollywood, it would be a long time before I could indulge in such foods. The camera loved to see the bone structure beneath the flesh. "Eat a piece of apple pie for me."

"That I can do." She was laughing when she said good-bye. "You keep your strength up. See you soon."

CHAPTER TWO

"Magnifico!" Federico Marquez's voice rang out through the studio, and though the scene was over, I couldn't pull my gaze away from Graf. His dark hair, so silken, fell forward, almost but not quite covering his compelling eyes.

We were lying on the floor of a studio set, acting the scene where Ned overpowers Matty with his passion, and her last restraint snaps. The teasing scent of Graf's cologne clouded my senses as the warm weight of his body pressed against mine. He leaned closer, the desire so evident in his eyes that I felt a blush creep up my neck, and I wasn't a girl prone to flushing.

"Cut, Graf!" Federico laughed as he grasped Graf's shoulder. "You look as if you mean to devour her."

"I do." Graf reluctantly eased off me and then offered his hand to pull me to my feet. It took a few seconds for me to become fully aware of my surroundings again, so deeply had I been captured by Graf's eyes.

"Sarah Booth, you are incredible!" Federico kissed both of my cheeks in the French style. "You are a star. You were born to make love to the camera."

"And me," Graf said under his breath but loud enough for all to hear.

A twitter rippled among the crew, and to my chagrin, I felt

another flush move along my skin. Graf noticed and gave me a knowing look. So far, he'd played the game by my rule book—no kissing or making love. But the movie scene had called for a kiss, and he'd delivered one that seared me to the tips of my toes and brought back memories of a time in my life when I'd lived for his embraces and the dream of being a star.

Sweetie Pie ambled onto the set and gave Federico a big sloppy kiss. "I think we must find a role for *el perro*." He lifted Sweetie's ears, holding them out from her head. She bore a strange resemblance to Dumbo, the flying elephant of the childhood story. "She is extraordinary." He turned to the scriptwriter, Ron O'Gorman. "Can we write her in?"

"Sure, Federico. Whatever you say." He shot me a glare as he walked away.

"Hollywood can't function without writers, but no one respects them," Graf whispered in my ear. "They're all so surly."

"I see his point. The original version of the movie didn't have a dog in it." I'd only seen the movie about a billion times.

"If Federico wants a dog, this one will have a dog. Let's hope Sweetie can pull it off. I wonder if we can get her in the union?"

I rolled my eyes and noticed that Federico was watching the two of us. He came over and took my hand.

"I want to see the takes, but I know how good you're going to be on screen, Sarah Booth. You're perfect to play Matty. And Graf is an exceptional Ned. The two of you will be hotter than Kathleen and Bill."

"I've loved this part for years," I admitted.

Federico put his hand on each of our shoulders. "You two share a magic that the camera relishes. Be careful. Love can turn to hate in an instant in this town. Competition, jealousy, betrayal. The camera will see all of that, too, so treat each other with kindness and respect. It's a lesson I've learned the hard way." His eyes reflected sadness and regret before he turned away.

"Federico, are you ready for lunch?"

We all turned to see a woman with legs that seemed five feet long come walking onto the set. She was beautiful, with silvery gray eyes and blond hair that swung about her face with each step. I recognized her instantly. Jovan. She was the number one Victoria's Secret model and the "sexiest woman alive" according to *People* magazine.

Federico made the introductions. Jovan, who was at least twenty years younger, was his main squeeze. In Hollywood, magnetism was often created by equal power. A man Jovan's age would find it difficult to meet her head-on. She was too beautiful, too sexy, too much for a young man's ego to deal with. Federico wasn't threatened by either her beauty or success. Hollywood was already teaching me some valuable lessons.

Federico put his hand on Graf's arm. "I need to shoot some footage of you with Jovan after lunch. The chemistry between you must be on the screen."

The tiny little flame of jealousy caught me unprepared. Jovan was so incredibly beautiful. I hadn't realized she had a part in the movie.

Federico must have caught my look because he turned to me. "Jovan is going to play Matty's sister-in-law," he explained. "She is beautiful, yes? A perfect complement to the dark sexuality you exude, Sarah Booth."

A bit soothed, I whistled up my dog and decided that I would take my insecurities to the ocean. If I was going to work in this town, I had to get a grip on my fears. In New York, I'd always played it a little too safe, a little too reserved. The stage demanded big gestures. Film, so much more intimate, was perfect for me—unless I let my own self-doubt erode my confidence.

I gave Graf a kiss and told him I was taking Sweetie to lunch at the Vineyard, a little place in Malibu that I'd heard so much about from Millie. Stars dined there on a regular basis. I was smiling when I left the building and stepped into a perfect, cloudless California day. I put an Eagles disk in the CD player as I edged the Thunderbird convertible, circa 1957, that Graf had rented for me onto the highway. Sweetie wore her sunglasses and a scarf. We reeked of Hollywood success.

The Vineyard was bare of celebrity but offered the best green salad I'd ever eaten. Sweetie was served grilled free-range chicken cubes, and after lunch, I took her to the beach. The sand was coarser, duller than the sugar-white powder that comprised the Gulf of Mexico beaches with which I was familiar. Instead of the gentle Gulf swells, this surf pounded the shore. While Sweetie ran into the waves and came out to shake the cold water all over me, I stayed well on land. The Pacific wasn't a body of water to tease. Like so much of California, it seemed designed for pleasure, but there was a definite undertow of danger.

When we got back up the mountain to the house, I was surprised to find the front door unlocked. I was certain Graf had locked it. I checked throughout the house, but there was nothing that I could find missing.

Perhaps the owner had come to retrieve some personal item. Bobby Joe Taylor was in the vicinity, holed up somewhere on Sunset Boulevard with his girlfriend, writing another brilliant script. He said he didn't like to taint the ambiance of his home with actual work, so he loaned his home out to friends while he finished a project.

It wasn't until I went in the bathroom that I found the note, written in bloodred lipstick. "Pack your hick ass up and head home."

Instead of frightening me, the message made me furious. I got the glass cleaner and a roll of paper towels and instantly scrubbed it away. It was only after I'd finished that I realized my actions were rash. Someone had broken into the house to leave that message. It might have been a smarter move to call the law and at least establish a pattern of craziness if the author of the note decided to act again.

Too late for smart thoughts. The lipstick was gone, except for the smears in the paper towels. I hadn't been in town long enough to make real enemies, and if jealousy was the motivation, the person had made his or her point. Whoever it was would probably never come back. I took my script and went onto the porch to study my lines.

Graf returned that afternoon with an armload of flowers and an invitation to the spring party at Michael Mainheim's. It was the place to see and be seen, and Graf cajoled and teased me into saying I would attend. He'd never been so tender and kind, and when I glanced up at him suddenly, I saw worry and compassion in his gaze.

"I know what you've given up to come here," he said, his hand warm on my arm. "I never really had a place to call home, a place where I belonged. Zinnia is your town, and you left it to come here and act with me. I don't think anyone has ever done something like that for me."

I'd come for myself as well as Graf, but there was no sense spoiling it for him with full disclosure. And I had a party to get ready for.

I had the beautiful dress Tinkie had so generously bought for me in Zinnia, a winter white creation touched with stardust sparkles that fit me to perfection. The idea of the party, while a bit intimidating, was also exciting. My first Hollywood bash.

As I got ready, Graf filled me in on details. He was borrowing Bobby Joe's tuxedo, and for this single evening, we decided to leave Sweetie home; she was exhausted from her play in the surf. As we slipped out the door, I caught a glimpse of myself in a window. My heart stopped. I'd never looked so much like my mother as I did in that dress with my hair swept up and my lipstick a peachy mango.

"What is it?" Graf asked.

"Just a ghost," I answered, my thoughts flying to Jitty. Where was she? Was she waiting at Dahlia House, or had she gone on?

"Are you okay?"

I'd chosen, and I refused to allow the road not taken to drag me down. "I'm fine." I put a smile on my face. I would make it so.

"If you don't want to go to the party . . ."

"But I do. See and be seen. This is part of it, Graf. In for a penny, in for a pound. I'll do everything I can to make this happen for both of us."

He bent to kiss my temple. "Sometimes you astound me." He took my arm and led me to the car, a Lexus sedan that he'd chosen for his own vehicle.

As he whisked me down the mountain toward the galaxy of lights that spread to the horizon, I closed my eyes and dared to dream. One of my worst habits was that I found it hard to believe when something really wonderful happened in my life. I hid from joy, because I feared it would be taken away from me. While Graf drove, I visualized the movie and all the pleasure of a dream realized. When we arrived at the party, I was ready to act the star.

The Mainheim house was everything I'd heard it to be. Michael Mainheim had done the music for a number of fabulous movies, and I knew Federico was courting him for our movie. A Mainheim soundtrack would be icing on the cake. From the looks of it, though, money wouldn't be the draw that brought M.M., as he preferred to be called, to the project. He had money, and he spent lavishly. The gathering in front of me was testimony to that.

The party was a star-studded gala—and everyone knew my name. Scarlet Johansson and Brad Pitt welcomed me to Hollywood as I walked toward the bar. I was green and taking it all in like a tourist. This was an A-list party, and I was a part of it all.

"I hear the screen test sizzled," Brad said. "Congratulations."

"Thank you." I moved on, hoping for a bar that stocked something as common as Jack Daniel's. I wasn't disappointed. A huge bottle sat on the shelf with my name on it.

"M.M. keeps a bottle for each guest," the barkeep explained. "He said that was your drink, and so the bottle is marked for you."

"Thanks." That was the password of the day.

Graf was busy talking with Ben Affleck and Matt Damon, and I eased upstairs, hoping for a bit of solitude and a place to take a breather. This stargazing was a bit wearing.

The house was a treasure trove of art. I took my time examining the paintings and sculptures as I looked for a bathroom. While I was staring at what had to be a real Picasso, I heard voices raised in anger coming from the room beyond. The door was opened a crack, and I started to walk by when I recognized Federico's voice.

"You must calm down," he said with a degree of forcefulness.

"I'm not a child. Don't you dare condescend to me. Don't you tell me what I must do!"

The second voice was female, and not that of Jovan, who had a cool, clear tone with the hint of some underlying accent that I couldn't place. This woman was one hundred percent California.

"Suzy, I'm sorry. This role was written for Sarah Booth Delaney. Something else just right for you will come along."

"You bastard!" There was the sound of a slap. "You promised me. You said I would be the perfect Matty. You said the role was mine."

Federico sighed loudly enough for me to hear. "That was six years ago, Suzy. I couldn't get the backing then, remember? I tried, but after all the things I'd been through, no one would put money on me."

"And now, because of me, you're in a position to make this movie and I'm cut out of it because of that slutty underwear model."

I'd finally figured out the woman's voice. Suzy Dutton. Big, big news when she was in her early thirties. She'd been the hottest property in Hollywood. Now, at forty, her flame was burning blue.

"Jovan has nothing to do with this."

"When you were in my bed, I was everything to you."

"Time passes, Suzy. You can't lay that at Jovan's door. We were finished when I met her."

"And soon you'll be done with her and screwing that Mississippi bitch, Sarah Bootless Delancy, or whatever her name is."

"You should go home and sleep. You look exhausted."

"I look forty, you son of a bitch. Not exhausted, not sick, not crazy. I look my age, and that's the biggest sin of all in this sick town."

I ducked into the offset doorway of another bedroom just as Suzy slammed out of the bedroom. I had no time to hide. The moment she passed the doorway, she saw me.

"You eavesdropping redneck bitch!" She drew back her fist to slug me, but I caught her hand and easily held it.

"I was looking for the bathroom." Why was I explaining my actions to a rude, mean actress? Maybe because Suzy Dutton had been a favorite of mine. I'd spent many a dark hour in a movie theater pulled into the characters she created.

"Did you hear enough to know what's going to happen to you? Federico will work you until you start to age, and then he'll cast you off and find someone younger and fresher." Her lip curled in a near perfect Elvis snarl. "Enjoy it while it lasts."

She pulled free of my grasp and stormed off down the hallway. When I chanced a look at the room where Federico remained, the door was closed. I couldn't be certain if he'd heard my encounter with Suzy or not. Federico was my boss.

I didn't really need to know about his love life. But at least I had a pretty good idea of who'd written in lipstick on the mirror. Suzy Dutton was thoroughly pissed off, but she wasn't a serious threat.

CHAPTER THREE

The moon hung in the western sky as I sipped the glass of wine Graf had brought me. Federico had only needed Graf on the set today, so I'd been able to stay on the mountain and explore with Sweetie Pie a few of the hiking trails that led down into the canyon. This Hollywood life was working on my hound, and she snored softly at my feet.

"This is delicious," I told him. It was very good wine, like everything else that seemed to come so easily to Californians.

Graf took a seat on the sofa and patted the cushion next to him. It was an invitation I wanted to take, so I eased into the nook of his arm.

"How did it go on the set?" I asked. I'd spent a lot of my hiking time imagining what was happening on the set.

"Mostly I heard everyone sing your praises, but I basked in the reflected glory." He kissed the top of my head. "I saw the screen test, Sarah Booth. You're amazing."

"Because of you." It was true. Graf made me feel safe enough to let myself go.

"Nonsense. We have chemistry, but you'll be great no matter who you're playing opposite. By the way, we have to be on the set at nine tomorrow."

"Let me get dinner finished." I'd driven down to this wonderful little store where everything was fresh and organic. "We're having asparagus and grilled tuna steaks. They even had a nice bone for Sweetie. I think she's already buried it in the canyon."

I got up and headed to the kitchen. It was a pleasure to cook in a space that was well designed, clean, perfectly lighted. His voice stopped me in the doorway.

"Be careful with Sweetie. There are coyotes in the canyon. Maybe mountain lions." I turned to see if he was teasing me, but his face showed sincerity. He signaled me back to the sofa, and I eased onto his lap. "And you be careful, too," he whispered against my neck, his breath sending chills of pleasure over me.

I yearned to kiss him, really kiss him, but I stood up and started back to the kitchen. I hadn't allowed myself to grieve over Coleman. I'd pushed back all of my hurt and disappointment and loss, because I was afraid if I confronted it, I would fall apart and never find the pieces to pull myself back together.

So Graf was too soon. No matter the physical attraction, if I cared about him, and about myself, I would give my heart a bit of time to heal.

"We'll be ready to eat in a flash," I told him. This cooking was so different from the way I'd grown up. I was still getting the hang of it, but I was a quick study when I wanted to be.

The tuna was marinating, and I had begun chopping fresh artichoke hearts for the salad when I heard Sweetie Pie baying on the porch. She had a lovely voice, all deep throat and warble. There is nothing better than the song of a hound, and I paused in my dicing to listen. Her cry went from lovely to aggressive, and I heard the scrabble of claws on the floor.

"Hey! Sweetie! Come back."

Graf burst into the kitchen. "Sweetie just took off outside. I'm afraid she's headed down into the canyon."

I'd never considered the coyotes a real threat—until I saw Graf's face. He was worried. "Let me get a light."

I turned off the stove, picked up a flashlight and Windbreaker, and headed outside with Graf. The night was brisk, the wind cutting through the canyon from the beach with the speed of a runaway train.

Beyond us, somewhere along the trail that led down into the darkness, I heard Sweetie Pie's baying mixed with an angry bark.

"We'll break our necks trying to get down that cliff at night," I told Graf.

"She's on the trail of something. I can hear her going deeper into the canyon."

Standing beside Graf on the lip of the cliff, I felt him tense. "What is it?" I couldn't see anything.

"Do you smell that?" he asked.

I inhaled and caught the tang of something burning. Wildfire! I'd heard about the California fires fed by the brisk Pacific breezes. The stories had always terrified me. There was nothing more frightening than the images of hungry flames raging up the ravines and over the mountains of the western states.

"Look!" Graf pointed down into the canyon. A dancing flame devil leaped up a hillside, shooting high in the pitch-black ravine.

"I'll call the sheriff." I dashed inside and placed the 911 emergency call, then hurried back out to Graf, who was frantically calling Sweetie.

The smell of burning brush and trees was distinctive on the wind, and far in the distance, I could hear my hound baying as she chased something. It sounded as if she was heading straight into the fire.

"Sweetie Pie!" I put all of my heart into the call for her. As I started down the trail, Graf pulled me back.

"She's a smart dog. She'll be okay." He put his arm around me, offering the comfort of his body and his words.

"She's a Mississippi dog. She doesn't know about wildfires and mountain lions." My heart was pounding while I could only stand helplessly by.

"Dogs are a lot smarter than people give them credit. Especially Sweetie Pie. And remember, wild creatures are afraid of fire. I'd say the only danger she faces now is the threat of being trapped by the blaze. She knows the way back up the trail. She'll be along any minute."

He was trying to comfort me, and I tried not to cry as I watched the flames build into a tower and begin to creep toward us.

A local fire station was only a mile below us on the main road. I knew because I'd driven past and seen the firefighters, all buff and tanned, playing volleyball in a court beside the station. I heard their siren as they came to the house. There was really no other place to take a stand and fight the fire. We were in an isolated area with no other houses around for at least five miles.

The truck pulled in along with a green and white patrol car marked with the sheriff's insignia and a van with a TV camera crew. I spoke with the reporters while Graf told the fire inspector what we knew.

While the firemen worked to stage a fire barrier down the ravine from the house, I answered the reporter's repeated questions in a monotone. I no longer heard Sweetie's bark or bay, and a hole the size of Kansas was opening in my heart. I should never have brought Sweetie to Hollywood. I should've left her with Tinkie and Chablis, the little dustmop Yorkie who was Sweetie's best friend.

The camera crew packed up and left, and I rejoined Graf and the fire chief.

"Why don't you folks go back in?" the fire chief suggested. "The smoke is getting thick here, and if there's any danger, we'll let you know in plenty of time to evacuate. It looks like we've found a good natural barrier to corral the blaze, though."

Graf took my hand and led me inside, where we stood on the porch, supper forgotten, and listened to the shouts of the firemen and watched the blaze draw ever closer.

"She's okay," Graf said, knowing that my thoughts were on my hound. "Sweetie knows how much you love her. She wouldn't risk herself."

I wanted to ask him why it was that everything I loved died, but I knew how terribly melodramatic such a question would sound. "Sweetie is smart." I said it aloud. Once again I was confronted with my own fears, and I was determined to master them. "She's plenty smart, and she'll be here any minute."

The words were barely out of my mouth when I saw her, framed in the darkness by the orange blaze.

"Sweetie! Sweetie Pie!" I dashed out onto the lawn, causing several firemen to look at me as if I'd lost my mind. I didn't care. "Sweetie!" She ran into my arms, a scrap of blue material in her mouth.

"What is that?" I took it from her and recognized it as the type of material used in athletic apparel.

Graf had followed me out and he bent to examine it. "Someone must have lost a jacket or something down in the ravine." He gave Sweetie's ears a rumple. "What say I finish cooking dinner and we can eat and keep an eye on the fire?"

Clutching my hound's collar, I nodded. "Sounds like a plan." Together the three of us walked into the house where we watched until an hour later, when the firemen finished extinguishing the flames.

Sweetie slept in the next morning while Graf and I went to work. Moviemaking can be a tedious affair. Except for the brief times when I was needed in a scene, I was free to roam the sound stage and explore costume potential with Dallas Brown, the designer. I'd been dreading the fitting sessions, but though Dallas tut-tutted at the size of my waist, she was congenial and merry and filled with wisecracks and fun.

Everyone at the studio had heard about the wildfire, and after I repeated my personal experience with it about six times, I'd begun to forget the terror of it and think what a great tale it made. I was beginning to really enjoy my place in the community of moviemakers when my cell phone rang.

"Ms. Delaney?" the male voice was clipped and businesslike.

"This is she." Aunt Loulane had taught me impeccable telephone manners.

"This is Sheriff Grady King. I've just received the fire report on the Lettohatchie Canyon blaze. It was arson. I'd like a word with you and Mr. Milieu."

"The blaze was set?" Who in his right mind would start a blaze in the tinder land of California? Thousands of acres could have been burned, homes destroyed, wildlife killed.

"That's right. It's definitely arson."

"Graf and I have no idea who would do such a thing. We've only been staying at Bobby Joe Taylor's house a few days. We're guests."

"I'll drop by about five this evening."

"But—" I didn't get a chance to protest. He'd hung up. And it was only after he'd done so that I remembered the lipstick message on the mirror. I should have reported it. As it was, I hadn't even mentioned it to Graf.

"Are you okay, Sarah Booth?" Dallas asked. She was holding a slender, short skirt and a pair of spike heels that looked to be my size.

"Apparently the fire last night was an arson."

"Oh, my." She frowned. "Surely they don't think the fire was meant to harm you." Her face brightened. "I'll bet some gal went after Bobby Joe Taylor. He's got a bad reputation with the women. Likes to love 'em and leave 'em, or so I've heard."

Sweet relief swept over me. The message on the mirror could as easily have been for Bobby Joe, calling him a hick and telling him to get out of town. He was from Alabama, and the hick title fit him as well as me. Even better, perhaps, if Dallas was right and he made a habit of rolling over people's feelings.

That thought sustained me through the rest of the work day. When Graf and I drove up the mountain to the house that afternoon, we found Sheriff Grady King waiting for us.

He was a handsome man—no surprise in a county where looks are part of a person's résumé. Tall, lean, with an elegant mustache, King's sharp gray eyes took in every relevant detail. His gaze shifted from Graf to me to our left hands to the house and Sweetie Pie's nose poking up at a window.

"You say you're visiting here?" he asked without even an introduction.

Graf went through the whole spiel about how we were borrowing Bobby Joe Taylor's house while we were getting ready to film. King didn't make a single note but listened with full attention. There were things about him that brought Coleman to mind, and I snuffed out the attending emotions that came up.

Graf gave him Bobby Joe's contact number, and we were about to walk inside when I turned back.

"Someone broke into the house two days ago, while we were at the studio. They left a message in red lipstick." I repeated the words exactly. "I was so angry I cleaned them up before I even thought."

I found myself caught between dual looks of concern and consternation.

"You didn't mention this," Graf said without even an attempt to hide the accusation in his tone.

"I figured the message was for Bobby Joe. I mean someone who had a key to the house." I shrugged. "I just assumed it was one of his ex-girlfriends who was mad. Bobby Joe is from Alabama and a reputed rounder. He could be called a hick as easily as me."

Sheriff King was strangely quiet, another habit that re-minded me of a Mississippi sheriff. "Would anyone leave such a message for you?" he asked me at last.

I was about to answer that Suzy Dutton might be a little pissed that I'd gotten the role of Matty, but Graf beat me to the punch.

"Everyone in town adores Sarah Booth. There isn't anyone who would leave such a note or even refer to her as a hick. Just because she's Southern doesn't mean she's a hayseed. She's sophisticated."

"Thanks, Graf." It was nice to have someone rush to my defense, even if it wasn't the complete and total truth.

"If you think of anything, give me a call." The sheriff pulled a card from his pocket and handed it to Graf. "I'd get the locks on the house changed. If Mr. Taylor has a harem of distressed women chasing him down, you don't want to get caught in the crosshairs."

"You think a woman started that blaze?" Graf asked. "Arson doesn't seem to be a female crime."

King tilted his head as if he were considering. "I thought you were an actor, Mr. Milieu. I didn't realize you were also a criminal profiler."

Graf didn't react instantly. He thought it through. "I gather you have some issues with actors," he said softly.

"No, no, that's not it at all. I enjoy the picture shows as much as the next one. What I have an issue with is a person who thinks they're so special they don't have to obey the law, a person who feels like celebrity is a ticket to any kind of bad or illegal conduct. That's what I have trouble with, Mr. Milieu."

"And what makes you think Sarah Booth and I are that kind of people?"

He nodded slowly. "Could be the report I pulled up on the two of you before I came up here. Let's see if I can remember it right. Ms. Delaney was charged with first-degree murder, and you were involved in a high-speed chase that resulted in a death. Ms. Delaney runs her own PI agency, no doubt aggravating every law officer in the vicinity. Am I leaving something out?"

"Sarah was innocent. The death was a suicide. If you'd done your homework, you would know that. Renata Trovaioli took her own life. Sarah Booth wasn't involved at all."

King only smiled. "You two have a good day, now. I hope your stay here is productive and short."

He walked away, never looking back.

"What a prick," Graf said.

I didn't respond. King was certainly unpleasant, but I had the feeling that he was also very good at his job. Why had he personally come out to talk to us? It was an interesting question and one without a ready answer.

CHAPTER FOUR

Graf put his arm around my shoulders as we walked into the house. "I'll be glad when we leave for location," I said.

"Don't let King get to you. Sometimes our fellow thespians make poor decisions in negotiating the legal byways."

"I wonder." I took a seat in the kitchen and watched Graf prepare coffee beans for a fresh pot. It was only five-thirty, too early for supper, and I didn't feel like a glass of wine.

He put the water on to boil for the coffee press and leaned on the counter, studying me.

"What?"

"I thought maybe my feelings for you were echoes from the past still sounding." He stopped and I felt my heart thud. "But you're not the same person you were in New York. You're different, Sarah Booth. All of the tentativeness is gone. You own the ground you stand on. I find that a little intimidating but also very attractive."

"If you add that I cast a big shadow, I'm going to deck you." The words came out nervous and silly.

"Don't play this for a joke, because I'm not kidding." His direct look said that this time he wouldn't allow me to escape with humor.

I held up a hand. "You promised when I said I'd come out here that you wouldn't press." Panic was rising in me. My emotions were in complete turmoil, and I didn't know what I wanted.

"I'm not going to press you to respond or reciprocate my feelings, but I am going to tell you the truth. It's taken me a long time to figure out what I want and what I feel. If I can't have you, if I lose you, I want it to be for a reason, not because I didn't try."

Giving myself a moment to think, I looked out the doorway. Wildflowers in vivid hues bobbled on a light breeze, and in the distance a wild mountainside rose up from the canyon floor, rocky and rough. This was terrain I'd never grow tired of seeing. As much as I loved Mississippi, I had to admit that California called to me.

"I won't say that I don't have feelings for you, Graf. I do. Strong feelings. But I'm not sure if what I feel is part of the past or for right now. I was so hurt when I left New York. You didn't even call me."

He looked down at the counter. "Because I knew you were leaving, and I knew there was nothing I could do to convince you to stay. You gave up on yourself, and the only thing you could do was go home."

"And lick my wounds?" I wasn't bitter. He was simply telling the truth. "I had to make some money or else I would have lost Dahlia House, and I was sinking in New York. I spent every penny I had trying to stay in the city long enough to get a role. I worked at it, hard, and it didn't happen for me."

He came around the counter and gently rubbed my shoulders. "I should have been more compassionate. I should have shown you what I was feeling. Instead, I let you walk away, and I let my pride dictate my conduct. I was hurting, but I didn't want you to see it."

How was it possible that I hadn't noticed? I'd waited for

him to rush out the door and stop me, beg me to stay, give me some lifeline to hold on to while my career wobbled. "I was proud, too."

Another case of two reasonably intelligent adults making a train wreck of a relationship. "I don't want to screw this up again, Graf. If we have a second chance, I don't want to find myself in your arms and thinking about—"

"Coleman Peters."

I put my hands on the counter to steady myself. "I want to be sure the past is dead and buried."

"And I think that's the right thing to do. But I'm falling in love with you, Sarah Booth. Whatever I felt before, this is deeper and stronger. I never realized I could feel this way."

I swallowed. Honesty was not easy, but I owed Graf complete truthfulness. "I don't know what I feel for you, other than an immense sexual attraction, which I don't want to act on yet." Liar! What a liar I'd become. I wanted to jump his bones right then and there and damn the consequences. I needed the weight and warmth of another human body to block out the emptiness I felt. But this was the classic mistake of the rebounder.

"Christ, Sarah Booth, you make it hard on a guy."

"No pun intended?" I had to get this conversation on a less serious track.

He groaned. "Please, we left high school years ago."

"You did, maybe. I feel I was gypped out of a real high school experience, so I'm going to go through it now."

His hands tightened on my shoulders and he leaned down and kissed my earlobe. "You can play it for humor all you want, but I know you feel something for me. That's enough for right now."

I turned my head and saw his lips. Before I could think it through, I was leaning toward them, hungry for his kiss.

The ringing of my cell phone brought me up sharp. "Shit." I answered with a gruff hello.

"Well, hello to you, too. By the tone of your voice, I gather you're still sexually frustrated," Tinkie said. In the background was a babble of voices and clinking dishes. She was in Millie's Café. I had a sudden hankering for a slice of Millie's homemade apple pie.

"What's going on?" I was hit with a wave of homesickness that made me almost gasp. Graf kissed my cheek and went onto the porch to give me privacy for my call. I kept finding new depth in him.

"Not so much here, but I see you've narrowly escaped a wildfire. You could have given us a call, you know."

Too late I remembered the reporters from the night before. The fire hadn't threatened us, but no telling what kind of story it had turned into. "We're fine. The blaze was contained before it got dangerously close."

"That's not what the story in *Hollywood Gossip* says."

"Tinkie, you know full well how some publications blow things way out of proportion." I was still a bit annoyed that the telephone had so rudely interrupted the kiss.

"True, but I don't know when the story is dead-on or when it's exaggerated. That's why you should call home and let us know."

I sighed. She was right. I'd been so caught up in my life that I'd forgotten my responsibilities to my friends. "We're fine."

"Are you?"

"Except that I'm missing you and Zinnia and everyone." Giving voice to that sentiment told me how real it was.

"How's the movie business?"

"The screen test was good. They're writing Sweetie into the movie. Graf is wonderful to act against. Everything is good here." I'd only been gone a couple of days, but it seemed an unbridgeable gap now. Tinkie no longer shared my life. We reported on events to each other. I thought of telling her about the message on the mirror in Bobby Joe's house, but I decided against it. While it would intrigue her, it would also worry her.

"Cece is planning a big story about you once the movie starts production. She hinted she'd like an invite to the set."

"Absolutely, and of course you and Millie might come with her?" My heart lifted at the thought.

"That's a distinct possibility."

"You've made my evening." I couldn't wait to see them, to show them the little I'd learned about Tinseltown.

"Stay in touch, Sarah Booth. Life continues here in Zinnia, but it isn't the same without you."

"I'll be a better caller," I promised before I hung up. I walked out to the porch to talk with Graf. He put his arm around me and kissed the top of my head.

"Let's start dinner. If I stay here with you, I won't be able to honor my word not to press you. I want to give you the time you asked for."

Before I could ask him to stay with me, he went into the kitchen and began rattling pots and pans. I was left with a million-dollar view and a body and heart at war with each other.

Graf had an early call the next morning, and Sweetie and I took advantage of a brisk March sunrise to head down the canyon for a hike. I'd lost at least fifteen pounds during my false murder accusation, and I was determined to keep it off. Climbing up and down the steep trails was the best exercise I could find, and I'd get to spend the morning with Sweetie Pie.

We went far down, dropping into cool shade and then barren patches of sun-soaked ground. When I got to the fire zone, I took great care. Sweetie stayed near me as I moved around the west side of the scorched area.

I was absorbed in trying to understand how the firemen had determined it was arson—I didn't see any empty gas cans lying around. Fire investigation was a talent I'd never looked into. Maybe later Tinkie and I could take a course.

Sweetie froze at my side. Her lips drew back and she bared

her teeth. A growl I'd never heard came from her. Instinctively, I reached for her collar. Before I could grasp the leather, she jumped forward with a wild, unearthly howl and disappeared into the brush.

"Sweetie!" I ran after her, remembering how blithely I'd dismissed Graf's warning about mountain lions and coyotes. "Sweetie Pie Delaney!" I made my voice stern as I pushed and panted my way through the dense underbrush that hadn't burned.

A long, low howl, as eerie as anything Sir Arthur Conan Doyle had created in *The Hound of the Baskervilles,* floated over the air. I struggled into a small clearing protected by jagged rocks in the shadow of one of the cliff faces. Sweetie stood over something blue, her muzzle lifted in a low, mournful cry.

"Sweetie." I rushed forward, my only thought to grasp her collar and snap on the leash that I wore around my waist.

I was upon her before I even looked at the blue object, which registered instantly as the size and shape of a human body.

Sweetie waited for me to get close enough to see that it was a woman. From the position of her body, I knew she was dead. Bones didn't grow at those angles. Sweetie nuzzled the dead woman softly with her nose and howled again.

"Stop that," I told her as I hooked the lead. The dog was creeping me out, howling as if she were in a ghost story.

I walked around the body, taking in the platinum blond hair, the manicured hands, adorned with expensive rings that seemed to clutch the dirt. I was no expert, but I'd be willing to bet the woman had been alive when she fell. I looked up the cliff face and saw where she must have slipped. Along with the blue athletic clothes, she wore hiking boots.

Sweetie had come home the night before—the night of the fire—with a piece of blue material in her mouth. I noticed that the dead woman's pants leg was torn, a piece of material missing. The poor woman had been lying out in the canyon with flames raging a short distance away.

"We have to call the police," I told Sweetie.

Sweetie had other ideas. She tugged the leash from my hand and went straight back to the body. She nudged the dead woman again with her nose. A draft of wind caught the woman's blond hair and shifted it.

"Oh, my God," I whispered. I recognized the woman. It was Suzy Dutton, the actress.

CHAPTER FIVE

"And you say you didn't know Miss Dutton?" Sheriff King asked me for the fiftieth time.

"Only as an actress." I gave the same answer I'd given fifty times before. In truth, the good sheriff was working on my last nerve. I'd called him to report the body, led him and some deputies to the place where I'd found her, and I'd been in his "custody" for the last few hours with only his aggressive behavior for my good citizen's reward. My butt was numbed by the hard chair in the sheriff's office, and I was worried about where they'd taken Sweetie Pie.

"There aren't any other houses near yours." Grady King spoke as if I'd personally destroyed a subdivision somewhere.

"Where's my dog?" I asked. King had finally allowed me to call Graf, and he and Federico were on the way. If I could keep from losing my temper until they arrived, things would get better.

"What reason would Suzy Dutton have for being in Lettohatchie Canyon?"

I shook my head. "I don't know. Sheriff, I don't know much about the canyon or the road that leads to the house or the lifestyle of movie stars. I just got into town." My words were a lie. I suspected Suzy was lurking around the canyon to spy on me because of the role of Matty that was mine instead of hers. But to tell King this would guarantee that I'd be a suspect in her death. I'd just played that role in Zinnia, and I had no desire for a repeat performance. I'd keep my lips zipped.

"Were you and Miss Dutton in competition for the same role?"

The question brought me up short. Grady King had some inside source into the movie business. "Not to my knowledge," I said. "Federico Marquez offered me the role after I took a screen test. I never heard it was offered to anyone else." That was all truthful. I had simply omitted the conversation I overheard between Suzy and Federico.

"When was the last time you spoke with Miss Dutton?"

"I met her recently at Michael Mainheim's house at a party. We passed in a hallway. That's the only time I've ever crossed paths with her."

"I hear that Miss Dutton was distraught because the movie role you're playing had been promised to her."

"I've already told you, I don't know anything about that."

"Miss Delaney, I shouldn't have to point out that you were charged with the murder of another rival in Zinnia not two months ago. This appears to be a pattern. Kill off the competition."

Anger made me clench my fists, an action that King immediately noticed. My sudden fury wasn't directed at him, but I wanted to throttle Coleman Peters. His false accusation of me would haunt me the rest of my days. "The charges were dropped. Renata Trovaioli committed suicide. She wasn't murdered by anyone, most certainly not by me."

"And you got the role she was playing, which resulted in your most recent film success." He sat back in his chair, his hands steepled in front of him.

"I got this role because I did a screen test and it was good." I shifted in the hard-bottomed chair, checking my watch. What was keeping Graf and Federico? "Have you found evidence that shows foul play in Miss Dutton's death?"

"I'm asking the questions here, not you."

"Fine, but that's a pertinent question, don't you think? As far as I could tell, it looked like Suzy Dutton slipped from the cliff. Maybe it's a simple accident."

"Or maybe not. Would Miss Dutton have any reason to want to burn you or Mr. Milieu to death?"

"That's ridiculous. That's a big stretch, Sheriff King, even for you. Have you found evidence that connects her to the fire?" I sat forward.

"We haven't finished the forensics yet, but we will find something, I promise you. We have state-of-the-art equipment, something you probably aren't used to in Podunk, Mississippi."

"No, Sheriff, in Zinnia, we rely on brains, not technology. Maybe you could hire someone with some smarts before you end up with egg all over your face." My temper overrode my good sense, but instead of getting angry, King smiled.

"I don't need to tell you that the media is all over this, Miss Delaney."

"That's not my problem."

He sat forward suddenly. "But I could make it your problem with very little effort."

"Are you threatening me?" I asked sweetly. "Let me point out that you should have found the body when you were investigating the fire. If it weren't for me and my dog, Suzy Dutton might have remained out there for a long, long time." I'd scored a point, but it was going to cost me. I could see it in the glitter of his pale eyes.

"You had a message written on the mirror in your house—"

"Bobby Joe Taylor's house," I reminded him.

"Telling you to go home. That sounds a bit personal to me."

"I have no way of knowing if the message was directed at me. I told you that."

There was a tap on the door and it opened to reveal Graf and Federico. The director looked slightly gray. The news of Suzy's death must have hit him hard. They'd been a couple for nearly four years before they'd split up.

"Is it true?" he asked. "Suzy is really dead?"

"She is. Her neck was broken in a fall." Sheriff King delivered the news without any attempt to soften it.

"This is terrible. What was she doing in that canyon?" Federico looked at each of us as if he hoped one of us could explain her death in a way that made sense.

"That's what I intend to find out." Sheriff King stood up. "You can go for now, Miss Delaney, but don't leave the county."

"Are you charging her?" Graf stepped forward and put a hand on my shoulder. "This is absurd."

Federico cleared his throat. "She must go, Sheriff. We're set to begin shooting day after tomorrow in Petaluma, Costa Rica."

Sheriff King's eyes narrowed. "Very convenient."

"The schedule was set months ago. The camera crews and set designers left this morning. Miss Delaney must go. Without her the filming will be halted. Each day of delay will cost thousands of dollars." His shrug was eloquent. "If you have no real evidence against Miss Delaney, you must allow her to work. Otherwise, I'll be forced to sue the county for any losses and damages to my film."

King's smile widened, and I was reminded of a barracuda. "You movie people think you're above the law."

"Do you have any grounds to charge Sarah Booth?" Graf asked. "What evidence do you have?"

Sheriff King gave him a calculated look. "Not enough. At least for the moment."

Federico nodded and gave a courtly little bow. "Thank you, Sheriff. If you need her to come back to Los Angeles, we'll see that she gets back. Until then, she needs to focus on her work."

Graf offered me a hand to rise. His arm came around me protectively. "Sarah Booth wouldn't harm a fly. Keep that in mind before you start making accusations you're going to regret."

"All of you get out of my office before I change my mind. The dog is waiting for you at the front door."

I didn't need another invitation. I meant to retrieve Sweetie Pie and get out of there. It was only when I was on the sidewalk, Sweetie's leash in my hand, that I heeded Graf's tug on my hand. He nodded to Federico, who was using one hand to support himself against the building.

"Can we do something to help?" Graf asked him.

He shook his head. "It's the shock. Suzy was very special to me."

"You were together for several years." Thanks to Millie's penchant for reading the celebrity magazines, I knew my share of Tinseltown dish.

"Do you really think someone pushed her off a cliff?" Federico asked me. The idea of such a thing brought him great pain.

"It could have been an accident. That's what I tried to tell the sheriff. Those trails are steep and difficult. I've almost fallen a few times."

"But what was she doing in Lettohatchie Canyon?" he asked. "She had no friends there. Suzy wasn't the kind of woman who would go hiking, and certainly not alone. Why was she even there?"

"Did she know Bobby Joe Taylor?" I asked.

Federico's eyes widened. "Perhaps. It's possible he was writing a script for her." The relief that touched his features told me a lot about his feelings for Suzy. He might have broken up with her and pulled the role of Matty out from under her, but he still cared about her.

"But if she was looking for Bobby Joe, why didn't she come to the front door and knock? Why would she be hiking around the canyon?" Graf looked from me to Federico.

I didn't have an answer, so I kept my mouth shut. It occurred to me that Jitty would be astounded and proud at this most recent display of maturity.

"Suzy often did things the hardest way possible," Federico said with sadness. "When we were seeing each other, she wouldn't ask a simple question. She created these complicated scenarios." He took a deep breath. "I'm sure the autopsy report will answer some of our questions. I'm just sorry that the last time I spoke with her was so long ago."

"When was that?" I asked. The question flew out of my mouth.

"I saw her at M.M.'s party, but we didn't get a chance to talk."

That was an outright lie. "King implied that you'd promised the role of Matty to Suzy. Is that true?"

"Sarah Booth, you got the role because you earned it." Federico straightened his jacket and squared his shoulders. "I never promised Suzy the role of Matty. She assumed it would be hers. Now I should get back to the set and you two get some rest. Tomorrow, Sarah Booth, you'll be flying to Costa Rica, and we begin filming the very next day."

I started to say something to Graf about Federico's shading of the truth. I'd heard him talking to Suzy. Arguing with Suzy. And she'd claimed he promised her the role. But as I turned to tell Graf, he kissed me. Concerns about Federico's messy relationship with Suzy Dutton were scorched from my mind.

By the time we got up the mountain to the house, both Graf and I had regained our senses. We studiously avoided any physical contact—even eye contact—and began the job of packing. We were both excited about going to Costa Rica. Federico had some family ties there, and we were filming the seduction and scenes between Matty and Ned and the murder scenes at an old family home. Between the excitement and the kiss we'd shared, I feared one or both of us were candidates for spontaneous combustion. We managed to steer clear of each other for the remainder of the night. The power of our attraction had frightened both of us, I think. Opening Pandora's box while we were acting together was dangerous.

Federico had hired a private plane for the entire cast, and we celebrated and drank our way across Mexico and into Central America. A shadow of sadness followed Federico, but he didn't mention Suzy to me, and I decided not to bring up her name. So they'd had an argument. I'd had plenty of them with friends, lovers, and even a ghost. That didn't mean I would be involved in violence.

Besides, I was certain that Suzy had accidentally fallen to her death. That was the only explanation that made sense.

The house at Petaluma was nothing less than spectacular— ochre stucco with a red tile roof, an interior courtyard complete with the most interesting sculptures of various Greek goddesses, enormous bedrooms lavishly appointed, and a staff that met us with trays of mojitos and canapés.

My room had a marble fireplace, and above it a magnificent portrait of a beautiful woman in a red gown, dark-haired with eyes of fire. She looked like someone I would have enjoyed knowing. I was about to unpack my luggage when I heard someone behind me.

A young woman stood in the middle of the room, her slender legs encased in breeches and boots. Her hair, lush and thick, was contained in an elegant French twist, and her white riding shirt was starched and immaculate. She'd opened the door and entered without me hearing her.

"She's lovely, isn't she?" the young woman asked, nodding to the portrait.

"She is."

"Her name was Carlita Gonzalez Marquez."

"Federico's wife?" I guessed.

"Federico has led a very interesting life." She spoke with contempt. "You should ask him sometimes. This was her home, a wedding gift to both of them from her father, Estoban Gonzalez."

"It's beautiful."

"Some people say it's haunted."

I couldn't tell if she was challenging me or not. "My home in Mississippi is also haunted. I think ghosts are drawn to me."

Her face hardened. "Don't humor me as if I were a child. If the film company stays here, you'll get more of a ghost story than you ever bargained for."

She swiveled and strode out of the room, her boots ringing on the stone hallway and then clattering down the stairs. I was about to turn to my luggage when the sheer curtains at the bedroom window puffed on a gust of wind. They took the shape of a slender female form before settling back against the wall.

Gooseflesh danced up my arms, causing me to inhale sharply. I exhaled, feeling foolish to have been so easily caught up in the ghost story of a young woman I didn't even know.

"Jitty would be amused," I said, wondering with a stab of pain if Jitty remained at Dahlia House or if she'd gone on to other lodgings. I had the strangest urge to call home, but I knew she wouldn't answer. So instead I dialed Tinkie.

"Hey, *muy bonita,* cha-cha," I said.

"Sarah Booth, you've finally found the Lord and are speaking in tongues. Do you need rescue or deprogramming or some holy water?"

"That's Spanish," I pointed out.

"Spanish by way of the cotton field. I don't know what you think you said, but it wasn't anything translatable."

I laughed. "I'm unpacking here in Petaluma, and we're all set to film tomorrow. This place is magnificent. It's like a huge old plantation set down in a tropical paradise. One of the staff said I could see the ocean from my balcony." I started toward the windows to see if the Pacific would wink at me. Just as I reached the open window, the outside shutters slammed together with enough force to make me jump backward and drop the phone.

"What was that? Sarah Booth, are you okay?"

I could hear Tinkie yammering away, but I ignored the phone and eased to the shutters. When I looked at them I saw that the latches used to hold them open had both broken. Simultaneously.

I picked up the phone. "Everything is fine. Just a gust of wind."

"Well, I'm glad you called, since we've all been wondering about your latest scrape with the law."

I groaned. "Finding the body of Suzy Dutton?"

"Front page of at least three tabloids. Millie has the story plastered all over the café. Harold and Oscar are on standby in case you need to hire a defense lawyer. Really, Sarah Booth, implicated in the case of another dead rival?"

"Oh, shut up. You sound like the sheriff."

"Is it the uniform, or perhaps the nightstick?"

"Tinkie!" I was suitably shocked. "You sound like Cece."

"I have to confess, she said it first."

"I'm okay. I didn't have anything to do with Suzy Dutton's death. We start shooting in the morning, and if I can resist Graf tonight, we should have enough sexual tension between us by morning to melt the silver out of the celluloid. Would you mind asking Millie what she knows about Carlita Gonzalez Marquez, former wife of my director Federico?"

"Will do. Call me when you finish shooting tomorrow. I want a blow-by-blow account."

"What are friends for?" I asked before I hung up.

I walked outside on the balcony for a closer examination. The metal latches that secured the shutters to the wall were snapped in half. Strange that both sides had failed at the exact same moment. Or perhaps they'd been broken and a gust of wind had caught them just right.

I had the creepy sense that someone was watching me, and I turned suddenly to survey the room, half expecting to see the angry young woman I'd seen earlier. The room was empty, but the eyes in the portrait of Carlita Marquez seemed to stare directly into my own.

Creeped out, I fled the room and hurried down the hall to knock on Graf's door.

CHAPTER SIX

"Joey, more wind chimes! I want tinkling and low notes! I want to *hear* the music of the wind!" Federico waved the young prop man to the balcony. "Hang them from the roof and trees!"

I sat in the shade, an electric fan sending a cool current of air over me, while they got the set ready. We were shooting Matty on the balcony, hot and sweaty, as a breeze springs up and sets off the chimes. My job was to look hot, in both meanings of the word.

Graf was across the patio, and he winked at me when he caught my eye. He'd already complimented me on the silk dressing gown that plunged almost to my navel. He arched an eyebrow and made me smile.

"Higher! Joey, hang them higher!" Federico yelled.

Joey leaned far out over the balustrade of the balcony, his long thin arms reaching for the branches of a *Cordia alliodora* tree whose branches hovered just out of his reach.

There was a grating sound and even as I started to rise to my feet, I watched the heavy balustrade begin to topple and Joey flail in the air as he plunged from the second story to the ground.

A cry rose from everyone on the set as Joey's body hit the hard earth.

"Joey!" Federico was beside him in an instant. He looked up. "Get an ambulance. Hurry!" He turned his attention back to the prop man and spoke in a low, soothing voice.

A handsome young man rushed from behind one of the cameras and knelt beside Federico and Joey. "I called the emergency number, Dad. Help is on the way."

Joey moaned softly, and Federico brushed sand from the side of his face. "You're going to be okay, Joey. Try not to move. Medical help is coming."

"The balustrade," Joey managed. "It gave."

"It's okay," Federico said. He looked up at all of us gathered around, unsure of what to do. "We'll film in the morning. We're done for the day. Please, leave us."

The cast and crew slowly dispersed. Graf came to stand at my side. "This is awful. Are you okay?" he asked.

"Yes, I'm fine. The question is, is Joey okay?" I wanted to go over and help, but there was little I could offer. Joey was conscious, and his breathing wasn't labored. It looked as if one arm might be broken, but he didn't appear to be fatally injured.

Graf put his arm around my shoulders and pulled me against him. "What a crazy accident. That balustrade is cement and at least six inches thick. Isn't that the balcony outside your bedroom?" he asked.

I nodded slowly. "It has the best light and Federico particularly wanted those white flowers from the tree." It was a beautiful shot, and the balustrade looked heavy enough to hold back a herd of zebras.

"Good thing Ricardo speaks fluent Spanish. I wouldn't know how to telephone for the emergency team."

That was a point of interest. "I didn't know Federico's son was on the set."

"Yes, assistant cinematographer. He shot your screen test. Didn't you know?" Graf's fingers drifted up to my hair, gently combing through my curls in a way that was both relaxing and exciting.

"I had no idea, but they look alike." I tried to keep my mind on the conversation. "I met his daughter yesterday. She's lovely, but . . . unhappy, I think."

"It's nice that Federico is giving his children a leg up in this business. Ricardo really wants to become a director, like his father. Estelle"—he shrugged—"Federico never talks about her."

"Listen. The ambulance is on the way." The sound of a siren came distinctly on the morning breeze. "I should change out of this dressing gown. Dallas will kill me if I get something on it."

He bent closer to my ear. "I'll be glad to help you get out of it."

His words affected me, but I gave him only a laugh as I turned and went into the house. Glancing behind me I saw the medics arrive with a stretcher. Graf remained behind to offer help.

The cast and crew had scattered, taking off for the beaches or hiding out in their rooms, or going back to the hotel in town where most of them were booked. Only a select few members had been invited to stay at the house, and for the moment the mansion was quiet and cool.

I walked up the stairs and into my room. Opening the balcony windows, I could hear Federico talking with the medics. Stepping outside, I watched them load Joey into a waiting ambulance. A gentle breeze tinkled the wind chimes, and I examined the balustrade. It was thick cement, and a section three feet wide had simply broken.

Or not so simply.

Bending closer, I saw what looked like chisel marks in the cement, as if a tool had been worked into cracks to weaken the structure. But who would do such a thing? And why?

The notion that I was being watched came over me with such certainty that I backed away from the balcony and ran inside. My gaze roved from one side to the other, but the room was empty. Except for the portrait of Carlita.

I could have sworn there was a hint of satisfaction in her smile that hadn't been there yesterday.

As soon as the medics were gone, I found Federico alone in the suite of rooms he was using with Jovan. The model was scheduled to arrive on the set any minute. She'd had a fashion shoot in Milan, so her scenes had been pushed back.

"Come in, Sarah Booth." Federico sat wearily in a chair before a cold fireplace. "What a day. The medics seem to think that Joey will be fine. His right arm is broken and he's badly bruised. They'll know for certain that there's no serious damage once they run some tests."

"I'm glad to hear that." I hesitated. The subject I wanted to broach wasn't going to be pleasant. "I looked at the balustrade, Federico. It's possible someone deliberately weakened the structure."

His eyes widened and he rose slowly to his feet. "Are you saying this wasn't an accident? That someone deliberately set out to hurt Joey."

"Maybe not Joey." It had occurred to me that had Joey not fallen, it might have been me. The script called for me to lean out into the breeze, letting it lift my hair and blow my dressing gown against my body while Ned watched from the lawn below.

He took my meaning instantly. "You think you were meant to fall?"

I frowned. "I don't know. It doesn't make sense. But something isn't right."

"This house has been empty for several years. It will be Estelle's on her wedding day, but until then, I've neglected it. I sent a cleaning crew out last month to prepare for the film, but before that, no one lived here." He paced as he talked. "Perhaps this happened when the house was empty, or somehow the cleaning crew did something."

I didn't disagree. Both scenarios were possible. "I'm not afraid, but I am concerned. I think you should hire some security here."

He stopped pacing and nodded. "You're thinking of Suzy, aren't you?"

"Two serious falls, one of them fatal. Yeah, it's an easy link to make." I saw the worry etch itself more deeply in the lines of his face. "There probably is no connection, but I heard what Suzy said at Michael Mainheim's party."

He dropped his gaze. "I'm sorry, Sarah Booth. You shouldn't have heard that."

"She felt I stole this role from her." I gave a wry grin. "I know what that feels like, and it isn't very nice. She was upset."

"Six years ago, I would have cast Suzy as Matty. But her time for that role passed. You *are* Matty, Sarah Booth. I've told you this before, but it bears repeating. I didn't give you anything you didn't deserve."

His words were high praise, but they didn't answer the question of what Suzy was doing out in Lettohatchie Canyon. "Do you really believe Suzy was climbing around that canyon because she and Bobby Joe Taylor are friends?"

He shook his head slowly. "I don't know. Suzy did say Bobby Joe was working on a script with her in mind."

Then it was possible she'd come out to the mountain to talk to Bobby Joe without knowing he'd let Graf and I stay in his place for a few weeks. But she never knocked on the door. She was climbing the ravine. It didn't wash.

"Suzy's death troubles me. Now Joey is hurt." I didn't have to go further. Federico took my hand and pressed it.

"I'll hire the security company now. Ricardo can check out several agencies and find the best one."

"I think that's a wise decision." I found a smile and pasted it to my face. Federico had enough to worry about. If someone was up to something on the set, maybe the presence of security guards would put a stop to it.

I awoke from a nap to discover that the entire day had slipped away. The rustle of papers made me sit up in bed. Graf sat in an overstuffed chair, his feet propped on an ottoman, reading *Variety*. Sweetie snored lightly at his feet. The soft late evening light struck Graf full on the face and I couldn't help but see how handsome he was.

"Would you like some coffee, Sarah Booth?"

I wasn't certain what I wanted, other than to pat the bed and ask Graf to come and lay beside me. That would open too many doors, though. I sat up and rubbed my face. "I feel like Dorothy, and this isn't Kansas anymore." The room was magnificent, especially with Graf there as if he were part of my family.

"There's some good noise about this movie," he said, folding the paper and offering it to me.

I shook my head. "Millie tells me everything I need to know about Hollywood. Part of it's true and part of it isn't."

He laughed. "You have good friends, Sarah Booth. I was watching you sleep and thinking that I've neglected to make those connections. I wonder if it's a gender thing or if I've failed somehow."

It was true that a lot of men never built friendships. Many developed "couple" friendships. "You'd probably be surprised at the people who count you as a friend."

He stood up and came to the bed. "I've been all about work or a romantic relationship. I want to have friends, like you."

I touched his face lightly, the evening stubble rough under my palm. "I'll be your friend."

He looked so innocent—before his fingers found the ticklish places along my ribs and hips.

Screaming and struggling to get away from him, I couldn't help but laugh. This was familiar ground for us. We roughhoused like kids, a trick way to experience the pleasure of physical intimacy. When at last I was panting for air, Graf pulled me into his arms and held me gently.

For a long moment we stayed that way before he let me go and stood up from the bed. "You're the hardest test I've ever met."

I only nodded. "I think coffee sounds good." We had to get out of the bedroom. The attraction between us was impossible to ignore.

"I'll go start it. Meet you in the kitchen."

Graf walked out of the room and I realized Sweetie Pie was still snoring. Some watchdog.

I put on jeans and a T-shirt and started down the hallway. The house was still quiet. In the morning everyone, including the caterers and set builders with their saws and drills, would be back.

Halfway down the upstairs hall, I had the sense that someone was watching me, but when I looked, the hall was empty, the hardwood floors shining in the peachy light. Maybe I was missing Jitty and hoping for a ghost.

As I started across the foyer, I heard voices raised in anger.

"You were responsible for Mother's death. No matter what you say, you were at the bottom of it."

The voice was young and female and filled with bitter emotion. I hesitated. It was coming from Federico's room. The door was open, and if the people arguing wanted privacy, they should have shut it.

"You can't begin to know what really happened." Federico's response was calm, sorrowful.

"Mother was so unhappy. You made her unhappy. That's why she overdosed. This is at your feet, Father."

Estelle was in the house again, and no happier than she'd been the day before.

"In one way, you're correct, Estelle. I am partially to blame for this situation right now. When you were younger, I did everything I could to protect you. I didn't always tell you the truth, because it was so painful."

"The truth! You wouldn't know the truth if it walked up and spit in your face."

"I can see you've inherited your mother's temper as well as her theatrics."

There was the sound of something breaking. "Mother doesn't want you in this house. She'll make sure you don't stay. What happened to that prop man is only the beginning."

"You should leave, Estelle. Before you say something you'll regret for the rest of your life."

"Make me! This will be my house. Mother meant for me to have it. She wouldn't want you and that filthy slut in here. I want all of you out!"

"I'm calling the security team. I'm having you removed, Estelle. This will be your house one day. Until then, I have a movie to make and I can't afford for you to do harm to yourself or anyone else. Leave now or I'll have you removed."

"You wouldn't dare."

Apparently he would dare, and he did. Not a minute later the front door opened and two burly men wearing blue uniforms with "PSA" embroidered on the chest came forward. They each wore a utility belt with what looked like Mace or pepper spray and batons attached.

I moved down the hall, pausing in the kitchen door, where I could hear the kettle Graf had put on whistling away.

"You bastard!" Estelle's angry scream came just as Graf lifted the kettle. I heard it clatter to the range top, and he was beside me in an instant.

"Take your hands off me!" Estelle, in the grip of the two security guards, was being dragged from her father's room and down the hall.

"You'll pay, Father! You'll pay the ultimate price for this! Mother won't allow it! You and that whore will pay, just like the last one did!"

"Take her off the property and release her," Federico told the guards. "Estelle, I'm calling Senor Martinez. If you step foot on this property again, you will be arrested and put in jail, where you'll remain until the filming here is complete. Don't make me do this."

She was escorted out of the house. The door slammed shut, and Federico was left standing alone in the hallway.

I pushed Graf back into the kitchen. Federico had enough on his plate without knowing that members of his cast had witnessed a terrible fight with his daughter.

"Holy shit," Graf whispered, "that was intense."

Graf hadn't heard the entire fight like I had. Several things were troubling me as I sat at the kitchen table. Graf placed a steaming cup of coffee in front of me and then took a chair.

"You look really worried, Sarah Booth."

I was. Several times Estelle made reference to her mother as if the woman were still alive. She wasn't—as far as I knew. Carlita Marquez had died of an overdose years back. Or that was the scuttlebutt. "Estelle seems seriously . . . unbalanced." The idea of her walking so quietly into my room was upsetting.

"She won't get back on the property. I'm glad to see Federico hired security."

"This was Estelle's mother's home. She knows it inside and out. Do you think Estelle was making reference to the death of Suzy Dutton when she said that about paying like the last one did?"

"Sarah Booth, don't borrow trouble." He picked up my hand and kissed it. "You're a movie star now. At least for the time being. You've taken down your shingle as a private investigator. If Estelle was involved in Suzy's death, let Sheriff King in California handle it." He kissed my hand again. "Besides, if I'm not mistaken, Estelle was here in Costa Rica. Hard to kill a woman in Malibu when you're a continent away."

"Good point." And it was. I sipped my coffee. Graf had hit

the nail on the head. I wasn't Sarah Booth Delaney, PI. I was Sarah Booth Delaney, star of *Body Heat*. One bitter lesson I'd learned in the last few years was that a person has to focus on what she wants. I couldn't keep one foot in the world of detecting and another in acting. I had made my choice and I owed it to myself and Graf to give it one hundred percent.

Estelle was a disturbed young woman. I could pity her, and her father, but it wasn't up to me to solve what had happened to Suzy Dutton.

"Let's take a walk, Sarah Booth. Then we can go into town and have a nice dinner."

I looked across at the man who was doing everything in his power to make me happy. I'd waited such a long time for this moment. "Sounds perfect, Graf. I'm ravenous."

CHAPTER SEVEN

It was a good thing Graf and I took a long walk, because when we got to the small restaurant and the delicious meal was placed in front of me, I ate like a politician at the trough. Graf was even amused. He teased me gently, and then ordered a rich and chocolaty dessert that was incredible. The man was spoiling me rotten, and I loved every second of it. No one except my parents had ever treated me with such love.

We were laughing as we walked up the cobbled street outside the café. I was slightly tipsy from wine, and Graf had proposed a skinny-dipping session in the calmer waters of the small cove behind Federico's mansion. The moon sparkled on the glassy water and silvered the sand.

I was reluctant, but I wasn't going to say no—until he got naked. Then I intended to snatch up his clothes and run. It was going to be payback for the tickle session earlier in the day. I was buzzed, but I hadn't forgotten that Graf had one-upped me.

We passed the drive to the mansion, and I glanced toward the house. My heart stopped. The silhouette of a man, backlit by the house lights, made my heart flip. Coleman Peters. I recognized the broad shoulders, the tapered waist. Coleman had come to Costa Rica to find me.

"What's wrong?" Graf asked. He, too, was slightly inebriated, but not enough that he missed the stricken look that surely touched my face. "You look like you've seen a ghost."

The silhouette walked toward us with that self-confident stride. My heart pounded and my mouth was dry.

"Can I help you?" the man asked in English with a heavy Spanish accent.

I tried to speak but couldn't. "No," Graf said. "We're going down to the beach before we turn in."

The security guard nodded. "The cove is nice for swimming. Not the ocean. It isn't safe."

"Thank you." Graf lightly grasped my arm and assisted me down the path. "What's wrong?" he asked.

"I was dizzy for a moment." I wanted to cry. Every time I thought I was beginning to heal from Coleman, something happened to rip the scab off and reveal the open wound.

It wasn't fair. Not to me and certainly not to Graf.

"Let's go skinny-dipping." I put a challenge into my words. Before he could react, I stepped out of my sandals and I ran toward the beautiful beach of the small cove. I left my sundress and underwear in a trail behind me as I skimmed over grass and then sand, determined to leave behind the hurt and disappointment of Coleman Peters before I hit the cold embrace of the water.

Graf was beside me when I came up for air, sputtering and gasping. The water was cold silk sliding over my body. Graf's hands, when he grasped my waist, were warm and familiar.

I turned to him and kissed him, blotting out everything except him and the freedom of the water.

"Are you sure, Sarah Booth?" he asked.

My answer was another kiss, one that left no doubt of what I wanted.

In the back of my mind I could hear Jitty. "Girl, you're jumpin' out of the fryin' pan and into the fire."

I tuned her out. She was another betrayer. She'd abandoned

me. It was up to me to craft the life I wanted, and right now I wanted to feel wanted. I needed the intimacy of Graf's kisses and his embrace.

He lifted me in his arms and carried me to the beach where he made a makeshift pallet of our discarded clothes. Beneath the rising moon, we made love, and I clung to Graf and the magic of his touch.

I awoke in the early hours of the morning, thirsty and with a headache. Beside me, Graf slept peacefully. It took a moment for me to recognize the sounds that had awakened me. Sweetie Pie was pacing the room, going to the door again and again on clickety nails, a soft whine telling me of her need to go out.

Slipping from the bed, I grabbed a gown and slid it over my head. Barefooted, I padded across the room and opened the door. Sweetie Pie bolted forward with a low growl that caught me by surprise. She was after something.

Or someone.

I gave chase. She was ahead of me in the hallway, almost to the stairs, her growl louder, more ferocious.

"Sweetie!" I whispered loudly, hoping to bring her back to me. When she didn't respond, I had no choice but to follow.

"Sweetie Pie Delaney!" I ran down the stairs just in time to see the hem of a red dress disappearing out the front door that closed on a soft slam. Someone had been in the house. Estelle? Out to cause more mayhem for her father? I grabbed Sweetie's collar so she couldn't follow and opened the door.

Outside, moonlight strong enough to cast shadows lit the grounds. There was no sign of anyone on the front lawn or down the drive. My heart raced, but I forced myself to take deep breaths.

"Can I help you?"

The male voice coming from less than five feet away almost made me scream. I swiveled and saw the security guard standing in the shadow of a porch column. "Did you see someone come out the door?"

He shook his head slowly. "No one left the house. I've been here all evening."

"But I saw . . ." What had I seen? "The door opened and—"

"No, senorita. The door hasn't opened all evening."

Still gripping Sweetie's collar as she tugged against me, I thanked the guard and closed the door.

Around me the house was silent, and I went to the kitchen for some water. The "ghostly visitor" had finished the job of sobering me up, and I sat at the huge kitchen table to think about the last few hours. I didn't regret the passion I'd shared with Graf, but worry nagged at me. My feelings for him weren't clear, and the act of making love seemed like a promise I wasn't certain I could honor.

Outside the kitchen window, I saw the sun brighten the horizon. Dawn would be upon me soon, and I had a hard day of shooting. Would the intimacy that Graf and I had shared affect our on-camera intensity? Anxiety rode me like a cruel rider with spurs.

Someone stirred in the depths of the house. Sweetie stood and wagged her tail as Federico came into the kitchen.

"Sarah Booth, what are you doing up so early?" When he looked at me more closely, he sighed. "What's wrong?"

"Nothing," I lied. "Too much wine and too little sleep."

"The doctor at the hospital said Joey is going to be fine, Sarah Booth. Go back to bed. I'll send someone to get you when you're needed on the set. Take some ice to put on your eyes. Michelle is an excellent makeup artist, but she can't compensate for lack of sleep."

"Thanks, Federico." I might not be able to sleep, but at least I could try. With some ice wrapped in a towel in my hand, I was almost back at my room when I heard my cell phone ringing. I dashed the rest of the way and answered it just as Graf gave me a sleepy "good morning" smile.

"Sarah Booth! Are you okay?" Tinkie's voice was worried. She had to be upset to be awake at 6:00 A.M.

"I'm fine, why?" I wondered if my friend had some kind of radar that made her aware of my indiscretion with Graf.

"Millie just called. It's all over the entertainment news."

"What?" I was lost.

"Someone is sabotaging your film. That young man was seriously injured, nearly killed!" The more she talked, the louder she got.

My first impulse was to calm her. "Joey is going to be okay. He took a fall. Broken wrist, two broken ribs. No serious injuries."

"That's not the way the media is playing it. They're calling this movie cursed. They're saying that the movie may shut down."

I considered telling her that the balustrade had been damaged, but it would serve no good purpose. She was already worried, and she was a thousand miles away. "Things are under control."

"That's not very reassuring."

Graf rose from the bed and came to put his arms around me. His lips found the sensitive spot on my neck and sent shivers all over me.

"Sarah Booth, are you carrying on with that actor?"

She did have radar. "Everything is fine here."

"That's not an answer." Her worry had turned to suspicion. "You sound . . . satisfied. You slept with Graf, didn't you?"

It was impossible to have this conversation with Graf nibbling at my neck and earlobes. "I have to get ready for my scene."

"Listen here, Marilyn Monroe, talk to Federico and tell him that your friends from Zinnia are on the next flight out. Obviously you need someone to come out there and keep you safe."

Happiness made me grip the phone harder. "You're coming? Really?"

"Me and Cece and Millie. Have someone pick us up at the Petaluma airport."

"I can't believe it." I was thrilled.

"You'd better believe it, and tell that gigolo he's going to answer to me if his intentions aren't honorable."

I didn't have to tell him. He was close enough to the phone to hear.

"I intend to make love to Sarah Booth until she begs for mercy," he said into the phone. "After that, it's up to her what happens."

"I'll see you soon," I said before she could respond to Graf. "I love you, Tinkie." I snapped the phone closed.

"Come back to bed." He put his words into action as he picked me up and placed me gently back in the bed. "Now let's pick up where we left off."

I didn't have a better plan for the early morning hours so I returned his kisses. If I couldn't look rested for the camera, at least I could look like the cat that got the canary.

Graf and I appeared on the set, causing a series of speculative glances in our direction. Had someone seen us on the beach, or heard us in the mansion? I wasn't ashamed of my actions, but I had a degree of modesty. I fought the flush that would betray me.

Federico had replaced the defective balustrade with a plaster piece, but it was clearly marked so that I wouldn't lean against it. The rest of the balustrade had been tested for safety.

I went up to my room and stepped onto the balcony. The wind fans were started and the chimes rang a beautiful song of light and dark notes. The silky length of the dressing gown blew against my body, reminding me of the feel of the water the previous night, which led to thoughts of Graf and the things he'd done to me . . . and the things I'd done to him.

"Close up on her face!" Federico directed.

I looked down and saw Graf walk onto the lawn, his shirt

rumpled and his tie askew. Desire licked at me like hungry flames.

Below I heard Federico ordering camera shots, but I forgot everything except the role I was playing and "Ned," a man I meant to seduce, use, and destroy.

When Federico yelled cut, I stepped back from the balcony and into my room. My heart was pounding. I'd gone so deeply into Matty that I'd lost myself. There was a rap on the door of my bedroom. When I opened it, Federico grasped me in a bear hug and kissed both cheeks.

"You are *caliente*! I thought you were going to melt the camera lens. I think Graf is worried, Sarah Booth. You looked as if you meant to eat him!" He kissed my cheeks again. "The camera loves you!"

I tried to blink myself back into the real world, but it was hard, moving from a character into my body.

"Go up to the ballroom and let Dallas help you get ready for the next scene," Federico said. "The clothes are all up there, and she's waiting for you, along with the makeup artist. Just a little refresher."

"Little refresher" my ass—I was sweating like a ditchdigger. The day was warm, but my thoughts had been so torrid that I'd worked up a sweat without moving.

"Thanks, Federico, I will."

He gave me another hug and then went back to his job. I went into the bathroom and splashed cold water on my face and neck. This was more than I'd bargained for. Maybe it was a sign, though, that I was becoming a better actress—that I could give myself to the part so successfully.

"Maybe it's a sign you're turnin' into a damn psychotic!"

I heard Jitty as clearly as if she were standing at my side. I looked up into the mirror, half expecting to see her. Instead, I saw a face filled with fury.

Long fingers dug into the flesh of my arm above the elbow.

"Mother doesn't want you here. Get out!"

I whirled, grabbing for her, but I was too slow. Estelle fled the room. I didn't bother to pursue her. She knew the house backward and forward. She'd elude me, as she'd done before. In the future, I would lock my door *and* I'd tell Federico that his security team was too lax. I was tired of Estelle popping in and out of my room like some demented jack-in-the-box.

Once I'd cooled off a little and gathered my wits, I headed up the stairs to the third-floor ballroom where Dallas Brown had set up the clothes for the shoots. She'd done a superb job of selecting for me. The designs were sexy in an understated, purely adult way, and it was a joy to gossip with her about her past work experiences. She was always insightful and never cruel.

Halfway up the stairs I caught sight of the swish of a red dress hem. It was a flicker of movement, the wisp of material at the corner of my eye. I thought of the red dress and the front door from the previous night—I'd seen it. I wasn't dreaming.

Here it was again, just ahead of me, tantalizing with the possibility of resolving at least one of the mysteries that seemed to populate the movie set.

I doubled my stride and took the stairs two at a time. As I got to the top, I looked down the hallway to the left. A dark-haired figure, slender and indistinct, disappeared at the end of the hall.

The ballroom was to the right, but I turned left, to follow the figure. I meant to find who it was taunting me with these visits set up to make me afraid. What they didn't realize was that I lived with a real-life ghost. Jitty had taught me a few things about the Great Beyond. If this apparition was a ghost, it couldn't hurt me, unless I let it scare me to death.

I ran down the hallway and stopped at a closed door. I rattled the knob. Locked. I moved back toward the ballroom, checking every door along the way. All were locked. Which proved nothing except that the person pretending to be a ghost had sense enough to lock a door behind herself.

"Sarah Booth, are you okay?"

Dallas had come out of the costume room into the hallway. She looked at me with concern as I rattled another door.

"I saw someone down here. What's in those rooms?"

She shook her head. "Federico said something about his wife's possessions. Her clothes, things like that. I guess he couldn't bear to part with them or kept them for Estelle. He said the doors were locked and he didn't want anyone in there."

"So only a family member would have a key to those rooms?" Damn Estelle. She was putting all of her time and energy into trying to run me off. Why me? Why not focus all of this on Jovan, Federico's girlfriend? I was merely an actor trying to make some money.

She shrugged, drawing me into the ballroom where screens had been put up for privacy. "Try this dress on, Sarah Booth. The fabric is perfect to give a soft reflection of the night lights. Federico loves it. He says it's you."

I looked at the dress she held up, fitted at the waist with a full skirt and a plunging halter top that made it totally backless. The fabric was brown, like molten chocolate. "This is incredible."

"Try it on." She held it out to me and I slipped behind a screen and let it glide down my body. Perfection. Dallas could look at a skirt or blouse or slacks and instantly know how they'd fit me.

I came out to show her. She was all smiles until her face fell into a frown.

"What's wrong?" I looked down at the dress. As far as I could tell it was perfect.

"What happened to your arm?" She looked across the room. "Sally, can you come over here. We'll need some makeup to cover these marks."

I looked into the mirror she indicated and saw the deep bluish-purple bruises just above my left elbow where Estelle had grabbed me. She wasn't a ghost. She was flesh and bones and dangerous.

"Who did that?" Dallas asked.

I shook my head. I wasn't about to say Federico's daughter. He had his hands full with her already.

"This place gives me the creeps." Dallas was suddenly unhappy. When Sally came up and began mumbling over the bruises, Dallas flopped onto a stool. "I've heard this house is haunted."

I tried not to react. Sally was brushing a concealing powder onto my arm.

"Posh!" Sally said. "Don't start that crap, Dallas."

"I didn't start it. Kyle, the cinematographer, told me this morning that someone had tampered with the cameras last night. He fixed them before shooting this morning. He said there was talk of seeing a ghost in the house."

They both looked at me. "Whose ghost?" I asked, playing it innocent.

"Most likely Carlita's ghost. There's talk that she didn't commit suicide." Dallas leaned forward. "I've heard rumors that she was murdered. That's why she haunts this place. She can't rest until the person who killed her pays."

CHAPTER EIGHT

Dusk had swallowed us in a warm mango glow by the time we finished filming for the day. While the end result of our labors might look glamorous, I was learning that shooting a movie was grueling work.

Anticipation of the arrival of Tinkie, Cece, and Millie had me to the point that I couldn't rest, though my body warned that I needed some shut-eye.

"Sarah Booth, why don't you try to relax?" Graf asked. "I'll make you something cool and delicious and you can rest until your friends get here. I'll even go to the airport and retrieve them."

I wondered where Graf kept his suit with the cape and the big "S" on the chest. "Will you really fetch them for me?"

"My pleasure. I owe them a lot. They helped me when I was in Zinnia."

If I had matured in the months that Graf and I were apart, he'd had a major growth spurt. This wasn't the same man I'd shared my bed with in New York. This was a conscious man, one who could put my needs ahead of his own.

"I'll make this up to you."

He shook his head. "This is nothing, Sarah Booth. I don't understand why I never got this until now. Maybe I've never truly loved anyone before. Now it's all so clear and simple. I'll do everything in my power to make you happy."

I felt a lump in my throat. "I'm not sure I deserve this."

"It isn't up to you to decide. This is my choice." He kissed my forehead. "Now take a hot shower and crawl in bed. I'll make you a Fuzzy Navel, lots of fresh orange juice and vitamins and a dollop of vodka to ease the tension. Then I'll dash to the airport. I should be back by dinnertime. We can all go out."

I started to make a smart-ass remark, but instead I kissed him. A good, solid smack that took his breath away. And then I left him standing at the front door while I went upstairs to follow his prescription for rest.

Federico had generously made two rooms available for my buddies, and I checked to be sure they were ready before I stepped under the stinging spray of a hot shower. The water was marvelous, pounding on my shoulders and melting away the tightness. I was wrapped in plush towels and sitting at the dressing table when Graf brought the drink. He'd squeezed the oranges himself.

"Drink this and I'll be back as quickly as possible," he said.

"Yassa, boss man."

"If you want to play roles, I can think of more interesting ones," he whispered in my ear.

He left while the pink still tinted my cheeks.

I sipped the drink and wandered around the room, examining the portrait of Carlita Marquez. She'd been incredibly beautiful, if a bit too thin. The version of her death I'd heard was overdose of prescription medication—ruled accidental due to Federico's influence, no doubt.

It would be interesting to talk to Millie about this. She was like a research database when it came to movie stars and celebrities. She knew things that no one else could possibly remember.

Though I stretched out on the bed, I couldn't rest. I was anxious. The day had been hard, but the good news was that, despite the lost hours from Joey's accident Federico had shot more usable footage than he'd anticipated. Minimal retakes meant we were ahead of schedule, and he was thrilled at the way things were going.

After twenty minutes of twisting and turning, I gave up trying to rest, slipped into my favorite black jeans and some walking shoes, and decided to explore the Pacific beach.

The sun had set, but the sky was still warm with light as I made my way along the half mile down to the shore. Venus had risen in the western sky, and soon the moon would lift out of the Pacific. Waves crashed against the shore, and I noticed a huge outcropping of rock that created a magnificent display of foam and spray as the waves crashed over it.

I removed my shoes and walked along the warm sand playing tag with the surf like a child. This was exactly what I needed. The tight knot of muscles let go as I inhaled the salt breeze and remembered the joy of being young and unencumbered.

By the time I turned back to the mansion, I was renewed and eager to see my friends. I was also ravenous. I hurried, wanting to slip into something cooler than jeans before Graf arrived with Tink and the crew.

The path that led to the mansion approached from the west, the side of the house where my room was located. I could see my balcony as I climbed the winding path that clung to the incline in a series of wooden steps and steep dirt.

From this view, the house was lovely. Many of the rooms were illuminated, and it looked like a palace waiting for a party. The wind chimes showered the night with music.

As I approached, I froze. Someone was standing on my balcony.

I eased closer, moving through the palm fronds and the small trees that contained heavenly night blossoms. When I had a clear view, I stopped. A slender, dark-haired woman gazed out toward the water. Something about her made me think that she had done this many times.

Night had fallen, and though the moon was full, I couldn't see clearly. Her features were indistinct. It could easily be Estelle. She was the same size and build, with the same flowing black hair. But I couldn't be certain.

I'd locked my door when I left, but that meant nothing in a house where the daughter would surely have keys to all the rooms.

"Hey!" I called out. "Hey, you!"

Either the figure didn't hear me or she ignored me. She continued to gaze out toward the ocean, as if she waited for some signal.

"Hey!" I yelled louder and jumped up and down, waving my arms. "What are you doing in my room?"

I was about to run the rest of the way to the house when I felt a firm grip on my arm. I turned to see one of the burly security guards eyeing me with suspicion.

"That woman is standing on the balcony outside my room." I pointed to the second floor, and we both looked.

The balcony was empty.

"Shall I help you into the house?" the guard asked in perfect English with a Spanish accent. I recognized him from the night before. He was the same man who'd been outside the front door when I'd seen the woman leave. He'd also claimed that the door hadn't opened.

"What's your name?" I asked.

"Daniel Martinez," he said. "The owner of Promise Security Agency, at your service." He almost gave a bow.

"Did you see that woman on the balcony?"

He shook his head. "I didn't see anyone, but it's dark. Let me check your room."

"Okay."

We walked into the house together. When we came to my room, the door was locked. I opened it with my key. Daniel did a quick walk-through of the room and adjoining bath and found nothing.

"The light here can play tricks," he said. His smile revealed strong white teeth and his dark eyes danced. "The locals say this house is haunted, though. Perhaps you saw the ghost."

"The ghost of whom?"

He gave a one-shoulder shrug. "The owner, the mistress, the murdered maid. Aren't the stories all the same? A ghost must be unhappy to remain behind to haunt a place." His smile widened. "And it's almost always a woman, yes? Something to think about."

Great, a security guard with a misogynistic comedy routine. "Thanks for your help, Mr. Martinez."

"Call me Daniel. I hear you're going to be a huge star when you return to the States. Perhaps I can get your autograph later."

I must have looked like a gaffed fish because he laughed. "No one has ever asked for my autograph," I confessed.

"Maybe if you leave one for the ghost, she'll go away happy."

"Clever."

"Call me if you need anything, Ms. Delaney. I'm at your service."

When he left I locked the door and searched the room myself. There was no evidence that anything had been tampered with. Then again, ghosts didn't normally move papers. If the ghost of Carlita Marquez was haunting the mansion, what did she want and why was she trying to get it from me?

"Well, this place puts the Delta to shame!"

Tinkie's lilting Southern drawl echoed in the huge foyer of the mansion, and I ran down the stairs to smother her in a hug. Right behind her were Millie and Cece, both wearing hats and huge sunglasses even though it was dark outside.

"Sarah Booth, dahling," Cece said, inching her sunglasses down her aristocratic nose. "You look underfed and overfucked. How do I get that job description?"

She gave me air kisses on each cheek before yielding to Millie, who gave me a big warm hug.

"The paparazzi took our photographs! They were like vultures fighting over a dead possum in the highway. It was wonderful!" Millie stepped back from me and began to ooh and ahh over the house. "I can't believe I'm here."

"She's afraid the café will close while she's gone," Tinkie said, a laugh in her voice.

"Don't worry about that! Everyone in town will show up and eat for days trying to pry gossip out of you," Cece told Millie. "In fact, you should set a twenty-dollar minimum. Not one shred of gossip about Sarah Booth unless the tab is at least twenty bucks."

"Where's Graf?" They were embarrassing me, and I wanted to change the subject.

"I think he's getting the luggage. We also brought Jovan with us from the airport." Cece gave a little *moue*. "Beautiful but not a great conversationalist."

"I couldn't stop staring at her," Millie said. "She's so gorgeous. They call her the Ice Princess in the tabloids. They say she's such a hot model because it's that contrast of Nordic cool and the hot Latino men they use with her in the ads."

"Graf has a surprise for you, Sarah Booth." Tinkie could barely suppress her glee.

"What kind of surprise?" I asked. Tragedy tapping at my door had made me suspicious of surprises.

"The kind you'll like." Cece put her arm around my shoulders. "Give us the tour. Millie especially wants to see the balcony where the prop guy almost fell to his death."

Millie pulled a shining digital camera from her purse. "I

brought my camera. I intend to document this entire trip. You would think Cece would do this. She is, supposedly, the journalist." She started snapping photographs. "Is the young man who fell doing better?" she asked.

"Joey is fine. His injuries aren't serious. In fact, he's back on the set already." And he was. He couldn't do much, but he was doing what he could. I led the way upstairs, unlocking my door to a curious look from Tinkie.

"Long story," I whispered under my breath.

While Cece and Millie toured the room, both stopping in front of the striking portrait of Carlita Marquez, Tinkie went straight to the balcony. Even in the dark she suspected the balustrade had deliberately been weakened.

"Were you the target?" she asked.

"I don't think so. There're some strange things happening in this house."

"Strange as in fatal?"

"Strange as in . . . supernatural." If I'd ever thought of telling Tinkie about Jitty, I knew better now. Her face showed clear doubt and a good measure of worry.

"Are you saying a ghost tampered with the balcony?"

"No." What was I saying? "Ghosts can't—" I broke off. Far be it for me to explain the rules and regulations of the Great Beyond. "Someone did that but it's possible it wasn't directed at me. It could have happened long before the filming started."

"Or not." Tinkie stared into my eyes, searching for some answer. "Suzy Dutton died in the ravine by the house you were living in. She was pushed off a cliff."

"Did the coroner rule homicide?" Being so far away from California and without access to a computer, I hadn't thought to check on the news stories about Suzy.

"The coroner's report hasn't been released, but law enforcement officials have been all over that canyon, and they hauled Bobby Joe Taylor in for questioning. They wouldn't do that if they felt Dutton's death was accidental."

"How do you know all this?" Foolish question.

"Millie keeps up with things. And it's a good thing, too. I'd never have known about the prop man falling if it wasn't for her."

"Things are going fine here. Federico is pleased with the work. We're ahead of schedule." I shrugged.

"The tabloids are saying the movie is cursed. They're hinting about some dark secret in Federico's past."

"Like?"

"Like murder."

I started to walk away and Tinkie grasped my arm. I winced, and she led me back into the bedroom and the light. "What the hell happened to your arm?" She looked toward the door. "Did Graf do that?"

"No. It was . . ." I was finding it hard to tell Tinkie all the things that had happened, because while I was determined not to add them up to get the score, she would do so instantly.

"It was what?" Cece said, coming over to join Tinkie. Millie was right on her heels. Angry expressions touched their faces when they saw the bruises on my arm.

"Federico's daughter. She's upset that we're using the house for filming. She says her dead mother wouldn't approve. She wants us gone, and she's a little hysterical."

"And so she grabbed your arm that hard? What did Federico say?" Millie asked.

I fudged a bit. "He had Estelle removed from the property." I almost left it there, but in fairness, I couldn't. "But she keeps sneaking back into the house. She must have her own keys."

"When her mother died, Estelle was sent to a *spa* for several months." Millie looked from one to the other. "Spa being a nice word for rehab. I remember the picture of her. She looked like warmed-over death. She was very close with Carlita, and there was talk that her mind had snapped."

"She's a little unbalanced," I said. "There's such anger between her and Federico. What I don't understand is why she's taking it out on me. I would have thought that she'd be dogging Jovan, her father's girlfriend."

"Jovan isn't the star of the movie," Tinkie said quietly. "You are, Sarah Booth."

"That's not the worst of it." I was on the verge of telling them about the ghost when I heard the distinctive sound of toenails on the floor. Sweetie Pie, followed by Chablis, burst into the room. Both dogs circled us and then jumped into the middle of the bed.

"You brought Chablis!" I was delighted to see the moppet.

"Heaven forbid that I should leave her. And I heard Sweetie Pie was going to be in the movie. I thought maybe Chablis might find a cameo role." Tinkie was grinning from ear to ear. "But you really need to step outside on the balcony."

"Right now?" I couldn't imagine why. We'd already been out there.

"Please," Tinkie said.

"Humor her," Cece instructed.

"Yeah," Millie chimed in.

Mystified, I followed Tinkie onto the balcony. When I looked down at the grounds, I saw Graf standing on the lawn lit by the set lights. He held the lead rope of a horse in each hand, a beautiful palomino and a lovely red roan.

"He borrowed them so you and he could ride together," Tinkie said. "He's very much in love with you, Sarah Booth."

I didn't know what to say. They were beautiful animals, and the idea that Graf had arranged all of this for my pleasure was almost more than I could absorb.

"Federico said they could stay in the old stables while you guys are working here." Cece put her hand on my shoulder. "I know it isn't Reveler and Miss Scrapiron, but I thought it was pretty dang sweet of him. For a person ruled by vanity and testosterone, he's a good guy."

I blew a kiss down to him, blinking back the tears that threatened. "So this was the surprise," I said.

"A good one, huh?" Tinkie asked.

"Yeah, one of the best ever."

CHAPTER NINE

Dinner was a happy time of margaritas and wonderful food, cool breezes and the simple joy of being in the company of my friends, and that included Graf. I'd never considered him a compadre in the past. He was my lover, my man, my passion. But his recent actions had moved him into the column of good friend, and my heart was opening to him. I had only to think of the sweet little roan, Flicker, and the palomino, Nugget, to know Graf was special.

We all walked home, laughing and talking and teasing. When we got to the mansion, Sweetie and Chablis came rushing out of Federico's quarters. I thought it was a little strange, especially since Jovan had arrived, and she didn't look like the kind of gal who appreciated dog hair on her size 00 black miniskirt.

When we got closer to the door, I heard sobbing.

"What in the world?" Millie said. She had the most maternal instinct of all of us, and I could see the worry in her eyes.

"There's a lot of emotion on a movie set," I told her, leading them up the stairs. "Nothing to worry about." But I was worried. Why had Sweetie and Chablis been in Federico's suite? I was almost afraid to find out.

Once the girls were settled, I gave Graf the kiss he deserved. "I need to talk to Federico," I said. "Would you entertain my friends?"

"Certainly. We'll wait up for you."

I hurried down the stairs to Federico's room and tapped lightly on the door. When it opened, I was shocked at his face. He'd aged ten years. "Are you okay?"

He stepped into the hallway and closed the door. "I'm only exhausted. Jovan is resting now. She isn't seriously injured, but she was badly frightened. The doctor examined her and gave her a sedative so she will sleep soundly now."

"What happened?"

"Someone pushed her down the stairs."

I felt the dull thud of my heartbeat. "She was pushed? For sure?"

"She insists she was pushed. She was going upstairs to look around, and she said she saw . . . a figure. Coming out of your room." He swallowed and looked at the floor. "A woman with dark, flowing hair and eyes that burned like hot coals."

Goose bumps raced up my arms and along my back. "Who was the woman?"

He shook his head. "There's no one on the set who looks like that."

"What happened next?"

"Jovan was frightened. She said the woman was strange. So she retreated, headed back to our room. She was looking down when someone gave her a big push. She could have broken her neck."

"Did this woman push her?" According to the rules of the Great Beyond, a noncorporeal being couldn't push a flesh and blood human down the steps. Only the most powerful ghosts—or evil spirits—could manipulate matter.

"She couldn't say for certain. She took a sedative and she's resting now. The only thing that calmed her was your dog and the other one. She felt like they guarded her—that they would sense an evil presence. She's finally relaxing."

"She isn't injured?"

"Some bruises, nothing serious. But it could have been. Sarah Booth, it could have been fatal. And if the media gets word of this, our film may die. No one wants to be affiliated with a movie that's cursed."

The media was already blowing things out of proportion. An "attack" on Jovan would send them into a real feeding frenzy. But the problems on the set couldn't be ignored, either.

I showed Federico my arm. "Estelle did this. She came into my room. She doesn't want us in this house."

"When? How?" Federico was shocked.

"Earlier today. She grabbed my arm and said her mother wouldn't approve of us being here." I cleared my throat. "Is she delusional, thinking that Carlita is still alive, or does she believe Carlita's ghost is here?"

Federico sat down heavily. "The past never dies, does it?"

"No," I said, "it doesn't." I spoke from personal experience.

"I've lied to Estelle about her mother's death, and now I'm afraid she's losing her mind."

I couldn't help that my heart rate accelerated. "How so?"

"I wasn't truthful about how Carlita died."

Jovan slept peacefully in the bedroom. I caught a glimpse of her through the open door from the sitting room where we were. "What really happened?" I asked.

"You see the picture of her in your room, yes?"

I nodded.

"She was a beautiful woman, lush and exotic even in that picture, where her illness was beginning to show."

I'd never heard that Carlita was ill, but I kept silent while Federico continued.

"Carlita wanted to be something else, someone other than

who she was. She suffered from the harshest of diseases. Self-loathing." He straightened his shoulders.

"Who did she want to be?"

"Someone European. Someone tall and slender and fair. She felt too short, too curvaceous, too Latino. She wanted to be considered a serious actress, and she felt she was typecast as the femme fatale because of her looks. She thought if she was thin, she would be viewed as a talented woman instead of a woman with looks."

I was stunned to hear this. "She was gorgeous. What a shame not to revel in that gift."

"And she was talented, Sarah Booth. Greatly talented. I was drawn to her beauty and her talent like a moth to a flame. But no matter what I told her, she could never see those things in herself. I have no idea what she saw when she looked in the mirror, but it wasn't the truth."

No one ever sees the truth in a mirror, which is the power of *Sleeping Beauty*. But none of this answered my question. "How did she die?"

"The medical term is anorexia nervosa. We were living in Los Angeles for my work. I got the finest doctors money could hire. The incredible truth is that she starved herself to death." He blinked tears from his eyes. "I've never endured anything more terrible. We force-fed her, we tried everything, from drugs to electroshock therapy. Before she died, her teeth were falling from her gums. To watch such loveliness descend into ruin was excruciating."

There had been a girl in college who was rumored to suffer from anorexia. I never knew for certain, because her parents came and took her home. I only knew that in one semester's time, she went from thin to skeletal.

"What did you tell Estelle about her death?"

"Estelle has always been self-conscious about her appearance. I was terrified if she knew her mother's true illness that she would mimic Carlita. They were so close. In appearance and temperament and emotions. So I sent Estelle and Ricardo to boarding schools in the East. Toward the end, I never allowed them to come home. Not even for holidays. And when Carlita finally died, I told them she'd accidentally taken a drug overdose."

"The coroner went along with this?"

He nodded slowly. "Which is perhaps why Sheriff King has no love for me. He feels I manipulated the system. That's why I had to lie to him about Suzy. He wants me to be guilty of some atrocity. He thought I was hiding something criminal in Carlita's death, but I was only protecting my children."

I blew out a breath and sat on the edge of the chair facing his. "You shouldn't have lied to Estelle and Ricardo."

"Hindsight is crystal clear, isn't it?"

"Right." I wondered what the best thing to do might be. "Should we leave this house? Surely there are other locations . . ."

"We'd have to reshoot everything, and the budget won't allow it. We'll finish before long, and then Estelle will be satisfied. I will be gone from here."

"Will that make her happy?" I asked the question gently. "She's so angry, Federico. She comes and goes at will in the house. There are obviously ways in that the guards don't know."

"She grew up in this house as a young girl. I'm sure there are passages. Not even I know them. But her grandfather would have shown her. He designed and had the house built. He never approved of me."

"Does Ricardo know the truth about his mother?"

He stood and walked to the mantel above the cold fireplace. He picked up a framed photograph I hadn't noticed and handed it to me. It was his family, all four of them smiling and hugging each other.

"Ricardo suspects. But whatever he thinks, it doesn't eat at him the way it does Estelle. He wasn't that close to Carlita. He knew she was very sick. He came home one holiday, unexpected, and saw her. He never asked any questions, and I sent him back to school."

"What a tragedy, Federico. I'm so sorry."

"If you could have known Carlita, you would have been charmed by her. Everyone was. And yet she could never love herself." He put the picture back. "But we must work tomorrow, Sarah Booth. You should rest, and I'll do my best to prevent Estelle from harming anyone else."

"And Jovan will accept this?" It didn't seem like much vindication for her near-death fall.

"She will. She understands."

"Estelle can't continue to terrorize us. My friends are here—"

"I know. I'll take care of it. Now get some rest."

He walked me to the door and brushed a kiss on my cheek before he shut it.

I went upstairs, following the sound of laughter to Cece's room. The gang was there, including Graf. They were waiting for me. I wasn't home, but I was pretty damn close.

That night I dreamed of riding the little red roan along the sandy beach as the ocean crashed mightily into the shore. When we got to the rock formation, where the spray rose thirty feet into the air, my horse suddenly changed into a creature of foam, and I was riding the sea, almost a mermaid but not quite.

I awoke in the early hours to Sweetie's gentle snores and the security of Graf's arms around me. The curtains in the room blew lazily on a soft breeze. Not once did I see the shape of a woman's body in them.

Outside were the sounds of the tropics, not the Delta. But my friends were all around me, and for that moment, I had happiness, peace, and contentment. My final thought before drifting back to sleep was that perhaps I'd begun to learn the Buddhist art of living in the moment. No mean feat for a Mississippi gal raised to gamble on the weather and a crop that was six months away.

The next morning, I woke Graf with a thousand kisses. I hadn't meant to fall in love with him. I wasn't sure that I had, but I had begun to trust the feelings that he stirred in me enough to at least explore them. There was the simple pleasure of the flesh. I was good with that one.

His body was a wonder to me. He was physical perfection, and I enjoyed looking and touching.

"I'll bet your friends are up," he whispered when we were both panting and sweating, spent from our efforts.

It was nine o'clock. Millie and Cece were up for sure. Tinkie—it was debatable. Unless she was on a case she liked the horizontal position in the morning.

"I'm starving," Graf said, gently biting my shoulder.

"Me, too." I didn't know if it was the work, the tension, or the lovemaking, but I was hungry.

"Let's see what's for breakfast." He slipped into his robe and held mine for me.

"Shall I bring you some breakfast in bed?" I asked.

"We can eat with your friends. I'll find out the filming schedule for the day and let them know so they can plan to be on-set for the scenes they want to see."

I smiled my thanks as we headed to the kitchen.

Halfway there I heard a burst of laughter. When we opened the door, Millie was flipping French toast and ten members of the cast, including heartthrob Ashton Kutcher, who was playing Teddy, the Mickey Rourke role of the bomb maker, were cheering and clapping.

"Sarah Booth, Graf, I thought I'd make breakfast," Millie said. "Tinkie is eating in her room."

"You can take the girl out of the kitchen, but you can't take the kitchen out of the girl." I took a seat at the huge table. "French toast? Yumm."

"It's wonderful," five people assured me.

"I can have it anytime I want in Zinnia, Mississippi." It was a point of pride.

By the time we finished eating, the kitchen was clear and I could ask Millie the questions that were on my mind. Graf excused himself and took the dogs out to the stables to check on the horses.

"What do you know about Carlita Marquez's death?" I asked.

Millie was washing dishes and her hands paused in the suds, a sure sign she was thinking through the implications of my question.

"It was a long time ago."

"Maybe twelve years." I was guessing, but I was fairly close.

"She was the Latino bombshell, sort of the Spanish Marilyn Monroe. My God, she was beautiful, but you can see that in the portrait in your room."

"Quit hedging and tell me what you know."

"Her death was ruled accidental overdose. Or that was the official version, but everyone thought there was something else going on."

"What in particular?"

"It was rumored that Federico was seeing a Danish actress. I don't recall her name, Alana or Alissa or something like that. I'll check. Anyway, there was talk."

If that was true, no wonder Carlita came up short when she measured herself. If Federico was dallying with a tall blonde it would go a long way toward explaining Carlita's image problems. The betrayed almost always assumes the blame—that's the destructive part of betrayal.

"I need to find out if that's true." I'd learned how the media could take a simple thing and turn it into a big deal. Perhaps Federico and the blonde in question were only friends. Or perhaps there was no blonde, only ugly speculation.

"I can do some checking," Millie said.

"How?" I was curious.

"I have membership in several different fan clubs. There are online lists where members are authorities on certain celebrities. I can post a question. If there's a computer I can use."

I shook my head. "Millie, you astound me. I'm sure I can find an Internet hookup among the cast and crew. Just be sure you erase your footsteps."

"No problem." Millie dried her hands. "I have to go put on my makeup and get ready for today. I heard that Pierce Brosnan was dropping by the set."

"He's not in the picture."

"He's a friend of Jovan's."

"I'll put the dishes away. You go get ready."

My aunt Loulane had always claimed she did some of her best thinking with her hands in dishwater. I knew it was a trick, so I didn't fall for it. But the rhythmic motions of drying and putting away dishes did give me a chance to order my thoughts and probe my feelings for Graf.

I had acted rashly in jumping into bed with him, but for the first time in months I felt as if I had a toehold on a precarious cliff. I had no doubt that Coleman Peters cared for me, but his actions toward me had not been loving. Torn between honor and love, he'd chosen honor. And the terrible predicament was that such behavior was exactly why I'd fallen for him in the first place.

But a woman can't always come in second, not even to honor. And I'd been third to his wife, Connie, producer of fake pregnancies and tumors, for I had no doubt that the latest of her cranial difficulties was fabricated.

As a point of honor I refused to ask Cece or Tinkie or

Millie how Connie's medical issues were progressing. I'd made a decision about Coleman, and now no matter what happened between Connie and him, I had moved on.

"Are you okay, Ms. Delaney?" I turned to find Jovan standing in the kitchen. "Is there coffee?" she asked.

"Yes and yes." She was a beautiful woman, but there was also sadness in her crystal blue gaze.

She poured a cup of coffee, black, and sat at the table. There was a large bruise on the orbital socket of her eye that ran down her cheek. There was also a cut on her lip, but she was able to work all of her limbs properly.

"You looked so sad when I walked in. My grandmother would say that you're too young for sadness."

"Chronologically speaking, your grandmother might be correct. But life doesn't wait 'til a certain age to dish out the hard spots."

"How well I know." She sipped her coffee. "Forgive my nosiness, but why are you unhappy today?"

I could ask her the same, but I didn't. "I was thinking about the people I'd left behind in my life."

"I suppose we all have our ghosts."

I knew she couldn't be referring to Jitty, but I was struck by a wave of homesickness. "What ghosts do you carry, Jovan?"

She shrugged. "Sometimes we're born burdened with the past."

She was smart for someone so young. "Tell me what happened last night, if you don't mind."

She went through the story Federico had told me, point by point.

"Do you think that woman you saw pushed you?"

She hesitated. "She was halfway down the second-floor hall. She would have had to move fast to get to me."

"If she didn't push you, who did?"

"That's the thing that's really scary, Ms. Delaney. I can't explain how she did it, and if she didn't, who did."

CHAPTER TEN

Federico was true to his word, and the next two days of shooting went without a hitch. There are rare times, sometimes only moments, when life is close to perfect. This was such a time for me. I had Graf, my best friends in the world, a job that I'd dreamed of and now discovered that I could do well, and a place that was close to paradise. If I'd been asked to make a wish, I would have had to say that I had everything I wanted.

Graf and I rode each morning on the beach, the waves crashing onto the sand and the seabirds calling. The brisk salt air made the horses frisky, and we rode and frolicked, and for those short hours I had no worries or cares. I embraced the happiness the gods had thrown in my path, and everyone on the set noticed, especially Tinkie.

The days had begun to run together, but Tinkie informed me that it was a Tuesday, and that she and Cece and Millie would have to leave soon. While I had started a new life, they were only vacationing from theirs.

The idea of saying good-bye almost made me cry, but I walled off my own sadness. "I wish you guys could stay forever."

"Oscar called three times last night. He's getting grumpy,

and that means it's time for me to head home. Cece says the newspaper is nagging at her, too."

Cece had worked too hard to overcome the stigma of being a transsexual to ever take her job assignment lightly.

"And Millie is worried about the café." Tinkie took my hand. "Let's take a walk."

We went to the beach and watched the surf strike the rock formation that looked like a castle from a distance.

"This is a beautiful place, Sarah Booth."

"Indeed it is. But we'll be heading back to California soon."

"I've been watching you act, and you do have a special talent. I'm so proud of you. You're going to have a big, big career in film."

She was the most generous of friends, offering freedom without guilt, even if it meant leaving her behind. "After the movie is finished, I'm coming home. We can have a big ole party at Dahlia House."

"That'll be nice." She turned to go back. "But Hollywood is where the parties count. No one in Zinnia can help your career."

"The party isn't for my career, it's for my friends."

She smiled and tugged me along behind her. "Millie is cooking dinner for Federico and Jovan and us. I promised her I'd go to the store and get some supplies. Want to come?"

I did but I had some lines to learn for the next day's shooting. "I'll help later in the kitchen."

"Good deal." We parted ways at the front driveway. Tinkie had borrowed the keys to a rental car and she had her list in hand.

As I walked to my room, I wondered how Federico had put the kibosh on Estelle leaping out of dark corners, but I didn't want to ask. The only thing that mattered was that he made certain she didn't frighten or harm anyone else.

In my room, I picked up my script and plopped into the comfortable, overstuffed chair covered in lush rose velvet. I wanted to be letter perfect for filming tomorrow. Several other actors were coming in for scenes, and it was a big day of shooting.

By the time I was satisfied with my rehearsal, dusk had fallen outside. My mother had called it "the blue hour," and I understood why. While dawn, with the pinks and roses of a new day, was promising, there was something about the fading of light from the sky that made me sad. Another day was ending, another cycle concluding.

Moving out to the balcony to stretch and take a breath of the fresh, wonderful air that blew in from the ocean, I saw movement in the gardens.

A slender figure in a red dress moved through the shrubs. My body tensed and I was on full alert. Somehow Estelle was back on the grounds and playing her games. I wasn't about to let her mess up Millie's dinner.

Sweetie and Chablis were nowhere to be found—gone with Graf, I presumed. The dogs had taken up with him, and while it did my heart good to see that Sweetie Pie had a father figure, I was a tad jealous. Especially in moments like this, when I needed my hound for a tracking job.

To my astonishment, the figure beckoned me.

"You bet your sweet ass I'm coming down," I mumbled, putting my words into action. "I'll be there before you can say Essie Mae Woodcock."

I slipped on my athletic shoes and crept down the stairs and into the blue dusk. From the kitchen I could hear Cece telling a story to some of the enthralled crew. My friends were hits with everyone, and I didn't want to disturb the joy of the evening. I'd have a few words with Estelle and convince her to let us finish the filming. If she left us alone, we'd conclude faster and get out of her mother's home.

The guard wasn't at the front door, but I assumed he was patrolling the grounds. Or sleeping. Obviously he wasn't keeping Estelle away.

My feet crunched on the shell drive as I jogged toward the gardens. Graf and I had explored them several times, finding alcoves where hibiscus grew in vivid shades and the sweet perfume of blossoms I couldn't identify seemed to drug the air. These were our secret canoodling places, and we sought them out when the urge to make out came upon us strong and irresistible. It was juvenile and naughty and thoroughly delicious.

I entered the garden. In places, the hedges were seven feet high, creating a wall of green that seemed impenetrable. But there were paths, small fountains, ponds and statuary throughout the five acres of formal gardens. I headed toward the place I'd last seen Estelle signaling me, a small clearing with a bench, a statue of Pan, and a fountain that babbled in clear, high notes. It was one of our favorite nooks.

"Estelle." I called her name as I jogged. I was eager for the confrontation.

The night fell softly around me, but in places the gardens were lit. I moved steadily west, or at least that's what I hoped. When I came out at the edge of the cliffs that led down to the ocean, I was a bit surprised. I hadn't thought I'd gone so far.

There was no sign of the woman in red, or Estelle, if that was who it was. No indication that she'd ever been in the gardens at all. Of course, she could be hiding beneath any hedge, laughing at me.

The chilling sense that someone was behind me made me spin around. "Estelle!" She was beginning to piss me off. "Come out and quit this foolishness."

The only sound was the soft cooing of a dove nesting somewhere in the tall shrubs. "Damn it, Estelle. This is getting old. Come out and talk. We'll be leaving in a few days so you can have the house to yourself."

No answer, no response. Even the dove fell silent.

"Great." I'd worked up a sweat jogging for no good reason.

But I was careful to keep my back to the drop-off. Jovan and Suzy Dutton had both been pushed. Suzy was dead, and Jovan was lucky.

And I was hungry, and I wanted to spend time with Graf and my friends. Before I left the gardens, I went to the edge of the cliff. In the pale moonlight, the waves, carrying a hint of green phosphorescence, were spectacular roaring onto the sand. Wild, savage, untamed, the ocean was the most mysterious of all earth's elements to me.

I was about to turn away when I saw the woman in red. She was below me on the sand, her right hand motioning to me. She touched her lips as if she meant to keep a secret.

"Damn it!" I spoke aloud. "I'm getting damn sick and tired of this bullshit." She was really pissing me off. I headed for the steep stairs that led to the beach. As far as I knew, there was no way off the beach except the stairs. I'd have her trapped, and then I meant to have a talk with her. I was sorry her mother was dead. I was sorry that she was so angry at her father that she'd ruin his career. But above all, I was tired of her playing dangerous games that could seriously harm some innocent person.

With a full head of steam, I charged down the steps and onto the beach. I was panting and sweating, even though the ocean breeze was cool. Far in the distance the woman beckoned me on. No matter how far I went, she was still ahead of me.

Either she was walking at the edge of the water, or she was a ghost. The fact that she left no footsteps registered on me with a chill.

In the distance, the waves pounded the rock formation shaped like a castle. White spray foamed over even the tallest outcropping, one that looked like a turret. It seemed she was going there, and I meant to catch her.

I put on a final burst of speed, so intent on catching her that I raced past a grove of trees that clung precariously to the cliff wall. With long, slender trunks, they seemed to reach out toward me in the moonlight, swaying in the breeze and causing shadows to dance and skitter on the sand.

The woman in the red dress ran ahead of me, stopping momentarily to turn and make sure I was following. I was gaining on her, and my anger was steadily increasing. Once I got hold of her—if it was Estelle, and I was pretty certain it was—I meant to shake some sense into her.

Dodging through the trees, I sprinted. I never heard anyone behind me. Not even a whisper of sound to alert me. The last thing I remembered was a blinding pain in my head and I dropped into unconsciousness before I hit the dirt.

The cold awakened me. That and the taste of salt. When my eyes opened, it took me a few moments to realize what had happened. Cold salt water washed over my feet and retreated, while spray doused my face and body. I couldn't move my arms or legs, and my only company was a million stars that winked in a perfect velvet night and the empty stretch of beach. High above me, on the cliff, I knew the lights of the mansion were warm and welcoming. But I was a long, long way from safety.

I was tied to the castle rock on the edge of the ocean.

Bad enough, but it got worse. The tide was coming in.

My first attempt to yell taught me that the pounding of the surf completely drowned me out. No one would hear me, and with each wave that smashed on the rocks below, the water inched higher and higher.

I'd never stayed on the beach long enough to determine if the rock was completely submerged by the tide. I'd never asked anyone. Unless I managed to get myself untied, I was going to find out the hard way.

"Help!" I screamed. "Help!" No one could hear me, but there wasn't anything else I could do.

From my blind side came the sound of a deep, warm

chuckle. Whoever had knocked me unconscious and bound me to the rock was hanging around to watch—and laughing about it.

"Untie me, you bastard." I sounded like Linda Blair in *The Exorcist*. "When I get loose, I'm going to cut your gizzard out and fry it up with some bologna."

My only answer was another warm laugh.

It was impossible, but I knew that laugh! "Jitty?" I didn't dare to believe it. I'd never known Jitty to leave Dahlia House. In my hour of need, had she come to save me?

"You sure know how to get your ass in hot water, or cold water in this instance."

I couldn't see her, but I knew it was her. "Untie me, Jitty. Thank God you came! I knew you wouldn't really leave me. Not when I needed you."

"You need something, but it may not be me." She shimmered into being sitting on one of the rocks not two feet away. She wore an eye-popping bikini and diving tanks and gear and she carried a spear gun and a huge knife. Halle Berry as a Bond girl.

"Cut me loose, and then tell me what in the hell you're doing with diving gear. You grew up in the Delta. Nobody in the Delta scuba dives."

"Sarah Booth, you're forgetting that I'm noncorporeal, as you keep insisting when you explain the rules of the Great Beyond to everyone." She smiled. "I can't untie you or cut you free."

"Then do something else! I don't care how you do it, just get me off this rock."

"I'm here to give you comfort."

"You're here pissing me off as payback for leaving Dahlia House."

"I'm not that kind of ghost, Sarah Booth. I'm not into extracting revenge. But I will say tick tock, Sarah Booth. You aren't getting any younger and if you don't pop out a young-un, what will happen to Dahlia House? I just don't see you on the baby track in Hollywood and that's been worrying me."

The nice Jitty, so tender and kind when I'd been heartbroken about leaving Dahlia House, was gone. Bad Jitty was sitting in front of me.

"I won't be alive to spawn if you don't help."

"Calm down, Sarah Booth, you won't drown."

The instant she said it, I did calm down. "How can you be so certain?"

"I know your friends. They'll go to your room and when you aren't there, they'll hunt for you. When they open the front door, Sweetie will bound out into the night and track you. They'll follow. Trust me, it's a done deal."

The water had risen to my waist, and I could only hope that Jitty had the wisdom of her years. If nothing else, she'd calmed me enough so that I was thinking clearly. With the water soaking the ropes that bound me, I might be able to get some stretch out of them. I began to wiggle my feet.

"That's my girl. You ain't no quitter, Sarah Booth. Remember that."

"Thank you, Jitty. For coming. How did—"

"Don't ask and I won't tell. That's the policy in the Great Beyond." She leaned closer. "It's like I told you, I'm never too far away. If you really need me, I'll come."

She was starting to fade. I didn't want to be left alone. "Jitty! Where are you going?"

"I got a date with a handsome man. We're gonna play 007. You're not the only member of the Delaney family who can hang out with stars."

She was gone. Just like that. Infuriating and terrifying all at once. And with her went all of my false courage. I was going to drown!

The sound of baying drifted to me, and my hope rose so rapidly that I gave myself a headache. It was hard to hear with the surf crashing around me, but I distinctly heard a hound—my hound. I'd recognize Sweetie's voice anywhere.

"Sweetie! Sweetie Pie!"

Her lovely bark rode the wind to me.

Mixed in with the bays and the surf, I heard voices. Graf called out to Tinkie and I also heard the Spanish accent of Daniel Martinez. They were drawing closer—and with no time to lose. The tide was rising rapidly now, up to my chest. I focused on wiggling the ropes until I finally got one foot free.

I used that to push myself higher up the rock, hoping that the abrasion of the rope against the rock would free me.

"Sarah Booth!" Graf was running toward me not twenty yards behind Sweetie, who was in a dead gallop.

"Here! On the rock!"

"Get down!" Graf hollered.

For one split second I wanted to beat him. "I'm tied to the rock. Hurry!"

I didn't think he could run faster, but that spurred him on. He was beside me, half running, half swimming. He didn't waste time but went underwater to find the knots that held me.

When he came up sputtering, I could see that he was terrified for me.

"Martinez, hurry! Bring a knife."

Tinkie didn't wait for Daniel. She snatched the knife from his hand and ran like a track star. I'd seldom seen Tinkie exert herself physically—the only running Tinkie did was in "running the Club" or "running Oscar's life." But coming toward me across that night-shaded sand, she was pretty damn spectacular.

She was beside me in a moment, and as soon as she gave Graf the knife, he dove into the water and cut the rope. In seconds I was free and we were all swimming toward shore and an impromptu welcoming committee that waited on the sand. Millie, Cece, and the dinner guests had all come to see what was happening on the beach.

And right behind them was a horde of photographers and reporters.

"Oh, shit," I said, gripping Graf's arm. "We'd better think fast. If word about this gets out, it'll be all over the place and the movie will tank."

Graf reacted quickly. He swept me into his arms and brushed past everyone. "She's fine, she's fine. She just got caught in the current. She's perfectly fine."

A cheer went up and Cece and Millie fell into step beside us. We marched triumphantly through the reporters, my arms around Graf's neck and my gaze upon "my hero." I was really getting the hang of the acting business.

"You may fool those other reporters, but you aren't fooling me," Cece whispered as soon as we were clear of the crowd.

Graf set me on my feet, and I discovered that my legs were weak and I was shaking so badly it looked like Saint Vitus' dance.

"Can you make it up the steps to the house?" he asked.

It was a steep climb, but I could—I would. I nodded. "Let's do it."

CHAPTER ELEVEN

Jovan and Cece had cleared the dishes, and we all sat around the kitchen table. Instead of a raucous, celebratory dinner, it had been solemn, and now everyone was gone except Federico, Jovan, Graf, and my friends.

Both Federico and I had insisted that the authorities not be called. His worries were about the movie; mine were a bit different. I was determined to find out who'd ambushed and tried to kill me, and I didn't want the local authorities mucking things up. If the police were called, there would be a leak to the media. No one doubted that.

Federico paced the room. And the things I was telling him were only adding to his worry.

"Was it Estelle?" he asked.

"I couldn't be certain. It could easily have been her, but it could also have been someone else slender. I mean she had dark hair, but it could have been someone in a wig." I took a breath. "Sally has an entire trunk of hair extensions, wigs, and things right up on the second floor."

Jovan dried her hands on a dish towel and gently rubbed Federico's shoulders. "I think we should leave," she said softly. "No film is worth a human life."

"If we continue at the pace we're going, we can complete

the scenes here in a matter of days. The rest we can do on the studio lots. I can't throw away all the work we've done. The studio would never let me reshoot the film at another location. In the moviemaking climate today, it would ruin me." Federico sipped a snifter of brandy. We each had a glass, and even though I'd had a hot shower, dry clothes, and Millie's delicious fried chicken, I welcomed the warmth of the liquor.

"Martinez said he had two men outside the house. Neither saw a strange woman," Graf said. "I spoke with Martinez and he said he was on the beach only an hour beforehand. He saw nothing."

"And none of the security team saw Sarah Booth, either." Federico swirled the amber liquid in his glass. "Ricardo said they were the best security crew in Petaluma. Maybe I should find someone else, though. I'm not satisfied with their work."

"Unless a security guard is assigned to each of us for twenty-four hours a day, they're not going to be able to protect everyone," I pointed out. "I went out into the gardens. I was angry and determined to put a stop to all of this. I should have gotten Graf or Tinkie to help me. I have to shoulder some of the blame for what happened."

Tinkie put her arm around me. "Sarah Booth can't leave behind her PI ways. There's something going on here, and we're going to figure it out."

"And the place to begin is with Estelle." Federico brought his cell phone from his pocket and placed a call. When he got Estelle's voice mail, he left her a terse message telling her to call him back immediately.

Jovan refilled his glass and wrapped her elegant arms around him. "Let's finish shooting and get away from here. The sooner the better."

That was a sentiment I heartily concurred with. But there were several key scenes up on the schedule for the next day, and I was in most of them. I'd checked myself in the bathroom mirror, and I looked like warmed over death. I had to get some rest.

I stood to excuse myself, and Graf was at my elbow. "Tomorrow I'd like to talk to Ricardo," I said. "Tinkie, can you help?"

"You bet. Oscar can wait another day or two." She picked up my hand and held it. "Millie and Cece have to go, but I can stay a bit longer."

Millie hugged me around the waist and whispered in my ear. "I didn't get any answers on the Internet research, Sarah Booth, but once I get to Zinnia and have access to my files and my contact list, I'll be able to turn something up." She kissed my cheek. "If you want me to stay, I sure can. You're more important than a café."

I hugged her tightly. "You don't have a clue what the café means to people in Sunflower County. Aside from the good food, it's a place to meet, a place to sit with a friend to worry through a problem. It's the hub of the town, Millie. Zinnia can't do without it, or without you."

"I wish you were coming home with us, Sarah Booth. I don't like this business about ghosts and phantoms hiding and jumping out."

The only good thing that had come of my near demise on castle rock was the arrival of Jitty. My family haint had arrived on-scene just in time to keep me from panicking and drowning. Now I wondered if she'd reappear.

Millie would flip if she knew I had my own ghost in Zinnia. "I'll be fine," I assured her. "And before you leave tomorrow, Federico has a surprise for you. Robert Redford is stopping by the set. He heard about your lemon meringue pie."

I thought I was going to have to hold Millie up. Aunt Loulane would have called it a swoon. Millie recovered and danced around me.

"I've got to roll out some pie crust and squeeze the lemons. I've got to—" She headed toward the kitchen.

"Have fun. I'm going to bed."

"Sarah Booth, can I speak with you alone?" Cece asked.

She was unusually solemn, but I figured she wanted to give me a personal good-bye. Tomorrow would be hectic, and there was no guarantee we'd have time for a real parting.

I followed her to her room, and she closed the door. "You never asked what we were doing while you were chasing down the beach."

"You were helping Millie cook," I said. I hadn't asked because I knew.

"We were. But before anyone realized you were missing, I found Sweetie and Chablis locked in a room on the third floor."

I'd gotten over my terror of nearly drowning, but this bit of news sent goose bumps racing down my arms. "A room on the third floor? The costumes and makeup are in the ballroom, but all the other doors are locked." I'd tried them while following the "ghost."

"I had to get a hammer and screwdriver to let them out."

I nodded, afraid that if I spoke my voice would quiver.

"They were both frantic. They nearly killed themselves getting to the front door, but I thought they had to go to the bathroom, that maybe they'd wandered into the room and somehow locked themselves in."

I watched her face. Cece wasn't the kind who worried, but a furrow between her eyebrows told me she was concerned.

"Once I opened the front door, the dogs were gone. Both of them. Like they were on fire. I yelled for Tinkie and Graf, and when Graf caught sight of them vanishing into the gardens, he ran after them."

"So everyone was chasing Sweetie and Chablis instead of looking for me?"

She nodded. "Initially. But Sweetie was acting so bizarre,

we knew something was bad wrong. And we knew it had to involve you. That's when I got really frightened."

"What did Graf say about the dogs being locked up?"

She shook her head. "I didn't get a chance to tell him. Or Tinkie either, but I'm going to call the police." She put her hands on her hips. "Someone set you up. This was premeditated and well planned. If we'd been ten minutes later . . ."

"I know it's dangerous." I took a deep breath. "But if this gets out, someone will leak it to the media, and it'll be in every tabloid. This one thing—that the dogs were deliberately confined—is something only you, me, and the person who did it know about."

Her head moved incrementally up and down. "I see what you're doing, but Graf can't protect you if he doesn't have the facts. Federico's daughter seems criminally deranged."

She was right about that, but it didn't change what I wanted her to do. "Just humor me."

"Until something else happens. Then I'm spilling the beans. Dahling, you can't be damaged before you rise to stardom. Without you, I'll never get a press pass to the Oscars."

We were giggling when there was a tap on Cece's door. She opened it to find an excited Federico. He shifted from one foot to the other. "I finally tracked down one of Estelle's friends here in Petaluma. Estelle left this morning for Los Angeles. She couldn't have been involved."

That information momentarily took me aback. I was pretty certain the woman I'd chased through the gardens and along the beach was Estelle.

"I'm concerned about her," Federico said. "I've tried calling her place in Malibu, but there's no answer."

"Estelle has a house in Malibu?" This was news to me. "Where?"

"Not too far from Lettohatchie Canyon, where you and Graf were staying." Federico seemed oblivious to the conclusion I'd drawn in a nanosecond.

"You never mentioned that Estelle lives in Malibu."

He looked at his shoes. So he had jumped to the same place, and he was ashamed of himself.

"Suzy Dutton is dead, Federico. Joey was injured here on the set. I was almost drowned. Serious things are happening, and your daughter is linked to all of it."

"She's disturbed, Sarah Booth, but she isn't dangerous. Besides, she couldn't have harmed you. She's not even in this country."

Federico wanted so badly to believe that his daughter wasn't someone who would murder. I understood that, but it didn't make it true. So far, I could say that Estelle could easily have been in the vicinity of Suzy Dutton's "fall" from a cliff. She could also have damaged the balcony where Joey fell, and she could have messed with the camera. It was possible she'd been in the house and pushed Jovan down the stairs. I'd seen her—or someone who looked a lot like her—before I was nearly drowned. And I knew for certain that Estelle had the means to slip in and out of the house undetected—and someone had locked up the dogs. The evidence was stacking up against her.

"Are you sure she left Costa Rica?" Cece asked.

"Regena says so. They share an apartment in Petaluma, so she would know."

"And who is this roommate?" Cece followed through.

"Regena Lombardi. She's a dancer."

I made a mental note of the name. Once I was through filming in the morning, I intended to pay Regena a call.

"Thanks for telling me, Federico."

He remained in the doorway. "Estelle has given me many problems, but she is my flesh and blood. She's an unhappy young woman, but I can't believe she would harm anyone."

I had a goose egg on my head that was all the evidence I needed that someone had meant to harm me. But I wasn't going to argue with Federico. Not now. Not in front of Cece, who was already worried enough.

"Tomorrow I'll see what I can find out. Let's give it a rest until then."

"Until the morning." He kissed both of my cheeks. "And have a safe trip home, Ms. Falcon. It's been a pleasure having you here."

"Thank you, Mr. Marquez. It's going to be a bang-up movie."

He left and I looked at Cece, who rolled her eyes. "Daddy doesn't want to believe his little darling is a murderer."

"When you get to the airport, can you check to see if Estelle actually boarded a plane today?"

"Sure. I don't think Costa Rica has the security issues we have in the States. Should be a piece of cake."

"Thank you, Cece. You're a good friend."

"Sarah Booth, you're going to be a huge star. I'm only doing this so you'll owe me."

I gave her a big hug and hurried to my room. Graf was waiting for me. Even though someone had tried to kill me, I was still a lucky woman.

To my bitter disappointment, the next morning when Robert Redford arrived, I was working. I caught a glimpse of him and Millie walking in the gardens. By the time I was due a break, Robert was gone and Millie and Cece were packed. Federico had assigned one of the security guards to drive them to be sure nothing happened on the way.

I kissed and hugged and held back the tears that would wash away all of Sally's artful work. When the car pulled out of the driveway, Sweetie sat at my feet and howled mournfully. "We'll see them soon," I promised her. I was ready for a trip back to Zinnia. I was homesick.

When I finished my scenes, I picked up the keys to one of

the rental cars and drove into Petaluma. It wasn't far, and I could have walked, but I wasn't certain where Estelle and Regena's apartment might be, and I didn't have time to walk if it was a distance away.

I checked a local phone book and found a listing for Regena Lombardi. There was none for Estelle. I rang the number and was surprised when a young woman answered. My Spanish was nonexistent, so I prayed Regena spoke English.

And she did—very well in fact. In less than thirty seconds she'd agreed to meet with me.

The apartment complex was lovely, sort of a 1950s Hollywood set where aspiring starlets might rent. Regena's apartment was 2B, and I knocked on the mahogany door, wondering how this interview was going to go.

The young woman who answered the door was petite, with hair colored a plum shade and a nose ring. She wore a leotard and leg warmers and was barefoot.

"I'm Sarah Booth Delaney," I said, trying hard to read her face, but she gave nothing away.

"I'm due to dance rehearsals in twenty minutes. It's a big opportunity for me."

"I'll be brief." I slipped inside before she could block me at the door. "Are you sure Estelle has gone to Los Angeles?" I asked as I took in the decor. Low-rent college kid furnishings were mixed with some expensive furniture and art.

"She said she was going, and yesterday morning she was gone."

"Did she take her things?"

Regena shrugged. "Estelle has things here, in Malibu, and in Europe. She doesn't have to carry things. They're there waiting for her when she arrives." There was no bitterness in Regena's tone.

"What kind of person is Estelle?"

She sank into a beanbag chair—an artifact from the seventies, I suspected. "She's very kind. She helps people when she can."

"And she hates her father."

She looked away, a telling gesture. "Federico was never there for her. After she turned ten, she was shipped off to boarding schools. Whenever she wanted to come home, he told her no. She wasn't even allowed to visit her mother when she was dying. How would that make you feel?"

"Pretty shitty, I'm sure."

"Her dad doesn't care about anything but himself and his movies. He even had Estelle thrown out of her house."

I thought of Federico's face as he tried to assure me Estelle couldn't be involved in the attack on me. "That isn't true, Regena. He's devoted to his work, but he cares about Estelle. He's worried about her right now."

"She doesn't think so."

And therein lay the rub. Perception was everything.

"Has Estelle been in Petaluma long?" I was curious to discover if she was in Malibu when Suzy was killed.

"She's been gone for a couple of weeks, and she came in the night before you guys arrived. She travels a lot." She went to the kitchen and returned with two bottles of water and handed me one. "She was in a state. She talked about booby-trapping the house. She said she asked her father not to film there, out of respect for Carlita. He just ignored her. The film was everything. Estelle's feelings didn't matter at all."

I sipped the water. "Has Estelle ever mentioned that her mother's ghost is in the house?"

Regena gave me a look that left no doubt she thought I was nuts. "Look, Estelle is angry, not insane."

"She's never spoken of a ghost or spirit in the house?"

She laughed. "Not to me. But it sounds like a good way to run off a bunch of unwanted company."

"You've never heard ghost stories about the house?" That

was peculiar. Daniel Martinez, the security guy, had mentioned the ghost stories as if everyone in town knew them.

She shrugged. "Any old house that sits empty is going to get a reputation in a small town. Petaluma isn't a big city. Kids used to go out there to park, until a couple of them got spooked away."

This was interesting, but impossible to track down. "Do you remember any of the stories?"

The blush that touched her cheeks was unexpected. "I was there one summer evening with a guy I used to date, swimming in the cove. I thought I saw a woman in a red dress on the balcony."

My gut tightened and my skin began to crawl. "Who was it?"

"I don't know."

"Did your date see her?"

She bit her bottom lip. "No. He thought I was making it up to avoid, you know. He got mad because I insisted that we leave. Anyway, there were a couple of people who saw something like that."

"No one ever investigated?"

"Nope." She walked to the door. "Now I have to go. I can't be late or they'll cut me from the rehearsals."

I followed her out the door. "Thank you, Regena."

"When you finally track Estelle down, ask her to call me, please. I've left twenty messages and she hasn't returned my calls. Sometimes she gets depressed and just sort of fades. That worries me and I have some things we need to talk about."

"Will do." I kept it perky and upbeat, but the talk about depression concerned me, too.

CHAPTER TWELVE

Another day in paradise was concluding, and I returned to the mansion with a mental list of people to talk to. Ricardo was right at the top, but I wanted to catch him away from his dad.

Tinkie, Chablis, and Sweetie were at the beach. I walked to the edge of the gardens and looked down to see her and the dogs scurrying around castle rock. It took me a moment to realize that the slick body in the surf wasn't a dolphin—Graf was in scuba gear examining the portions of the rock that were underwater.

They were looking for clues. My heart surged with warmth. Graf really seemed to care about me. And Tinkie, well, she was the best friend ever.

We were an odd couple for a business team. When I'd first come home, licking my wounds and in dire financial circumstances, I'd failed to see past the Daddy's Girl exterior that Tinkie projected.

I'd sold her short.

But she was far more than her five-carat engagement ring, her banker husband, and her Dun & Bradstreet report. Tinkie, for all of her slavish devotion to glamour and fashion, was smart. And loyal. And caring.

Watching her and Graf and the dogs, I again thanked whatever lucky stars had brought her into my life. I'd lost a lot, but I'd also gained.

Tinkie and Graf went into a huddle, and then they packed it in and started back toward the mansion. I changed into some cool shorts, sandals, and a sleeveless T-shirt and went down to greet them.

Graf swung me into his arms, making me giddy with laughter, as Tinkie looked on with approval. "It's good to see you happy, Sarah Booth." She punched Graf's arm lightly. "I never thought this celluloid playboy could do it, but I was wrong. I think he's good for you."

"And she's good for me," Graf said.

"And we all have to be good detectives to get this whole mess resolved." I put my arms around their waists as we walked to the front door. When I told them my plan, they readily agreed.

Tinkie distracted Federico, while I talked to Ricardo. Graf was going to the third floor to see if Sally and Dallas had heard or seen anything unusual.

Ricardo had a room on the second floor in another wing from my room. I knocked on his door, half expecting that he wouldn't be in.

The door swung open and he stood there, shirtless, in a pair of shorts. Like his father, he was handsome, and he knew it. While his conduct on the set was impeccable, I'd heard he was something of a rake and a scoundrel with the young women who were part of the crew.

"Dad send you to talk to me?" he asked, leaving the door open so I could enter or not.

"No. Why would he?"

He flashed his perfect white teeth. "Because Dad doesn't like confrontation of any kind."

"And what have you been doing that would lead to a confrontation?"

"Sleeping with Dallas. Dad is afraid if I dump her she'll quit in the middle of the film." His grin was just a hair too smug.

"Your father has legitimate concerns, Ricardo. No one likes to be used like garbage." Dallas was a beautiful young woman. She could have her pick of any number of men, but Ricardo could make her feel like trash in a ditch.

He shrugged, picked an apple from a table, and bit into it with a loud crack. "I'm giving her what she wants."

"Somehow, I doubt that."

"Come on, you older people don't get it. We hooked up. She knows that. When we get back to Los Angeles, she'll go her way and I'll go mine. That's how it is." He took another huge bite of apple.

"As long as she knows that upfront. We 'older people' and most younger ones, too, like to know the rules before we begin the game." I wasn't insulted by his rudeness. In terms of maturity, the fourteen years between us was a huge distance. He was handsome, privileged, and felt entitled. "I didn't come to talk about Dallas. I want to ask you some questions about your sister."

"Estelle, the psycho queen?" He took the last large bite of the fruit and tossed the core into a garbage can. "What's she done now?"

"Do you know where she is?"

"Ah, hiding in the attic?" He grinned big, proud of what he viewed as his cleverness.

It was peculiar, but I'd talked to Ricardo before, and he hadn't been such a jackass. "Do you know where Estelle is?" I asked patiently. "Federico is worried about her and so am I."

The mask of superiority dropped for a moment. "Why? What's she done now?"

"Nothing, for sure. She's not answering her cell phone." I wasn't certain how to proceed. I'd expected Ricardo to be more cooperative. Our prior conversations had been pleasant; now there was antagonism.

"Sometimes she gets down and doesn't want to talk to people," he said. "Maybe she wants to be left alone."

"That's a reason for concern. This anger she carries toward your father could be . . ." I let the sentence fade. He'd supply his own ending.

"She'll be fine. She's just pissed about the house. He could have asked her, you know."

"I don't know. I don't know any of the details. What I'd like to know is how stable is your sister?"

He dropped all pretense of being the smartass he'd been earlier. Motioning to a comfortable chair for me, he sat down on the floor. "Look, Estelle has her ups and downs, but she's not going to harm herself."

"Could she harm someone else?"

That really got his attention. "She likes to pretend to be crazier than she is."

"Someone tried to drown me last night. It wasn't kidding around. Joey was seriously hurt in that fall. Another woman associated with your father in Los Angeles is dead."

"And you think Estelle is doing all of that?" The idea shocked him.

"I didn't come to tell you what I thought. I want to know what you think."

"What does Dad say?"

"What do you think, Ricardo? Tell me that and then we'll talk about Federico."

He considered for a long moment, one hand aimlessly brushing up and down his shin. "She hated Suzy Dutton. She thought . . ." He looked at me, suddenly much younger than his twenty years. "Estelle wasn't rational about sex. She has it in her head that Mom died because of Dad and his liaisons with other women."

"And why did your mother die?"

"She hated herself."

It was a pretty succinct summation of the terrible disease that had killed Carlita. "Does Estelle know this?"

"In her heart she does, but she won't admit it. If she accepted that Mom was mentally ill, that Mom starved herself to death, then she'd have to forgive Dad." He sighed, suddenly tired. "This is all so boring."

"If Estelle is trying to sabotage Federico's film, we're going to have to stop her before she really hurts someone."

"Good luck. She knows this house inside and out. Grandfather showed her all of the secret passages, the places he had built into it just for her."

I'd been curious about this. "Why would he construct a house like that?"

"He liked puzzles. He liked playing games with us when we were children. He could hide and we would never find him. He enjoyed that." He was smiling as he talked. "Estelle adored him. He gave her his undivided attention and I think the only time she really felt loved was when she was with him."

"I've never heard Federico talk of him."

"For good reason. Dad and Granddad hated each other. Pappy Estoban didn't believe Dad was good enough for his daughter. He did everything he could to break them up before they married. He told me once that if Mom hadn't married Dad, she would be alive and happily married."

"And I suppose he told Estelle the same thing?"

Federico lifted a shoulder and let it drop. "When Dad moved us to California, Pappy was furious. He tried to get the police to stop Dad from taking Mom and us. He had Dad arrested. It was awful."

I could only imagine the horror of that scene to a child—caught between the grandfather she loved and the family she felt didn't love her.

As sorry as I felt for Estelle, I still had to know if she

was capable of harming another person. "Estelle went to a private boarding school, as you did. Was she ever in trouble?"

His gaze dropped and I knew he was thinking about lying. For all of his sexual suavity, he wasn't as sophisticated as he thought.

"Tell me the truth, Ricardo. I'm not out to harm Estelle, but if she is behind some of these things, she has to be stopped."

"Why don't you ask Dad about this?"

I considered my answer, but I told him the truth. "Whatever Estelle thinks of her father, he's doing everything he can to divert suspicion from her. I'm afraid he'd color the truth to protect her."

"And you figured I'd be a stool pigeon?" He was quick to insult.

"No, I figured you'd want to help your sister and could see that the truth was the best way to get there."

He rose to his feet in one fluid movement. "How about a banana? They're fresh from a plantation not far from here."

"Sure." The bananas available in Petaluma were totally different creatures from the ones in supermarkets.

He brought back two and began to peel his. I thought perhaps he was going to ignore my request, but he began talking. "Estelle was expelled from one school for a stunt she pulled that resulted in injury to another girl. It was harmless, but it looked bad then and it could also look bad now."

"What happened?"

"No one knows the exact details, because Estelle would never talk about it. Not even to defend herself. But Lisa, a girl in her dormitory, fell from a second-floor window. The headmaster said Estelle put Lisa up to edging out on the brickwork and pretending that she was going to jump. This was a diversion so Estelle could sneak out of the dormitory."

"She was trying to get home?"

"Yeah." He ate the banana. "She was miserable at boarding

school. She hated being away from Mom, and she hated the other girls."

"You went away to school also. Was it like that for you?"

"It was okay for me." He took my peel and tossed it in the trash. "I hated being at home and I made friends easily. For Estelle, it was torture. She was shy and self-conscious, and she had this need to be at home to protect Mom." His laugh was bitter. "She didn't understand that no one could protect Mom from Mom."

"How seriously was her classmate injured?"

"Two broken legs. Nothing fatal."

"I'm guessing she slipped?"

"Yeah. There was never any doubt about that. Estelle was already headed out the gate of the school where she'd finagled a ride to the train station. She was held accountable, though, for thinking up the plan."

Estelle had a cunning mind and an interesting ability to get others to go along with her plans. Had she convinced Suzy Dutton to meet her in the canyon so she could push her over the cliff?

That reminded me that I needed to check in with Sheriff King to see what the final determination in Suzy's death was.

"If you hear from your sister, will you let me know?"

"Sure. But I'm going to tell her you're looking for her. I'm not going to betray her."

That wasn't exactly what I wanted, but it wasn't worth an argument. "Fine. Tell her to please call me or your father. On a related topic, do you know who damaged the cameras on the first day of shooting?"

"That was probably Estelle. She all but said she'd done it. Lucky for Dad she doesn't know enough about cameras to really tear one up."

"Yeah, lucky." I rose and walked to the door. With my hand on the frame, I paused. "Ricardo, have you seen anyone strange here in the house?"

He rolled his eyes. "The ghost?"

I nodded.

"Dallas and Sally were asking me about it, too. There's some old story that this house is haunted. My grandfather would love that. Heck, he may have started it."

"Do you know who supposedly haunts the house?"

"Estelle always believed it was Mom. Some people say it's a woman in a dark dress, which sounds like the portrait of Mom in the room you're in. I think people want a little thrill, so they see a shadow and create this whole legend."

"So you haven't seen the ghost and you don't believe there is one?"

"That sums it up."

"Thanks." I hurried down the corridor toward my room. At the stairs that led to the third floor, I hesitated. It was late in the day. Graf had gone to talk to Sally and Dallas, but he was surely finished by now. The third floor, by all rights, should be empty.

I took my shoes off and crept up the stairs. A lot of mysterious things were happening on the third floor. Disappearing ghosts, locked-up dogs. It was hard to snoop when people were going to and fro to costume and makeup. This was a perfect opportunity.

I eased into the hallway and listened. I heard only silence, except for the gentle tinkle of the wind chimes that still hung outside.

Moving silently along the wall, I paused before each door to listen. If Estelle was hiding in the house, she was quiet as a church mouse. I thought I heard a dull pounding, but it was only my heartbeat in my ears. The silence was downright scary. I'd never heard a house so soundless, as if even the past had been sucked from it.

The doors to the ballroom were open, and I glanced around, half hoping someone was still working in costume or makeup. I'd managed to frighten myself just a tad, and some company would have been welcome.

White screens made small dressing rooms that were like ghostly alcoves all over the huge room. Dresses and outfits hung on dressmaker dummies, giving the illusion that someone was there. It was a creepy place. I was about to leave when I heard a soft thumping sound. This time I knew it wasn't my imagination.

I couldn't be certain, but it sounded like kicking. Or something thudding, step by step, down a flight of stairs.

Something really awful was nagging at the back of my mind, but I pushed hard to keep it submerged.

Walking through the sheet-draped alcoves, I felt like every idiotic teen in every idiotic teen horror movie. I'd sat in many an audience screaming, "Don't go up the stairs! Don't open the door! Don't go in the laundry room!" And yet here I was, walking through a room that looked like a set for some psycho lurker to jump out and grab me.

I heard the thudding again, but it seemed neither closer nor farther away. In the maze of the screens, I'd lost my bearings in the huge room. I kept walking, slowly, moving and wishing that Tinkie or Graf or Sweetie or Chablis would appear and laugh at my foolishness. I'd just spied the exit and began to make my way there and back to the safety of the second floor when the strange notes of a pianoforte came from a corner of the ballroom.

In the times I'd been in costume and makeup, I'd never noticed such an instrument. The skin on the back of my neck and my arms marched crazily around in goose bumps.

I recognized the tune, though I couldn't name it.

A woman's voice, low and sultry, began to sing, "Hush, hush, sweet Charlotte."

My blood literally ran cold. I knew that song. The movie had terrorized me as a child when "John's" head tumbles down the stairs and lands at Bette Davis's feet.

That was the thudding. That was the sound. John's head thumping step by step as it rolled to the bottom!

I wheeled and spun to beat it back to the second floor when I heard a delicious giggle, warm and rich.

There was something about that giggle that stopped me. It came again, far too amused to be dangerous. I knew who it was.

"Jitty!" I'd been had by a haint. "Jitty, you'd better show yourself!"

She came out from behind one of the screens wearing the layered tulle ball gown that Bette Davis had worn in the movie. The front of the dress was covered in a huge bloodstain.

"John!" She came toward me holding out bloody hands. "John! Don't leave me!"

"Stop it." I backed away from her. I couldn't help it, even though I knew she wasn't "Charlotte." She was thoroughly convincing.

She wiped her hands on the gown. "See, you're not the only Delaney who can act. You should see your face. You thought my heel whackin' the floor was ole John's head tumblin' along, didn't you?"

"If you weren't dead I'd probably kill you." I was exasperated and panting from fear, but I was also glad to see her. "What are you doing here?"

"Watching out for you."

"Thanks. You've got a real unique way of showing it." I took a deep breath and regained my composure. "Got any good tips for me?"

She looked around the room. "There's something really strange about this house. I haven't gotten a handle on it yet, but I'll get back with you. In the meantime, you'd better check in with that man of yours. He's looking for you."

She shimmered away, and before she was completely gone, I heard Graf calling my name.

"Be right there!" I yelled and beat it out the door before I had a chance to get lost again.

CHAPTER THIRTEEN

I ran into Graf's arms with enough force to make him stagger.

"Sarah Booth." He hugged me tight. "What's wrong?"

"I scared myself." It was as close to the truth as I would go. While I hadn't hesitated to tell him about the woman in the red dress who seemed to haunt Federico's house, I wasn't about to tell him about Jitty.

He eased me back so he could look into my eyes. "I'm sorry. I didn't learn much from Dallas or Sally. They've heard noises, but nothing that really bothered them." His beautiful eyes twinkled. "But Tinkie hit pay dirt."

I didn't want to look away from Graf. In his eyes I glimpsed an extraordinary image of myself. I was valuable, desirable, necessary. I liked that reflection far better than the one in my mirror. Graf saw the best in me and ignored the rest. What a wonderful gift.

I'd held back, but I needed to tell him something. I could make no guarantees, but I could be honest. "Graf, each day my heart opens a little more to you."

He kissed me lightly. "I have no great faith that somehow I won't screw this up. But I am trying."

"Me, too." It was all we could ask of each other, and the

possibilities were terrifying. I changed the subject to something more manageable. "What did Tinkie find?"

"I'll let her tell you." He escorted me to the kitchen where Tinkie was whirling up a blender of celebratory margaritas. She met me with a full-wattage smile that reminded me of expensive orthodontic procedures.

"What did you find out?" I asked as I took a glass of "that frozen concoction" and passed one to Graf.

Tinkie licked the salt from the rim and arched one eyebrow—a newly acquired trait. "Federico said there was a floor plan for this house at an architect's in Petaluma. I called, but the office had already closed for the day. Tomorrow morning while you're filming, I'll visit Senor Lopez and pick up a copy of the plans."

"Tinkie! That's perfect." I checked my watch. It was six o'clock, which meant it would be four in Los Angeles. "I'm going to call Sheriff King and check on Suzy Dutton's autopsy report. It's peculiar that we haven't heard a word from him. I figured for sure he'd have me taken back to the States in chains."

"You do have a way with lawmen, Sarah Booth." Tinkie turned on the blender to whip up another round of drinks, effectively blocking my reply.

While I took the telephone to the front hallway to make my call, she turned ice cubes into delicious tequila slush.

Sheriff King was leaving his office when my call went through, but he took it. My first question was direct and to the point about Suzy's autopsy.

"Well, well, Miss Delaney. It isn't every day that a suspect calls to check in with me."

"Have you gotten the autopsy report on Suzy Dutton?" I asked for the second time.

"I'm trying to keep the coroner's ruling out of the press," he said, "but I don't reckon you'll be spreading the news. Word all over Los Angeles is that your movie is cursed. Rumors abound, and most of them center on your director. Folks are saying some of his past deeds are coming home to roost." He paused for dramatic effect. "Talk like that isn't good for a movie."

"I wouldn't have believed that the sheriff of a California county would be susceptible to ghost stories and curses." I couldn't help myself. King brought out the very worst in my antiauthoritarian nature.

"I've been in law enforcement long enough to know that sometimes the factual explanation defies logic. Bad luck is the same as a curse, except a curse makes for better head-lines."

"Right, and the boogeyman is haunting the cast and crew." I had to force the sarcasm into my voice, but I wasn't going to let King know he was getting to me. He was a smug bastard. "What did the autopsy determine?"

"I don't have to tell you this, but I will. It was a homicide. She was pushed."

"How did the coroner come to that conclusion?" I wasn't questioning the coroner, but I was curious.

"He found grass and dirt under her fingernails. She clung to the cliff. Her knuckles were scraped and bruised—"

"As if someone stepped on her hands?" I couldn't keep the shock out of my voice.

"More like stomped them with cleated hiking boots."

That was even more horrific. "Who would do such a thing?"

"That's what I'm going to find out. We've questioned Bobby Joe Taylor at length, and though he knew Suzy, he doesn't believe she was visiting him. They'd had an argument about a movie script and she wasn't speaking to him. He also says the note on the mirror wasn't directed at him, that he'd given up his womanizing ways and had been dating his cur-rent girlfriend exclusively."

"And what else did you expect him to say?" Was King slow

or just determined to devil me? He believed everyone except me. Because he was determined that Federico was guilty of something?

King's voice was lazy. "I figure most all of you actor types will lie to cover your asses, so I didn't expect anything else."

"If I were involved in Suzy's death, do you think I'd be calling right now?"

"You would if you were smart and trying to look innocent."

There was no way to win with King. "Do you have any other suspects except for me and Federico?"

He hesitated, and I wondered if he was actually going to be honest with me.

"Who?" I pressed.

"There were several phone calls made to Ms. Dutton's home. The calls came from pay phones in the Malibu area."

"I didn't—"

"Your actions for the specific times when the calls were made have been accounted for. You were on the set and filming. You and Marquez have alibis, so don't bother professing your innocence."

Even when he was being sort of nice, King was a pill. "So who else is a suspect?" I deliberately withheld Estelle's name. I couldn't decide if I was trying to protect Federico, or if I simply wasn't comfortable pointing the finger of blame at a young woman who was already emotionally troubled. It was possible that Estelle made those calls to Suzy, but the bottom line was that only circumstance seemed to implicate Estelle. I had no real evidence that she'd done anything wrong except tinker with her father's cameras—and that was hearsay from her brother. I knew what it felt like to be falsely accused, and I didn't want to inflict that on someone as delicate as Estelle.

"We're working on it."

"Sheriff, have you determined a motive for Suzy's death? I mean, looking at it from my point of view, why would I kill her when I already have the part?"

Silence stretched between us. At last he spoke. "You might not have as much to gain as Marquez, when it comes right down to it."

"I'll take that as a compliment," I said sweetly, "but what does Federico have to gain from the death of a former girl-friend?"

"Oh, I'd say there could be numerous answers to that question. Marquez is something of a legend in the Hollywood Hills. A lot of people had scores to settle with him, and maybe Suzy Dutton was trying."

Arguing with King was like spitting into the wind. "Am I still a suspect?"

"That sheriff in Sunflower County speaks highly of you, Miss Delaney. He assured me you were never a serious suspect in the murder of Renata Trovaioli, but that he had to arrest you because of the evidence that had been planted to frame you."

Coleman was a day late and a dollar short with his explanations. But there was no point going into that with Grady King. "So am I off your suspect list?"

"Maybe."

He was as thorny as a Devil's Walking Stick. "I'll take that as a yes. Sheriff, could you possibly check on Federico's daughter, Estelle?" I gave him her Malibu address. "She's been here in Petaluma, but she left Costa Rica suddenly yesterday and we're concerned that we haven't heard from her. She isn't answering her phone."

"Why concerned?"

I didn't want to overplay it. "She's high-strung and she's had emotional problems in the past. Just a call or drive by her place to make sure she's okay would be great."

"I'll get an officer out there as soon as I hang up. I'm sure we have someone in the Hollywood Brat Babysitter department. Hey, if Federico's daughter was in Malibu—"

"She was in Petaluma, according to her roommate, at the time of Suzy's death." That wasn't a proven fact, but I didn't want King giving Estelle the rough treatment until I knew she was guilty. "Even though you're ill-tempered, I thank you." I meant it, too. If I knew Estelle was truly in Malibu—and okay—it would give me some necessary answers about what was happening in Petaluma.

"When is the film crew returning to the States?" he asked.

"In a couple of days. We're almost finished."

"Tell Marquez to check in with me as soon as he gets into town. And let me remind you, Miss Delaney, that if you aren't involved in the murder, then it's possible you're a future target. Bobby Joe Taylor has convinced me that the note left on the mirror was meant for you. So take that into account when you're flitting around the area."

"I feel better knowing that you're concerned for my safety. Have a good afternoon." I hung up. Even though I enjoyed my moment of one-upsmanship, King's words troubled me. Bad things were happening around this movie. Someone had a burn on for Federico or someone involved with the film. And until we found out who that person was and stopped him or her, things could get worse.

Once Tinkie and Chablis were safely tucked in bed, Graf and I found some time alone. Instead of a stolen few passionate kisses in the garden alcoves, we had the night to ourselves. With all of the commotion going on, I hadn't been able to focus on Graf and my feelings for him. As the moon peeked in the bedroom window, I set about putting that to right.

A breeze with a trace of salt rumbaed with the sheer curtains and teased our superheated skin as we made love. We were different, both of us, than we'd been in New York. We were gentler in some ways and more savage in others. But there was no doubt that we were kinder to each other in every way. The sense that time would run out for us—an emotion that had dominated our relationship in New York—was gone. We took our time with each other, savoring each touch, each sensation.

There is no aphrodisiac like self-confidence, and I found a willing partner in Graf. In our bed, there wasn't room for fear. In that wonderful way of passion, the more I had, the more I wanted.

Graf had just begun a wicked exploration of the backs of my knees with his mouth when there was a loud crash from downstairs followed by an eardrum-piercing scream.

Sweetie began barking and clawing at the bedroom door with such franticness that it sent a shaft of fear through me. Tinkie was alone in her room with only Chablis to protect her. Chablis would do her best—and could be a fearsome adversary if she had the element of surprise on her side—but she only weighed three pounds.

Galvanized into action, Graf and I threw on robes and hurried into the hallway to peer down the stairs. Sweetie didn't wait for us. She took the steps four at time, landing at the bottom in a dead scramble for the kitchen.

Hysterical sobbing came from there, and Graf and I ran. Along the way he picked up a heavy candlestick, and I clutched one of my beautiful spike heels.

Pale and shaken, Federico joined us. "Jovan is missing," he whispered.

But not for long. We found her in the kitchen hunkered in a corner and crying. She was so terrified she fought Federico when he captured her in his arms to console her.

"She's afraid," Graf said, looking around. Nothing in the kitchen was out of place except for a platter that was smashed

on the floor. I examined the broken pieces and realized it had
been valuable, a handmade piece that was signed by the artist.

As Federico and Graf lifted Jovan from the floor and into
a chair, I gathered the large pieces of clay and swept up the
sharp shards. Sweetie patrolled the kitchen, whining at the
sink and clawing at the cabinet door.

I opened the cabinet, but only neat rows of cleaning supplies were in evidence. I had no idea what was wrong with
Sweetie Pie. She kept nosing the cabinet like a rib eye had
been dropped there, but I couldn't find a thing.

Tinkie, rubbing the sleep from her eyes, joined us. "What's
going on? I thought I heard a scream and a crash."

Jovan whimpered before she answered. "There was a
woman, here in the kitchen. A stranger." She was shaking so
violently that her teeth chattered. Her pale blue eyes were
glassy with shock.

Federico put his arms around her and held her. "You're
safe," he said, but he looked around the kitchen as if he expected to see the intruder hiding in a corner. I couldn't help
but wonder if he was looking for his dead wife. A chill swept
over my body at the thought.

"What did she look like?" Tinkie asked gently. She took a
seat at the table and patted Jovan's hand. "Can you tell us?
Then we'll find her."

"She had on a red dressing gown." Jovan inhaled with a
shudder. "She was standing right there, at the sink, and she
turned to face me." Tears ran down her cheeks and she choked
back a sob.

"Jovan, darling, take a deep breath." Federico rubbed her
arms and kissed her head as he did his best to give her comfort. "You're safe now. We're all here with you."

She inhaled deeply and continued. "She was so beautiful,
at first. I thought she was an actress I hadn't met yet, someone
dark and exotic and beautiful." Her eyes welled with tears
again. "But then she glared at me. Her eyes were dark and

hey burned like hot coals." She sobbed in earnest. "It was awful. She looked at me with such hatred, and then she lunged at me and said, 'Get out! Get out of my house before you die!' " She closed her eyes. "She said we were all going to die."

Even though we were all in the kitchen with the lights on, I edged closer to Graf. Tinkie, on the other hand, took practical action and went to check the door that led to the outside. It was locked. From the inside.

"Which way did she go?" Tinkie asked. "Did anyone else see her?"

We all shook our heads.

Jovan wiped her tears away. "I don't know. That platter shot off the counter and smashed. I was startled and glanced at the broken dish. When I looked up, she was gone."

Federico rubbed the right side of his face. "That platter was made for Carlita by Pablo Rameriz."

"The famous artist?" Tinkie knew exactly who he was.

"Carlita sometimes modeled for him. He adored her. She valued that platter highly."

Jovan turned so that she could look at him. Her eyes widened. "She broke it so we couldn't use it. She is haunting this house, like everyone says. She hates us so much she'd destroy a work of art to keep us from using it." She burst into wild tears.

"I'll check the front door and the windows," Graf volunteered.

"Take Sweetie with you." My hound was pacing the kitchen. When she went with Graf, Chablis followed.

"Jovan," I said, "are you sure you haven't seen this woman before?" I refused to name her Carlita. If the idea that Federico's dead wife was out to get us circulated through the film crew, we would shut down.

Jovan covered her eyes. "The first night I came here. When someone pushed me down the stairs. I saw her upstairs. I think she must have pushed me."

"You're positive it was the same woman?" I'd resisted believing that a ghost could harm any of us—or even that a ghost was involved. But Jovan had evidence.

She nodded. "I'm sure of it now. It was her. The same woman I saw on the second floor. The one who pushed me and could have killed me. And she said we're going to die."

I spoke before I thought. "She has to be in the house somewhere."

My matter-of-fact tone made Jovan look at me. "She doesn't have to be here. If she's a ghost, she can come and go as she pleases."

"Ghosts can't push humans." When everyone turned to look at me, I realized I'd spoken with authority. "I mean, ghosts aren't supposed to be able to manipulate matter." In all of the time I'd spent with Jitty, the best she could muster was a breeze.

"Evil spirits have powers," Jovan said in a whisper. "Her eyes burned like hot coals. She was evil. I know she was. I know it." She turned her face into Federico's pajama top and cried.

Tinkie looked at me. "Do you believe this?" she asked in a whisper.

"I don't know." I'd seen a woman in red. She'd lured me to the beach where I'd been attacked and nearly drowned. But I wasn't certain I believed this entity could push Jovan down the stairs or fling a platter. I needed to consult with Jitty, but she was being coy and evasive.

"Let's go back to our rooms," Federico said as he assisted Jovan to her feet. "Perhaps we should go to the hospital and get you checked out. Maybe the doctor can prescribe a stronger sedative."

"No, no, I'm fine. I have my big scene with Graf and Sarah Booth tomorrow. I don't want to see a doctor." She swayed on her feet and Federico steadied her.

It was true that Jovan was slated for the big confrontation

scene between Matty and the sister-in-law about the will. Ned, representing Matty, gets his first clue that he doesn't know everything about the woman he's become embroiled with. It was going to be Jovan's finest moment in the film, and if she didn't get some rest, she was going to look awful.

"I'll check with Graf and make sure the house is locked up," I said.

"Me, too." Tinkie stood up beside me.

"You can't lock out a ghost," Jovan said, blinking back a fresh round of tears. "Be careful, because if you see her, she's going to try to hurt you, too."

I took Jovan's limp hand. "Please don't tell anyone about this until we have a chance to investigate."

She looked at me as if I were dense.

"Jovan, this film is already plagued with rumors about curses and other problems. If this story gets out among the cast and crew, it could cause a lot of problems."

"She's right," Federico said. "This kind of story will add fuel to a dangerous fire."

"And none of you care that I was nearly frightened to death." Jovan stepped away from Federico, the glint of battle in her eyes.

"It isn't that," I assured her. "Tinkie and Graf and I will search the house from top to bottom. We'll do everything we can. If this woman is real, we'll find her."

"And if she isn't?" Jovan challenged.

"I don't know what we can do about an angry ghost."

"We can get out of this house." Jovan stalked across the room and paused in the doorway. "She's already injured me. Next time, she may break my neck."

She had a point, but I had a suggestion. "I think none of us should wander around the house alone. We can stay in teams."

"You think that will stop her? She can hurt two of us as easily as one. I don't like living in a place that's dangerous."

My response was cut short when Graf returned, a worried

look on his face. "All of the doors are locked from the inside. The downstairs windows are also locked."

"Then we need to conduct a search." Tinkie was all business. "We'll put an end to this foolishness once and for all."

CHAPTER FOURTEEN

Once the door to Federico's rooms was closed, I turned to Graf and Tinkie. "Let's take this place apart."

"What have you figured out?" Tinkie asked. We'd only been partners for a year, but she knew me.

"I'm beginning to find it strange that Carlita's ghost—or whoever this apparition is—has appeared only to women." I turned to Graf. "Have you seen it?"

"Not even a flicker of strange light." He looked around the foyer and up the staircase. "Now that you point it out, it is odd that the ghost would appear only to you and Jovan."

Tinkie gave me a foxy look. "Unless there's some special attraction between Sarah Booth and the spirit world."

For one brief instant, I wondered if she'd somehow learned about Jitty. But that was impossible. Jitty refused to show herself to anyone but me. As she explained it, she was my personal haint and no one else could see her.

So if Carlita's ghost was in the house, why was she haunting two actresses? Jovan I could understand—because she was Federico's lover, and the jealousy card would play perfectly there.

But why me? I had no interest in Federico, except as a

director and a friend. I had no history in Hollywood, no past sins to be punished for.

Except for my love of a married man.

And with that the door I'd shut so carefully in my mind burst open and Coleman stepped into my head with such force that I stepped back from my friends. I wasn't over him. Not yet.

"What's wrong?" Tinkie asked.

I stammered, but I managed to say, "I'm trying to figure this out, and I keep going in circles. It's making me dizzy." Even as I talked, my brain was whirling. Was it possible Carlita's ghost meant to punish women who came between married couples? But Federico was single. Had been since Carlita's death more than a decade ago. Why punish him now?

"Sarah Booth, we should start searching." Tinkie put her hand on my shoulder to pull me back from my thoughts. "You don't look well."

"No, I'm good." I found a smile of encouragement. "You and Graf take the dogs and begin the search. I want to call Millie."

Tinkie checked her watch. "This is probably a good time to call her. She's up."

I glanced at her wrist. Five A.M. would be good. I'd catch Millie before the crowds flocked into the café.

"Sarah Booth, I don't want to leave you alone," Graf said. "We agreed to work in teams."

I hadn't given it a thought until he said it, but I gave him a hug. "Leave Sweetie with me. She'll protect me. And I'm going to stay right here where cell phone reception is the best in the house."

"Sweetie would give her life for you." Graf kissed my forehead and then my cheek. "Dogs have a sense about ghosts, or so I've heard." He turned his affections to my hound and gave her ears a rumple. "Yell if you need us."

"Oh, don't worry, I will. Start upstairs, and I'll sit here

near the staircase. If anyone tries to sneak out this way, I'll scream like a banshee."

"We need those floor plans of this house," Tinkie grumbled as she and Graf climbed the stairs.

She was right, but even if we went and camped at the architect's office, there was no way he'd appear for several hours.

I placed the call to Millie and she answered on the third ring. "I was going to call you this morning," she said. "I found some interesting things in my research."

"We can stand some help here."

"Let me get a cup of coffee," she said, "and then we'll talk."

Across the long air waves, I heard the familiar clatter of Millie's Bunn coffeemaker. I could visualize her, already dressed, apron tied on her waist. It was early morning, yet she'd have her hair done and makeup on. Millie had survived loss, as I had, yet she'd always held on to who she was and the life she loved.

"I'm back," she said. "And I'm not certain exactly what I've found, but I think you need to know it."

"Shoot," I said.

"You actually owe this one to Tinkie, but she won't take credit for it."

I gripped the phone tighter. Once my gal friends started disclaiming the credit for something, I knew it was going to be good.

"Millie, quit stalling or I'll tell Robert Redford that you think he can't direct!"

"Okay, okay, don't you dare say a derogatory word about Robert Redford. So check this out. Back in the eighties, Federico was involved with two large-budget films that were complete disasters. The only way he recovered his career was that an outside investor threw some money in to cover some of the debts."

"Who was that investor?" Money was always a good motive

for revenge. If Federico had, willingly or not, screwed someone out of millions, that would be excellent cause for that person to try to wreck the current film.

"Harold hasn't been able to get a name yet. The money
was given anonymously, but Harold says to give him time,
that there are ways to find these things out."

"Tell Harold I owe him a Hollywood dinner." Harold
Erkwell had once been a suitor, but more importantly, he'd
turned into a good friend—and president of the bank in Zinnia. He had financial contacts that had helped me and Tinkie
solve cases more than once.

"That and a lot more. Sarah Booth, why don't you give
him some serious consideration once you get home to Zinnia? He adores you."

A pain as violent as a knife wound stabbed into my heart.
It was Millie's honest assumption that I would return to
Zinnia once the movie was finished. No matter what, she
believed I would come home. Because Zinnia was where I
belonged. And that's where people lived, where their hearts
were.

"Millie, I can't promise—"

"I know. I'm not asking for promises. But I did pay a visit
to Madame Tomeeka."

My old high school friend, Tammy Odom, had a talent for
peering into the future. The pictures she got weren't always
clear, but Tammy knew things. I wasn't about to argue with
Millie on this one, because I couldn't say for certain what my
heart wished for most of all—fame and Hollywood or home
and security.

"And what about Graf?" I asked.

"He loves you, Sarah Booth. I don't doubt that for an instant."

"But what?" I didn't want to hear this, but I couldn't help
myself. At this moment, Graf was upstairs with my partner
and best friend, hunting for a ghost in a red dress that neither

of them had seen. But I had seen her. So therefore they were searching. Could any woman ask more from a man?

"But Graf is a movie star."

"And I'm not?"

"Oh, you certainly have the talent. No one doubts that. Sarah Booth, no one ever doubted that but you."

"So why am I not a movie star?" I sounded a little huffy even to me.

"Because it isn't talent that makes someone that thing. If you could balance and contort your body on a trapeze, that wouldn't make you a circus performer."

"Unless I ran away to join the circus."

"Exactly!" Millie was triumphant.

"But I'm making a movie."

There was an uncomfortable pause.

"What did Madame Tomeeka say?" Millie had me worried. The movie was having difficulty, but the actual filming was incredible. I was my own worst critic, and I thought the dailies were superb.

"Tammy talks in riddles."

She was hedging. "What did she say?"

"That your parents would guide you in the right decision."

That took my breath away. Since their deaths in a car accident when I was twelve, I'd dreamed and fantasized about their reaction to the accomplishments and disappointments of my life. No matter how hard I'd imagined or prayed, I'd received no clear word from the Great Beyond regarding their wishes or opinions of my plans.

Jitty didn't count, because she had her own agenda, normally involving viable male sperm and a screaming baby on my hip.

"Did she say my parents would tell me something?"

"Oh, Sarah Booth, that's not what she said at all, and I sure didn't mean to imply anything like that. I know how much you miss them."

No point denying it. I did. "I'd give anything for ten minutes to talk with them."

"Tammy said they were with you, protecting you."

My heart was filled with sadness. "That's a good thing to know. Thank her for me." It didn't answer a question, but it did give me hope that someone was somehow looking out for me.

"So what else did you find out about Federico?"

"The good stuff was back in the archives of some of the magazines. A place you might start is with Vince Day."

"The French director who did all of those terrific post-apocalyptic films?"

"That's him. He and Federico were like brothers at one time. Then there was a falling out—over Carlita. The gist of what I could find out was that Vince and Carlita had an affair, and there was talk that Estelle wasn't Federico's child."

"Holy cow. That puts an entirely different spin on Estelle's attitude toward Federico."

"It sure does. And from what I could read between the lines, it seemed Carlita never really cared for Vince. She used him to taunt Federico with her infidelity. But the end result was that Vince's wife left him. The whole thing with Carlita—whatever it was—destroyed his family."

Hollywood could be a vicious town, where personal lives played out in public. "And yet Federico took Carlita back and raised Estelle as his own." This was the total opposite of the gossip about Federico's marital flings—but it could also explain Carlita's self-hatred. What was the real story, though?

"That would seem to be the case. But that's what you need to find out—the truth about Federico and Carlita's past."

Millie was smart. What got printed in a celebrity gossip magazine in the eighties and early nineties would be only the tip of the iceberg. In those days, there was some restraint by the media, some assumption that a celebrity had a right to a private life. And also the celebrities made an effort not to expose themselves and their emotions in front of cameras.

"Millie, thanks so much for digging this up."

"My pleasure, Sarah Booth. It gave me a chance to look back on some of the best moments in film and my life. Back in the eighties, I was a pretty hot chick."

"You're still a pretty hot chick," I said, "but one with a lot of wisdom."

"When is Tinkie coming home? Oscar is here at the café for every meal, and I'll bet his cholesterol is off the charts. The man doesn't eat anything unless it's fried."

That didn't sound good. "She'll be home soon."

"And you?"

"We still have a lot of filming to do, but as soon as I'm finished, I'll be home to see my friends and my house and my horse."

"You are a star, Sarah Booth. Your dream came true, and that's something very special."

"Good-bye, Millie. I love you."

I hung up just as Graf and Tinkie clattered down the stairs.

"Find anything interesting?" I asked.

They shook their heads.

"And we couldn't get into the locked rooms on the third floor. Shall I get a key from Federico?" Graf looked handsome and ready for action.

"I think it can wait," Tinkie said. "I'd like to have a copy of the keys to those rooms so we can periodically check them, but let's not disturb Federico and Jovan."

"Something strange is going on in those rooms," I agreed. "Keys would be good. We'll talk to Federico tomorrow."

I started to tell them what Millie told me, but it was nearly six o'clock. Filming would start soon, and neither Graf nor I had had much sleep.

"Let's grab some shut-eye and come up with a plan in the morning when Tinkie gets back with the blueprints of the house," Graf suggested. He put his arm around me. "We'll find that ghost or woman or whoever she is, Sarah Booth, and once we do, we'll find out what's really going on around here."

The next morning, we were all yawning for the confrontation, with Ned finally seeing the possibility of an awful truth—that he'd been played by the love of his life. But once the cameras were on and Federico yelled "action," we came alive. Tinkie watched for a while before she took off for Petaluma and the architect.

When I wasn't needed on-camera, I studied Graf and Jovan. Their performances were nuanced and strong. I had wondered if Jovan was a good actress or if Federico had thrown her a bone because she was his love interest. I should never have underestimated him. She was good. And she played well off Graf, who was nothing less than stunning. Watching him as the truth dawns, I could almost see his brain churning toward the reality of Matty and yet not wanting to believe it.

When Federico finally called "cut," everyone applauded. I wasn't needed in the next scenes, which were between Ned and the little-ole bomb maker played by Ashton Kutcher. I only wished Millie could be there. She was a huge fan of the young man.

I went up to my room, doing my best to avoid falling into the bed. I was tired, but there were things to be done. And the one person who could help me needed to put in an appearance.

I closed and locked my bedroom door. "Jitty!" I whispered, but it was a loud one. "Jitty! I need you." While she might ignore my demands, she would never ignore a plea for help.

I walked around the room, waiting.

"Jitty, this is serious!" Hell, she didn't have to fly over from Zinnia. She was a ghost. She could just materialize, so what was keeping her?

I saw a form on the balcony outside my window, and my heart skipped a beat. Someone was out there. I'd locked the windows and my door before Graf and I left the room. So who was it?

The figure crossed the window, a shapely silhouette in a long, dark gown. The elusive woman in red! I hurried to the French doors and yanked them open, determined to find out who was playing such a dangerous game.

Jitty, wearing a blond wig and a long, sleek black gown that hugged her bodacious curves, put one gloved hand on her hip. Her other hand held a long, slender cigarette holder and a glowing fag.

"Is that a pistol in your pocket, or are you glad to see me?" she asked, a perfect imitation of Mae West. She strutted past me into the room.

"Jitty!"

"You called, didn't you?"

"I thought you were the ghost." My heart was still pounding.

"I am. So what's going on?"

"Can you tell if there's another spirit in this house?"

She looked at me as if I'd suddenly grown a large, cabbage-shaped tumor on the side of my head. "Sarah Booth, I'm not a medium like James van Praagh or John Edward."

"I didn't ask you to communicate with the ghost. I just need to know if there's one here in the house, or if the things that are happening are from a human source."

Jitty puffed on her cigarette, making me want one. Being dead had some real advantages. "I'm not allowed to tell you."

"And if you do, what will happen?" I couldn't believe the red tape in the Great Beyond.

"Nothing good. I might get a permanent recall."

I wasn't willing to barter Jitty's presence for a scrap of information that I could determine for myself. All I had to do was grab her—and if I caught her, she was flesh and blood.

But so far, the lady in red had been fleet of foot. "Is there a test to determine if this is a spirit?"

"Check out a mirror. Ghosts don't have a reflection." She frowned. "Or is that a vampire? I get the rules confused sometimes. Now I've got business of my own." She started to fade, an undulating shimmer of energy that grew dimmer. "Keep up the bedroom activity, Sarah Booth. Think what a child star you and Graf could produce."

Her laughter was the last aspect of her to depart, a throaty chuckle that even while it irritated me, made me smile. For whatever reason, Jitty was unwilling to help me with this. That in itself had to be a clue.

CHAPTER FIFTEEN

Tinkie had rented a purple car that looked like a cross between a Scion and a VW bug—it had the best air conditioner of any car in the fleet. She pulled up to the front of the mansion with her hair blowing in the chilled breeze. Chablis, too, was enjoying the air-conditioning. Her little ears were standing straight up.

Both of them jumped from the car, and Tinkie carried a roll of architectural plans almost taller than she was. Her dress-to-impress outfit she'd chosen to visit the architect included five-inch stiletto sandals, lime green, a linen minidress, backless, and a floral matador jacket. The outfit was completed with a straw hat. She looked like a million dollars.

"I not only got the plans, I got a bit of history on the Gonzalez family from Senor Lopez. Fascinating stuff." She waved the plans at me.

"Let's have a look at those," Graf said. He was as eager as I was to put an end to the visits of the phantom woman. "I'll bet there're secret passages where someone is hiding." His eyes narrowed. "She's popping out and doing stuff, then hiding again. And when we find her and catch her, she's going to face an assault charge against Jovan."

"There are passages," Tinkie said. She'd drawn her own

conclusions and was having a hard time not spilling everything right then and there.

"Let's go up to my room," I said. "It's more private and—" I broke off when Ricardo came around the corner of the house.

"Ladies, Graf." He smiled, and I thought again what a handsome young man he was. What a perfect contrast to Estelle, who was beautiful but so angry that it distorted her lovely features.

"Dad needs you back on the set." Ricardo spoke to Graf. "He needs a retake of a shot with you and Ashton."

Graf hid his disappointment. "Certainly, Ricardo. I'll be right there." He looked at us. "You girls continue without me."

"What's that?" Ricardo pointed to the roll of drawings Tinkie held.

"Sarah Booth and Graf are building a home back in the States. I wanted to go over the plans with them, since I'll be in charge until they return." Tinkie was cool as a cucumber in chilled dill sauce.

"It must be a big house." Something cold had drifted into Ricardo's big brown eyes.

"They're movie stars, Ricardo. Of course the house will be palatial. It's expected. Part of the packaging. Maybe your father can explain it to you." Tinkie's voice had an edge to it.

Ricardo was either smart or lucky. "Be sure and include a gym with a Jacuzzi and lots of workout equipment. Being a star is difficult. One extra ounce of fat, one bad hair day . . ." He gave his signature one-shouldered shrug. "You guys can have it. I'll take anonymity behind the camera and a big paycheck anyday."

"Let's see what your dad needs," Graf said, stepping in front of Ricardo and leading him back to the set.

Tinkie and I stood in the shade of some lush tropical tree. The scent of roses wafted to us from the gardens.

"There's something about that kid that gives me the willies," Tinkie said.

"Could be testosterone untempered by experience."

"Could be sociopathic tendencies and a subverted hatred of his father."

"Wow, Tink, I'm usually the one to say the harsh things."

"This family is seriously screwed up, Sarah Booth. And I'm not just whistling 'Dixie.' I've got the proof right here."

"My room?" I asked.

"Absolutely not."

She was so adamant that I put a hand on her shoulder and got her to face me. "What's wrong with my room?"

"It's perfectly lovely, and whoever matched those sheers to the wallpaper and the bedspread did a perfect job, but—" She held up a hand to stop me from interrupting. "There's a passageway behind the bathroom wall. It's large enough for someone to stand in, and there are peepholes cut so that you can be watched. Behind one of the tapestries. I'll show you later."

A million thoughts collided in my head. Someone could have been watching Graf and me make love. That was creepy enough. But it went deeper than that. Someone was spying with the intention of hurting one or all of us.

The mental image of Norman Bates leaped into my mind. I turned to Tinkie.

"You're white as a sheet," she said, grasping my elbow and moving me into the shade of the porch. "Take a breath and let's go up to my room. As far as I can tell, the guest rooms don't figure into the secret passageways and hidey-holes that Estoban Gonzalez built into his daughter's wedding gift."

We entered the cool of the house and hurried upstairs to Tinkie's room. Chablis and Sweetie trotted with us, flopping on the floor as we spread the house plans on her bed.

"See, here's the space in your room," Tinkie pointed out. Sure enough, there was enough space between the walls for a person to stand. Entry was gained from the hallway, a panel that slid to the side.

My initial shock gave way to anger. The idea that someone had been spying on me, in my most intimate moments, made me furious.

"Calm down," Tinkie said. "You don't know for certain anyone has used that hidden area."

She was right. Just because Estelle had appeared in my room unannounced didn't mean she was spying on me. The hidey-hole wasn't an entrance to my room.

"But why would Estoban Gonzalez build a room to spy on his daughter and her new husband?" That was sick. So sick I didn't even want to think about it.

"Is it possible he feared for Carlita?" Tinkie posed the question softly.

"As in he thought Federico would harm her?" That hadn't occurred to me.

Tinkie kicked off her heels and flopped on her stomach, her feet crossed in the air behind her. I couldn't help but notice her perfectly manicured toenails, a pretty pastel mango. Tinkie had color coordination down to a science.

"Either that, or perhaps he thought she might harm herself." Tinkie arched one eyebrow. "With all of that anorexia, he might have been worried about depression or something. I mean, is it possible that Carlita suffered from her eating disorders *before* she married Federico?"

"So why not tell Federico and let him take care of his wife?"

"Federico had a career. I'm sure he wasn't home all the time. Perhaps Estoban only wanted to make certain she wasn't harming herself."

Tinkie was putting the kindest possible spin on the situation. I settled on the bed, realizing for the first time how tired I was. It had been a long night and a hard morning. I needed a nap.

Tinkie shifted the documents until she had the kitchen in

front of her. "Look! There's a passageway from the pantry up a flight of stairs to the second floor!"

This was a big discovery and could easily explain how someone had frightened Jovan, broken a dish, and then escaped with all the doors and windows locked.

I studied the prints in earnest, following Tinkie's pointer finger as she flipped to the page that showed the second floor. Right at the top of the stairs was another false panel. Someone could take the kitchen pantry passage up to the second floor and escape. Or they could wait in the passage until the house was empty enough for them to make a getaway.

"What about the third floor?"

Tinkie flipped the sheets until we had the floor plan for the ballroom and the locked rooms. The ballroom was the heart of this floor, but there was something off about the room at the end of the hall. I leaned closer to try to figure it out.

"It's a dumbwaiter," Tinkie said, her breath coming out in a rush. "It could work just like a passage. A person could sit on it and be moved up or down, like an escalator."

"Where does it come out?"

We found the second-floor plans, and Tinkie looked at me. "In the linen closet in your bathroom."

"And the first floor?"

The blueprints made a crisp sound as we flipped to that page.

"Behind the kitchen cabinets," I whispered. I remembered that on the morning Jovan was attacked, Sweetie had been nosing there, trying to tell me. So there were two ways to exit the kitchen secretly.

Tinkie rolled to her back and then sat up with the ease of a sixteen-year-old. "That tells me there is no ghost, just someone trying to scare us."

"And trying to hurt us." Jovan could have been killed in her fall. I'd come close to drowning. "This is a dangerous person, Tinkie."

"Dangerous, desperate, and perhaps deranged. A deadly combination."

When my cell phone rang, I made a little squeak of surprise. The caller ID showed the sheriff's office in California. Now that was a shocker. I couldn't imagine Sheriff King was calling to ask how the filming was going.

"What can I do for you, Sheriff King?" I asked.

"Are you certain Estelle Marquez came back to the States?"

Though Cece had used all of her many charms at the airport in Petaluma, she'd been unable to confirm that Estelle had actually boarded a plane to the States. King had the legal authority to find out for sure, though. "That's what her roommate said, but you're the man with the badge and subpoena power."

"Somehow Costa Rica doesn't give my badge a lot of weight. LAX has no record of her landing here, and there's no sign of Ms. Marquez at her place. This morning, we got a call from the neighbors. Her house has been ransacked."

That got my attention. "Any idea who did it?"

"The crime-scene guys are still there. There wasn't evidence of forced entry that we could find. I'll know more later." He sighed. "I'm worried. The neighbors said she was fragile and prone to depression. Is it possible that Estelle Marquez is so disturbed that she killed Suzy Dutton?"

I thought about the "apparition" that had attacked Jovan. It was possible that Estelle was building herself an alibi in the States. "I can't answer that question, but there's a chance she's still here in Petaluma, Sheriff. Some strange things are happening on the set."

"You think Marquez's daughter is the source of the curse?"

"I don't have any solid evidence, but I'll call you when I find something." I hung up fast and turned the phone off in case he tried to call back.

* * *

Graf wanted to take the house plans to Federico and talk to him, but Tinkie and I persuaded Graf that it would be better to wait until we'd had time to examine the secret passageways we'd discovered. Federico looked haggard, and there seemed to be tension between him and Jovan. Besides, we had to tell him that it was possible that Estelle was missing.

Of course, I was elected to do that.

I found Federico and Jovan sitting in the falling dusk, sipping red wine, on the patio outside the kitchen. I'd showered and changed, and later Graf and Tinkie and I were going into town for one last dinner. Tinkie had to get back to Zinnia. She couldn't delay any longer. Oscar was going crazy without her. He'd even begged to speak to Chablis over the phone.

I could hear Jovan's low-pitched voice, and she sounded serious. As much as I hated to interrupt, I had to.

"Federico, I need to speak to you about Estelle," I said.

Jovan leaned forward. "Is something wrong?"

I'd hoped to talk to the director alone, but I could see that wasn't going to happen. "She's not in Malibu, and there's no evidence she left Costa Rica."

Federico sighed. "This is one of her stupid games."

"She's done this before?"

"Even when she was a child. She'd disappear in the house and Carlita and I would hunt for her for hours. Then she'd reappear. It was frustrating."

I could see where that would make parents nuts. "I'm worried, Federico. She told her roommate she was going to Malibu, but she isn't there, and the sheriff told me someone ransacked her home."

Concern swept over his face. If the gossip was true and Estelle was not his daughter, he seemed to care about her regardless. "Is there any indication that she was injured?" he asked.

I shook my head. "No, there's no trace of her at all."

"She's probably still here, in Petaluma. She's hiding out to punish me and try another tactic to ruin my film."

"Federico, she's your daughter," Jovan said. "She wouldn't—"

"She would, and before you rush to her defense, I suspect it was Estelle who shoved you down the stairs and scared you senseless. She's disturbed."

"And that's my point," I said. "She could be in serious trouble."

"And she could be doing this to see if I'll give up the film to hunt her—which is what I suspect. With Estelle, it's always been about choosing. She's her mother made over. Always pitting herself against my work. If I work, then I don't love them." He stood up so abruptly that his wineglass tipped and shattered against the tile.

The red stain spread across the slate like blood.

"Federico!" Jovan stood and grasped his arm. Her eyes were wide and her face contorted in misery. "That's a terrible omen. I think we should hunt for Estelle. What if she's in trouble?"

Federico looked at me and then at Jovan. "I've spent two decades trying to keep Estelle from harming herself. If I don't bring this film in on time and on budget, my career will be ruined."

Jovan let her hand trace down his cheek. "She's your daughter."

I thought about the rumors Millie had told me—that Estelle was really Vincent Day's daughter. I wondered if that was what Federico was thinking. How much could he sacrifice for a daughter who hated him? A daughter who might not be his?

"Sarah Booth, would you find Daniel Martinez and send him to me?" Federico asked. "I'll pay him to find Estelle. If she's in Petaluma, he'll find her. And make certain she's okay. But I must focus on this film."

That sounded like a reasonable plan, because if Estelle was actually in the house, Graf, Tinkie, and I planned to rout her out.

Jovan kissed Federico's cheek. "I can help hunt for her, too. Surely, if she's playing the spoiled daughter, she'll be staying somewhere comfortable. I'll tour the hotels and guesthouses tomorrow and check."

It was a good idea. "Perfect, Jovan. I'll talk to the authorities and see if they'll give us any assistance."

"And I will speak to her brother." Federico's tone was grim. "If he knows anything, he'll tell me."

"Federico, when you get a moment, I need to speak to you about something else." I hated to lay the hidden rooms and secret passageways on him, but he had to know.

Jovan gave me a look that held curiosity and something else I couldn't pinpoint. She had no need to worry about me. My interest in Federico was strictly professional, and I'd done everything I could to show it.

"Is it about the ghost?" Jovan asked.

My smile was tired. "Not really. I think you were pushed by a real person, Jovan. I wouldn't worry about the ghost." Especially not once we blocked the secret passageways. That would put an end to a lot of the ghostly maneuvering around the house. But I didn't want to tell Jovan, and on second thought, I wondered if I should keep this between me and Tinkie and Graf.

CHAPTER SIXTEEN

When the sun had set and the full moon rose big and fat and filled with liquid silver light, Graf and I saddled the horses. Our time in Costa Rica was coming to a close, and I wanted to ride on the beach and smell the salty tang. This was a magical place, a gentle place. In Petaluma, my heart had begun to heal, and I'd found myself yielding to the tender feelings growing for Graf.

He was a handsome man, his dark features and chiseled jaw *GQ* perfect in the moonlight as he rode Nugget. He could play a highwayman or a cowboy or a corporate exec. His features were classic and combined with his talent, they would take him far. Had it been destiny that brought him to Zinnia to perform a play originally slated for the Mississippi Gulf Coast? It still surprised me to think how radically my life had changed, almost overnight.

We rode along the beach where the sand was firm and the footing good for our horses. The waves seemed to chase us, rushing to cover the sand we'd left behind. Sweetie Pie bounded beside us, her silky ears flopping in the breeze and the salt spray flying from her paws. It was exhilarating.

We passed the castle rock and continued on, letting the horses canter. They slowed on their own accord, dropping into an ambling walk. Graf and I were side by side. He reached across and put his hand on my thigh.

"As lovely as this is, I'll be glad to get back to Los Angeles." He squeezed my leg lightly.

"Why?" I was surprised.

"I'm worried about you here, Sarah Booth. You were almost killed, and it seems that no one takes that seriously except me and Tinkie. There is someone in that house up to no good. It isn't a prank or mischief, this is dangerous."

We'd discussed the secret passageways, and our plan was to block them off during the night, while everyone else was asleep. "We'll put a stop to the problem," I said.

"Someone who goes to this much trouble isn't going to be easily deterred."

One of the best things about Graf was that he didn't pretend to be an investigator. He was happy to help with the searches, but he didn't spew theories. He waited to be asked. "What do you think about Estelle?" The wind lifted my hair, creating a cool breeze on my neck.

"It's hard to say. I don't really know her. I mean, she seems like the logical suspect, and she's certainly acted crazy enough . . ." He let the sentence die.

"But what?"

"I can't put my finger on anything. I do believe we should hunt for her, though. If she's still in the area, we need to know it. And if she's in trouble, we need to find her."

"Amen to that."

With the moonlight bright on the water, the waves looked tipped with silver. I felt so connected to Graf that I put my hand on his arm and pressed. Whatever mistakes he'd made in the past, he was a good man.

"Do you believe in ghosts, Sarah Booth?"

He couldn't see my smile because I turned away. "I do, Graf. Wholeheartedly. I know they exist."

He hesitated, and the only sounds were the waves on the

shore and the wet footfalls of our horses. "Will you hold it against me if I'm a skeptic?"

"Not at all. In fact, I'm counting on it."

"And why is that?"

"If I told you, I'd have to kill you." I slapped Nugget on the rump and asked Flicker for a gallop as we turned and headed home.

The moon on the waves leaped and crested, and the horses flew along the sand, their shadows dancing behind them. It was a moment of perfect happiness, one of those rare times when there's no need to fret or project. My world was *magnifico*.

By the time we got back to the house, we were late to meet Tinkie for dinner. She'd insisted that she needed to pack and talk to Oscar on the phone. Horseback riding, though she claimed she could do it, wasn't one of her specialties. Tinkie could put together an ensemble from shoes to matching hair color in thirty minutes or less, but she wasn't particularly attracted to outdoor sports.

While Graf unsaddled the horses and rubbed them down, I went to find her. It was her last evening, and I wanted this to be special. There were many wonderful restaurants in Petaluma, and one very elegant dining establishment. If her heart was set on elegance, I was prepared to make the sacrifice of dressing up. I could "borrow" one of Matty's dresses from the ballroom.

When I tapped on her door, there was no answer. I tapped again, louder. "Tinkie!" Silence. I pushed the door open. Her bags were on the bed, half-packed. And her dress for the evening was laid out, along with shoes. But there was no sign of her or Chablis.

I tried her bathroom, but it was empty. Her makeup was still out on the counter. She'd insisted she was going to pack because her flight was early in the morning. So what had she done in the two hours that Graf and I had been riding?

There was no trace of her in her room, so I went to mine. Graf had said he would shower in his bathroom, avoiding the whole issue of the passageway. For a man who had no problem with a camera recording his passionate kisses, he was modest about showering with an audience.

I checked the balcony—no Tinkie. I went to the kitchen and out on the patio where Federico and Jovan had earlier been sipping wine. No Tinkie.

And more troubling, not even a peep or a bark from Chablis. She was a lovely and well-behaved dog, but like any creature of short stature, she made up for what she lacked in size with loudness. Normally, when Chablis sniffed Sweetie Pie, she went wild to play with her. I checked each floor of the house, calling Tinkie's name. It seemed no one was in the mansion at all. Ricardo's door was locked, and so was Federico's. Everyone had obviously gone into town for dinner.

I met Graf on the path from the stables and told him that Tinkie and Chablis were missing.

"Did you check the secret passages?" he asked.

Dread rippled through me. "Tinkie said she would wait for us to return so we could explore them tonight while everyone was asleep."

"You said the house was empty. She might have seized the opportunity."

Graf wasn't a private investigator, but he was pretty darn smart. "Let's go."

While I cleared canned goods and staples from the cabinet shelves in the kitchen, looking for the mechanism that would open the wall, Graf found a flashlight. Sweetie was at my side, sniffing and whining. The idea that Tinkie was trapped in the dumbwaiter scared me. Why hadn't she yelled or cried out? Why hadn't Chablis barked? If the base of the dumbwaiter was structurally unsound, Tinkie and Chablis could have had a nasty fall. Dire images plagued me as I shoved things out of the way and pulled and tugged at the wooden cabinet.

At last I found what sounded like a hollow panel. A false wall covered the opening of the dumbwaiter, but Graf popped it off with little trouble. To my sweet relief, the cubicle that rode up and down on cables was there, empty.

"Look." Graf pointed at a place where the dust had been disturbed.

Someone had been inside it. And not so long ago. But there was no sign of Tinkie or Chablis or that the equipment was dangerous.

Graf found the button that sent it up and when he pressed, the dumbwaiter disappeared slowly and noiselessly upward.

Because I'm a victim of a vivid imagination, I looked down into the shaft to make certain my friend wasn't there. The hole was empty.

Graf, Sweetie, and I moved on to the passageway that started in the pantry. This was easier to manage, and as soon as Graf found the button that released the sliding door, Sweetie bounded into the darkness, her hunting bay echoing back to us.

Graf led with the flashlight, and I held his hand as we hurried forward and then up a flight of wooden steps. We had to be heading for the sliding panel on the second floor, but in the darkness it was so easy to become disoriented.

To negotiate the stairs safely, we had to slow our pace. We were almost at the top when I heard a heartrending moan.

"Sweetie!" I called my hound, but there was no response. I'd never heard her make a noise like that.

A keening wail echoed off the walls of the narrow passageway. It was so sorrowful that my eyes teared up. I grasped Graf's hand as he pulled me forward to the top of the stairs.

The flashlight beam led the way, and the first thing it struck was Tinkie, slumped against the wall. In her arms she cradled Chablis.

Tinkie cut loose with a wail and then turned to us. "She's hurt," she said. "I can't get her to wake up."

Graf and I surged forward. Sweetie was already there, licking her little friend's face and licking Tinkie, too. While I took Chablis's limp form into my arms, Graf pulled Tinkie to her feet. She was bleeding from a huge goose egg–sized lump on the side of her head. Someone had really whacked her.

When I tried to examine her head, Tinkie pushed me away.

"I couldn't get the panel to slide open." Tinkie was sobbing. "I heard someone coming, and I tried and tried, but I couldn't find the release. Then Chablis rushed back down the passageway and attacked. I think she was kicked."

Now wasn't the time to question Tinkie. I held the flashlight in one hand and Chablis in the other while Graf searched for the release. We were at the second-floor hallway wall, and there had to be a device that would slide the panel aside so we could get out of the passageway.

"Aha!" He pressed something and the pale, soft light from the hall sconces illuminated a rectangle in the darkness. We all stepped into the light, and I glanced down at Chablis. The little girl was unconscious.

"Graf, bring a car around." I spoke calmly, because I didn't want to upset Tinkie further.

God bless Graf, he didn't argue or ask questions, he flew down the stairs and out the front door to find one of the rental cars always left on the property.

"Is she dead?" Tinkie asked, holding back her sobs by sheer force of will.

"She has a heartbeat." And she did, but it was weak. Her breathing was labored and her gums were too pale, a sign of shock. I wasn't a vet, but I knew we had to get help for Chablis. "Tinkie, find a telephone book and an emergency vet clinic."

She rushed to the foyer where a telephone and book waited. Though her hands were trembling, she found the number, placed the call, and had an English-speaking veterinarian promising to wait for us as Graf pulled around front. All of us, including Sweetie, got in the car.

Graf nearly took down the security guard at the gate, who didn't move fast enough. We careened into the road and sped to town. In ten minutes we were parked at the clinic.

Chablis was still breathing, and Tinkie was sobbing softly. I did my best to comfort her, but there was nothing I could say. We were helpless.

Dr. Milazo took Chablis with great care and disappeared into an examining room. In several moments, he came back out.

"I'm afraid I need to operate," he said. "Her ribs are broken. One has pierced a lung."

"Do whatever is necessary," Tinkie said bravely. "Can I wait here?"

Dr. Milazo looked around at the empty waiting room. "It would be best if you went home, Mrs. Richmond. I will call you when I have news."

"But—" Tinkie started to protest, but Graf put his arm around her and drew her to his chest.

"It's okay, Tinkie. We're ten minutes from here. If Chablis or the doctor needs you, I'll bring you."

"I don't want to leave her!" Tinkie's wail was muffled by Graf's shirt, and I turned away to keep from breaking down completely.

"We can be here fast," Graf said. He was gently moving her to the door. "We need to leave and let Dr. Milazo take care of Chablis. That's the best we can do for her now."

He was so gentle and caring that I stayed out of it. He moved Tinkie out of the clinic and into the night. Instead of following, I went to the veterinarian. "How bad is it?" I asked.

"Serious. Someone meant to hurt this dog." His dark gaze was level. "Who would do this to such a small creature?"

He had no clue what was happening in our lives, and it was possible he suspected us of abuse. "Tinkie was attacked by someone. Chablis tried to protect her. The attacker injured Chablis."

"Have you reported this to the police?" he asked.

I sighed. That would make logical sense, and he wouldn't understand why I hadn't. "The dog was our first priority. Now I need to attend to my friend's head wound and then call the authorities. Call me as soon as you have word on Chablis."

He nodded and went back to the treatment rooms and surgery. As he shut the door, I wanted to sit down in one of the ugly plastic chairs and cry. In fact, I sank into one, trying hard to get my act together so I could badger Tinkie into getting medical attention. What I couldn't escape was the awful truth: Tinkie was injured and Chablis was seriously injured—because they'd come to help me.

The clinic door creaked open, and Graf came to me. He pulled me into his arms. "Chablis is going to be okay."

I wanted to believe him. I needed to believe him. But I couldn't stop the sob that tore out of me. He held me tighter.

"Pull yourself together, Sarah Booth. We have to make sure Tinkie doesn't have a concussion, and she's not going to want to go to the hospital."

He was right about that. Everyone accused me of being hardheaded, but Tinkie could match me any day. She was simply better at manipulating than I was.

"Is Sweetie in the car?" I finally asked.

"She's comforting Tinkie, but we need to go." He took my elbow and led me to the passenger door. In a moment we were in motion and headed toward the emergency room.

To both of our surprise, Tinkie didn't really protest. She sat placidly while the young doctor examined her, took X-rays, and pronounced that she had no serious injuries.

On the way back to the mansion, she called Oscar to tell him that she wouldn't be flying home the next day. When she started to talk about Chablis, her composure broke, and I took the phone and explained.

"I want my wife and dog home," Oscar said. He wasn't angry, he was scared. "You two are going to get killed one day, Sarah Booth."

I couldn't argue with him. We'd both been hurt on numerous occasions. "I didn't come here to get involved in a mystery," I told him. "None of us did. But as soon as Chablis can travel, I'll put them on the first flight out."

"Is Chablis going to—" His voice broke.

I almost couldn't answer. "We must believe she's going to be fine. Nothing else is acceptable."

"Send them home to me, Sarah Booth. Both of them."

"I'll do my best, Oscar." I hung up, remembering a time in the past when Oscar wouldn't give Tinkie enough money to ransom Chablis from a dognapper. He'd changed. We'd all changed, and now I'd give almost anything I had to guarantee that the little dustmop dog that I'd once abducted would get well.

CHAPTER SEVENTEEN

I'd managed to get Tinkie into bed, and Jovan, when she and Federico got home from dinner, loaned us a mild sedative. Because Tinkie was so distressed, I chose to stay in her room, at least for a while. Graf had volunteered to talk to Federico about the secret passages and a method of sealing them. Distraught by what had happened to Tinkie and Chablis, Federico would agree, I felt sure.

When we'd gone to the hospital, we'd told the attending physician that Tinkie had accidentally struck the side of her head. We gave no details. Federico didn't have to warn me that the movie didn't need another "cursed" incident. So far, we'd been able to avoid the paparazzi. Having the security people at the gate—while they weren't exactly keeping us safe—at least deterred the most aggressive of the photographers.

After I was sure Tinkie was asleep, I took her cell phone and hurried out in the hallway to meet Graf. He'd been busy, too. He had two-by-fours and nails and a hammer. He was serious about blocking the passageways.

We started in the kitchen, hammering loud enough to wake the dead, a phrase that gave me mild discomfort. It was a good thing Graf was doing the carpentry work, because I had Tinkie's phone in a death grip. I willed the veterinarian to call and give me a good report. Chablis had to be okay. She had to be.

After twenty minutes of hammering, the pantry entrance was blocked off, as was the dumbwaiter. Still clutching the phone, I started putting the canned goods back.

"Hey," Graf said, grasping my shoulders as he swung me into his arms. "Chablis will be okay."

I looked into his eyes and searched for the lie, the soft truth, rotten at the core, that he was peddling. All I saw was calm certainty. "How can you be so sure?"

He shrugged. "I'm not psychic or anything like that, but the vet looked confident."

"He didn't say—"

He put his finger on my lips. "Words don't guarantee anything, Sarah Booth. You know that. But I'll make a deal with you."

My poor heart cracked wide open then. The last lingering doubts I felt about Graf melted. Here was a man who cared enough about my worries to bargain with me, even in a situation where he had no control. "Okay," I whispered, "what's the deal?"

"If the vet hasn't called in another hour, we'll drive back to the clinic. We'll sit there until he has some word for us."

"We have to work tomorrow. We're both going to look like crap." Even as I argued, something strange and wonderful was happening. Graf had touched me with the most precious of gifts—trust. He'd seen a great weakness in me, and he'd moved to protect it. By action, he'd shown that my feelings were safe with him.

He kissed my fingertips. "We'll work, because we have to. What difference does it make if we stay awake at the vet clinic or here?" His arms pulled me into his chest, and I clung there, listening to the steady thrum of his heart.

I would have stayed forever, safe in the haven he created

for me, but Tinkie's cell phone rang. Graf took it from my hand and answered.

My first reaction was to protest, but I realized what he was doing. If the news was bad, he would tell me. I would not have to hear it from a stranger.

While I waited, I imagined Chablis, sun-glitzed hair rumpled by the wind as she hung out the window of Tinkie's Caddy. I saw her romping through the fields of Dahlia House with Sweetie Pie, two unlikely friends. I remembered her bowed up and barking, protecting Tinkie or me or Sweetie. Even Oscar. She only weighed three pounds, but she had the heart of a wolf when it came to those she loved.

I couldn't look at Graf, and his voice was a low murmur. When he grasped my arm, a sob escaped.

"It's okay," he said. "It's okay, Sarah Booth. She made it through surgery and she's doing fine."

I made some sound that was only half human and flung myself against him.

"Thank you, Doctor," he said. "We'll be by first thing in the morning to check on her. Yes, a couple of days. I understand. Thank you again."

We tiptoed into Tinkie's room to share the good news, but the sedative had kicked in and she was out. Graf placed a call to Oscar. In a few moments he'd updated Chablis's father on the good news. He snapped the phone shut and kissed me, hugging me tight. "I'd hate to see your reaction if the news was bad," he teased.

I tried to speak, but the only thing that came out was a pitiful bleat. Instead of laughing at me, he cuddled me against him and stroked my head. "That little dog has everyone's heart, doesn't she?" he asked.

"She's like Tinkie's child," I managed to get out. "And Oscar loves her, too. I'll call him again in the morning. As much as he protests, Chablis is his family."

"And well she should be." He lifted my chin. His gaze

was definitely wicked. "But maybe it's time to start thinking about a real baby, Sarah Booth. I want that. I want to have children with you. I want a family."

"Have you been talking to Jit—" I stopped just in time.

"Who?"

"Never mind." There was nothing like nearly giving away a secret to dry up a girl's tears.

"I haven't been talking to anyone. But I've been thinking. Sarah Booth, I want a future with you. I never thought I'd hear myself saying these words to anyone, but you've changed me. When I see you in the morning with the sun slanting on your face and hair, I want that every morning for the rest of my life. I want to grow old with you."

"We're only in our thirties." He had surprised me, and I wasn't sure of my own feelings. I'd grown to care for Graf, and I was falling in love with him. But children? I'd been so busy fighting for survival I'd never given a child serious thought. Jitty was always on me to spawn, as she so lovingly called it. Somehow, I'd managed to think such decisions were far in the future, but Graf was right. I was thirty-four. My biological clock was marking the passage of the seasons.

I'd always assumed I would have a child, but the offer Graf was making wasn't some distant dream like being a rock star. It was real and imminent. "I don't know." It was as honest as I could get.

"I'm ready to be a husband and a father. Not this month or next, but once the film is over and we're permanently settled." He stroked my cheek. "I'll work to be the best husband. I know I'll be a good father."

"Graf, I don't doubt you in either capacity."

"Then you'll think about it?"

"I will." Once Chablis was safe, I'd likely think about nothing else. He'd just rearranged my entire life's priority. "You've surprised me, but I will think about it."

He grinned. "I always thought the woman I proposed to would fling her arms around me and kiss me while saying, 'Yes, yes, yes!'"

I felt heat rush to my cheeks. He was right. My reaction was unnatural. "I'm sorry—"

He kissed me lightly. "No, you're not, and you shouldn't be. You're cautious when it comes to your heart, Sarah Booth. I like that. I want you, but only if you're dead certain. I'm not interested in a temporary marriage or a part-time post as a husband and father. I want 'until death do us part.'"

"You sure know how to turn a girl's head." I matched his smile. Graf knew the bargain he was striking. The most remarkable thing was that he knew it and still wanted me.

"I won't ask again until the movie is done. Now, let me tell you everything the vet said. Chablis is in good hands."

"How badly is she hurt?" I was almost afraid to ask.

"He patched the hole in her lung and put the ribs back in place. She's going to be delicate for a while, but she should heal perfectly and be back to new in a couple of months."

It was going to be hard to contain Sweetie and Chablis— the two were such mischief-makers. But we'd manage it. And Chablis would heal.

"When I find the person who did this, I'm going to do something vile." It wasn't a threat, it was a promise.

"I'll hold them for you." Graf held out the hammer. "We can break every bone in his feet."

He was kidding, but it made me feel better. He knew how to give emotional support to a Mississippi woman.

"Graf, let's not talk about children publicly. Tinkie wants a child, but there's a medical problem." I wondered if Graf could really understand that longing. "She hasn't been able to conceive. If something happens to Chablis . . ."

He put his arm around me and directed me toward the stairs and our bedroom. "I don't know how we can help with a conception problem, but if we can, we certainly will. But for now, let's get some sleep. I took care of the peepholes in the tapestry in your room."

I opened the door and saw my best pair of red lace panties tacked over the tapestry. My laughter rang through the huge old room, and I knew that the release would allow me to sleep.

"Chablis, my precious baby." Tinkie stroked Chablis's head as she reclined, torso bandaged, in a kennel. An IV fed into one of her tiny little veins, but her eyes were alert and she licked Tinkie's hand.

Tinkie turned to the veterinarian. "Thank you, Doctor. Thank you."

"She's a lucky little dog. Not all animals are so fortunate to have someone who loves them or who can afford medical care." He started to turn away.

Tinkie caught his arm. "On my next private investigation case, I'm going to donate all of my salary to your clinic, for health care for indigent animals."

He was very solemn. "Thank you, Mrs. Richmond. I thank you for those who can't speak."

"I'll check on Chablis later today."

Tinkie and I hurried out to the car. I had to be on the set by nine, and we were cutting it close. "Chablis is healing, so how are you?" I asked her.

The knot on her head was swollen and ugly, and I was glad she couldn't go home to Oscar looking like she might hatch a Mini-Me from her temple. Oscar's tolerance for the private investigative work Tinkie did never ceased to amaze me. He'd married the daughter of the owner of the town bank. Tinkie was the epitome of a sorority girl—long on social skills and masterful at manipulating men. She wrote the Daddy's Girl manual. But she was also smart and loyal and brave and really good at math. And Oscar had begun to recognize those qualities and step aside as she developed them. Injuries, though, rattled his conviction to leave her alone.

"Tinkie, can you remember anything from last night?" I told her Graf's supposition of the chain of events.

"He's right. I made it all the way to the panel, and I couldn't figure out how to open the door. I was so focused on that, I didn't see who snuck up behind me." She felt the knot. "What the hell did they hit me with?"

"Your assailant didn't leave a weapon in the passageway."

Tinkie bit her bottom lip. "Someone had been in there before me. The dust was all disturbed and cobwebs had been knocked down."

"We'll find this person. I'm just sorry your trip home is delayed. I know you want to take Chablis somewhere safe."

"To be honest, Sarah Booth, that's not what I want at all." She turned her beautiful blue eyes on me and I saw contained fury. "I want to find the son of a bitch who kicked my dog hard enough to break her ribs, and I want to make them pay."

"That's one thing that you and I and Graf agree on." I pulled into the driveway of the mansion just in time to see Ricardo talking animatedly with Daniel Martinez, the security guy. It looked as if they were having a heated argument.

"I'll check that out," Tinkie said. "You get ready to work."

I did just that, and when Sally had my makeup on and Dallas had me dressed, I hurried down to the set. Graf met me with a worried look. "Federico's not feeling well. He's nauseated."

My gut took a dive. "Damn it, I dropped the ball. If someone is trying to destroy the film, it stands to reason they might go after him. Do you think he's been poisoned?"

Graf shook his head. "He insists he's fine. He said Jovan gave him something to sleep and he must have had a bad reaction to it. The thing is, Jovan is sick, too."

"We need to get that prescription checked." I looked around. Tinkie and Daniel were nowhere in sight. "Is Jovan in her room?" After the attack on Tinkie, I didn't know if it was safe for the model to be alone in the house.

"She was out here a moment ago, bringing some medicine for Federico. She was a little green around the gills, but she was ambulatory."

"Let's get these scenes done. We've got to find out who's doing this." I started toward the set.

"Sarah Booth." The tone of his voice stopped me. When I saw the worry in his eyes, I couldn't resist touching his face.

"What is it?"

"When I went to the set, Ricardo was talking with his father. He was upset and loud. He thinks his father has had Estelle committed."

"Where did he get that idea?" I couldn't read Ricardo, but I was going to give it another try.

"I don't know," Graf said. "He sounded worried."

"What did Federico do?"

"He told Ricardo that if Estelle showed up here again, he would have her arrested. That really bent Ricardo. He stormed off."

"I think I'll have a word with him." Ricardo was standing in the shade of a tree drinking a bottle of water. He still looked hot and angry. And worried.

Graf lifted my hand to his lips. "I'm due on the set and you're up next. If you want to wait in your room . . ."

I kissed him, lightly but with a serious promise of more. "I'm not the kind of actress who hides in her trailer waiting to be called."

"Behave, Sarah Booth, I need to concentrate on being Ned."

I watched him go back to his mark as Federico resumed his place and waved everyone back into position. Ricardo remained in his spot, sulkily smoking a cigarette. When I approached, he gave me a bored look.

"Do you know something about Estelle?" I asked.

"Why bother answering. No one believes me."

"If your sister is still in town, I'm worried that she'll harm someone."

He exhaled cigarette smoke and stared at me as if he could assess my sincerity. "Daniel Martinez was looking for her last night while everyone was gone."

"The security guy?"

"He has a crush on her. She stood him up for a date a few days ago, and he's been going by her place, calling her cell phone, questioning her roommate."

"And?"

"No one has seen her. The cell phone has gone dead." Ricardo lit another cigarette, pretending to a nonchalance I saw through like smoked glass.

"Have you talked to Estelle?"

He shook his head. "Not for days. She was upset that Dad had her removed from the property."

"She's been in some of the secret passages, harassing me and others."

One shoulder came up and dropped. "She's angry, okay. But it isn't like her to disappear." He swallowed and finally looked at me. "I'm worried about her. Look, there's someone in the house." He dared me to interrupt him with a look. "Someone who doesn't belong there. I heard something this morning . . ."

I didn't know whether to believe him or not. "We've searched the secret passageways. We've searched all the rooms except for those on the third floor, and we're going there when the filming is over for today. If someone is hiding in the house, we'll find them."

"I tried to follow the noises, but I couldn't. No matter where I looked, there was no one."

"Ricardo, if you're messing with me, don't. Someone hurt my friend last night. It was serious."

Concern was quickly replaced with anger. "I knew you wouldn't listen. No one does. Did you ever think that might be the reason Estelle is so mad? No one listens!" He crushed out his cigarette and stalked away.

CHAPTER EIGHTEEN

By the end of the day's shooting, light had fled the sky, leaving bruised mango colors on the horizon. I was exhausted, and even Graf looked fatigued. Federico, a shade of bilious green, disappeared into the suite of rooms he shared with Jovan, who'd been resting most of the afternoon.

Tinkie was waiting for us in the kitchen with a pitcher of homemade lemonade and glasses filled with ice. It had been a long time since I'd tasted something that good. It was the perfect blend of tart and sweet, and it took me back to long-ago summer days when my mother would pack a hamper with sandwiches and lemonade and take me to one of the small amber creeks that fed the Tallahatchie River.

These were times my mother earmarked just for us—girl time. And she would talk of her love of the land and my father and her dreams for me to be successful and happy at whatever I chose. Jitty had said my folks were proud of me. I so hoped she was correct.

I put the past aside, and Tinkie, Graf, and I took our drinks outside to the patio where we were relatively sure no one could overhear us.

Tinkie's face was aglow. Not even the goose egg at her hairline could detract from her joy. "I spoke with the veterinarian, and he said I could get Chablis in a day or so." Tinkie played with the swirl of lemon peel decorating her glass and a shadow fell over her features. "He said if we hadn't acted so quickly, she would have died."

"But she'll be good as new, right?" I asked. "No permanent side effects?" Chablis could not be crippled.

Tinkie sighed. "He's almost positive. But he's cautious."

"Chablis is tough," Graf said. "She'll heal."

"I want to go home." Tinkie blinked back her tears. "I take Oscar for granted sometimes, but I realize how much I rely on him. He's irascible and self-involved, but he's also there when I need to lean on him, and I've got to say, I'm feeling like letting him play the big, strong he-man."

"That's what the best relationships are about—you rely on each other," Graf said softly. He reached across the table and picked up my hand. "I know you miss Oscar. As soon as Chablis can travel, we'll get you a flight home."

"But that's like abandoning Sarah Booth with this criminal stalking the film crew." Tinkie put her hand over ours and squeezed. "I may be short, but I'm generally the one who saves Sarah Booth's behind."

"True," I easily agreed. "She's arrived in the nick of time more than once. If it weren't for Tinkie and Sweetie, I'd be dead. But on this case, which I might point out isn't really a case since no one is paying us, I think the film is the target."

Tinkie swirled her drink. "I'm not in the film, but I was still hurt. If we could find Estelle, I'd feel a lot better."

And so would I, but Tinkie needed to go home as soon as she could. She didn't need to hang around, worrying about a young woman who might or might not be in trouble.

"I have some news," Graf said. "Federico said something today about wrapping the filming here tomorrow. He's ready to head back to L.A."

That was news to me, and I must have looked shocked.

"He was planning on filming some of the other interior

scenes around here, but he says he can do it as well on one of the studio lots. He wants to leave. This whole thing with Estelle so angry and Jovan getting injured—it's taken a toll on him." Graf drained his glass.

The idea of going back to California should have excited me, but it didn't. There were still questions unanswered about this house and what was going on. "I didn't expect to leave so quickly." The truth was, the sooner everyone was out of that house, the better. Still, I found myself reluctant to go.

Graf stood up and stretched. "I want to visit Chablis." He checked his watch. "The clinic is open late this evening. Tinkie, what about a trip to cheer the patient?"

"Wild horses couldn't stop me." She jumped to her feet. They both turned to me.

"You two go ahead. I want to talk to Ricardo again."

Graf put his hands on my shoulders. "Are you sure you want to stay here alone?"

"I'm not alone. Federico and Jovan are here. The security guards are outside. I saw Daniel Martinez walking toward the gate not half an hour ago. I think Ricardo may open up to me if I'm alone."

"Good luck," Tinkie said. "He's like a split personality. All charming one minute, and then all surly and rude the next. At the best of times, he's not the most forthcoming person I've ever met."

"That's why I want to talk to him. He sounded genuinely upset earlier. He said no one ever listened to him or Estelle. I want to give it a try. If he's got something to say, I want to hear it."

Graf came up behind me and pulled me against his chest. "Be careful. Take Sweetie with you wherever you go."

"That's a promise."

Graf leaned around to kiss me, a warm kiss that was fiery and tender. "That's my girl," he said.

"Give Chablis a kiss for me. When you get back, we'll have

some dinner." As much as I wanted to see the little dustmop, I needed to talk to Ricardo. Alone. He was sulky, charming, angry, uninterested. His emotional range made me wonder about several things, including drug use.

I walked Graf and Tinkie to the front door, then turned back to knock at Federico's room. No one answered and I pounded louder. My heart rate did triple time as the possibilities of what could have happened zipped through my brain. I was about to put my shoulder to the door when Jovan opened it a crack.

"Federico is asleep," she said softly.

"Sorry." It looked as if I'd awakened her. "Are you feeling better?"

"A little. I think we'll all feel better once we're back in the States."

I couldn't argue that, so I excused myself and went to look for Ricardo. Sweetie padded along with me as I walked through the west wing of the mansion. Portraits hung on the wall, most of them bearing some family resemblance to the painting of Carlita in my room. There were oil paintings of my mother's and my father's family throughout Dahlia House, but I'd never had my portrait painted.

It was traditional for a Daddy's Girl to have her image rendered on canvas at the time of her debut into society. My parents were dead by then, and I was strong-willed enough to sidestep Aunt Loulane's attempts to give me a debutante ball. The ball gown and portrait went hand-in-glove.

A long Persian carpet covered the hallway and muffled our footfalls as Sweetie and I made our way to Ricardo's suite.

According to the floor plans of the architect, there were no secret passages in this part of the house, which had been designed for guests, not family members. Old man Gonzalez obviously hadn't felt a need to spy on houseguests, only his daughter and son-in-law. No matter how I tried to explain that away, it was still creepy. What man would attempt to watch what was happening with his daughter and her new husband?

Ricardo's door was open, but his rooms were empty. I hesitated, standing in the hallway, wondering if I should search his personal belongings. Sweetie took the decision in hand and entered the room.

Glancing left and right down the hallway, I didn't see a sign of Ricardo or anyone else. I followed my hound straight to his suitcase on the floor. Sweetie nudged the bag, whining softly. Sweetie is an above-average dog, but she hasn't had drug training. Yet that was the first thing I thought. Drugs would explain Ricardo's Jekyll-Hyde behavior.

Before I had time for second thoughts, I opened the soft leather bag and began to move his clothes around. The only pills I found were health food vitamins, a blend with green tea extract for additional energy. I kept searching, and my efforts were rewarded with a slim journal. Sitting on the bed, I opened it. Pages were filled with the long, fluid scrawl of Ricardo's handwriting. I wasn't a big fan of private schools, but I had to admit that his penmanship was excellent.

I eased down onto his bed for a quick read. My theory on snooping is that if a person is going to do it, then do it one hundred percent. Don't invade someone's privacy and do a half-assed job of it.

The journal was a running account of the filming and what Ricardo had learned working under the tutelage of the cinematographer. The passages were filled with enthusiasm about different shots. If I'd wondered if Ricardo was serious about a career in film, I held the evidence.

I also saw a side of Ricardo he was loath to show—one where he worshipped his father. In comment after comment, he raved about Federico's brilliance. I thought how much this journal would please Federico, but I also knew that I could never show it.

I was about to put it away when I noticed Estelle's name.

The entry was dated the day she supposedly went back to California.

> *My sister continues her crusade. I'd hoped that Daniel might talk some sense into her, but I guess not. She's obsessed with the idea that Mother is still here, in this house. Sometimes I want to believe her, but Mother is gone. Her body stayed, but her spirit left. Perhaps that's the greatest sadness of all.*

An additional entry written this morning noted that he was "worried about Estelle." It didn't elaborate, and there was nothing else of interest in the small book.

I put the journal back and did a cursory exam of the rest of the room. Sweetie had fallen asleep with her nose in one of Ricardo's shoes. I found a small amount of marijuana and lots of dirty clothes. Nothing that would cause the mood swings I'd seen Ricardo display. When I was ready to leave, I woke my hound.

Something was nagging at me. Federico had said that Ricardo had arranged for the security crew, and Daniel was mentioned in Ricardo's diary as someone who had influence with Estelle. Perhaps it was time to have a little talk with the head of Promise Security Agency, Daniel Martinez.

I took a few moments to wander down the west wing hallway and open the doors to beautifully decorated—and unused—bedrooms. It was a huge place where Estelle could still be hiding.

I found a small study and stepped inside to admire some of the artwork. The vivid swirls of color in a contemporary oil were particularly fascinating. I couldn't make out the name of the artist, but I made a mental note to ask Federico later. Just as I was turning away from the painting, I heard what sounded like a moan, the old haunted house version of a haunting. The noise was muffled and unclear, but it was definitely someone—or something—in distress.

It wasn't an auditory hallucination. Sweetie spun, looking in all directions, a low whine coming from her. We both held perfectly still for a moment. The faint sound came again. Distant and indistinct, I couldn't tell where it came from or even if it was human. It could have been a dove in a chimney or even someone out on the grounds.

The latter was easy enough to check, and I went to a window and forced it open. The sun had set completely, but the driveway was well lit. This wing gave a good view of the front slope of lawn, the border of trees, and the white shell lane that meandered to the main road. The grassy lawn was in darkness, and someone could be hiding behind a tree or shrub, but I was fairly certain the sound hadn't come from outside.

Ricardo had said he'd heard something. A water pipe with a low-pitched complaint? An animal in the upper regions of the house?

Or someone deliberately messing with him—and me.

I closed the window with a bang and marched back toward the east wing and my room. Someone was playing me for a fool.

"If Ricardo is messing with us," I said to Sweetie, "we're going to find him."

Sweetie gave a soft yodel of approval. She always backed my play. We'd almost made it to the staircase when Sweetie froze. I nearly tripped on her. It was as if she'd been turned into stone.

"Sweetie," I said, nudging her with my knee. "Get a move on."

She remained stock-still, her gaze riveted at the end of the hall. The hairs on the back of my neck did a little dance, and I slowly shifted my gaze to the end of the hallway.

A woman in a red dressing gown stood at the top of the

staircase. Her dark hair was pulled softly back off her face, and she held something in her hands—a piece of material of some kind. She seemed to waver and shift in and out of focus.

"Help me." The sound came to me not like speech, but like something underwater. The words were indistinct. I put out a hand as if I could touch the air and feel the words.

"Stop it," she said. Her mouth didn't move when she spoke, but I heard her.

"You'll di-i-i-ie." The last word was a wail, and her dark eyes seemed to glow with a red light.

Before I could react at all, Sweetie growled low in her throat and bounded toward the figure. In the three seconds it took for her to reach the place where the woman had stood, there was nothing there. Not a trace of her.

From above me I heard what sounded like the footsteps of a running child. My heart seemed to catch in my throat. The scream that wanted to escape couldn't.

With Sweetie Pie at my heels, I ran down the stairs and out the front door into the warm embrace of the night.

Fifteen minutes later, I'd managed to calm myself and ventured back in the house as far as the kitchen. The smell of brewing coffee gave me some comfort, and I'd found some grilled chicken in the refrigerator for Sweetie.

I poured myself some strong black java and took several deep breaths, calming my body and trying to remember exactly what I'd seen and heard.

It was possible that we'd failed to discover all the secret passages. If that was the case, then the figure I'd seen could easily be a normal, flesh-and-blood human. A human who could move quickly, for sure. And I chose to believe that because the alternative was unacceptable. A ghost who made threats was more than I could handle.

"Jitty," I called my ancestral haint. "Jitty, I need you."

Outside, a tree limb brushed against the window and I

bolted out of my seat. When I picked up the chair I'd knocked over and looked around the room, my heart lurched again. A woman in a dark dress, white apron tied at the waist, stood in the doorway.

"That's not the way Mrs. DeWinter does it," she said in a severe tone that matched her hair pulled tight in a bun at the back of her neck.

By the time I recognized Jitty, I thought I was in the first stages of a heart attack. "If you weren't already dead, I'd be tempted to kill you."

"You're a poor imitation of Rebecca," she said, walking around me and examining me as if I were a hunk of rancid beef. "So callow. So young and desperate to please."

"Damn it, that's not funny." I was steamed. "And those aren't even the lines from the movie. You're just making that up."

Jitty laughed. "You look like you've seen a ghost," she said.

It was pointless to get angry with her. She was having a blast playing Mrs. Danvers from the movie based on Daphne du Maurier's book, *Rebecca*. "I would have thought you'd want the role of the ingenue. Joan Fontaine was quite pretty in the film. Mrs. Danvers was old and mean."

"Mrs. Danvers had all the best moments in the film. She was really creepy. But I have to say, it would be nice to kiss Sir Laurence Olivier. Maybe I'll put that on my to-do list."

Even if I was still angry with her, I was glad to have company, especially a spirit who was on my side.

"You look peaked, Sarah Booth. What's wrong?" she asked.

This time I was determined to press her. "Is there another spirit in this house?"

Jitty took a seat at the kitchen table, unpinned her hair, and let it fall around her shoulders. "I don't know if I can answer that question."

"Can't or won't." I was still a bit testy. "I saw a woman upstairs. I've seen her before, but never that close. She said I was going to die."

Worry shifted across Jitty's face, and when she looked up at me, I thought I saw a tear in the corner of her eye. "Sarah Booth, there are bad spirits as well as good ones. There are those who stay behind to exact revenge, or because they lost their way. They're confused and they can lash out."

The hair on my arms was standing straight up. "Is there such a spirit in this house?" I asked.

"What do you believe?"

"I don't know."

"And that's why I can't help you. If you told anyone about me, they'd think you were crazy."

"But—"

She held up a hand to stop me so that she could continue. "Whatever I say, you'll believe, because you believe in me. You've walked a long way to bein' a grown-up woman, and this is a road only you can walk. You have to decide."

"But—"

She stood up abruptly. "Listen to your heart, Sarah Booth. And while you're at it, listen to your womb. That good-lookin' man is offerin' to plant a crop. I foresee a mighty fine harvest."

And before I could even protest, she was gone and I heard the front door open on the *click-click* of Tinkie's high heels.

CHAPTER NINETEEN

"Chablis was so excited to see us!" Tinkie bustled into the kitchen, unloading a shopping bag filled with tequila. "I thought we'd have some drinks tomorrow, before everyone started leaving. Sort of an end of shooting in Petaluma party."

Even in Costa Rica, Tinkie was the perfect hostess. She thought of the things I should have done. As a failed Daddy's Girl, I was smart to have partnered up with her.

Graf had also been pulled into her plans. "I told Tinkie I'd man the grill. Maybe some shrimp and steaks. This place is paradise, and we need to bid it farewell in style." Graf was so handsome, it hurt to look at him. He'd become the man I needed him to be.

"That sounds like fun." I was still trying to accept that we would leave this house without resolving the mystery of the ghostly presence and who'd been hurting my friends and the crew.

"And the best news is that Chablis may be able to be here with us," Tinkie added. "The doctor said if she continues to heal at this pace, she'll be released tomorrow afternoon."

"That's wonderful!" I grabbed my friend and almost picked her up in a hug. Now that was something to celebrate.

"Did you discover anything from Ricardo?" Tinkie asked as she began to help tidy up the kitchen.

I told them about his journal and the marijuana. "No serious drugs. No amphetamines or things like that."

"No prescriptions?" Graf asked.

I shook my head. "I think his mood swings are emotional. He's worried about Estelle."

"While we were in town, I stopped by Estelle's apartment. Regena still hasn't heard from her, and now she's getting worried," Graf said.

"She was very willing to talk to Graf," Tinkie said, a teasing note in her voice. "She would have told him anything he asked, I think."

"I have a very effective interrogation technique," Graf said.

"You have a handsome face, a beautiful body, and a way with the women," Tinkie responded. "We could use that at Delaney Detective Agency."

Tinkie looked as if she wanted to take the words back, but she couldn't. There it was, the question that we each knew had to be faced eventually. Was I an actress or a private investigator?

"Almost all of the television PIs are handsome." Graf was doing his best to patch the silence. "Magnum, Rockford. A man can have good DNA *and* a brain."

"Both of those stars are delicious," Tinkie agreed, "but are they really intelligent? I mean, can a man be both things at once?" She hid her smile as she began pouring liquor in a blender. "This isn't the time to worry about tomorrow. Where are we going for dinner?"

I hadn't told them about the woman in red at the staircase, or what she'd said to me, and as I took the margarita that Tinkie offered me, I debated whether I should. The problem was, I couldn't get her out of my mind. She'd been a terrifying presence.

"Are you okay, Sarah Booth?" Graf asked.

"I need to speak to Daniel Martinez. He was mentioned in Ricardo's journal. While you two get ready for dinner, I'm going to find him. It won't take ten minutes."

Graf and Tinkie exchanged a glance I couldn't read. "He was at the gate when we came in," Graf offered.

"I'll wait for you there. And I'm starving." Still clutching my drink, I headed out the front door and down the drive to the gates.

I saw Daniel's silhouette standing in the doorway of the small office where a security guard checked vehicles in and out. Since the last days of filming had gone without incident, most of the paparazzi had moved on to fresher meat. Without the scent of tragedy or scandal, they had nothing to follow, so they'd left.

I recognized Daniel from a good distance away, and I slowed my pace as I realized he was talking to someone on a cell phone.

When I got close enough to hear what he was saying, he saw me and snapped shut the phone.

"Ms. Delaney, what can I do for you?" he asked.

"Tell me about Estelle."

"I believe she's returned to California," he said. The man was smooth, I had to give him that.

"Really," I said with a hint of sarcasm. "Do you know that for a fact?"

Concern slipped into the furrow between his eyebrows. He cleared his expression with an effort. "Her father told me she'd returned to Malibu. I haven't seen her hanging around the house."

"And would you report it if you had?" I asked.

He knew I was on to him, and in the light from the guard booth, I watched him decide how to play his hand. "So you know Estelle and I are . . . friends." It was a statement, not a question.

"Don't you think that was something you should have told your employer?"

He rubbed a hand over his jaw. "Perhaps. But maybe not. I've done the job he paid me to do."

"Let me count the ways I disagree with you. I was nearly drowned, Jovan has been pushed down stairs, my friend Tinkie was attacked in the house—"

"Attacked! No, that's not possible. And anyway, Estelle is gone."

"So you admit you knew she was responsible for what happened to me and Jovan."

He sighed and waved me into the guard shack where two stools were almost knee to knee. "I'll tell you what I know," he said. "The truth is, I'm worried about Estelle. I've called her house in Malibu repeatedly. She doesn't answer. Her roommate in town hasn't seen or heard from her. Estelle is like the wind—she blows from place to place. But she always calls and checks in. Always."

Not everyone on the set could be an actor, so I believed the worry in Daniel's face. He cared about Estelle, and he was concerned for her. "When was the last time you saw her?" I asked.

"Her father made me escort her out of the house. You were there. You saw it."

I nodded.

"I took her back to her apartment. Regena was there and we both talked to her. We told her she was going to end up in jail. Federico is Petaluma's star. He's like a national hero, and if he snapped his fingers, the local authorities would lock Estelle up, at least until Federico finished filming."

I hadn't realized that the director carried such weight in Petaluma, which begged the question of why he didn't want some officers to check out the mansion once Joey had fallen and nearly been killed. That was when action should have been taken. He could have stopped this before it got started.

"What did Estelle say? What were her plans?"

"She promised me that she'd stop bothering the film crew. She'd meant to frighten you with the ghost stories. That's all. She never meant for anyone to be hurt. She was going to Malibu. She'd given up, she said."

"Did she admit to any of the incidents that happened at the mansion?"

He shook his head, and the furrow deepened. "Only the cameras and the balustrade. But she never meant for anyone to fall. She thought the railing would give only enough to halt filming. She insisted that her mother was unhappy with the film crew in the house." His gaze dropped, but he continued talking. "She truly believes her mother's ghost is there, angry at the people in her home."

I cleared my throat softly. "And what do you believe, Daniel?"

When he looked at me, I was unprepared for the direct-ness of his gaze. "I love her, Ms. Delaney. She's troubled. I know that. She was hurt so deeply in her past that she can't overcome it without help, but I'm willing to see that she gets that help."

I put a hand on his knee. "Does Federico know how you feel about his daughter?"

He shook his head. "Ricardo knows. I told him when he of-fered me the job. I think that's one reason he made sure my se-curity firm was hired. He loves his sister, even if he thinks she's insane."

"And what do you believe about the ghost of Carlita?" I was cheating, trying to get a consensus of opinions before I made up my mind.

"I've never seen the ghost. Other people claim that they have. And Estelle certainly believes it. But she's still that lit-tle girl desperate for her mother's love and attention. She wants it to be true, because that's the only chance she'll ever have to know Carlita."

Daniel was not only a security guard, he was also familiar with human behavior. "What's your story, Daniel?"

He looked surprised, then sheepish. "I'm working toward a degree in psychology. I want my own practice. I met Estelle in class at the local university." He rubbed his chin again. "Estelle is messed up in some ways, but she isn't dangerous. She wouldn't push Jovan down the stairs. And she wouldn't have tied you up to drown or attacked Mrs. Richmond."

When I looked at him, hard, he held his ground. "She wouldn't do that," he said. "She might try to scare you out of the house, or even threaten. But she would not harm anyone."

"How can you be so certain?" I asked.

"Because I know her. I love her. It's as simple as that."

And perhaps it was—or not. Because Daniel believed her, he might not have been as vigilant in watching her as he should have.

"You're positive you haven't seen or heard from Estelle since that time you escorted her from the building?"

The way he licked his lips was a dead giveaway. He was going to lie.

"I haven't," he said.

"Thanks, Daniel." There was no point backing him against the wall, but I believed Estelle had been in the house—and that Daniel Martinez knew it.

The only thing I knew for certain was that the security forces hired to protect all of us were not as effective as Federico thought.

I left the guard shack and was standing in the pool of light when Tinkie and Graf came tearing down the driveway, ready for dinner.

When we returned, I would talk with Federico. Perhaps I would seal my fate as an actress. But I had to do it.

* * *

Graf pulled me into his arms and kissed me, long and thoroughly. My body yearned to yield to him and forget the chore I'd set for myself. When we'd come in after dinner, Federico's door was closed, and there was no sign that he or Jovan had been in the kitchen. They were most probably sound asleep.

Graf and I were in the hallway outside my room. I'd hoped that he would wait for me in bed while I had a talk with Federico, but Graf had other ideas.

Tinkie had gone to her room, full of a wonderful seafood dinner. Chablis was healing, and she knew she'd be winging her way back to the Mississippi Delta in little more than a day. Graf was of the opinion that we'd done all we could for the moment. He wanted to make love to me—an option that was becoming more and more difficult to resist.

"Sarah Booth, come to bed," he whispered in my ear, knowing full well the effect it would have on me. Shivers raced along my skin. Graf was not above applying unfair tactics.

"Give me ten minutes," I said.

"No." He kissed my neck, moving up to my earlobe. "Come to bed."

He was turning me from a responsible actress/private investigator into a wanton. My will crumbled, and I put my arms around his neck, kissing him back. As much as I wanted to talk to Federico about his past with Vincent Day, I wanted Graf more.

I found the doorknob of my room with one hand, opened it, and pulled Graf inside. The night was warm, and the doors to the balcony were open. The curtains puffed on the breeze, and for one indefinable moment I thought I saw the figure of a woman in the billowing material. But then it was gone, and I gave Graf every shred of my attention. I meant to bring

Graf to his knees, literally. And I spent the next hour doing just that.

After Graf had fallen asleep, I couldn't stop thinking about Jitty and her insistence that Graf and I would have a beautiful child. Graf had mentioned wanting children. I'd always assumed that I would have one eventually. Or maybe two. Not more than that.

My parents had had only me, and once I'd asked Loulane why. She'd frowned and said, rather sharply, I thought at the time, that my mother said that once she achieved perfection, there was no need to try again. The memory of that conversation made me smile. Aunt Loulane was never one to give out such bounteous praise. She was afraid she'd spoil me and I would become worthless, or worse.

Graf turned in his sleep, and I shifted so that I spooned against him. It was funny how love came in such different varieties. I had loved Coleman, but it was different from the love that was growing for Graf. Coleman was arid soil. No matter how much I'd cared for him, nothing could grow there. Not that he didn't care for me. I understood that he did. But not enough to change his life or give up his idea of who he was. Honor had claimed him, and kept him tied to Connie and her lies. There was no room to grow the love that had sprouted between us.

I heard the jingle of silver bracelets, and I was aware that Jitty was in the bedroom. I pulled the sheet up to my shoulders, causing her to give a low chuckle.

"I've seen you in your birthday suit since the day you were born," she said.

"You can't be in here," I hissed at her. "This is private time."

"Graf sleeps sounder than that hound dog. He won't never know we had a chat."

"I'm not in the mood for a chat." All I needed was for Graf

to wake up and hear me talking to what he would assume was myself. Psycho ward for sure—right beside Estelle. And perhaps that was why I had such sympathy for her, I suddenly realized. She wanted to be haunted, and I was.

"How long does it take cotton to grow?" Jitty asked.

I couldn't get a good look at her. The room was too dark. "Why are you asking that now?"

"Just tryin' to calculate the maturation of a crop."

I scooched up in the bed and turned on the light. Something was amiss with Jitty. She wore her bracelets, but she wasn't decked out in some film star's costume. She was wearing my old sweats and a T-shirt that advertised a local Zinnia blues club, Playin' the Bones. She hardly ever abandoned her costume theme. Clothes defined her.

"You've never been interested in cotton before," I pointed out.

"Crops have caught my interest. I like the idea of things growin'." She laughed again.

"You're not talking about cotton." I saw to the heart of her question. "You're talking about a baby."

"The finest crop you could grow, Sarah Booth. A future Delaney. Someone to carry on the name and add to the fine tradition of the line."

"Don't get the cart ahead of the horse. Graf and I are just getting to know each other. We want time to explore each other. We—"

"Just made love."

"I'm not stupid," I told her. "I take care of that."

Her only response was another laugh that faded into the shadows of the room.

"Sarah Booth! Sarah Booth!" Graf's voice came to me, his hand lightly shaking my arm. "Wake up, you're having a nightmare."

When I finally opened my eyes, he'd switched on the lamp

and was sitting on the edge of the bed. Relief made him smile. "You were thrashing and shaking your head and saying, 'No, no, it's not true.' What were you dreaming?"

I took a deep breath. "I was being deviled by the ghost of a family member." I yawned and sank back into the pillows. "But don't worry, I'll get even with her tomorrow."

Graf laughed. "You're still half asleep. You've got ghosts on the brain."

"And bats in the belfry," I answered before I fell back to sleep, content in the knowledge that Graf was right beside me.

CHAPTER TWENTY

Because movies aren't shot in sequential order, I'd focused solely on projecting Matty's emotions in each scene that involved her character. On this last day of shooting, Tinkie and I had parked our chairs behind the cameras to watch. My work in Petaluma was done. I had no more scenes until we started again in Los Angeles.

"I don't know how you keep up with where you are," Tinkie said. "And I certainly don't know how someone edits everything together to tell a story."

"I just do it one scene at a time and let Federico worry with stitching it into a seamless story." And novice though I was in the business, I could clearly see his genius. He had an ability to conclude a scene with a sound or image that would connect viscerally to the next moment of the story. Whether it was technique or style or simply the way he saw the story, it was brilliant. To do it, though, he had to know in his head how everything would fit together.

The film and all of the problems were wearing on Federico. He'd lost energy, and his skin was sallow. He kept glancing toward the house. Jovan hadn't been out of their rooms, as far as I knew. While the actual movie seemed to be going well, all of us were paying a high personal price.

Around noon, Federico shut down the cameras and or dered the crews to begin packing to go home. He'd rented a private plane to take the equipment and all of us back to Los Angeles, and he announced that we would leave early the next morning.

While he smiled and congratulated all of us on fine work, I could see that he was forcing himself to be jolly. Some thing was eating at him.

Everyone scattered in different directions, and at last Fed erico was alone. Tinkie excused herself to drive into town to check on—and hopefully bring home—Chablis. I pulled the director aside.

"Can I ask you some personal questions?" I dove right in.

"Is this about the accidents on the set?" He'd stopped pre tending to be hale and hearty, and he looked awful.

"Yes." I motioned toward the gardens. "Let's take a walk. The grounds really are so beautiful. It's going to be hard to say good-bye."

"Carlita loved this place," he said as we stepped into the shade of an arbor. "Me, not so much. I recognize the beauty, but there was always the sense that this wasn't my home."

"Clearly your father-in-law wanted you to feel that way." I'd told Federico about the passageways. He'd been surprised, but he hadn't been angry. Now, he seemed more saddened than anything else.

"Estoban thought that I wasn't good enough for Carlita. The Gonzalez family came from old money, banana and coffee plantations. My father was a merchant, and I went to film school on scholarships. Estoban had no use for the cin ema, especially not since Carlita was so in love with it. He hoped to marry her off to a planter or a banker, someone who could provide for her and give her security. Someone of her class."

We passed several beautiful statues, women with flowing hair and gowns, caught in a moment of rapture or action.

When we came to a bench in the shade of some lush plants, we took a seat.

"Surely after your career took off, Estoban got over his initial distrust."

Federico's chuckle was dry. "Hardly. He hated me even more. Carlita was cast in several films, and he felt that was my doing. He had the idea that all actresses were whores, and he made her feel like one. She was exotic and sexy, and he made her dislike those things about herself. Her biggest problem was that the man she most loved refused to recognize her talent."

I could draw a lot of parallels, but I wasn't being paid to do that. In fact, I wasn't being paid to stir this pot at all. But no one was going to attack my partner and get away with it.

"I've been trying to put together a list of people who might want this film to fail." I gave him a moment to think it through. "When was the last time you saw Vincent Day?"

"Vincent," he said softly. "I haven't thought of him in a long time now."

"Have you seen him lately?"

"No." He stood up and started walking. I followed him, giving him a moment to find the memories I needed.

"I understand the two of you were great friends?"

"Yes, and we parted bitter enemies."

"Because of Carlita?"

He glanced at me, a sidelong gaze that assessed me in a new light. "I thought the whole business about you being a private investigator was a story Graf made up, some Hollywood hype. But it's true, isn't it?"

"Finding out about Vincent Day didn't require a whole lot of experience, just the right person who's interested in movie stars and has a good memory." Millie was invaluable.

"Hardly anyone working in Hollywood remembers Vincent. And he was brilliant. That was twenty-five years ago or better."

"Is he Estelle's father?" I thought the question would shock him, but it didn't.

"I never asked Carlita. I didn't care. Estelle never belonged to me or Vincent, she was her mother's daughter. She was born with an attachment to Carlita that no one could sever, not even for her own mental health."

We'd passed through the main part of the gardens and were almost at the cliff that gave onto the beach. It was still early afternoon, and the sun cast stark shadows. The wind was warm, a caress, and tropical blossoms grew in abundance all around me, creating a scent of such poignancy that I wondered if Carlita had been happy in this house.

"Where is Vincent Day?" I asked.

Federico shrugged. "I don't know. It's been years since we spoke."

"Do you think he might be behind this scheme to ruin your film?"

Federico slowed and then stopped. He put his hand up to shade the sun from his eyes as he glanced out at the surf pounding below us on the beach. "Why would he do this now? So much time has passed. We've both accepted Carlita's death."

"Did he know she was starving herself to death?"

He looked to the left and I couldn't see his expression. "I never told him. Even as Carlita was dying, I wanted her to be mine." He made a sound of disgust. "That sounds so pathetic, but you had to know her. She was fire and ice. She was so magnificent—"

"That you had to sleep around on her." I said it quietly, and that only heightened the impact of my words. Federico looked as if I'd slapped him.

"It doesn't make sense, I know."

Even though I waited, he didn't attempt to explain it further. So I pressed. "If you were so in love with your wife, why did you sleep around on her?"

He sighed and reached out to pick a perfect rose from a vine growing along the fence at the back of the garden. He held the blossom, turning it slowly in his fingers. "Can you begin to imagine what it was like for me when I finally realized that Carlita would never be mine? Not truly mine."

"She loved Vincent Day that much?" Somehow, I'd gotten the impression that Vincent was someone Carlita used.

"Not Vincent." He laughed, but there was no mirth in it. "If it had been Vincent, perhaps I could have understood."

"Then who?"

"Carlita loved her father. He was the only man that mattered to her."

"Are you saying—"

He looked appalled. "No. Not that. Certainly not. There was no sexual bond between them." A flush stained his cheeks. "Or perhaps there was, and I was too blind to see it."

"What do you mean?" Federico's emotions were like an angry abscess, and I was the one jabbing around with a needle. It wasn't going to be pretty if he ever really let go.

"Carlita was a virgin when I married her. In fact, she was unbelievably innocent. I knew she was pure, but I found myself in the position of teaching her everything. How to kiss, how to accept a touch of affection. It was as if she'd been . . . walled away from most human emotion that had even a hint of sexuality in it."

"This was the eighties, Federico. Sex was all over television and the movies and—"

"You've just made my point," he interrupted me. He sniffed the rose and then held it out to me. I took it, careful of the thorns. "Carlita's innocence was unnatural. I believe Estoban honestly felt that all sexual feelings were dirty, so he raised Carlita to deny all such urges."

"Holy cow. That's a sick and twisted thing to do to a young woman."

"Indeed." He waved a hand around him. "He built her this

temple to virginity, and then he had to spy on us so that he could manipulate her. I didn't know about the secret passage-ways, the listening spaces, the panels where he could watch a peep show." Anger crept into his voice and I saw his features harden. Here was the hatred I'd expected.

"I was gentle with Carlita. And patient." His dry and hollow laugh came again. "Imagine such a fool. I was proud that I was the only man my wife had ever known. That I was the one to teach her to please me. And that bastard Estoban watched, so that he could punish her for each thing she did that gave her pleasure."

I leaned against the fence, slightly queasy. "I'm so sorry."

"I was a coward," he said. "Instead of confronting Esto-ban about the way Carlita took such pleasure in some inti-macy and then later lashed out at me for teaching it to her, I buried myself in work."

"Federico, you didn't know. How could you know what Estoban was doing?"

He moved so quickly that I almost yelped when he lashed at the roses with his hands. He swung at the beautiful blooms, sending a shower of petals on the winds that blew them out toward the ocean and the beach. The sweet scent, old-fashioned and heartbreaking, filled the area where we stood.

He didn't stop until the last rose was demolished and he was panting from exertion. He wiped the sweat from his fore-head and gripped the railing of the fence. "She hurt my ego. She said things that—that I was a bad lover, that I would never satisfy her, that I was dirty. She drove me insane, Sarah Booth. And I paid her back by sleeping with the woman I knew would hurt her the most, a tall blonde."

I understood, and the truth of it was unbearably sad. "It was Carlita's father who made her self-conscious about her looks, because she was so sexually charged. She was the Latin Marilyn Monroe." I repeated what Millie had told me.

"When the film world saw her, she got offers from every director working. She was so exotic, so sensual, and she could act. She could also sing and dance, but that wasn't important in that first rush of offers. I told Carlita that her true talent would be acknowledged, but that her feminine power was what everyone saw first."

"So the roles she was offered fed into the misgivings her father had set up in her. She was typecast as the seductress, the role her father had taught her would send her straight to Hell."

He nodded once and then turned away. His hand went to his face and I wondered if he was wiping away a tear. "I utterly failed her, you know. Instead of helping her, I cut her to the bone."

"Hindsight is always twenty-twenty, Federico. Neither of us can say whether you could have changed anything had you behaved differently. Estoban set those behaviors and beliefs from infancy."

"And that's why I sent the children away from her. Not to be mean, not to punish her, but to protect them. I thought if I could keep them from seeing the way she behaved, the things she did to herself, they wouldn't learn them." His tone had turned bitter. "Estelle certainly proved me wrong. It's genetic. It comes in the blood."

I put a hand on his arm and felt the tension in his muscles. "Estelle can choose to change."

"You say that as if it were so simple." The anger was gone and he was left with sadness again.

"Change is the hardest thing, for human or animals. Even plants have difficulty, and many can't survive it." I felt the corners of my mouth tug upward, but it was merely the ghost of a smile. "But the most amazing thing is that we keep trying. As long as we're alive, we continue to try. So we have to find Estelle and make sure she has all the help we can give her, if she chooses to try."

He put his arm around my shoulders and moved back the way we'd come. "You're a wise woman, Sarah Booth."

I laughed, and this time it was full and real. "Not me. I happen to have some very smart friends."

He leaned down and whispered in my ear, "But you listen to them, and that's what makes you wise. Now let's head back to the house and find Jovan. I'm sure she's wondering where I am. I can't leave all the packing to her."

But as we rounded the hedge in the garden, I realized Jovan wasn't worried about packing. She stood on the balcony of my room and stared down at us. Her expression was blank, but when she noticed my gaze on her, she turned and went inside. She'd witnessed Federico putting his arm around me and whispering in my ear. She couldn't know that he was talking about something innocent. From her vantage point, I doubted that the gesture looked anything except guilty as sin.

I started to tell Federico, then stopped. He had so much on his mind. And besides, I couldn't be certain Jovan was the jealous type. After all, she'd been spending mornings, evenings, and nights acting opposite Graf in scenes from which I was excluded.

That didn't exactly equate to a private walk in the gardens, but it was Federico's call. If he wanted to tell her, he could. I was going inside to pack. If Tinkie got the nod for Chablis to head home, Tinkie would fly back to Zinnia with the dustmop in the morning, and Graf and Sweetie and I would hop the private jet to L.A.

As soon as this film was wrapped, I was heading back to the Delta for a dose of down-home common sense and some of Millie's cooking. I was fairly certain the problems in the Marquez mansion stemmed from Estelle. She was somewhere on the premises, pulling pranks and still trying to sabotage her father's film. Like Carlita, she wasn't ready to change the patterns of her behavior, and I wasn't willing to spend my time trying to solve a mystery that would have no real resolution.

Estelle was the only person who could stop her personal crash and burn.

"Chablis!" I hailed the returning heroine. Tinkie parked in front of the mansion and carried the little moppet, all done up in fashionable hospital white, into the foyer where Graf, Sweetie Pie, Federico, and I waited.

"When Sarah Booth does her next film, you must bring Chablis to Hollywood," Federico said, stroking the pup's silky ears. "Now that Sweetie Pie has a role in a film, we must cast this darling creature."

Tinkie beamed, though I couldn't help but wonder if she'd ever risk Chablis on another trip again. The dustmop was healing, but it was a close call.

"I made her some chicken and rice," Graf said.

He'd disappeared into the kitchen and threatened me if I tried to enter. But Graf, cooking comfort food for a dog?

"I'm skeptical," Tinkie said, voicing my exact thoughts. "You're a good man, Graf, but I don't buy this at all." She bustled past him, Chablis in her arms.

We weren't far behind, but when I heard her exclamation, I had to give Graf a kiss. He was a man of his word. Two doggie bowls of chicken and rice were on the counter, warm to the touch. He'd even washed up the mess he'd made cooking.

"If Sarah Booth lets you get away," Tinkie whispered loud enough for everyone to hear, "I will have her put in the mental institution we've been threatening her with."

"She can't shake me this time," Graf assured her. "We're a team. Better together than either is solo."

How is it possible that words that can bring so much pleasure can also bring pain? I'd thought the same could be said of Coleman, but it hadn't panned out. And each time I found myself drifting to the past and my feelings for Coleman, I was cheating Graf.

"Is something wrong?" Federico came up beside me and

spoke so softly that neither Graf nor Tinkie heard him. They were busy hand-feeding Chablis. Sweetie Pie was scarfing her food down in fine Delaney tradition.

"I'm fine," I said. "It's hard to leave here."

"Once you're back in L.A., the work pace will keep you so busy, you won't have time to miss Petaluma."

He was right, of course. "I think I'm going up to my room for a quick shower," I told the gang. "Graf, since you're playing chef tonight, rustle up some vittles so we can all eat on the patio and enjoy the last evening here."

"Your wish is my command." He nodded his head like a certain television genie and I ducked out of the room and hurried upstairs. I wanted the water pounding down on me to wash away my self-destructive tendencies. I cheated my own happiness by clinging to the losses of the past. If I had to have a lobotomy or an exorcism, that was one pattern of behavior I intended to break.

I'd gathered fresh clothes and turned to go into the bathroom when I caught a glimpse of a figure standing on my balcony. My heart hammered against my chest, and my fresh clothes slipped to the floor. I almost ran back to the kitchen, but I didn't. It was Estelle, and she wasn't going to get my goat this time. She couldn't get past me; the door—or jumping twenty feet to the ground—were the only ways out of my room.

"I'm not afraid of you," I said. I walked toward the balcony. So my knees were a little weak; my voice was strong and steady. "If you've got something to say to me, you'd better come on in and say it."

The figure didn't move, and it took me a few seconds to realize it was dressed in a floor-length gown of fine gray silk, with a high-necked, fitted bodice and flaring full skirt. The dress rustled in the breeze that was coming off the ocean.

The figure turned toward me and I saw pale skin, hair in a chignon. My mouth was suddenly dry. This wasn't the woman in red. This was another figure entirely, and one that seemed to fade and shimmer in the dying light of day.

"What do you want?" I asked.

"Quinton. I want Quinton. He loves me, you know. The children see him in the stables. He's waiting for me."

Try as she might to imitate a Victorian governess from one of the scariest movies I'd ever seen, *The Innocents,* Jitty couldn't completely lose her Southern accent. A desire to wring her neck came hand in glove with the knowledge of what she was up to.

"Damn it, Jitty, you scared me."

"I'm a ghost, Sarah Booth. It's in the job description."

I picked up my clothes and turned back to the bathroom. I didn't have time for her antics. "I'm heading home tomorrow."

"To Zinnia?"

There was such hope in her voice that I stopped and turned back to face her. "To Los Angeles. But once I'm done with this film, I'm going to Dahlia House. I need a break from all of this movie hustle and bustle."

I could see that my explanation did nothing to soothe the wound I'd so innocently inflicted. She'd really thought I would give up this movie in midstride and head home. "Why are you on my balcony?" I asked.

"I was thinkin' of perception. You know, how you can see somethin' and another person can see the same exact thing, but if you both tell it, you each have a different story."

"And?" She'd given up all attempts to speak like a governess. Her voice was rich and soft and lilting with the soft "g" endings that made a Southern drawl so appealing.

"You're packin' up to leave Costa Rica. I've never known you to leave a case half-finished."

It stung a little, which let me know she'd hit an exposed nerve. "First of all, I'm going to L.A. to finish a job that I'm committed to do. Secondly, this isn't 'a case.' No one is paying me to straighten out Federico's daughter. I did what I could, but now it's time to move on."

"Are you so certain that Estelle is the perp?"

I hated it when Jitty used television language. She sounded like such a phony. "Estelle may or may not be 'the perp' but she damn sure has motive, means, and opportunity. She's at the top of the suspect list."

Jitty remained on the balcony, the sheer curtains lifting and falling around her in the breeze. Even in her governess garb, she was beautiful.

"That's what I mean about perception, Sarah Booth. Maybe, for just one minute, you should try lookin' at this from her point of view."

"I would if I had any idea what her point of view might be." But I was already talking to air. The balcony was empty. The curtains billowed once and then hung straight. Jitty was gone, and I was left with a feeling of dissatisfaction.

CHAPTER TWENTY-ONE

My hair was still damp from the shower, and my mind was on Jitty's message as I locked the door of my room and started for the staircase. The lessons from my haint were always cryptic, but this one had me puzzled. How did Marlon Brando as Quinton, the horse master in a movie based on a delicious short story, relate with anything that was happening around me?

I'd forgotten all about my "moment" in the gardens with Federico, but obviously Jovan had not. She waylaid me at the foot of the stairs.

"Is there something between you and Federico?" she asked.

At least she had the guts to come to me to get an answer, and I gave her points for forthrightness. "No, Federico is my boss. I'm concerned about his daughter." I matched her look for look. "I saw you on the balcony of my room." I checked my impulse to ask her why she was there. It would be more interesting to see what she volunteered.

Jovan's smile was amused. "Your door was open, and I heard something, like someone shuffling around. Creepy. Since Federico and I both have had that virus or whatever it was, I went in to check on you. I thought you might be sick."

I knew what happened next. "But the room was empty."

"Yes, the room was empty, and as soon as I went to the balcony, the noise stopped. I checked the bathroom and around, but I couldn't find anything. It had to be a water pipe or something in the walls." Her blond hair caught in one of her beautiful earrings, and she tugged it free. "It was so eerie. I honestly thought someone was there. Maybe the ghost that everyone is talking about."

"And then you glanced out and saw me and Federico in the garden."

She nodded slowly. "You looked pretty cozy. Federico and I are together because it suits us, but if he's developing a new interest, I don't want to be the last to know."

"Like I said, we were discussing his daughter. He's worried about her, and for good reason." No matter that we'd sealed all the secret corridors we knew about, there were others. There had to be. Old houses made strange noises, but it also seemed that someone floated through that house like it was a poltergeist honeycomb.

"The little bitch is working him." Jovan showed her first spark of Nordic heat. She was usually so cool, so unemotional, but Estelle had been pushing her buttons, too. While she might not show Federico her true feelings, she had no such reservations where I was concerned. "Estelle is a manipulative, dangerous woman," she continued. "I've told him he should stop all contact with her. Every time he gets worried and upset, she wins."

Estelle was manipulative. But dangerous? Yes, that, too. She'd hurt Joey, Jovan, Tinkie, and Chablis. And me. I could easily have drowned. "If we find her before tomorrow, I think Federico will put her in a facility for medical care. He's afraid she's going to harm herself."

"Instead of a country club mental institution, I'd rather see her sit in jail." Jovan frowned. "I hate to sound like a shrew, but she could have killed me. And your friend was hurt, as well as her dog."

I nodded in agreement. "To be honest, I don't think we'll discover Estelle before tomorrow. And once we're out of this house, she has no reason to bother us again."

"Tell that to Suzy Dutton." Jovan's blue gaze held mine for a moment before it broke. "I'm afraid, Sarah Booth. If she killed Suzy in Malibu, she might try to harm me again. Or you. Or someone on the film like Joey. He was lucky he didn't break his neck."

"We don't know that Suzy's death involved Estelle in any way."

"Right. It's just a coincidence that Federico's ex-girlfriend is dead and everyone on this film has been hurt." Her face shifted into shock. "Except for Graf. Nothing bad has happened to him."

I laughed. I couldn't help it. I didn't intend to be rude, but what she was implying was ridiculous. "Only women and teenage boys have been injured. Graf is a strong man. Perhaps that's why he hasn't been targeted. And you're forgetting Federico. No one has pushed or slugged him." I moved past her. I was ready to join my friends in the kitchen. Chablis was home and I needed some pampered pooch kisses.

"Federico may have been a victim, too. I'm thinking someone tampered with our food. We had seafood delivered and he and I both have been sick."

That brought me up short. Sick was one thing, but if Estelle, or someone else, was poisoning the food, it could also be deadly. Or it could merely have been a mild case of accidental food poisoning. Seafood and sun were a breeding ground for bacteria. "We should have had that food tested."

"I know, but Federico threw it away." Jovan walked with me toward the kitchen. "Look, we're leaving in the morning. If that's the end of all of this, I say let it go. Estelle is nuts, but she's also Federico's daughter. But what if this continues in Los Angeles? What then?"

"I'll mention that to Federico, but I honestly think once we leave, you're safe."

"I hope you're right," she said, pushing the door open. "Graf asked me to hurry you up and I've detained you, jabbering about my fears. Graf said the steaks are almost ready."

We entered the kitchen together, talking about the scenes that would be shot as soon as we unloaded our gear in Los Angeles. Jovan had a far better understanding of how the movie would be edited. But, of course, as Cece would point out, she was sleeping with the director. That did give her a slight advantage.

Throughout the meal, Chablis was alert and wagging her tail, but she didn't leave Tinkie's side. And Sweetie remained near her, attentive and protective. Like me and Tinkie, they were best friends.

Federico tapped his wineglass with a spoon and stilled the conversation that was buzzing around the table. "The plane leaves at ten in the morning. Be at the airport at nine." He turned to Tinkie. "And what time is your flight out?"

"I have one last checkup with the veterinarian, so I won't leave until the afternoon."

Federico frowned. "I can leave Ricardo here to stay with you. He can catch a commercial flight the next day."

"I wouldn't think of such a thing." Tinkie's glitzed hair bobbed with the vehemence of her answer. "I'll be perfectly fine."

"I've offered to stay and so has Graf," I said.

"It's a checkup for Chablis. There's no need to worry, and I'll only be a few hours later than you guys in taking off."

Conversation buzzed back to a mild roar, and I found myself leaning against Graf, feeling the reassurance of his strong chest as my support. For many women, this might be the norm. For me, it was a moment to treasure. I wasn't the leaning kind—but it was nice to find someone solid when I did.

We broke up early, all eager to conclude in Costa Rica

nd head back to the States. Graf, Tinkie, and I volunteered
o put the kitchen to rights and we set about our chores after
he others went to attend last-minute chores.

"It's been a wonderful trip," Tinkie said as she dried the
plates I'd just washed.

"Right. It isn't every day you get knocked on the head and
our dog kicked." I gave her a grin to show I was kidding.

"No, this is a lovely place. Your coworkers are wonderful,
Sarah Booth. This has been an experience. I'm sure Millie
nd Cece will pump me for information as soon as I get
home."

"Make it up, and make us look good," Graf suggested. He
was cutting the remains of a steak into tiny little bites for
Chablis.

"Maybe I'll just take you and Sarah Booth home to show
them what a nice couple you make."

There were so many things I wanted to say in answer to
this, but I kept silent. I wasn't certain where my life would
take me, and I made no promises.

We finished the cleanup and headed to our rooms. Chablis
had fallen asleep, and we were all tired. Our lives would
change yet again in another few hours. I wondered if I was
getting better at handling these sudden shifts, or if since I'd
torn my roots from the soil of Sunflower County, I would
forever be rootless. The prospect of that made me want to
snuggle into Graf's arms and hide.

We went to bed, exhausted, but not too far gone to forget
that this was our last night in Costa Rica. We made love slowly
and with care for each other. Graf could be both fiery and tender, and he was always a surprise. He aroused me with kisses
that were sweet and familiar, and in other new ways. In bed
with him, I had the sense that time stood still for us. Curled together, we fell asleep.

The room was filled with darkness when I awakened. It
took me a moment to realize the thrum and hammer I heard

was the sound of Graf's heart. My ear was pressed against his chest and his arms held me protectively. But there was another noise. A soft whimper, like someone crying in an empty church, broke and rippled around me. There was the dull thud, like the fictional John's head thudding down uncarpeted stairs in that old black-and-white movie. It was impossible to tell if the sounds were noncorporeal or real.

My first impulse was to nudge Graf awake, but instead I eased from bed. The sounds were elusive. I heard them, but maybe I was imagining it. Grabbing a robe, I slipped out into the hallway.

I heard the eerie keening again, so soft that it almost wasn't there. It echoed, as if it came from a chest devoid of heart and lungs. Almost as if it rippled from the very walls themselves. It was impossible to tell which direction it came from. I had the sense that I'd stepped into *The Haunting of Hill House.*

Creeping along the hallway, I didn't make a sound. Movement in a recessed doorway made me freeze.

Someone was in the hallway. Hiding.

I paused for a few seconds. If this was the woman in red, I intended to catch her. If it was Estelle, then our mysteries would be mostly resolved.

Tensing my muscles, I launched myself forward, turning and diving into the small hidden area. My forehead connected with something solid and sharp, and I let out a yelp and struck the locked door of an empty bedroom with my shoulder. Slowly, I sank to the floor, momentarily stunned.

"My God, Sarah Booth!"

I recognized Tinkie's voice instantly, but when I looked up she was slightly out of focus. She held one of her stiletto heels in a tight grip.

"I'm so sorry. I thought you were attacking me." She sank down beside me and her fingertips brushed at my forehead, which was beginning to throb. "I clocked you. Let's go to the kitchen and put some ice on that."

"You hit me?" I was a little slow to gather the facts.

"With my shoe. The heel sort of dug a hole in the center of our forehead." She cleared her throat. "I'm afraid it's not going to be very attractive tomorrow."

I wasn't worried about my looks, I was afraid that I'd been lobotomized. "I don't think I can stand." I wasn't playing the pity card, either. Tinkie had brought that shoe down with force.

She got me under my arms and helped me to my feet. Tinkie is only shoulder height on me, but she's all wiry muscle. We ambled down the hallway, pausing at the stairs. I wasn't sure if I could make it or not.

"Shall I get Graf?" she asked.

"No." I felt slightly foolish. "I'll be fine." To prove it, I took the stairs slowly. By the time we got to the kitchen, my forehead was on fire and my ears were ringing.

Tinkie made an ice pack and we sat at the table while I chilled my wound.

"I'm so sorry. I heard this scary sound and I went to investigate. Then I heard someone following behind me. I assumed it was Estelle or whoever has been attacking people. So I hid and waited." She bit her bottom lip.

"It's okay." The ice was helping. "I would have done the same thing."

"What is that noise?" she asked.

"I don't know." I didn't know much. I'd just had my brains scrambled. "But if I had to guess, I'd say this house has a past. A tragic past." The truth was, the sounds I'd heard scared me.

"It's so sad, Sarah Booth. Do you think it's a ghost?"

This was the same question I'd posed to Jitty, and her answer had been totally unsatisfactory. Yet I was about to give to Tinkie.

"I can't say."

"Do you believe in ghosts, Sarah Booth?"

Her question was asked with such innocence. Like a child

asking about Santa Claus. "Yes. Unequivocally." That que[s]tion I didn't have to dodge.

"Then this crying person in the house could really be [a] ghost. Someone who's here because she can't leave. Tha[t] would be terrible, to be dead and be caught between that worl[d] and this one."

Jitty didn't seem to mind, but I wasn't about to tell her tha[t] "Caught here or staying here voluntarily, I think ghosts ca[n] stay behind to help, or for revenge."

"Good and bad ghosts, just like people." She smiled, an[d] I could see the fatigue in the tender skin under her eyes.

"Right. Just like people."

"This ghost, I think we should help her."

I was stunned. Tinkie had always disavowed a belief in th[e] supernatural. But then I remembered Tinkie's interest in on[e] of our clients, a woman named Doreen Mallory, who was sai[d] to heal people. Tinkie had found a breast lump, but someho[w] she'd convinced herself that she could heal it herself. Th[e] bottom line was that when we finally convinced Tinkie to a[d]dress the lump with a medical doctor, it was gone. Vanishe[d.] Dissipated. Tinkie had never claimed that the lump had bee[n] healed. She simply said nothing. Now she wanted to assi[st] dead people.

"How can we help a ghost?" I asked.

"First we have to find out why she's haunting this house[."]

"And how do you propose we do that?" My forehead wa[s] swelling, and I was feeling cranky.

"We ask her."

I rolled my eyes. "Okay, I'll wait here and hold the ice o[n] my forehead while you track her down and ask her what th[e] problem is."

"You are grouchy when you're in pain. I'll be sure and te[ll] Graf, just in case you try to talk him into natural childbirth[.] You're definitely one of those who should have the epidur[a] *and* general anesthesia."

"Don't worry about my breeding abilities. If you're going to help a ghost, you'd better get on the stick. We're leaving in less than ten hours."

Tinkie took a deep breath. "I'm not leaving, Sarah Booth."

Surely the blow to my head had affected my hearing. "Oscar is having a conniption to get you back to Zinnia. And Chablis is cleared to travel."

"I'm staying."

"Tinkie, you can't stay here alone." The idea was upsetting. Tinkie had already been injured. She had to clear out and go back to the safety of Mississippi.

"I won't be alone. Chablis is here." The set of her chin told me argument was useless.

"Oscar will kill me if I leave you here by yourself."

"I love Oscar, but he isn't the boss of me."

"God forbid that anyone try to boss you." I pressed the ice harder to my forehead. A really big headache was blossoming.

"I know you have to go, Sarah Booth. The movie is your priority. But something is going on in this house. Something bad. I can't just walk away."

I removed the ice pack and got a gander of my forehead in the reflection on a toaster. It looked like I was developing a third eye. "I'm staying, too," I said.

"Don't be ridiculous." She lifted her chin another notch. "You can't go AWOL on a movie."

"And I can't work with a hole in my forehead. I'll give it a day or two to heal while I'm here with you. I don't think Sally has enough putty to fill this crater. I may as well do something useful."

She picked up my free hand and squeezed it. "Thank you, Sarah Booth."

"Don't thank me. I'm not sure this is a smart choice."

"What will you tell Graf?"

That was a good question. "I think I feel a stomach virus

coming on." It wasn't a total lie. I did feel a little queasy every time I looked at my reflection in the toaster. I wondered if there might be room for me on the circus midway.

"I'll volunteer to take you to the doctor while they head out to Hollywood." She patted my fingers. "It'll be like old times. Me, you, Sweetie, and Chablis. We'll have this ghost thing knocked out in no time."

"Right," I agreed. "No time at all." If someone didn't push us down a flight of stairs or hit us in the head with a hammer first.

CHAPTER TWENTY-TWO

Before he got in the car to go to the airport, Graf kissed me passionately. When I was weak-kneed, he put his lips beside my ear and whispered softly, "I'm not buying this whole stomach virus story *or* that you slipped in the bathroom and hit your head. You're up to something."

I started to pull away, but he held me closer. "I'm your lover who won't blow your cover, but you have to promise me you won't get hurt." His lips moved along my neck. "I might die if something happened to you."

"I'll play it safe. As soon as Chablis can safely travel, I'll be on my way to Hollywood. Tinkie has to stay, and she doesn't want to give up yet." I leaned against him as I spoke, already missing him.

His answer was another long, searing kiss, and then he got in the car. "I'll call to check on you as soon as we're on the ground. If you don't answer, I'll have police swarming over this place."

I nodded and turned to Federico and Jovan, who were openly examining the bandage that Tinkie had plastered to my forehead. Or maybe it was the makeup job that she'd done to give me a "virusy" look. My skin tone was slightly green and bilious.

Jovan stepped closer to me. "Come with us, Sarah Booth. You can't stay in this house. It's dangerous."

I was touched that she cared. "I'm going to the emergency room," I told her. "I'm too sick to stay here. I think I'm dehydrated, and my fever is high. If they don't keep me, Tinkie and I will get a hotel room. As soon as I can travel without throwing up, we're out of here."

Relief touched her features. "Thank goodness. Anything can happen in this place. I think the house is damned. You're already weak, and someone could really hurt you."

Tinkie had walked up and overheard her comments. "Once Sarah Booth is feeling better, she'll be on the next plane home," Tinkie said. "I'll stay with her until then. She'll be fine."

"What about the dogs?" Jovan asked. She rumpled Sweetie Pie's ears. "They could be hurt again."

"We'll take them to the vet clinic." Tinkie picked up one of Jovan's suitcases and started toward the waiting car. "Federico can't miss this flight."

"I know." Jovan hugged me. "It's so hard to find a real friend in Hollywood, Sarah Booth. I'll see you soon."

When they were gone, I whipped off the bathrobe and revealed my jean shorts and a T-shirt. My running shoes were behind the door. All I had to do was wash the makeup off my face.

"Where to first?" I asked.

"I think Senor Lopez hasn't told us the entire truth." Tinkie had a look in her eyes that made me shiver. One thing about Tink—she took it personally when someone played her.

When we were in the car, the dogs riding in the backseat happy as clams, Tinkie glanced at me. "I should handle this alone."

"I'm fine. I'm not really sick. It was all an act."

Tinkie flipped the passenger visor down so that I was staring at myself. My face was puffy and the bandage made me look like an ax murder victim. Even without the makeup, I looked bad.

"I can take the bandage off. That'll help." I peeled the tape free, looked, and slapped it back into place. "Maybe not." Tinkie had really clocked me. The lump looked like a misplaced horn.

"Stay in the car," she said as she parked. "I'll be back."

"What if he gets aggressive?"

"He's, like, sixty-five."

"Remember Virgie?" Virgie Carrington was an older woman who ran a finishing school for girls who also happened to be a serial killer. She'd almost snuffed both Tinkie and me, not to mention Sweetie Pie. She'd shot Coleman and drugged Oscar. All in all, she was pretty spry for a senior citizen.

"Senor Lopez isn't dangerous, but I am." She slammed the door. "Stay still. If someone sees you they might think the virus in *28 Days Later* has infected Petaluma. Somehow, I get the sense that reanimated dead aren't part of the Costa Rica tourist scene."

Likening me to a slobbering, jittery zombie was a low blow, but I leaned back in the seat and let the cool breeze slip over my face. If Tinkie wasn't out in twenty minutes, I'd ride to the rescue.

When the allotted time had come and gone, I ambled into the small office. I could hear Tinkie, her voice raised. The reception desk was empty, so I knocked on the partially open door of Lopez's private office and stepped inside.

My appearance obviously hadn't improved in the half hour Tinkie was gone. Lopez glared at me. "Who are you and what happened to you?"

I pointed at Tinkie. "She nearly killed me with her stiletto heel." I mimed the action. "She's small, but she's deadly."

Lopez dismissed me with a glance. "If you want to know more about the Marquez house, you'd better get a court order."

His smile was foxy. "Or perhaps you should talk to Senor Estoban Gonzalez."

Tinkie's mouth dropped, and so did mine. And Tinkie thought zombies weren't part of the Petaluma scene. "He's dead," I pointed out.

"No, senorita, he's very much alive."

"And no one bothered to tell us this, why?" Tinkie asked, her voice tight with fury.

"You never asked." Senor Lopez rendered a perfect Latin shrug. "You asked for blueprints of the house. I gave them to you without a fuss."

"Not the complete blueprints," Tinkie pointed out. "There are other secrets in that house."

"Why didn't Federico tell us that his father-in-law was alive?" I asked, thinking aloud.

Lopez glared at me. "Perhaps because he carries the burden of his wife's death on his head." He sat back in his desk chair as if he'd resolved everything. "If you want more information, you'll have to speak with Senor Gonzalez. I've told you all that I'm authorized to tell."

"Where is Senor Estoban Gonzalez?" I asked.

"He lives mostly out of the country now. In Venezuela. But he maintains a home here." Lopez scribbled an address on a slip of paper and handed it to Tinkie.

"Call him and tell him we're on the way," I said.

"I'm not going to disturb Senor Gonzalez. I'm going to call the police," Lopez threatened.

"Call them," I said. "Do it fast, because I think you're involved as an accessory in a series of serious assaults."

My words were as effective as a lip zipper.

"Let's go," Tinkie said. "Before the stink in this office rubs off on us."

As we were leaving, I heard him scrabbling for the phone and dialing. Senor Gonzalez would be waiting for us.

* * *

The day was warm and pleasant, and we left Sweetie and Chablis in the car once we found the Gonzalez address in the heart of Petaluma. We rolled the windows down and parked in the shade of a lush tree. The pups would be fine for half an hour.

The house, which occupied almost a city block, was surrounded by a high, stucco wall painted a lovely pale cardamom. Tropical vines climbed the exterior and vibrant blossoms gathered in clusters. I knocked at a solid wooden gate.

"Sarah Booth, you look awful. You really should stay with the dogs," Tinkie said.

"Not on your life." I wasn't at my best, but I had no idea what Tinkie would confront with Estoban Gonzalez. I wanted to be backup in case he was as nutty as the rest of his family.

The gate was opened by a middle-aged woman in a maid's uniform. She ushered us into a shaded patio and through the front door of a lovely Spanish-style home.

The house, filled with a beautiful golden light, was completely silent. Our footsteps echoed on the tiles, as if we'd stepped into a place where time and sound were self-contained.

The maid never said a word. She opened a door, indicated with a nod that we were to enter, and then closed the door behind us. Lopez had let his master know we were paying a call.

Tiger-oak wainscoting was offset by a pale plaster wall. It was a spacious room, the north end in dark shadows.

"I get the sense we're meeting the Godfather," I said.

"Shush!" Tinkie warned, but she was too late.

"I can see your mind has been rotted by the film industry. I expect nothing less from an actress."

The voice that came from the deep shadows was old and dry, like the touch of a frail decaying leaf.

"Mr. Gonzalez," Tinkie said, unfazed, "we're here to talk about Carlita and the house you built for her."

"I wanted to know what you looked like," he said. "Now I do. Get out."

"Your granddaughter is missing." Tinkie stepped forward. "Don't you care about her?"

"Estelle was lost to me years ago. Her father saw to that." The filtered light in the room touched his forehead, nose, and chin. The rest of his features were hidden.

"Mr. Gonzalez, Estelle left for the States a couple of days ago. No one has seen or talked to her since. Do you know where she is?" I asked.

"No."

"Do you care?" Tinkie's voice rose.

"It wouldn't matter if I did. Federico took my grandchildren away from me. They never visit. I don't know who they are."

While another person might have felt pity for an old man mourning the loss of family, I didn't. Estoban Gonzalez had done everything in his power to sabotage his daughter's marriage and her self-confidence. From what Federico said, Estoban had browbeaten an already fragile young woman. No wonder Federico kept Estelle and Ricardo far away from their grandfather.

"You loved Carlita a lot, didn't you?" I asked. My voice was deceptively smooth. Tinkie cut a glance at me.

"She was my light, the most perfect thing in my life."

"And Federico took her?"

"Yes. He stole the thing I loved most. He took her and didn't appreciate her."

I didn't know how deep his self-centeredness went, but I took a wild stab at it. "Carlita would have been happy here in Petaluma had she never met Federico. If Federico had never shown her the world of movie stars, she would still be alive."

He leaned forward into a shaft of light that illuminated

his face. He was old. His features had begun to fall in on themselves. "Federico tempted her with being a film star. He turned her into a whore and a fool. Men could pay five dollars and watch her strut across the screen in her underwear, showing off her body like a strumpet."

"I see your point," Tinkie said, catching on to what I was doing. "It must have been difficult for you, knowing that men everywhere watched her. And wanted her."

"They never knew her, the sweetness and innocence. They saw only her flesh. It was obscene." Estoban was deep in his memories of a young daughter who was his alone.

"When you built the house for Carlita, why did you put in the hidden passageways?" I asked. "You did it for her, but why?"

He gave a soft chuckle. "When she was a child, she loved for me to read stories. Her favorite was about a house with secret passageways and rooms. We must have read that book a thousand times, and she would always say she wanted such a house."

"And you gave it to her because you loved her, even though you didn't approve of her marriage." Tinkie was leading him exactly where we needed to go.

"I took that storybook to Senor Lopez. He created the house exactly as the one in the story, or as exact as an architect could."

"Ricardo told me there were games of hide-and-seek. Exciting times," I said. "He spoke of it with fondness."

He shook his head. "Ricardo was a dullard. He was never part of the secret. He never knew about the passageways and secret places. When I looked at him, I saw his father, and I told Carlita that she could never show him."

"The house was only for Carlita and Estelle," I said.

He nodded. "Those were the best times. Estelle was very clever. She was even better than Carlita at hiding. She could move around the passageways, slipping from one floor to another, hiding in the smallest corner. She was a beautiful child with such intelligence. The games we played."

Tinkie and I exchanged a look.

"Sometimes," he continued, "when there was a big dinner party, Carlita and I would move through the passages, listening to the gossip in different rooms."

I kept my features blank. "You must have heard some interesting things."

"People are not discreet when they think they're alone. Especially not men who have power. There were women desperate to flaunt themselves in a movie and men who willingly took advantage of it."

It appeared that Estoban Gonzalez may have set his own daughter up to witness her husband's flirtations or even adultery. He had stopped at nothing to undermine the marriage he found unacceptable.

"Federico never knew about the passageways, did he?" Tinkie asked. "Carlita loved her husband, yet she never told him."

"He wasn't part of the family. He was an outsider. I told Carlita he would never be allowed to know."

Poor Carlita. The man she loved wasn't accepted, and so she was torn between her own feelings and her father's harsh demands.

Tinkie was tired of his cancerous narcissism. "We got the architect's drawings of the house, but there are other secret passages, aren't there? That's your specialty. Secrets among secrets. Layers revealed slowly, like peeling an onion."

"Complexity makes life interesting."

Tinkie walked to within a few feet of him. "Someone is hiding in that house. Someone dangerous. I was injured. Another woman was pushed down stairs. And your granddaughter is missing. If she's in that house, she may need help. Can you step outside yourself long enough to realize that Estelle may be in danger?"

"If Estelle is in her house, she's safe." The hint of a smile touched his features. "In the last years, I've often had the sense that someone was watching me in that house. I walk down the halls and feel a gaze on my back. Sometimes I catch the tail of a red dressing gown going around a corner, but when I get there, nothing."

His statement was like a shower of ice water. "When was the last time you were there?" I asked.

"Officially? That would be when Carlita died. There was a family service there, a wake."

"And unofficially?"

"The house is empty. Sometimes I go there to look at the portrait of my daughter. I miss her."

I knew exactly which portrait. The day was pleasant and warm, but my body had grown cold.

"I gather Federico doesn't know you visit there?" Tinkie was having a hard time keeping her tone neutral.

"He doesn't know I come back to Costa Rica at all. He said that to him, I am dead. He won't speak my name." He laughed. "Why should he care if I go there? I built the house for Carlita. It will pass to Estelle in a few years. If I go there, it's none of his business. He drags filthy movie people there. He takes his whores there. No one in the movie business has morals."

"That's a blanket condemnation of a business you don't know about." I'd had enough. "A lot of people in film have ethics and—"

"And you're sleeping with Graf Milieu."

I didn't deny it, and I had the most awful thought that perhaps he'd watched us from the peephole behind the portrait. It was a Norman Bates concept.

He laughed. "I haven't been watching you, Ms. Delaney. But film crews talk in town, and eventually everything of interest filters back to me. My network of sources is impeccable."

"I'm flattered that I'm of interest," I said. "But does your network of impeccable sources tell you where your grand-daughter is, or who's in the house attacking people?"

"Some say it's the ghost of my daughter."

"And what do you say? Are you responsible for the attacks on Tinkie, Jovan, Joey, and me?" I walked up to him, and it took me a moment to realize he was in a wheelchair.

"And your question has been answered," he said with only a hint of bitterness. "I've been in this chair for the past eight months. I'm not capable of frolicking through the secret passages for mischief or spying."

If he hadn't been such an old roach, I might have felt sorry for him. "But you are capable of hiring someone to do so."

He nodded. "A smart man would pay someone to do his dirty deeds." He paused a beat. "Though I'm innocent, of course."

"Where is Estelle?" I pressed.

"She refuses to see me because I told her the truth. That her father wanted her mother gone so he could live his profligate life. I told her about the affairs and the way Carlita came home from Los Angeles to cry and berate herself that she wasn't beautiful enough to keep her husband." His forearms rested on the wheelchair, but he couldn't keep his fingers from dancing in the air.

"Why did you do that?" I asked. "Why would you hurt your own granddaughter like that? Federico is her father."

"The Gonzalez family always faces the facts, Ms. Delaney. We look life in the eye and spit."

"And you may have cost your granddaughter her happiness." Tinkie leaned forward into his face. "You are a vile, unhappy old man and you want everyone around you to be the same. You stole Estelle's chance at a relationship with her father and filled her head full of anger and suspicion."

"I tried to protect her."

There was a terrible second when I thought Tinkie was going to punch him. She controlled herself and stepped back.

"Your soul is rotted. You'll die alone and that's what you deserve. Let's go, Sarah Booth."

I was almost out the door when he called out to me.

"Ms. Delaney, you won't last a year in Hollywood. The cannibals will eat you alive. They're already nibbling."

I didn't bother to respond. He was still hurling bile when we walked out the front door and into the sun.

"We didn't learn anything new," I pointed out. My head had begun to throb.

"Not true. We learned a lot about the family dysfunction, and that the old bastard has access to the Marquez house and money to hire someone to do dirty deeds. He's capable of anything."

I sighed. "Poor Carlita and Estelle."

"Do you think he was trying to set us up when he mentioned seeing someone in a red gown? That sounds like your ghost."

"Unless he's manipulating all of this. He didn't exactly say he'd seen her ghost."

Tinkie opened the wooden gate that led to the street. "Maybe she's haunting the place, waiting to kill him."

"Always the eternal optimist, Tinkie. Let's get our things out of the house. We aren't going to find an answer and I don't want to be there after dark.

CHAPTER TWENTY-THREE

Tinkie was in a funk as she drove back to the mansion. She gripped the steering wheel, drummed her fingers, sighed, and generally showed her discontent. When we pulled up to the gate, I was glad to see three security guards still there.

Federico had insisted that Promise Security Agency remain on the premises until Tinkie and I were completely clear of the house. The interview with Estoban Gonzalez had disturbed both Tinkie and me. It was difficult to look into the abyss and not be affected. He was unhinged, and in a way that I would never understand. How had his love for Carlita and Estelle become so twisted that he'd deliberately destroyed them trying to make them hate Federico?

And why hadn't Federico told us that the old man was alive? That nagged at me. Even if he thought Estoban was in Venezuela, surely it was worth a mention that he was still breathing and meddling.

As we stopped at the entrance, I recognized Daniel. He and two additional guards were checking a horse trailer that had come to pick up Nugget and Flicker and return them to their home. Seeing the horses gave me a pang, because I'd grown fond of them, but it also reminded me that I missed Reveler and Miss Scrapiron. It seemed like a million years since I'd ridden my wonderful gelding through the vast expanse of the cotton fields.

The horse trailer pulled through, and Daniel turned to us. "Did you forget something? I thought everyone had left."

"We're getting our things," Tinkie explained.

He looked at Sweetie in the backseat and gave her ears a rub. "Federico was explicit that I remain here until you leave, so I and these men will stay." He frowned. "I've sent all my men to other jobs but I can call them back."

I hesitated. It was true that the security guards hadn't been able to protect us, but it was nice to know someone with a weapon was on the premises. "We'll be fine with you watching the gate. If we need something, we can call."

"Senor Marquez made it plain that your safety was my first priority."

"It's okay, Daniel. We won't be all that long." My emotions were mixed. Tinkie and I had a perfect success record with our cases. We'd solved every one. It went against the grain to simply walk away without knowing who was behind all the problems at Casa Marquez.

Daniel shook his head. "So many unfortunate things have happened here." He looked at the mansion, beautiful and elegant in the distance. "I never thought it before, but perhaps this place is really cursed. Thank goodness no one died here, but you came very close, Ms. Delaney. I just can't imagine who would do such a thing."

I could imagine, but I wasn't going to say it out loud. It could be Grandpa Psychopath or Estelle the Demented. "Have you heard anything from Estelle?" I asked.

He shook his head, a furrow deepening between his brows. "I'm very worried. I know she's been . . . difficult about her father and the film crew being in the house. She's not like that really. You don't know her. Estelle is a kind person. It's only her family that makes her act crazy."

"I'm concerned about her, too," I said, and I was sincere. Even if she had tried to kill me, I was apprehensive that something untoward had happened to her. She literally had disappeared, and while her father and grandfather could dismiss that fact, I found it unsettling.

"Were you aware that Estelle's grandfather was in town?" I asked Daniel.

I could tell by the look on his face that this news came as a shock to him.

"I never asked Estelle, but I assumed he was dead. In all the time I've known her, she never mentioned him once."

"He's very much alive," Tinkie said. "And let's just say that his obsession with Estelle isn't exactly healthy."

Daniel checked to be sure his employees were out of earshot. "Estelle never talked about her grandparents. She didn't want anything to do with her family. She can't speak of her father without getting furious. She hates them, except Ricardo. She speaks of him as if she really loves him."

"Do you think Estelle is behind all of this because she's trying to ruin her father's film?" Tinkie asked.

"Estelle would attempt to frighten you out of the house, and she would damage property like the cameras. I have no doubt of that. Would she push a woman down a flight of stairs? Would she try to drown you, Ms. Delaney? No. I can't believe she would go that far."

"Did Estelle ever talk about the house?" I asked. "Like there were special rooms or secrets here?"

He thought about it. "It's strange because she seemed to seek out the ghost stories, but I also had the sense she was afraid of the place. I tried to get her to take me here one night for some wine and . . ." He had the grace to flush. "But she refused. All of those empty bedrooms, and she wouldn't even walk through the front door."

"You honestly think she was afraid?"

"I do." He blew out a breath. "And I let her down."

"How so?" I asked. Tinkie was staring at the place as if she could use X-ray vision to see into the heart of the house.

"Once Estelle wanted to talk about the house, about how her mother might be here, and if she could only talk to her." His fingertips dug into his forehead as he rubbed the sweat away. "I didn't take her seriously and I teased her. After that, she wouldn't say any more about the house or Carlita. I blew my chance. If I asked about her family, she said she hated them, except Ricardo. I don't understand. Senor Marquez seems like a nice man."

"Did Estelle ever mention growing up in the house?" Tinkie asked. "Playing games, maybe."

Daniel shook his head. "The only thing I remember is that once she said when she was little, she used to believe the house made her mother cry."

That was a bizarre statement, but knowing what we did about Estoban and his spy system, I understood why Carlita might weep. To a child, that could have been very confusing. "Did Estelle say how the house made her mother cry?"

"If she did, I don't remember." His gaze went back to the house. "Do you believe in evil, Ms. Delaney?"

"I believe in evil people," I said.

"And you, Ms. Richmond? Do you believe in evil?"

Tinkie considered longer than I had. "I believe people can be evil," she said, "and I also believe that sometimes negative energy gets trapped in a place. Maybe it's evil or maybe it's not. What do you believe, Daniel?"

"I think this place is bad. Estelle would drive by here and look. It was like she was drawn here by something greater than herself. Even when it made her unhappy, she still came. Just to look."

"This was her link to her mother," Tinkie said. "Perhaps she merely wanted to feel close to Carlita."

"Maybe," he said. "Or maybe there's something in that house that pretends to be Carlita and isn't."

Now that was a cheerful thought. "We should go, Daniel," I said. "We need to pack."

"Call me if anything suspicious happens," he said. "I'll be here all night."

"We'll be fine," Tinkie assured him. "I just hate that we have to leave without figuring out what's going on."

He put a hand on the door. "If you hear anything from Estelle, will you tell me?"

Tinkie nodded. "I will. And the same from you. If she calls, please tell us."

He saluted and stepped back as we drove away.

When we were parked in front of the house, Tinkie killed the engine and sat. She finally looked at me. "I'm not ready to give up. I know something is going on here, but I don't know that we'll get to the bottom of it."

"Tinkie, everyone is gone."

"What if Estelle is still here?"

"Then she'll have the house to herself once we leave."

"I'm not sure that's what she really wants, and to be honest, I'm ready to go home. I miss Oscar." She looked up at the empty windows. "I may be a coward, but I don't want to spend another night here."

She was selling herself short. She wasn't window dressing in the detective agency. She took action when it was necessary. I had a flashback of her running across an open field toward Virgie Carrington as Virgie held a gun trained on Coleman. Virgie had drugged Oscar and taken him hostage, and Tinkie meant to save her husband. She was willing to risk her life to do so. To prevent her from running straight into gunfire, I had to tackle her. Good thing she had a penchant for high heels or she might have outrun me.

When she opened her car door, Sweetie jumped out and began to patrol the property. The house looked dejected. I was reminded of a film star I couldn't name—so beautiful, until the camera closed in too much and revealed the tiny sag of flesh and wrinkles. Casa Marquez looked as if the people who loved her had left for good. I swallowed a lump of unexpected emotion. The place seemed sad and abandoned.

Did our homes miss us? I wondered. Was Dahlia House waiting for my return? For some a house was merely a structure, a place of shelter. But for a Delta girl, home was a place where the past met the future. It was part heritage and history, a place of comfort and safety. This mansion, though more modern and larger than Dahlia House, had been Carlita Marquez's home. Her children had grown up here, laughing and playing games with a grandfather they adored.

And probably should have feared.

We entered and went straight to the kitchen, where Tinkie examined Chablis and found her to be coming along satisfactorily. Chablis would be able to fly tomorrow without any ill repercussions.

Per the vet's directions, we gave the dustmop a tiny tablet for pain and let her snooze on a plump pillow in a corner of the kitchen. Sweetie settled in beside her, friend and guard. With Sweetie on call, Chablis was safe and we could go and collect our things.

We were halfway up the staircase when we both heard it. Tinkie grabbed my arm. It sounded like a child running, and every movie with an evil child popped into my head. If a little blond child peeped around the corner—

"We're getting our things to leave, Estelle!" Tinkie yelled the words. "You can stop this foolishness. We're leaving. The house is yours."

Somewhere on the upstairs hallway, a table crashed. I remembered the beautiful Chinese vase and knew what had happened.

"Damn it!" Tinkie started up the steps. She was angry. "I have had enough of this. Stop being a spoiled child."

Just as she got to the top, the lights went out. Even though it was still daylight outside, the hallway was plenty dark.

"What the hell?" she asked. "She's acting like she doesn't want us to go."

"Well, we're leaving anyway." I'd had it with the flying glassware and the tables that went thump in the night. The things that were wrong with Estelle couldn't be fixed by me or Tinkie. Or even Daniel's love.

"Could we just take a look through the east wing?" Tinkie asked. "We didn't really search there."

I checked my watch. "We'll try for two hours. Then we're leaving. I don't want to be here after dark. Why risk getting hurt?"

"It's a deal."

I gathered the high-powered flashlights Graf had bought and we took off down the second-floor hallway. Tinkie had purchased a stethoscope from a drugstore so we could listen to the walls. My plan was to find any additional secret passageways, check them and leave. Estelle was too clever for us. We'd never catch her. But if we did manage to hem her up, we were going to drag her out and turn her over to the authorities—either legal or mental health. She was going to pay for kicking Chablis.

The house was L-shaped, with the main wing extending north to south and the east wing jutting off. And then there were the stables and other outbuildings. I'd begun to wonder if there might not be tunnels that linked the buildings together underground. Hell, anything was possible where Estoban Gonzalez was concerned.

Because we hadn't spent any time to speak of in the east wing, it was creepy and unfamiliar, even in broad daylight. I kept having images of Jitty as Mrs. Danvers standing at a window saying, "It's a lovely view. Why don't you jump, Sarah Booth? Just jump and put an end to all of it."

"Sarah Booth, is something wrong?" Tinkie asked.

I shook my head. "Just thinking of an old movie, *Rebecca*."

"I've thought of that film more than once," she said as we

moved down the hallway, tapping the plaster, moving portraits and tables, as we tried to find some place that sounded hollow. "The parallels are a bit uncomfortable."

We searched several bedrooms and finally ended up at the small study. The painting I'd admired was there, and Tinkie knew the artist. While she talked about the composition and use of color, I remembered something else.

"Tinkie, I was thinking about being tied to that rock in the ocean."

"Not a good thing to think about." She removed a shelf of books and began pressing on the built-in mahogany bookcase.

"When I was tied to the rock, Cece told me Sweetie and Chablis had been locked up in a third-floor bedroom."

Tinkie turned slowly and looked at me. "So someone in the house knew you were going to see that ghost and chase it. And that someone didn't want the dogs to mess things up, so they confined them."

I nodded. "Because the dogs can run so much faster than I can. The dogs might have caught the person I was chasing."

She nodded. "So there have to be at least two of them. Our ghost has an accomplice."

"So it would seem."

"Why didn't you tell me this before?" she asked.

"I thought you were going home. I didn't want to worry you. Then so many other things happened, it slipped my mind. If Estelle was the person I was chasing, who was the person who locked up the dogs? Even if Estelle is a sprinter, she couldn't be in two places at once."

"Who else was here? Never mind, because if someone was hiding in the house, in the passageways, we'd never know." She turned back to her shelf. I moved to help her, and we worked our way toward a lovely fireplace that held Indian pottery.

I moved the pottery. "This is the whole problem. With these hidey-holes all over the house, a battalion of miscreants could be involved."

"Press the stones around the edge of the fireplace. There has to be a trigger." Tinkie was taking books from another shelf. She had one wall denuded.

"Why the fireplace?"

"It's always the fireplace," she said. "Don't you watch any detective shows?"

The soft sound of thumping froze me on the spot. It was the same sound I'd heard for the past few days, but fainter, maybe weaker.

"Doesn't that sound like someone kicking the floor or a wall?" Tinkie asked. She rubbed at the chill bumps that had sprung to her arms.

"It does. Or a head rolling down stairs, à la *Hush, Hush, Sweet Charlotte*."

Tinkie got out her stethoscope and put it against the wall behind the empty shelf. Her face told me everything. She handed the listening device to me.

Someone, or something, was definitely thumping in another part of the house. The sound was traveling through the walls. I swallowed and strained to hear.

A heartrending sob trembled down the dead space of the wall and straight into my heart. In the past, I'd felt the strange noises were designed to frighten me. This was different. "Someone's in trouble," I said.

Tinkie touched my shoulder. "Or else it's a trap."

My chest constricted painfully. "Or it could be the ghost."

Tinkie's eyes widened. "Or it could be both—the ghost *and* a trap." She picked up a heavy candlestick. "What should we do?"

CHAPTER TWENTY-FOUR

We had three choices. We could continue on the search, or we could get Daniel to help us, or we could run like hell. Tinkie was moving from skeptic to believer in wraiths of the supernatural realm, but I was way ahead of her there. I had the sense that the ghost who haunted the Marquez mansion was bitter and angry and filled with enough negative energy to truly harm us. But I wasn't certain what we were hearing was made by a noncorporeal being. This sounded like someone in distress.

But someone in distress wouldn't likely be shutting the power on and off and breaking things. Were both partners in this deadly game of destruction in the house?

"It sounds like it's coming from inside the wall." She held the candlestick in one hand and her flashlight in the other.

"I—" Before I could finish, both of our cell phones began to ring.

We answered simultaneously, looking each other in the eye.

"It's Daniel Martinez," Tinkie mouthed before she turned away so she could hear him.

"Hey, Millie," I said, delighted to hear her voice. "What's going on?" Now wasn't the optimum time for a call, but Millie wasn't someone who chatted. If she was calling, she had something to tell.

"I've been doing some research," she said, "and I thought you should know that Vincent Day has a criminal record. An old one *and* a recent one."

I could hear Tinkie making soothing noises, and I wondered what in the hell Daniel was telling her. Millie was my priority now, though.

"How recent?"

"As in less than a year ago."

"What happened?" I asked.

"The reason the media didn't pick it up was because it happened on location in Canada. Both Federico and Vincent were directing films in the same province. You know, the production costs are cheaper in Canada, and it's so beautiful there."

Millie could work for the Canadian government as a PR person. "Okay, so they were working on different films on the same continent. And?"

She ignored my sarcasm and continued. "They both ended up in this trendy restaurant. From the account in the Canadian newspaper I found, Vincent walked over to Federico's table and said something. Federico stood up and responded. Then Vincent said, 'You righteous bastard, you ruined my life.' That was a direct quote, and then Federico said, 'Everything you lost, you lost by your own hand.' And he sat down. Vincent then attacked him, turning him over in the chair and trying to stomp him."

The scene Millie was describing sounded like utter chaos, and also the behavior of teenagers rather than grown men, and they were fighting about a woman who'd been dead for a long time. What really troubled me was that Federico had lied. He'd told me he hadn't seen Vincent Day in a long time.

"So Vincent Day was arrested?"

"That's right. He had a list of charges against him, and Federico gave the police a damning statement about the encounter."

"How did you find all this out?" Millie had tactics and sources that I needed to learn. When it came to digging up dirt on celebrities, she was incredible.

"There's this photographer, or he would be called paparazzi now. Long ago, when I was young and pretty enough to think about going to Hollywood, I contacted him. He was hungry and shooting wannabe star portfolios. Funny thing, he's from Elba, Alabama, so he was down-home folks."

"And you've stayed in touch with this guy all these years?" Millie was the kind of woman that men didn't forget.

"Not really in touch, but I knew how to find his e-mail. His name is Tor, or that's his professional name. Like Cher. Speaking of which, Tor did an exquisite spread on her. He sent me some photos that she autographed to me."

I hated to halt her trip down her star-studded memory lane, but Tinkie was talking low and intensely to Daniel. It sounded like something was seriously wrong. I needed to know Vincent Day's criminal history. What if he'd snatched Estelle to get even with Federico?

"So you called Tor, and he told you about the Vincent-Federico ruckus in Canada?" I interjected.

"Right. He was on the set of Vincent's movie doing some still work. The whole crew was upset about the fight. They lost a couple of days' work because Vincent was in jail. And Tor overheard Vincent say that he was going to get even with Federico one way or the other."

"What was the old charge about?"

"Apparently Vincent has a terrible temper. He was charged with domestic abuse by his wife, Ivana Day, back in the eighties. He was booked, but she later dropped the charges. Tor said she looked bad. Black eye, swollen face, bruises, that kind of thing. He took photographs when she came out of the hospital emergency room, and yes, I did check the hospital records. It took some help from Coleman, but I found out that Mrs. Day was seen at a Los Angeles hospital."

I heard everything she said, but she had also invoked the name of Coleman. Tinkie was busy with her call and Graf was gone; I could ask the question that immediately sprang to my lips. But I didn't.

"Are you going to ask about Coleman?" Millie asked, saving me the bother of trying to decide if asking was a betrayal of Graf.

"I was and then I wasn't."

"Caught on the horns of a dilemma, huh?"

"That would describe it."

"Coleman is okay. He's lost a bunch of weight. In fact, he's downright thin. Looks like a high school kid again. He's living in the old Marston place."

I swallowed. He'd left his home and rented a place. That implied that he was no longer living with Connie.

"And because you're so concerned and asking and all, Connie is out of the hospital and in Jackson with her sister. Coleman didn't say, but the brain tumor was apparently another invention." Millie was going to tell me whether I wanted to hear it or not.

"It doesn't matter now." I wasn't being dramatic. I'd given Coleman plenty of chances to make this move and he hadn't. He'd held back and withheld and postponed. Now that I was gone, he'd taken action. "Did it ever occur to you that Coleman may have used Connie as an excuse so he didn't have to commit to me?"

"In fact, it did, so I asked him that," Millie said. "He was in for lunch the other day, and I just sat down and asked."

My mouth was terribly dry. "What did he say?" I couldn't help myself. All of my good intentions not to play into this conversation had fled.

"He said he'd made some bad mistakes, and he didn't

know if he could ever correct them. But the one thing he'd learned was that opportunities of a lifetime didn't come at moments of convenience, and that the next time something he wanted was put in front of him, he was going to take it, no matter the consequences." She cleared her throat. "He said that's what you'd done, and he admired you for it."

That last statement made me want to weep. Why couldn't he say that he was a fool, that he'd let me and himself down, that he saw now what he hadn't seen before. But it was his damn nobility in seeing how I'd done the best thing that made it impossible to allow myself to care for him in any way other than as a friend. Coleman would always put others ahead of himself—and therefore me. Love requires a certain degree of selfishness, and Coleman could never truly love me as I needed to be loved.

"Coleman is a good man," I told her. "He's one of the best. I hope he does grab his next opportunity. And thanks for the information, Millie. That's going to help a whole lot. Really good work."

"Any message for Coleman?" she asked.

"No, none." No point in prolonging the pain. "Tinkie and I should be heading out tomorrow. Chablis is fine. Healing as we speak." I knew Oscar had told everyone that his "child" had been injured in the line of defending Tinkie. "I miss you, Millie, and I'm planning a trip to Zinnia as soon as we finish filming."

I hung up and looked over at Tinkie. She was still talking into the phone. "Daniel, I'm sure there's more to this than meets the eye. When we find Estelle, I'll speak on your behalf." She nodded her head. "I promise. And thanks for calling."

She closed her phone and heaved a big sigh. "Daniel really cares for Estelle."

"And?"

"And she dumped him."

"He heard from her?" I was surprised at how relieved I

was that she was okay. The idea of Vincent Day holding her hostage to get at Federico had really concerned me.

"He did. He got a text message from her and a photograph from her phone saying that she was in Maine at a friend's house, and that she wouldn't be back to Malibu or Petaluma for the next few months. She told him she cared for him, but that she couldn't sustain a relationship right now. She's considering therapy."

Maybe Estelle wasn't as crazy as I thought. "I wish she'd contact her father."

"Daniel messaged her back and asked her to do that."

"What a helluva way to break off a relationship—through a text message. Like what? 'We R 0-ver.' That's pretty cold."

"Estelle couldn't confront him, not even on the phone. That's sad, Sarah Booth. Have you ever broken up with someone long distance?"

My romantic past was too sordid to even wade through. "Not interested in answering," I said. "Now let's search this house. Since Estelle is in Maine, I doubt we'll find much of anything. But we can search and then pack up. Oscar will be glad to see you."

"You're one hundred percent correct. I can almost taste one of his mint juleps."

Tinkie was making me homesick, but I had committed to finishing the movie. After that I could hop a flight home for some R and R with my buds.

"If Estelle is in Maine, why don't we cancel this exploration?"

"You said two hours. There's still time on the clock. If it isn't Estelle, then it's someone else. And that someone could turn up in Hollywood doing the same stuff there. Let's end it here and now."

We continued the tedious process, moving things, tapping walls, listening. It would've been a lot easier if Estoban Gonzalez had simply cooperated with us and told us where to look.

Concern for his granddaughter should have been motivation enough. But now we knew Estelle was far away and safe, so whatever was happening in the house didn't involve her at all.

So who—or what—were we tracking? I needed a confab with Jitty, but she wouldn't appear in front of Tinkie. And she probably wouldn't tell me anything useful anyway. Jitty was a big believer that the best lessons were those learned the hard way.

If she didn't help me, though, the vessel to carry the prized Delaney heir might be injured. Now that was a threat I could use against her.

"Tinkie, I have to go to the bathroom, and I'll check on the dogs."

"Sure." She was moving paintings.

"I'll be right back."

"Yeah." She was so absorbed that she didn't notice when I left.

Sweetie and Chablis were fine in the kitchen, both snoozing. Now was my moment.

"Jitty! I need you."

I turned slowly, hoping for a shimmer or fade-in.

Nothing.

"Jitty, damn it! I'm the only person who can bear the Delaney heir. If you don't help me, I'll have myself sterilized."

"If you do that, people will talk."

Her voice was cultured, mature, and I spun around to find her standing in the door in a tight black dress, her hair suddenly blond and in a French twist. She made a beautiful Lana Turner, though I hadn't realized she was so buxom.

"We're leaving tomorrow. I have to find out what's going on here. There's no guarantee this won't start again in Hollywood."

She paced the kitchen, her voice coming New England cultured. "You're not the only person with troubles, I have my own. Why don't you dust somewhere else?"

She wasn't going to help me until I figured out what role she was playing. I flipped through the movie images in my mind. "Give me another clue."

"There's an illegitimate daughter, a scandal, and fear of gossip in a small town." She did a turn worthy of any runway model. "Hollywood is just a small town, Sarah Booth." The Lana Turner voice was giving way to plain ole Jitty.

"This isn't helping me," I said. "Is Carlita in this house, and is she here because she was murdered?"

Jitty sighed. "She's here, but it isn't because she was murdered."

"Then why?"

"Perhaps you should ask Daniel Martinez. They say a picture is worth a thousand words. Isn't that what makes movies so exciting?"

I realized who she was. "*Peyton Place,*" I yelled at her fading image. "*Peyton Place.*"

The last I heard was her chuckle.

I thought Sweetie would rouse at the sound of my cursing, but she slept on, her body curled around Chablis. I ran down the driveway to the guard post. The two security men were there, but not Daniel.

"Where is Mr. Martinez?" I asked.

"He went into town. He'll be back in fifteen minutes," one of them answered.

"Tell him when he gets back to come to the house as fast as he can," I said. Reversing, I ran back to Tinkie, suddenly afraid that she'd been left alone.

Tinkie didn't even look up when I burst into the room, breathless and sweating. "It has to be the fireplace," she said.

"You've watched too many B movies," I told her. "Be careful or Vincent Price will be standing behind the secret panel. What do Lana Turner and *Peyton Place* have to do with this situation?"

She took time to roll her eyes at me. "I can't say for sure, but in *Peyton Place* there's a scandal involving the daughter's legitimacy, and there are the layers of lies and deceit and also a fear of what others will think. There's also a murder of a father by a daughter . . ." She stopped and stared at me. "But Estelle is in Maine."

"Maybe not," I said.

"Shit." She leaned against the fireplace and the stone mantel behind her gave. To my amazement, the entire stone structure shifted to the left. The opening in front of us was dark, and a cool odor came to me, reminding me of marsh grass and some of the river brakes beside the Mississippi.

Tinkie started in, and I grabbed her arm and held her.

"What?" She had her flashlight on probing the depths of the dark hallway that were revealed.

"I do believe in ghosts," I said. "I do, I do, I do."

"You're the one who's always telling me that ghosts can't hurt us. They're noncorporeal."

"I think maybe I was misinformed," I said, stepping into the darkness behind her. "Maybe we should wait for backup."

A low wail echoed down the cool passage. It was followed by the sound of dull thudding.

"Help me." The cry was weak, but we both heard it.

Together we stepped into the darkness and the smell of rot and decay.

CHAPTER TWENTY-FIVE

The passageway was narrow, just large enough for us to go sideways. I would have taken the lead, but Tinkie was there and it was impossible to wedge past her.

When the corridor took a ninety-degree turn, I figured we were moving between rooms, but in the darkness, I'd lost all sense of proportion and direction. I was about to speak when muffled sobbing came to me.

Tinkie halted so abruptly I rear-ended her. I suppressed a moan as my sternum slammed into her bony head.

"Ouch, Sarah Booth. That hurt. When we find the ghost, what do we do?" she asked.

Run wasn't an option because in the narrow confines we had to move like crabs. "Ask her how we can help?" I'd read somewhere long ago that a human could, sometimes, assist a ghost in moving on to the next plane. I'd never actually asked Jitty if this would work, and I'd certainly never tried this tactic on her because—I'd come to admit—I wanted her in Dahlia House. Even though she was an unmitigated pain in the ass, she was part of my heritage, part of Dahlia House, and part of my family. Somehow I had invited her to live with me, and that's right where I wanted her.

Tinkie swung her light beam in front of us. "What if the

ghost says that what she needs is to kill us? I mean, not all ghosts want to 'go to the light,' you know. It only stands to reason that some are going to the dark side. And then there are those who want to hang out here and screw with people."

Tinkie's logic was sometimes illogical but always intriguing. "We want to help her, why would she want to harm us?"

"Because she's an evil entity that's already lured you to a near death by drowning, and she pushed Jovan down the stairs and—"

"We don't know any of those things involved the ghost." I hung hard to fact. Ghosts were real, but not all of them were vengeful spirits. Besides, if Tinkie panicked, even as small as she was, she might stampede over me and finish me off before the ghost got a chance. "Maybe it's not an entity at all. Perhaps it's someone dressed as the ghost." The idea was exciting. "Someone who wants to blame a supernatural being. Think of all the things you could get away with if you had a ghost to blame."

"Like . . . ?"

I didn't have time to answer. I glanced over Tinkie's head, and standing in the flashlight beam was a translucent figure dressed in a flowing red dressing gown. The woman was beautiful, though terribly sad. She was closer than I'd ever seen her, and in the unforgiving illumination of the flashlight, I could see the sharp bones of her face. Her eyes were large and burned with an inner fire.

"Tinkie," I whispered. "Ghost." The word seemed to tear my throat as it exited.

Tinkie stepped forward and turned her shoulders so she could look. I heard the sound of a loud whump, and she fell backward against me. I caught her as she slid to the floor.

"Tinkie!" She was out cold, and when I shone my light, I saw the support trestle she'd struck with her forehead. I eased her to the floor as best I could, all the while fighting the horrible sensation that the entity was on the move—toward me.

When I finally picked up a flashlight and shone it down the passage, the woman in red was only twenty feet away.

The apparition, for it was most definitely something from beyond our world, lifted a hand that held a white cloth. She put it to her mouth and coughed, a racking sound that ended in a choking noise. When she finished, she lowered the cloth toward me in a pleading fashion. "Help."

The word seemed to waver in the air, moving like an echo rather than speech.

Whatever this ghoul was, she bore no resemblance to my lovely Dahlia House haint. Jitty was sexy and beautiful, voluptuous and groomed to perfection. If this was Carlita Marquez in her last days, I could only say that Federico was right to keep the children away from her. No child should have to see a parent dying in such a manner. Carlita was a skeleton barely covered by skin, her suffering etched into every plane and angle. The beautiful woman in the portrait hanging in my bedroom had evaporated, leaving only the dregs of who she'd once been.

Tinkie moaned softly. She was coming around. Her full weight was pressed against my shins and I had to brace myself to stand steady. Even if I could get away, I couldn't take Tinkie. We were jammed like sardines in the secret hallway.

"What do you want?" I asked. My voice quavered, and I wished with all my might that Jitty would appear to intervene for me. I could handle a family member's ghost, but not this pathetic creature that looked to be in agony. Even though she hadn't spoken again, I could feel her pain like waves rolling over me.

"Help," she said in that strange voice that was like air molecules colliding together and moving to me.

"How?" I dreaded her answer.

"Help me," she said again. She seemed to move closer, but she wasn't walking.

Tinkie moaned and shifted. "Tinkie, wake up." I needed her to see this. "Tinkie, wake up."

"Help me," the ghost said again. "Too late."

I had her pinned in the beam of the flashlight, and I could tell she was starting to fade.

"What can I do?" I asked.

"Save . . ." But she didn't finish. Just as Tinkie sat up, the figure disappeared.

I knelt down beside my friend, using the flashlight to reveal the lump swelling on her forehead. She'd had a rough time with her noggin these past few days. While she'd taken a fairly good lick, the swelling was coming out, which Aunt Loulane always said was a good sign.

"Damn, I nearly knocked my brains out," she said.

I took it as a favorable omen that she knew what had happened. "You saw her, didn't you?"

"Saw who?"

"The ghost."

She grabbed my knee and used it as a brace to push herself up. "I can't believe you're trying to scare me after I just slammed my head into a board."

"But I'm not. She was there. She asked us to help her. She said we were to save . . . someone or something." The more I talked, the more I realized Tinkie was having no part of this. She'd been unconscious, lying on the floor, while I'd spoken with the 'Ghost of Marquez Manor,' and now she'd never believe it.

"This is *not* amusing, Sarah Booth. And it's in poor taste, I might add." With my assistance, she got to her feet. She was unsteady for a moment, but then she regained her equilibrium. "Did you really see a ghost? You're positive it wasn't some trick of lighting?"

"Carlita Marquez's spirit is here, in this house, and she wants us to save someone or something. I don't think she's evil."

Tinkie bit her bottom lip. "I wish I'd seen her, too. I want to believe you. It's just that why would she appear right at the moment I get knocked out?"

That wasn't a question I wanted to ponder while still crammed into a crawlspace without good ventilation or a speedy path of retreat. "We should go back to the study," I said. I would come back later to look for evidence.

Even if Tinkie didn't believe me, I knew I'd seen Carlita Marquez, and she'd asked me to save someone. Federico? Estelle? Both were safe. Then who? Maybe save her spirit from her father? It was very complex.

"You know, you and Jovan are the only people who've seen the ghost." Tinkie was inching her way out, following my lead. She was wobbly but doing okay. If I didn't get her on a plane and back to Zinnia, she might damage her brain for good. She couldn't take a lot more bumping and whacking.

"There are stories in town," I pointed out. "So kids have seen her standing on the balcony."

"Or they just like telling the story. Good date material. Gives the girl an excuse to cuddle close."

"For a woman who healed her own breast lump with the help of a faith healer in New Orleans, I find it strange you're so determined not to believe this house is haunted."

"I just find the timing interesting. And a little convenient. Maybe you want to see a ghost."

Now that was the regular Tinkie—a zinger lurking behind every multiglitzed curl. "Thanks."

"Why do you think the ghost presents to you?"

We were almost back to the study. "Because I'm willing to see her?" I didn't add that it might be because I had my own ghost and had learned to listen.

Thinking of Jitty brought back the remarks that she'd made earlier in the kitchen while acting out *Peyton Place*. I stopped dead still and Tinkie bumped into me with a curse.

What's wrong? I'm not going to have an inch of skin left that isn't bruised."

Jitty had said a picture was worth a thousand words. "Tinkie, we can't be sure Estelle is in Maine."

"Daniel said he had a photo sent from her phone. He was torn up because he figured some new guy had taken it. Do you think he's lying?"

"No, but a photo doesn't prove anything."

She swung her light so that it was directly in my eyes, blinding me. I pushed it away as she spoke.

"You're right. What if—"

"What if Estelle is who we're supposed to save? What if the ghost of Carlita was talking about her daughter?"

Tinkie aimed the light down the passageway we'd just sweated down. "We're going to find out."

"You should go to the kitchen and check the dogs. I can do this."

She ignored me and reversed down the tunnellike path. We'd gone only fifteen or so yards when we both stopped dead in our tracks.

Soft sobbing wafted to us, and this time it was closer. It sounded like a woman, exhausted and ready to give up.

"Estelle!" I called. "Estelle, can you hear us?"

The answer that came chilled me to my bones. "Please. So . . . much . . . blood."

After stumbling and banging our way down the torturous passage and climbing the narrowest stairs I'd ever seen, we finally found Estelle in the back of a cupboard in one of the rooms in the third-floor east wing. In my searches of the house and questioning of the staff, I'd been told the room was a linen closet. I'd even searched it once before.

There were stacks of sheets and towels, but there was also a false front that concealed a space large enough for Estelle's

body. Her hands and feet were tied so tightly, I wondere
if the lack of circulation would necessitate amputatio
She'd also been gagged, but she'd managed to work th
loose. She was bleeding from a head wound and a sever
cut to her thigh. Blood, dried and oozing fresh, had pud
dled around her.

The exterior door of the closet was locked, but using ou
shoulders, Tinkie and I managed to split the wood at th
hinges and crash it open. While Tinkie called an ambulanc
I untied Estelle and dragged her out into the hallway.

Estelle had slipped into a thrashing sleep, and I could te
by the heat coming from her body that she had a high feve
She was also dehydrated, but I was afraid to try to rouse he
to drink. I wasn't sure what to do, so I sat on the floor an
cradled her head and talked to her, even though she was s
delirious she couldn't possibly understand my words.

I didn't want to think how long she'd been in that cubby
hole, unable to move and without water or food, bleedin
from two serious wounds. I could only hope that her cond
tion wasn't fatal.

Tinkie came running back upstairs. "The ambulance is o
the way, and I put in a call to the Petaluma authorities an
Daniel." She saw the look on my face. "I think he was dupe
Sarah Booth. I talked to him when he thought Estelle had bro
ken up with him. He was devastated. I don't think he had any
thing to do with this."

Tinkie had good gut instincts, but I wasn't as trusting i
the area of love as she was. She'd married once and wel
She'd lived a life where fairy tales did come true. That hadn
necessarily been my experience, but I let it go.

"We'll find out who's responsible for this when Estelle re
gains consciousness." I spoke with more authority than I fel
Looking at the unconscious young woman, skin taut fro
dehydration, her face pale but hot with fever, and her hand
and legs still an unnatural gray color from the lack of circu

tion, I wondered if she would ever wake up. We had found er, but maybe too late.

Footsteps pounded toward us, and Daniel Martinez came the stairs. If his expression could be taken at face value, e was shocked and horrified at what he saw.

"Estelle." He slid across the polished floor on his knees. He cked up her hand and held it to his chest. "Holy *Madre*," he hispered. "What's wrong with her? Who hurt her?"

Tinkie gave him a rundown on how we'd found Estelle, nd how we didn't know who might have hurt her.

I could see the anger building behind his eyes, and when e spoke, the flash of fury was in his speech. "I'll find the erson who did this, and he will pay."

"Any ideas who it might be?" I asked.

He considered. "Estelle sometimes behaved like a spoiled ild. She made enemies, but not the kind that would do is." He waved a hand over her unconscious body. "Will she ve?"

I didn't have an answer to that, but I heard the sirens of e paramedics. At least the presence of the movie crew and y friends had helped the local economy by keeping the ospital and vet clinic busy.

"Estelle." He rubbed her hand frantically, as if he could ase the gray tone and bring it back to the full flush of life. Wake up," he begged.

I eased her head into his lap and stood. There were things be done. At a signal from me, Tinkie backed away so we uld talk privately.

"So it couldn't have been Estelle who was haunting the ouse. She's been in the closet awhile." Tinkie was watching Daniel stroked her hair from her face. If he wasn't acting, e was truly grief-stricken.

"The timeline is everything. Was Estelle in the closet when was lured onto the beach?" I'd always assumed it was Estelle aying the role of her dead mother for dramatic effect. Now

my theories were blown to hell and I needed to rethink the se
quence of events. "Estelle could have pushed Jovan."

"Or the ghost could have." Tinkie met my gaze. She wa
choosing to believe me and what I'd said I had witnessed.

"I saw Carlita up close. She didn't have enough meat on he
bones to push a pea across the table. She looked awful."
shook my head. "I had this crazy idea that ghosts got to choos
their bodies and how they looked at any time in their life. Poc
Carlita. She died a terrible death, and she's stuck in the phas
just before she passed on."

"Carlita didn't do this to Estelle," Tinkie said, "and w
have to find out who did."

"I'm afraid that answer is going to be in Hollywood, n
Petaluma." It had to be someone on the cast and crew. If
wasn't Daniel, and I believed Tinkie was correct in her assess
ment, then it had to be a member of her father's movi
ensemble—or someone who'd passed himself off as part c
the crew. Each day there were dozens of hangers-on—peopl
who catered or drove cars or cleaned clothes and brough
them back or provided some special service like a massage c
bottled water of a certain brand. While the core group of th
movie was fairly well known to me, there were people comin
and going all the time.

"What about the grandfather?" Tinkie asked.

He was an evil and unhappy man, but why would he pur
ish Estelle in this manner? Yet he'd refused to divulge th
floor plans of the house even when he knew Estelle wa
missing. "He's a possibility."

We heard the ambulance pull up in the yard and right be
hind it was a squad car with two police detectives. I ran dow
to let them in and direct them to Estelle. The paramedic
wasted no time putting her on a gurney and moving her int
the ambulance. The medical experts gave me and Tinkie th
strangest looks, but they said nothing and focused their skill
on Estelle.

"I'll ride with her," Tinkie said. "Sarah Booth, you can give a statement to the detectives."

"Please, let me go with Estelle." Daniel was distraught. "I should never have left. She was obsessed with her father. I knew she was doing things she shouldn't, but I never dreamed she was lying in that hole, hurt."

"Go with her," Tinkie told him. "We'll be there soon."

After the ambulance was gone, we told the police officers the sequence of events, showed them the secret passage, and then answered their questions. Before they began the forensics work, they told us we could go.

I turned to Tinkie. She had a huge lump on her forehead. I touched my own head, where the heel of her stiletto had done its work. We looked at each other.

"Frik and Frak." She shook her head. "Jesus, Sarah Booth, we look like members of some religious cult that batters their foreheads. No wonder the paramedics were giving us the evil eye."

"The good news is, I can't work looking like this so I might as well solve this case."

"Oscar is going to throw a hissy, but that's too bad."

"Let's ride," I said, though I wasn't certain which direction we needed to take.

CHAPTER TWENTY-SIX

With Sweetie and Chablis riding shotgun, we drove into Petaluma. I'd left word for Federico to call me, but I felt we needed to tell Estelle's roommate.

When we got to the cabana-style apartments, we ran into Regena in the courtyard. She took one look at us and winced. "Who whacked you two?" she asked.

"We're fine," Tinkie told her. "It's Estelle you should be worried about. She's at the hospital."

We filled her in on what had happened; I watched closely for some sign that she knew more than she was letting on, but she was floored.

"Is she going to be okay?"

"We don't know." I glanced at my watch. Time was slipping away from us too fast. "If there's anything you can tell us about Estelle and who she's been talking to or seeing, it might help."

Although Regena was anxious to get to the hospital, she motioned us to a seat in the shade of a big tree.

"When Estelle first heard the movie was going to be filmed in her mother's house, she was upset. I know she got some calls from someone in the States, and there was one time when I overheard part of her conversation. It was pretty extreme."

If only Regena had come forward with this information sooner, I thought, but I refrained from saying so.

"What did you hear?" Tinkie prompted.

"She said something like she'd never forgive her father for what he'd done, and that Carlita would not go unavenged."

This was old hat. "Who was she talking to?"

"It was a woman. That's all I know. I tried to question her, but she said it would be best if I didn't know anything about her plans."

"She was right about that," Tinkie said, "but it doesn't much help us figure out who hurt her. Or who was hurting us."

Regena frowned. "She was so bitter toward her dad. I tried to talk to her about it a couple of times. I mean, what's the point? Her mom is dead. Her father is all she has. It just seemed senseless to hate him for something from so long ago."

She was preaching to the choir—unless Estelle knew something we didn't. Federico had always been a weak suspect, and I couldn't believe he'd hurt his own daughter in such a way, but it was a lead and I had to follow it.

"Did she say why she hated Federico?"

"She never said specifically." Her eyes widened. "Except for one comment. She said her dad and his friends used women as brood mares and dropped their sperm and then forgot about them."

Tinkie and I looked at each other. "Thanks, Regena."

"I have a dance lesson scheduled, but I'm canceling and going to the hospital."

"Daniel is there," Tinkie said.

She smiled, and for the first time I realized she was a lovely young woman in her own right. "He loves Estelle. If she'd only wake up and see that people care about her, she could have a very different life."

We left her at the parking lot, where she revved the engine of her little car and took off. "Sounds like she has her head on straight." Tinkie cast a sidelong glance at me.

"What's that supposed to mean?"

"I didn't want to get into it with you, but I can't leave Costa Rica without telling you. Coleman loves you, Sarah Booth."

"And I love him." I didn't see any reason to lie. "But that doesn't mean a thing. Graf loves me, too. And I'm falling deeper in love with him with each passing day."

She put her arm around my waist. "I can see that. I thought at first he was shallow and a user, but he has depth and strength, and the two of you are wonderful together. That's why I've been quiet about all of this. But I wanted you to know the truth. You can't make a fair decision unless you know everything. And whatever you decide will be right."

"Thanks, Tinkie." I couldn't give her any more than that, because I didn't know more myself. I'd spent so long waiting for Coleman, wanting him to be a real partner. But I'd given up hope.

"Where to next, fearless leader?" Tinkie asked and gave my waist a firm squeeze before she let go.

"Maybe we need to consult with Millie?"

"Or that Tor person she told you about."

"Good idea." I put a call in to the café and got the answering machine. It was the lunch hour and the place was hopping. Millie was waiting on customers, ringing up tickets, laughing and talking and planning the menu for the next day. And Tor's number was unlisted; I'd have to wait for Millie to give it to me.

"Let's grab some lunch," Tinkie said. "My head throbs and my stomach is growling. And you look like something from a *Star Trek* episode that involves a brain leech."

"If I was ever inclined to get the big head, my friends would deflate it instantly."

"That's our job." She linked her arm with mine and we headed to the rental car.

* * *

Lunch was delicious, and it was a pleasure to sit on the patio of the small café and indulge in Tinkie's company. From the moment she'd arrived, we'd been in one crisis or another. We'd had no time to talk, to giggle and do the girl things we loved.

Sweetie Pie and Chablis were allowed to sit beneath the table as long as no one complained. We slipped them morsels of food, and I was relieved to see that Chablis was perking up with each bite. She still couldn't jump into Tinkie's lap, which was a good thing since we would've been thrown out of the restaurant.

"I think this movie is going to be a smash," Tinkie said, stirring some mango concoction that looked cold and luscious.

"It still doesn't seem real," I told her. "It's like a dream, a fantasy. I'm doing the one thing I've wanted to do since I was a child. And people say I'm good at it. That I have talent. This is balm to an old wound."

"They speak the truth." She pushed her plate back. "You're also a good detective."

"Then why am I stumped on this case?" I'd been going over and over it but couldn't come up with a single reasonable explanation for all the things that had happened.

"It's strange that Federico never called back." Tinkie signaled the waiter for our check. "I left a voice mail saying to call one of us instantly and that it was about Estelle."

"Jovan may have erased it," I said. "She feels Estelle is deliberately sabotaging the film by claiming all of Federico's attention."

"He is her father."

As a practicing Daddy's Girl, Tinkie had rigid criteria for the father/daughter relationship. Putting a movie, no matter how great, ahead of a daughter was totally unacceptable.

"I'll call Graf." I'd held off telling him about Estelle, but someone needed to let Federico know. Graf could relay the message and perhaps that would inspire the director to call back.

"I'll call the hospital and check on Estelle," Tinkie said.

We whipped out our cell phones and had a moment of dueling digits as we tapped in numbers.

"Hello, darling." Graf had the leading man vocal timbre down pat. He melted me with two words.

"Graf, we've found Estelle. She was beaten and tied up and hidden in another secret passage." The words spilled out.

"Sarah Booth, are you okay?"

"I'm fine. So is Tinkie. And both dogs."

"Thank God. Who would do such a thing to Estelle?"

"We don't know." I told him about our visit to Estoban Gonzalez and how Estelle would have died if we hadn't found her.

"Can she remember anything about who attacked her?"

"She's delirious. In fact, Tinkie is checking on her condition right now." My partner gave me a thumbs-up, but also a shake of her head. "I think she's holding her own. Critical but stable. We don't have a lot of information right now." Tinkie nodded that I'd interpreted her signals correctly.

"Can you bring her to the States?"

"I'll ask the doctor later today, but I'm waiting for Federico to call. Have you seen him?"

"Actually, no. He left the airport and went straight to editing."

"I've left several messages. Would you see that he knows about Estelle? He might want to be here."

"I'll go back to the set and look for him."

"Graf, be careful. The person who did this to Estelle could be in the crew."

There was a pause. "What are you saying?"

"Only that Estelle was tied and locked in a closet a while

before y'all left. So it could easily be someone in the cast and crew. I think this has to be an inside job. I'm just saying be careful."

"Now you've creeped me out." He tried to make light of it, but he was disturbed.

"And I saw the ghost again." I had to tell him.

"Where?" he asked.

"In the secret passage. She sort of led us to Estelle."

"Did Tinkie see her?"

Now why was that relevant? I'd seen her. That should be enough. "No, Tinkie hit her head and knocked herself out."

"At least she did it to herself this time."

"You aren't even going to ask me about the ghost?" I was disappointed. I wanted Graf to believe me.

"All of this talk makes me want to hop a plane and get down there to load you up and bring you home. Ghost or not, someone is dangerous and determined to harm members of this production."

"Tinkie and I are heading out in the morning. You don't need to come and fetch us." The idea of seeing him again made my stomach knot with anticipation.

"I'm worried for you and for Tinkie." Graf spoke with passion. "It wasn't the ghost of Carlita who pushed Suzy Dutton off a cliff, Sarah Booth. It was a real-life, flesh-and-blood murderer. And if that person is still in Petaluma, I want you out of there."

"And if that person is in Los Angeles, intending to sabotage the film further?"

"I'll talk to Federico. It might be good to get some security around the set. To protect the cameras and all."

"Call Sheriff King." Although the California sheriff was difficult, he also had the ability to protect Graf and the rest of the crew.

"Not a bad idea," he agreed. "I'll do those things if you promise to hop the first flight out of there tomorrow."

"Wild horses couldn't stop me," I assured him.

"I love you," he said before he hung up.

Tinkie closed her telephone about the same time. "Estelle has stabilized, but they're not sure they can save her hands and feet." She shuddered as she spoke. "She hasn't regained consciousness."

"And Daniel?"

"He's with her."

"Let's stop by there on the way back to the mansion."

Estelle lay in the hospital bed, dark hair spread on the pillow. Someone had done his or her best to wash her hair and remove some of the blood, but nothing could be done to hide the wide gash that ran from her temple across the top of her head. The doctors had shaved it and done what they could to close the wound.

Daniel sat beside the bed, rubbing her hand and then her foot. He was trying to bring the circulation back to her limbs by sheer force of his will.

"This can't be happening," he said.

"I'm so sorry." I put a hand on his shoulder. "Has she said anything at all?"

"She's mumbled some. It's incoherent. Sounds like a nightmare."

"We need for her to wake up and talk," I told him.

"Ms. Delaney, if she loses her hands and feet, I hope she never wakes up." He looked as if he'd been stabbed in the heart. "She won't be able to handle this. It'll drive her mad, and then . . ." His voice broke and he turned away.

"Whoever tied her and left her meant for her to die, Daniel. That person could still be out there." I wasn't trying to come down hard on him, but he had to realize the danger. Just because Estelle was in the hospital didn't necessarily mean she was safe.

"If she wakes up, I'll do my best," he said.

"Call us. We're trying to help her."

He nodded as he shifted to the other side of the bed and began rubbing her left hand briskly between his own. "I know." He kissed her hand. "I knew something was wrong. Estelle would never have disappeared like that. But I didn't listen to my heart. I believed she'd grown tired of me and simply left to avoid the confrontation."

"Daniel, we all act from weakness sometimes," Tinkie said. "You heard what you dreaded most to hear."

"And I failed to search for her."

"But we were looking, and we didn't find her either," Tinkie said. She put a hand on Estelle's arm. "We did the best we could do with the information we had. She's a young woman who had disappeared before, moving from one place to another at the drop of a hat. Her disappearance was normal behavior. This isn't your fault." She gave Daniel a hug and followed me out into the hall.

"If the person who murdered Suzy Dutton is the same person who tried to kill Estelle and that's the same person who's been in the house, hurting you and me and Jovan, then it all goes back to the movie."

"But why and who?"

That was the weak spot in my theory. "I don't know. But whoever it is knew Suzy was going out to the Malibu house Graf and I leased. They also knew that Estelle was prone to disappearing acts—that no one would take it seriously until it was too late."

Tinkie's blue eyes widened and she did that little thing with her lip popping out of her mouth that drove men wild. "It's someone on the inside."

"Without a doubt. As much as I'd like to hang this on Esoban, I don't think he's guilty of it."

"So now we begin to narrow our suspects. We need a cast and crew list."

"Exactly."

"Where do we begin?" she asked.

"In the stacks of the national gossip sheets. Let's find a library." It would be easier to call Millie, but we didn't have time to wait.

CHAPTER TWENTY-SEVEN

To our utter delight, the research librarian at Petaluma was a misplaced South Dakotan named Patsy Kringel. She was a demon of research *and* bilingual. By the time we'd warmed our chairs, she had us on the Web and surfing the thousands of sites and archives dealing with the movie cast and crew. The only stars we left out were me and Graf. Everyone else, we did at least rudimentary checks on, narrowing our focus mostly to Federico, Estelle, and Ricardo.

Our searches came up with little that Millie hadn't already told us. The Marquez family had seen its share of sorrow and success. The story of Carlita's "devastating illness and death" was reported almost everywhere, but not a single newspaper or tabloid had unearthed her anorexia. It was a kinder and gentler media back when she'd died.

"Look at this," Tinkie said. She'd taken Jovan as her next prospect. Since she was living in the house when many of the incidents took place, Jovan was a logical suspect even though she'd been the victim of an attack.

I rolled my chair over beside Tinkie's computer to read the Web site. She pointed to the visitor counter at the bottom of the front page.

"Holy cow," I said. "This says one million eight hundred

and eighty-nine thousand visitors to this Web site since January." I couldn't believe it. Jovan had more Web site hits than Tom Cruise.

Tinkie was unimpressed. "She's part of the fashion world as well as movies, and she has devoted fans that follow her every move. These great pictures don't hurt, either. She photographs even better than she looks in person, which pretty much makes her a goddess." Tinkie moved around the Web site. "Says she was born in Stockholm to working-class parents, went to high school, was seen by a talent scout while playing sports, and the rest is history."

She scrolled down to a photograph of Jovan with a pretty middle-aged woman and a middle-aged man.

"So what did you want to show me?" Jovan was interesting, but I didn't have time for fashion gossip or celebrity schmoozing.

"Do you think she looks anything like those people?" Tinkie asked.

"Her parents?" I wondered what tangent Tinkie was off on now. "Not really, but so what. Genetics are strange things."

"Could she be adopted?"

I shrugged. "Possibly." Tinkie and Oscar were thinking of adoption, and Jovan might prove to be the poster child to help her bring Oscar around. I studied the picture closer. "That might explain her attempts to control Federico when he wants to rescue Estelle from her own bad conduct. Jovan may feel a little threatened when he shows unlimited love to his daughter—especially a daughter who's done everything to defy and ruin him. I mean, if she feels her father didn't want her."

"Aren't you little Miss Freud."

"If you're going to call me psychiatric names, I'd prefer to be Little Miss Jung. Freud and all the emphasis on penis envy sort of leaves me cold."

Tinkie laughed, and several patrons glanced at us—right,

the rude Americans were in the library. I mimed an apology and went back to my computer. "Take a look at this on Ricardo," I whispered.

She rolled over and we examined the Web site for the younger Marquez, which included photos of him with his heavy metal band in Venice, California, and several black-and-white photographs he'd taken, which were beautiful.

"He has a feel for light," I whispered. "He'll be a great cinematographer."

"And not a single word about Federico on the Web site," Tinkie pointed out. "You'd think he might mention his dad is one of the premier Hollywood directors."

"Which could mean he doesn't want to trade on the old man's name."

"Or it could mean he hates his father and wants to sabotage his film." Tinkie rubbed the lump on her forehead and I knew she was tired and getting cranky. Our time to solve this case was running out. We'd dropped the dogs off at the vet clinic. Chablis was due for a checkup and Sweetie was hanging with her.

"We're getting a lot of background on people, but nothing really useful," I told her. "I wonder why Federico hasn't called yet?" I'd turned my cell phone to vibrate, so I knew he hadn't. "And neither has Millie."

"It's like we've dropped into the black hole of Calcutta. No one is returning our calls." Tinkie's tone was huffy. In Zinnia, Tinkie's calls were never ignored. As the premier Daddy's Girl, by virtue of the fact that her father owned the bank and her husband was president of it, Tinkie was used to people sitting up and taking notice of her. It was a fact that had worked to the Delaney Detective Agency's advantage many times before.

We thanked the librarian for her help and made our way into the afternoon breeze. For all of the problems we'd had here, Petaluma was one of the most beautiful places I'd ever been. The town was clean, filled with bright colors and hand-painted tiles decorating the walls of buildings and gardens. It had some feel of old New Orleans, but with a definite Latin twist. The cobbled streets were baked in the sun, old and worn and authentic. Looking at the vista of the town sloping down a gentle incline, I wondered if I'd ever come back. Maybe Graf and I would honeymoon here.

"You look pensive," Tinkie said.

"I was considering Petaluma for honeymoon potential."

She started toward the car. "That would be lovely," she said, and I could hear how she forced the happiness into the words.

"It was just a thought."

"Whatever makes you happy, Sarah Booth. That's what I want for you."

And she meant it. If she had her wish, I would go home to Zinnia. As much as she'd once deviled me about Coleman's lack of commitment, now she wanted to return to that time when I was at Dahlia House, Coleman was on the horizon, and our partnership was not impeded by the distance of a continent.

"Where to now?" I asked. We'd done pretty much all we could using the Web for a research tool. If Federico didn't call back soon, we'd be winging our way home to the States. Tinkie had booked a flight to New Orleans for 6:00 A.M. the next morning. My flight to LAX left at 7:10 A.M. We had early calls to meet the guidelines of the international flights.

"I don't want to go back to the mansion," Tinkie said.

"Me either." The memory of Estelle was too fresh. And there was the sense that Carlita was still there, waiting for another chance to talk to me.

"Maybe we can catch a flight out tonight."

Tinkie was ready to go, and I didn't blame her. "If you can get out, I'll stay and make sure Estelle is stable and improving before I go." I touched my forehead. The swelling had gone down, but I still wasn't ready for the camera.

Tinkie longed to leave, but she shook her head. "I'm here until you go."

"We both believe the person behind the attacks is in Los Angeles. It's okay for you to go, Tinkie. Take Chablis and go home to Oscar. Talk to him about adopting. There are a lot of children who would love to have you for a mom."

She nodded her agreement. "I'll deal with my family issues when I get home. Right now, we need to think about a possible killer. It's true, we *believe* the attacker is in California. But until we have proof, I'm not willing to leave you here alone."

My cell phone rang and I snapped it open. Millie's voice came through loud and clear.

"I'll give you Tor's private number," she said when I told her what I needed. "Since you're a friend of mine, he'll tell you what he knows."

"Thanks, Millie."

"Sarah Booth, you should see the spread Cece did on you in the newspaper. She got some photographs from the filming. You're magnificent. Everyone in town is raving about it. Several men are desperate for you to come home."

"Several?"

"Harold Erkwell had the newspaper matted, framed, and hung in the café. He's so pleased for you. I had no idea he harbored such deep affection for you."

"Give Harold a kiss for me," I instructed her. "He's been a good friend."

"And what shall I give Coleman?" she asked.

I closed my eyes. Why was it that I had to keep making this break over and over again? "Give him my regards and tell him I'm happy and fine."

There was a pause. "I will."

"Thanks for Tor's number, and tell Cece I'm going to get

even with her when I get . . . home." No matter what, Zinnia would always be home.

I hung up and Tinkie suggested that we get the dogs and go back to the mansion to make the call to Tor. We still hadn't retrieved our things, but we weren't going to stay there overnight.

On the way to the vet's clinic, we stopped by the Petaluma police. One of the officers who'd come to the house, Sergeant Calla, told us they'd gathered a number of prints, but they were waiting for Estelle to regain consciousness. If she could identify her attacker, they would be all over it.

Sergeant Calla did have one interesting thing to report—aside from the prints Tinkie and I had made, there were two other sets. Estelle's and a stranger's. While the forensics team had collected a pretty good impression of a size nine and a half athletic shoe, they hadn't matched it with anything in their system. They were working with Sheriff King for some help in the States.

"We're more hopeful on the fingerprints recovered from the dust in the passage and closet," he said. "We take it seriously that Ms. Marquez was nearly killed. We'll find the perpetrator and he or she will be punished. Estelle's father is an important man."

"Thank you, Sergeant," Tinkie said, batting her eyelashes in a way that looked helpless and sexy. "We'll be in touch."

We picked up the dogs—Chablis's glowing recovery report going a long way to making Tinkie ecstatic—and headed for the Marquez place.

Night was falling. Another day had come to a close, and we both knew we had to leave Costa Rica. Despite Tinkie's generosity with her time, she had her own life to manage. So far, the filming of the movie had proceeded without me, but my scenes were coming up and quickly.

Which made me wonder again why Federico hadn't called me back.

I put in another call to Graf, who was delighted to hear from me but could shed no light on what was happening with the director.

"He's disappeared, Sarah Booth," he said. "Ricardo is trying to track him down. Jovan is frantic. I did call Sheriff King. He told me if this was a publicity stunt he'd put all of us in jail, but he is checking into it."

"Is there a chance this is a publicity stunt?" I had a terrible feeling. What if everything that had happened in Petaluma—the falls, the attacks, everything—was a way of getting buzz going for the movie? Maybe someone had seen Suzy Dutton's death and the resulting publicity as an opportunity to promote this film.

I'd assumed that being "cursed" was a bad thing, but what if it translated into box office interest?

And what about Estelle? She was severely injured. This wasn't a bump on the head or a tumble. She might lose her hands and feet. Surely Federico would have no part in harming his own daughter. Surely.

"Find Federico, Graf. Do whatever it takes, but find him. Get him to call me."

"I'll go back to the edit room."

"I love you," I told him before I hung up.

"You look awful," Tinkie said. "What is it?"

"What if all of this started out as a publicity stunt and then went too far?"

"I don't believe it," Tinkie said. "A dead daughter isn't going to translate into very good press."

"What if he didn't intend for her to die? Maybe he expected us to find her much sooner." But that was crazy. He hadn't given us a single clue.

"And what about the ghost?" Tinkie asked. "Did he manipulate that, too?"

"I don't know," I had to say. There were visual and special effects tricks available to Federico that I'd never heard of.

I was spared further Tinkie interrogation by the shrill ring of my cell phone. When I answered, it was Sergeant Calla.

"Could you and Mrs. Richmond come to the station?" he asked. "My men found a pair of shoes in the garden that match the print in the passageway. We'd like you to identify them if you can."

"We're on the way." I motioned for Tinkie to do a U-turn, and we headed back to town.

When we got there, Sergeant Calla met us in a small, sparsely furnished room. Another officer brought in a pair of beat-up athletic shoes. He put them on the desk in front of us. I felt Tinkie tense, but I kept a poker face.

"Do you recognize those shoes?" he asked.

I could hear Jitty in a corner of my mind, calling me a stool pigeon and worse, but I had to answer. "Those belong to Federico Marquez." I'd seen them numerous times. He wore them for walks on the beach with Jovan. "Where did you find them?"

"Hidden in the garden beside the house. They'd been buried beneath some mulch and leaves. Daniel Martinez was very upset over Estelle's attack, and as a special favor to him I brought in the tracking dogs. They found the shoes."

I didn't look at Tinkie. She really adored Federico, and I knew she was crushed. I wasn't feeling so great, either. Aside from the larger issue that Federico was a monster, I didn't think he could get a pass from jail to finish his movie. My bright and shining career was suddenly in shambles.

"Why would Senor Marquez want to harm his daughter?" Sergeant Calla asked.

"I don't know," I answered.

"I'm not certain he did this," Tinkie said. "Someone could have planted those shoes. He wore them on the beach and left them at the back door. Everyone and his brother had access to them."

"She has a good point," I said.

"We have calls in for Senor Marquez to contact us, but he hasn't done so." Calla looked at me as if I could explain it.

I shrugged. "I've been calling him most of the day. He's disappeared from the set. No one can find him." I realized after I said it how suspicious it made him look.

"We're afraid someone has harmed Federico," Tinkie said, taking the bull by the horns.

"What makes you think that?" Calla asked.

"He has a multimillion-dollar movie three-quarters of the way made and he disappears? The timing doesn't make sense. None of it. Why do all of these things now, when he has a shot of really getting back on top as a director? Rumors around Hollywood for the past six months have been that this movie is going to make him the most sought-after director working today. Why would he jeopardize this when the movie is going great?"

Tinkie's passion was unexpected, but her logic was impeccable. "Yeah, why?" I brilliantly echoed.

Calla was unimpressed. "I intend to find out. If you hear from Senor Marquez, explain to him that he should contact me immediately."

"Will do," I said.

"My advice is not to stay in that house. Daniel tells me that he's had men on the gate since filming began and yet accidents continue to happen there."

"We're getting a room in a hotel," I assured him. "We just have to go and gather our belongings."

"I wouldn't linger. Especially now that it's night."

His words touched me with an acute chill. Night, ghosts, spirits a'calling. "Let's get our stuff," I said to Tinkie as we left the police station.

"And then let's check on Estelle. If she would only wake up, she could resolve this whole snarl."

"Either that or put the nail in her father's coffin, which she might do just for spite."

CHAPTER TWENTY-EIGHT

The old mansion was too quiet. I paced my room, knowing that this was my last chance to figure out what was really happening in the house. I'd placed a call to Tor and left a message, and Tinkie was in her room with the dogs, packing her four suitcases.

With my one bag ready to go, I paused for a moment and stared at the portrait of Carlita Gonzalez Marquez. Why in the world hadn't she been happy with her beauty? I could look at her and see what she never could—she was stunning—and I was left with a sense of the total waste of it all. She'd never seen herself as she really was, and it was a shame.

From behind me an emotionally choked voice spoke. "You're on your own, Cat. You're better off being independent. You don't need me or anyone else."

I whirled to find Jitty, rain-sodden, wearing a tightly belted raincoat and sobbing. Instantly I recognized the scene from *Breakfast at Tiffany's* that had deviled me as a child. Holly Golightly has just released the yellow tabby, Cat, into an alley, thinking that independence in trash cans was better than the disappointment of needing someone and being rejected.

"Jitty." I stepped toward her. She was distraught. And dripping. Water had pooled around her on the floor.

She twirled, and in an instant the raincoat was gone and she was wearing a black Chanel dress, her hair swept up in a bun, a fringe of bangs emphasizing her gamine eyes. She was the glamorous Audrey Hepburn, albeit in a shade of mocha.

"Do you prefer this image?" she asked. "I'm certainly more comfortable. I never cared for the soppin' wet look. Works for blondes much better, doncha think?"

"How did you do that?" Jitty was always dashing about in some new wardrobe, but I'd never seen a quick-change like that one.

"Exterior don't count, Sarah Booth. Beauty's not always a ticket to anything except heartbreak and disappointment. Your mama knew this. As beautiful as she was, she never traded on her looks. She taught you better, too."

"I've never traded on my looks." I was indignant.

"No, you never have. And you've never seen yourself clearly, either. You're standin' here wonderin' how Carlita couldn't see herself, and you're floatin' in the same boat."

"That's just not true. I've always been clearheaded about my talents . . . and my . . ." Jitty had hammered me. "When I was in New York, I never felt beautiful." It was true.

"And now?" Jitty asked.

The realization that dawned on me was interesting. "And now, I don't think about it."

That was obviously the right answer, because she did another twirl, and the black dress was replaced by a beautiful white gown that made her look both vulnerable and elegant. She was still Audrey, but she was a happier version.

"This conversation is fascinating, but it doesn't help me solve the case. Have you seen Carlita's ghost?" I asked her.

"I can't do nothin' to help Carlita. You and your partner did what she needed. You found her daughter and got an ambulance."

"Maybe too late." I hated to think about what might be happening to Estelle. "Is Carlita gone now? Is she at peace?"

"I don't know." Jitty sat on the edge of the bed. "I'm here because you need me. I don't know why Carlita's in this house." She shrugged. "I don't know everything."

The rules of the Great Beyond were not any clearer to me, either. The more that happened, the less I understood. "Tinkie and I have to go, and I don't have a clue what really went on here. Was Carlita involved in the attacks on me and Tinkie and Jovan?"

Jitty put on a pair of round sunglasses that almost hid her face. "There's really only one person who can answer that question."

"The ghost doesn't answer questions." I gave her a sharp look. "She's a lot like you in that regard. She does pretty damn much what she wants." I put on a pout. "This will be our first unsolved case. A sterling record broken."

Jitty crossed the room, her silver bracelets tinkling. "I doubt that."

I was about to ask what she meant when my cell phone rang. I looked down to check the number, and when I looked up, there was no sign of Jitty. The hospital was calling, and I answered.

"This is Dr. Valdez. Estelle Marquez asked me to call. She wants to speak with you and Mrs. Richmond."

"We're on the way," I said. "How is she?"

"She's stabilized."

"And her hands and feet?" I didn't want to ask but I had to know.

"We're working to save them. It's touch and go, but she is improving."

"Thank you," I said, feeling a weight lift that I hadn't been aware I carried. "Thank you, Doctor. We're on the way. Is Mr. Martinez there?"

"Yes. He gave me your number."

In a matter of minutes, I had Tinkie's and my bags in the trunk of the car, the dogs in the backseat, and we were on the way to the hospital. We stopped at a lovely old hotel and took a room, failing to disclose that we had hounds with us. They could charge us double, or even triple, but we couldn't leave Chablis and Sweetie Pie alone in that house, and we couldn't take them to the hospital.

We arrived breathless from our sprint across the parking lot. Estelle was in a private room, and Daniel sat at her bedside. She had tubes running into veins and an oxygen line in her nose. The bank of machines behind her blinked and beeped in a steady, rhythmic way that I associated with recovery.

When we entered, Estelle opened her eyes.

"Thank you," she said. "Daniel told me you found me." Her voice was dry, whispery—and very much like Carlita's.

"Thanks aren't necessary. I'm just sorry we didn't find you sooner." Tinkie was the epitome of graciousness. She put a hand on Estelle's blanket-covered shin.

"Who did this to you, Estelle?" I asked.

She looked at Daniel, who nodded.

"I don't understand why this happened," she said.

I could tell that she was having a hard time, but I honestly wanted to shake her. She'd been creeping around the house, putting all of us in danger. She might not be responsible for what happened to Tinkie and Chablis, but she was to blame for part of it. Had she not been playing hide-and-seek, Tinkie wouldn't have been hunting her.

"Who hit you, tied you up, and left you to die?" I asked.

She started to cry. The machines that beeped and pulsed behind her began to light up.

"Calm down, Estelle," Daniel said. He looked at me. "Give her a minute. She's been through hell."

I started to say something sharp, but before I could get the words out, my cell phone rang. Again. *Phonus interruptus* was getting to be a regular—and annoying—habit. I knew when Tinkie made me get the cell phone I was going to regret the thing.

I checked the ID and it was Tor. "I have to take the call," I said.

"I'll handle this," Tinkie whispered as she leaned toward me. "We'll do good cop, bad cop. You've already proven that you're the bad one."

I stepped into the hall to answer my phone. Tor still retained a soft Southern drawl beneath his California accent. "Millie said I should help you," he said.

"Where is Vincent Day?" I asked.

"Millie also said that you could be rude. She was right."

"Sorry, but it's a time thing. I do apologize but we have only a few hours. If Vincent Day is in this area, I have to find him before my flight leaves." It was logical to me, and I hoped Tor understood.

"I haven't seen Vincent since he came back from Canada. I'd heard he stopped over in Sweden to look up his ex."

"Ivana?" I struggled to remember. The cast of characters in the infidelity quadrangles of the Marquezes and Days was a bit confusing.

"Yes, she lives in Stockholm. I think Vincent was trying to make atonement."

"What makes you think that?"

"He said something about how he'd walked away from the one person who gave him real joy."

"Ivana?" The story I'd gotten from Millie was that Ivana had left him and returned to her native country because of the romantic intrigues and domestic violence.

"I got the sense it wasn't Ivana. Hey, I knew her and she was a bitch extraordinaire. She left no stone uncast when she got riled up, which was about every twenty minutes. I think she hated Vincent."

"So why would he go and see her?"

There was a pause. "Technically, he didn't say he was going to see Ivana."

"Then who else could it be?" He didn't even have to answer.

A dozen little balls tumbled into place in my brain. "Did he have a child?"

"Not a word was ever spoken about a child."

But I could hear it in Tor's voice. He was making the same connections. "What happened to Ivana after she left Day and went home?"

"She was a beautiful woman, but she wasn't part of the Hollywood royalty."

"She dropped out of sight."

"Exactly."

"So she could have had a child?"

"Possibly." There was another pause. "Damn. Day could have a son or daughter."

"Thanks, Tor." I had to get off the phone and fast. There were calls to be made. Calls of life and death. "I'll give Millie your regards." I'd already proven I was rude so I hung up.

As I pushed against the hospital door, it opened. Estelle was weeping silently in the bed. She looked at me. "I only meant to mess up the movie. I never meant for anyone to be hurt."

"Who hit you and put you in that closet to die?" I asked, even though I knew the answer. Jovan.

Her response was an echo of the name in my own brain. I looked at Tinkie. "We've got to get to Hollywood. Federico is missing."

Estelle was crying in earnest now. There were only a few other questions that needed an answer in Petaluma. "What role does your grandfather play in all of this?"

"He paid off Daniel's security men to allow me to slip around the premises. Daniel didn't know. He wouldn't have helped me."

"You could have died, Estelle. Had Sarah Booth and Tinkie not searched the house, you'd be dead now." Daniel was hurt and angry, and I didn't blame him.

"Grandfather didn't know I was injured and in the house. Like everyone else, he thought I'd gone back to the States.

He truly didn't know." She reached for Daniel's hand, and
could see that her dexterity was clumsy. The price she migh
pay for this would be far higher than any a judge could met
out to her.

"And Suzy Dutton?" I asked.

"I had nothing to do with that. Nothing."

"We have to call Sheriff King," Tinkie said.

I handed her my cell phone. I had another question fo
Estelle. "Why did Jovan turn on you?"

"I realized she meant to kill someone if she had to. We ar
gued. I told her it had gone far enough. That I'd come to re
alize that my mother loved my father, and that it was he
own illness that killed her, not his infidelity."

Tinkie was waiting for the secretary to find King and rin
her through.

"How did you discover that?" I asked.

Estelle never faltered. She never even blinked. "Mam
told me. When I was in the house one night and everyone els
was gone, I saw her. She told me to stop, that Father wasn't t
blame. She said she'd never rest in peace until I knew th
truth."

Chill bumps danced along my arms.

"You don't believe me, do you?" she asked. "I'm heade
to a mental institution anyway."

"The problem, Estelle, is that I do believe you," I said. I
was cold comfort, but it was all I had to give.

With the cell phone still pressed to Tinkie's ear, we hur
ried out of the hospital and into the night. If there was
flight to LAX tonight, we were going to be on it.

CHAPTER TWENTY-NINE

When Sheriff King answered, he was brusque but courteous. Tinkie gave him the information and then rang off. I called Graf. My heart began to thud when there was no answer. Graf always kept his cell phone with him.

"It's okay, Sarah Booth. I'm sure Graf is fine." Tinkie spoke the words with a valiant heart, but she couldn't hide the tremor in her voice. She was worried, too. A psychopathic killer was on the loose in Los Angeles, and she'd targeted Federico and the cast and crew of his film. Graf was one of the key players in the movie.

"We should have figured this out quicker," Tinkie said.

"The running shoes that Valdez found. Jovan had access to them. She planted them." As crazy as it was, it gave me hope. Maybe she intended to frame Federico for murder rather than kill him. Maybe he's still alive."

"Maybe." Tinkie drove like a bat out of hell. She normally drove that way, but she upped it a notch on the narrow Petaluma road. We had our luggage and the dogs, and we were only minutes from the airport. A plane had to be there. It had to. We couldn't wait to get home.

I dialed Graf again. I had this horrible image of him, broken and dead, at the bottom of a cliff. As hard as I tried to shake it I couldn't.

We tried Federico again, no answer. Ricardo, no answer. Was it possible that Jovan had pulled a Jim Jones and given them all a lethal dose of poison-laced Kool-Aid?

When we pulled into the airport, I knew we were in trouble. The place had that desolate look of an empty train station. No one waited on a flight because there weren't any planes going out.

Since I was almost in tears, Tinkie negotiated with one of the sleepy airline employees. For the wad of cash Tinkie produced, the man would have built a plane for us if he'd had the ability. "Sorry, senoritas. There are no planes on the ground here. None will come in until tomorrow." He eyed the money reluctantly.

Tinkie walked to the window that gave a view of the air field and pointed. "Then what is that?"

He followed her finger to the beautiful jet that seemed to perch, briefly, on the ground.

"That is a private jet, senoritas. We have no public transportation available."

"Who owns the jet?" I asked.

"It is an actress. Charlize Theron. She was here to do a benefit and she is leaving very soon."

I looked at Tinkie and she looked at me. We handed the dogs' leashes to the attendant and ran out the door and across the tarmac. Tinkie and I were getting into good physical shape despite ourselves with all this running to and fro.

We got to the gangplank just as they were about to push away. "Wait!" I screamed, mounting the stairs even as they began to move.

The ground crew scrambled to stop it before I was injured, but they gave me a murderous look. I beat frantically on the door of the plane. "Please, open up," I said. "Please."

An incredibly beautiful woman peeped through the small window. She assessed me and finally opened the door.

"We need a ride to Los Angeles," I explained. "It's a matter of life and death." As soon as the words were out of my mouth I realized what a cliché they were.

Charlize looked beyond me at Tinkie.

"Just the two of you?" she asked.

"And two dogs."

"You want to put dogs on my plane?" Her tone was cool.

"They have to come. We can't leave them. But we're trying to prevent the murder of Federico Marquez. And possibly Graf Milieu."

"Federico Marquez, the director? And Milieu is the new actor he's working with?"

I nodded. "It's a long story, but I swear, Federico's life is in danger and Graf may be missing."

"Are you the actress from Mississippi he hired for the film he's doing?"

Relief almost made me stutter. "Yes, yes, I am, and that's Tinkie Bellcase Richmond, my partner in a private detective agency."

A smile touched her lips. "I don't know anything about murder or PIs, but I have a dog and anyone who loves animals is good with me. Grab the dogs and come on."

The attendant had already brought Sweetie and Chablis out to the tarmac. Tinkie gave the attendant a wad of cash to forward our luggage and return the rental car, then she took the leashes, and as I waved her on board, she picked up Chablis and ran toward us.

While we prepared for takeoff, I called Graf. He still didn't answer so I left a message telling him I was headed back to Los Angeles. I also called Federico—to no avail—and Sheriff King's office, letting him know I would soon be back in town. Tinkie, with her phone, arranged to have a car ready and waiting for us.

* * *

For most of the flight, I compiled a list of things to do as soon
as I got on the ground. My cell phone was worthless in the air,
and I desperately needed to talk to Graf and know that he was
safe. I hoped that Federico had reappeared, and that I could
call Sheriff King and tell him what I'd learned and that he
would rush out to arrest Jovan. But mostly I made a list of the
places that Graf could be where he wouldn't have access to
his cell phone.

There had to be a reason, other than the obvious, as to why
he hadn't returned my calls. So I made a list of those reasons.
I made a list of things to tell Jovan when she was finally arrested. Then I wrote down groceries to buy when Graf and I
were safely together. Lists gave me comfort and a sense of ac-
complishment.

I remembered that Aunt Loulane once told me that negative
thoughts could lead to a negative reality. With that in mind, I
steadfastly refused to allow my mind to linger on why Graf
hadn't answered his phone.

Tinkie and Charlize chatted, and I watched my partner
with pride and a smidgen of envy. The Daddy's Girl rulebook
had mostly been an easy target of my ridicule, but there was
something to be said for a Nazi-like indoctrination into eti-
quette. Tinkie was amazingly poised and able to handle almost
any social situation. She was versatile and flexible, and those
were good things in the life we'd chosen to lead. She could
talk with royalty or rabble. That was my partner.

We landed at LAX in the early morning hours. We thanked
Charlize profusely and headed for the car rental counter. To
my utter relief, I had a message from Graf. He'd obviously
called while I was in the air.

"Sarah Booth, I'm at the house in Malibu. Meet me
there."

I frowned as I closed my phone.

"What is it?" Tinkie asked. We were headed toward the

adillac she'd rented. Tinkie had a certain standard in vehi-
es, and this merlot Caddy suited her well.

"Graf says to meet him at the Malibu house."

"And?"

"He didn't say a thing about Federico or the movie or any-
ing. And he called at three in the morning. Graf normally
n't awake at that time of night."

"Maybe he's missing you," Tinkie said, but her frown told
e that she, too, found this suspicious.

"Or maybe he called when he knew I'd be in the air and
ouldn't answer. Maybe he doesn't want to talk to me." The
securities I'd worked so hard to bury were poking their
nds out of the grave.

She got behind the wheel. "Which way?"

I was torn. The film crew was supposed to be on a sound
age at the studio lot. Even though the night was black,
ere were scenes of the script that called for darkness. It
as possible the cast and crew were at work. But Graf was in
alibu. I didn't know which direction to head in first. "Hold
," I said.

I tried calling Graf, then Federico, both with negative re-
lts. I wasn't certain where to go. I called Sheriff King.

"Tell me you've found Federico," I said when he came on
e line.

"I could, but it would be a lie, and I wouldn't want to lie
a little lady like you."

So now he was going to pull out his charm. I wanted to
omp his cowboy-booted toe. "Have you spoken to Graf?"

"I haven't, but I guess I don't have to tell you it's not light
t. Dawn is still an hour away, Ms. Delaney. It might be best
you wait until daylight. I thought we'd meet at the set
ound eight o'clock. If Marquez hasn't shown up by then,
'll launch a full investigation." He yawned. "I don't care for
u movie types, but I've never seen an acclaimed director de-
erately screw up his own project."

"I'm going to find Graf," I told him.

"I don't envy Mr. Milieu," he said, but he was chucklin[as he hung up the phone.

"Perfect. The sheriff wants to be a stand-up comedian," told Tinkie.

She was already flying along the highway. Tinkie could tal[her way out of a ticket in Mississippi, but I wasn't so certai[the California state troopers would be as easy to hornswoggl[Then again, if she did that thing where her lip popped out (her mouth, she could probably talk her way out of a murd[charge.

"Try calling Graf," she suggested.

"Brilliant." I placed the call as we sped through the nigh[His phone rang and rang and rang. Just as it had before I le[Costa Rica. Finally it rang through to voice mail and I le[another message.

"I'm on my way to Malibu, Graf. I . . . can't wait to s[you." I glanced at Tinkie who kept her gaze on the road.

We were away from the city lights, headed into the hil[and canyons that were so wild and beautiful. Soon we were (the road to the house Graf and I were borrowing. I'd driven t[road plenty before now, but I'd never really realized how is[lated everything was. We passed the fire station, all dark f[the night. The firemen were inside sleeping, like normal pe[ple. We climbed higher, winding around and using switc[backs for some of the steeper inclines. This terrain was call["hills" but in the eyes of a Delta girl, they were mountain and not the gentle green giants of the Smokies but a more ba[ren, harsher cousin.

"You've got to get a place in town, Sarah Booth," Tink[said. "This is too far out and the road is dangerous."

"It's only temporary. But it is beautiful."

She made a sharp curve, the tires giving a low sque["Beautiful and isolated. This road gives me the willies, and[

isn't even raining. I can imagine when the rains come and the mudslides start and—"

"Give it a rest. Your point is made."

We pulled into the parking area of Bobby Joe Taylor's house. My little T-bird rental was there, but no sign of Graf's vehicle.

"Shit," I said, opening the door to let Sweetie and Chablis out to take a whiz. After Tinkie's driving, I needed one myself.

I used my key to the front door and Tinkie and I entered. The house had a stale odor—one that I associated with a place left empty for a while. But Graf had supposedly come home the day before, and his intention was to stay in this house. Or so he'd led me to believe.

"Graf!" I called his name loudly. "Graf!"

There was no response.

We'd brought the dogs in with us—I couldn't take a repeat of the fire or coyote scenario. Tinkie and I split up. She took the interior and I checked the porch and balcony that ran along the exterior.

While I was checking out the back balcony, I heard Sweetie and Chablis "pack up." They began barking at someone or something, and my heart lifted with the hope of Graf. By the time I got to the front of the house, though, the dogs had quieted and there was no sign of Graf or anyone else.

When Tinkie and I rejoined in the kitchen, neither of us had found a sign that showed Graf had ever made it back to this house. His bags weren't here and the house looked exactly as we'd left it.

"Where could he be?" I asked, not even trying to hide my worry.

Tinkie knew I didn't want to hear the answer, so she wisely said, "Call the sheriff."

It was a good suggestion, and I did. King wasn't any

happier to be awakened again, but he did take me seriously. "Let's meet at the set," he said. "I'll bring some deputies. We need to find out what happened to Federico and Mr. Milieu from the moment they got off the plane."

"Thanks, Sheriff King."

"I'll meet you as quickly as you can get there. I'll see if I can find someone who can bring in the whole cast and crew."

Sweetie Pie and Chablis were exhausted. Although I didn't want to leave them alone in the house, I also didn't want to haul them back down the mountain and into town again, where they'd be forced to wait in the car or a dressing room while Tinkie and I investigated.

"Let's leave them in the house," Tinkie said.

Although I agreed with her, I had that unsettled sense that I was going to regret my decision.

With Sweetie and Chablis standing in the glass doorway watching us go, Tinkie and I headed back down to the movie set. We hadn't slept in hours and hours, but adrenaline had kicked in and we were wired.

"I hate this road," Tinkie said. She'd allowed me to drive only because she had a headache. I kept my mouth shut and my attention on the asphalt. I drove considerably slower than Tinkie, but going downhill, it was hard not to pick up a lot of speed. The Caddy was a larger car than I normally drove, and I was still adjusting when we came to a hairpin curve.

I stomped the brake and my foot went all the way to the floorboard.

"Pump it," Tinkie said. "I thought the brakes felt a little soft."

I pumped as hard as I could while still keeping the car on the road. As we nosed downhill, we picked up more speed.

"The brakes are gone." I spoke quietly. It felt as if my fingers had broken around the steering wheel. My grasp was so tight that I couldn't let go.

Sawing the wheel back and forth, I did everything I could to reduce our forward momentum. There was a dangerous curve approaching, and at the speed we were traveling, close to fifty miles an hour, we'd never make it. It was a hard turn to make at fifteen.

"Pump the brakes again," Tinkie said. She pulled out her cell phone and placed a 911 call for an ambulance.

"Don't you think that's a little premature?" I asked as I barely made a curve.

"We're going to crash. It's just a matter of how bad it's going to be. I want medical attention as soon as possible. Oscar will never forgive me if I die."

I flashed her a smile to show I appreciated her spirit and her humor.

I saw the caution sign for the turn that was almost 180 degrees. A yellow light blinked a warning. It was less than two thousand feet ahead. On one side was solid rock and the other was a sheer drop.

I pumped the brakes like one of the Riverdance performers. When there was no response, I did the only thing I could. I turned the wheel and rammed into the side of the mountain.

We slammed into solid rock. I heard the squeal of tires sliding on asphalt and the rattle of stones raining down on the top of the car. The air bags inflated with such a rush that it pushed the oxygen out of my lungs with terrific force. I was thrown forward and then back and then forward again until I felt as if I'd been shaken by a giant hand.

When I looked over at Tinkie, my heart almost stopped. Her face was turned toward me, her eyes closed, and a trickle of blood leaked from her mouth.

"Tinkie." I struggled to get away from the air bag and my seat belt. Steam was coming from the car, and I could smell gasoline. It could go up in flames at any time.

There wasn't another vehicle in sight, and in the darkness, I was afraid anyone coming up on the curve might not see the wreck until it was too late. But there was nothing I could do about that. My concern was Tinkie.

I managed to force my door open and hurry around to her side of the car. "Tinkie!" I choked back the tears. "Tinkie, come on."

Her door was jammed, but I pulled and tugged until I got it open. She was so small that the air bag had struck her full in the face rather than the chest as it had me. But the good news was that I could easily pull her out of the car once I'd undone her seat belt.

"Tinkie," I whispered urgently. "Wake up."

She had to wake up. This whole movie adventure had been a nightmare from the get-go. Tinkie had been hurt numerous times. Normally I was the one who was injured, and that was far easier to take than seeing her so lifeless.

I felt for a pulse and found one, and it seemed strong and steady. My worst fears began to dissipate, and I lifted her into my arms and walked across the road, away from the car, to a small gravel area by the shoulder.

I gently eased her down onto the ground. For such a petite person, she was rather heavy. I looked over at the car, and in the darkness I could see it was a total loss. The front was accordioned almost to the driver's seat.

"Tinkie, that was a close one." It made me feel better to talk to her, even if she was unconscious.

"Could you carry me to another place? These rocks are uncomfortable."

"Tinkie!" I knelt down beside her and helped her into a sitting position. "I thought you were knocked out."

"I was, for a bit. I came to while you were carrying me. I'm glad I didn't have to try to lift you."

"Good point." I sat down beside her so we could lean against each other. "I'd be willing to bet ten thousand dollars that someone damaged the brake line on the car. Probably a small puncture so the brake fluid leaked out slowly."

Tinkie was feeling her face to see how much damage had been inflicted. She ignored my bet, which told me she agreed with my deductions.

"You don't think Graf has been abducted, do you? You think he's involved." I spoke softly.

She hesitated. "I think he could be. He left you that message luring you up to the house when he wasn't there. Sarah Booth, he wasn't at the house and he hasn't been. That was a setup. And we know there were at least two people involved in all of this."

She was right. I couldn't argue it if I wanted to, but I also couldn't believe Graf would do such a thing. "But why, Tinkie? Why would Graf do it?"

"I can think of a few reasons, but so can you if you put your mind to it."

Greed, sex, revenge, lust, envy—always the same basic motivators when it came to murder. None of them looked good on the man I'd grown to care about. And none of them truly fit him, either.

We heard the sound of a siren in the distance. Sound travels a long way in the clear mountain air, so we knew we still had a bit to wait. "You're overlooking the possibility that Graf might be another victim," I said.

"No, I'm not, Sarah Booth. I just don't want to think what may have happened to him if Jovan got to him first."

Tinkie's dark words hung in the sky as the red lights of the ambulance strobed around the hairpin curve that could have killed us.

CHAPTER THIRTY

To my utter amazement, Sheriff King showed up as the paramedics were giving us both a nearly clean bill of health. While we were banged and bruised, we weren't seriously injured. King had heard the call and come to check on us. I was even more stunned when he sent a deputy to sit with Sweetie and Chablis because Tinkie refused to do anything until we knew the dogs were safe.

The tow truck pulled the totaled Cadillac away, and King gave Tinkie and me a ride down the mountain to the movie lot. He was quiet, but the look on his face made me anxious. I was used to snappish, not pensive. The fact that he was nice scared me.

As we rode to the studio, dawn brightened the sky. Funny, but the weather in California was seasonless—paradise by anyone's measure—but I found it annoying. The last winter at Dahlia House had been lonely and on some mornings bitterly cold. The summers were often unbearable. But weather marked the passage of time in a rhythm that was familiar.

We were almost to the studio when King began to talk. "I have some information on the situation," he said. "I've got men at the studio, and I just talked with one of my captains. We believe Jovan is holed up on a sound stage with hostages."

"Hostages? Plural?" My voice broke.

He cast me a quick glance. "Two or more. We can't be sure. We've got surveillance equipment trained on the building, but the visibility isn't great."

"Are the hostages alive?"

He rubbed his chin. "As far as we can tell. But I'm not going to kid you, this is a bad situation."

"Has anyone tried to talk to her?" Tinkie asked.

"A hostage negotiator called and she said if we called again, she'd kill the people she's holding. And I believe she will. She's coming unraveled fast."

As I watched the sun come up on one of the most beautiful places I'd ever been, I was paralyzed by dread. The car seemed to crawl forward, and while Tinkie asked questions, I couldn't make out any of the words.

I felt her hand on my shoulder, and I squeezed her fingers to let her know I appreciated all she was doing. Graf was okay. I had to believe that. Somehow he'd gotten caught up in this mess, but there was no reason for Jovan to kill him.

Except that she'd killed Suzy Dutton and almost killed Estelle, not to mention taking a swipe at me and Tinkie. Homicidal maniacs didn't need a reason.

As we turned into the studio lot, I saw the patrol cars, a line of eight, waiting for the sheriff. Snipers with high-powered rifles stood talking beside the cars. This was serious business, and while Grady King was calm, he was prepared for anything.

"Graf is okay, Sarah Booth." Tinkie spoke with the confidence of a friend. "Feel it? He's fine. Don't worry."

"Sure," I said, though I felt only the sensation of dropping into a void.

King stopped and we got out. He talked with several of the SWAT team members, then came back to us.

"It's like this. We can see one man we believe to be Marquez tied in a chair. There's no sign of the second man. We can see Jovan pacing back and forth, talking to the man in the chair. We've used the bullhorn to alert her that we're law enforcement and that she should surrender. She's not inclined to listen."

"What's your plan?" I asked.

"We can't get a clear shot on her. We need someone to try to talk to her. She won't answer her cell phone."

"I'll go talk to her," I said. I had to get to Graf and make sure he was alive.

King assessed me. "You'd risk your life?"

"Yes." I didn't want to. I had a pretty good life. If something happened to me without producing the Delaney heir that Jitty kept hounding me about, I'd never hear the end of it. Jitty would haunt me in the afterlife just as she did now.

"No!" Tinkie stepped forward. "Let me do it. She has reason to hate Sarah Booth because of the movie. I'm not involved with any of it. She may listen to me."

"She whacked you on the head and kicked Chablis," I reminded her. "You're as vulnerable as I am. And you look like a raccoon. She won't talk to you."

The bruises from the wreck had already begun to settle around Tinkie's eyes. She did look remarkably like the masked bandit of the animal world.

"She'll be a lot more receptive to me," Tinkie insisted.

"Ladies." King held up a hand. "I've never seen two civilians argue for the chance to get shot."

"You've never met a true Mississippi gal," Tinkie said.

"And hope never to again," King said under his breath. He looked at me and then Tinkie. "She's going in." He pointed at Tinkie. "Get her a vest and as much protection as we can," he said to one of the men, who led Tinkie away to make a Kevlar selection.

"You can't let her risk herself," I told him. "She has a husband and friends who love her."

He only arched an eyebrow. "All we need is for her to get

the door open. She's short and if we have to, we can take the shot right over her head."

The idea was awful. But I could see from King's and Tinkie's faces that they were going full ahead. "I've got to find a toilet," I said. "I'm going to be sick."

"That way," a young deputy pointed.

Vomit was such an effective threat. They were only too glad that I was ambulatory and could clean myself up. I slipped away without anyone giving me a second thought.

The sound stage looked to me like a huge warehouse with metal doors that slid on runners. Inside, there were different sets and climate-controlled conditions. I had no idea which set Jovan might be occupying with her prisoners, but I would find out.

As I passed a patrol car, I saw a canister of pepper spray on the seat. I reached in and took it. Then I was running, heading behind the building, hoping that there might be a way for me to slip inside before Tinkie could risk her life.

I heard Sheriff King cursing a blue streak, but I was too far away for him to stop me, unless he shot me, and I was reasonably sure he wouldn't do that. Not yet.

When I made it to a corner of the building, I pressed myself against it and took some deep breaths. To my horror, I saw that Tinkie was proceeding toward the building, too. She was going straight to the doors.

I pushed off the wall and began circling behind. Although I couldn't see them, I knew snipers surrounded the building. Moving quickly, I ran along the back looking for a window or door or some opening where I could push myself inside. I had to hurry. Tinkie and Graf both were in danger.

I was on the north side when I found a window with a cracked pane. If I did this wrong, tragedy could result. Using my elbow, I cracked the glass more and began to pull it out piece by piece. When I could get my hand and arm inside, I unlocked the window and gently raised it.

In another three minutes, I was inside, completely disori-ented but able to hear the sound of someone knocking.

"Go away or I'll kill Milieu," Jovan yelled.

I followed her voice, tracking silently through the huge building.

"It's Tinkie Richmond," I heard my partner say. "Will you please talk to me? Jovan, your mother is worried sick about you."

"Yeah, right. She was so worried she gave me away at birth."

The last and final piece clicked. Tinkie had been right. The parents on Jovan's Web site had adopted her. Her mother, the lovely Ivana, had not wanted to raise the daughter that was a product of . . . her marriage or an affair? Was Federico Marquez her father?

I moved steadily closer to the sound of Tinkie pounding on the door. "I can help you, Jovan. You have a career and fans and Federico cares for you. You don't want to hurt him."

Don't go there, Tinkie, I wanted to shout at her. Federico might be her father. And her lover. Shades of *Chinatown*. Don't go there. But it was too late.

I saw a flood of daylight as the door opened and Jovan reached out and snatched Tinkie inside just as several slugs whammed into the side of the building.

"You were trying to set me up to be shot."

I crept forward. Jovan gripped Tinkie's shirt.

"It's not too late for you to give up," Tinkie said. "I'll try to help you."

Jovan pushed her back so hard that Tinkie fell. She stayed on the floor.

"You can help me," Jovan said. "You can watch as I gun the man who destroyed my family and my life." She stepped around Tinkie and went to a set designed as a bedroom. Fed-erico was sitting in a chair, tied so tightly that he couldn't move.

Jovan stepped behind him and picked up a knife on a small table. Quick as a flash, she grabbed Federico's hair and pulled his head back, revealing his throat. She passed the blade in front of him, and for a moment I thought she'd slit his jugular.

"Federico Marquez slept with my mother to get even with my father." Jovan kept repositioning the knife. At any moment she could easily kill him.

"So Vincent Day is your father," Tinkie said. She walked closer. She was calm and poised. Tinkie had courage.

"That bitch Carlita seduced my father. She used him to try to manipulate Federico. And then Federico turned on his best friend and tried to ruin him. My father's last two films ended in bankruptcy because Federico convinced the backers to pull out."

The man tied in the chair began to struggle and fight against his bonds and the gag.

"Why don't you let Federico speak?" Tinkie asked. "Have you given him a chance to tell you his side?"

"I don't need his side. His pathetic daughter told me how he'd killed Carlita and wouldn't allow the children to see her. He's a vile man and he deserves to die. I'm going to make sure it happens."

"Carlita died of anorexia," Tinkie said. "No one killed her. She killed herself."

Tinkie was getting to Jovan. I inched around to the flank position. If Tinkie could just distract her, I could knock her down and douse her with pepper spray.

"Federico loved his children and his wife. Carlita was ill. She needed validation of her beauty, and she did some bad things to people, especially to Federico and his children. And to you and your parents. Federico is as much a victim as you are."

"That's not true!" Her rage was instantaneous. "How dare you!" She started to lunge at Tinkie and I hurled myself out of the shadows and at her legs. I took her down at the knees like an Ole Miss tackle. She hit hard and before she could recover, I pressed the button on the pepper spray and sent a thin jet of it directly into her eyes.

"I'll kill you," she raged, thrashing and choking. "I'll kill all of you."

Tinkie found an extension cord and together we bound the model's hands behind her back. "I think you're killing days are over, Jovan. And just so you know, Estelle is going to be fine."

We left Jovan on the floor and untied Federico. He looked like he might keel over, but he assured us he hadn't been harmed. While Tinkie went to signal the deputies inside, I knelt beside Jovan.

"Where's Graf?" I demanded.

"Screw you," she said. "He's as good as dead."

I grasped a fistful of hair. "I swear to you, if you don't tell me where Graf is, I will snatch you bald-headed."

Something in my tone must have convinced her. "In the trunk on set eight."

As King and the deputies entered the building, I was rushing to set eight. It was built to be an attic, and I saw the trunk instantly. It opened with a creak, and I found Graf bound and gagged.

For a moment I thought he was dead, but he opened his eyes when I removed the bandanna she'd wadded into his mouth.

"Sarah Booth," he said. "I knew you'd come."

Tinkie had walked up behind me. In the background, Sheriff King was reading Jovan her rights. Tinkie helped me loosen the bonds that held Graf, and he climbed out of the trunk bruised, but none the worse for wear.

I can't say for sure who embraced whom, but we were holding each other like we intended to graft.

"Oh, no." Tinkie spoke so softly that I thought something had happened to her. But when we followed the finger she was pointing, we saw it.

What looked like miles and miles of film had been pulled from canisters and burned. Cameras were bashed and destroyed.

We ran toward the devastation, but I knew what it was. Jovan had achieved her goal of destroying the movie. Every scene Federico had shot was ruined. In one vengeful, insane act, she'd changed all of our lives.

CHAPTER THIRTY-ONE

Graf, Sweetie Pie, and I stood on the tarmac of the private airport and waved good-bye to Tinkie and Chablis. On the flight to Los Angeles from Costa Rica, Tinkie had formed a strong friendship; Charlize was loaning Tinkie her private jet for a quick trip home.

My heart ached as she waved out the door and then disappeared into the plane. She reappeared at a window, waving Chablis's little paw.

"What's Federico going to do?" I asked Graf.

He'd spent the morning with the director. Not a single frame of the movie was salvageable.

Jovan was in jail, charged with Suzy Dutton's murder, kidnapping, and a dozen other offenses. Estelle was recuperating in Petaluma. She was scheduled to fly to L.A. to stay with her father.

"Federico doesn't know. He can't afford to reshoot the film. His backers have abandoned him. They don't care that none of this was his fault."

"I'm not so certain I want to do it again." I couldn't believe I was speaking those words. "I mean, it's fun and all, but I—"

"You were far more involved in solving the case than you were in acting."

Graf said it so well.

"I don't know. Can't I do both?"

He smiled. "I don't see why not. You can be biprofessional."

My cell phone rang and I saw with surprise the number from the Sunflower County Sheriff's Office. I answered cautiously.

"Sarah Booth, I'm trying to find Tinkie. It's important." Coleman's voice was strained.

"She just boarded a plane to head home," I said. "What's wrong?"

He hesitated, and I felt a sharp blade to the gut. Whatever had transpired between us, I'd never given him reason to doubt me.

"It's Oscar," he said. "He's deathly ill."

He could have slugged me and I wouldn't have been more shocked. "What's wrong? What happened?"

Coleman took a breath. "We're not certain, but it's bad. Remember the old Graystone Estate? The bank has held the mortgage on it for years, and Oscar had a buyer, so he went out to check the property. When he got back, he wasn't feeling well. Two hours later, his secretary found him in his office, unconscious."

Before I could even think, I was signaling frantically at Tinkie to stop the plane. She quit waving Chablis's paw and made a face at me.

"Stop the plane," I told Graf. "You have to stop it. I've got to get on."

"What's wrong?"

"Just stop that plane."

While Graf went to find someone in authority, I ran to the plane with Sweetie right at my heels. Tinkie's face reflected horror, but in a moment the door of the plane reopened. She came out.

"What?" she yelled above the roar of the airport.

Before I told her, I had to know the extent of it. I spoke into the telephone. "Coleman, how bad is Oscar?"

"Sarah Booth, it could be fatal."

I made my decision. "We're both headed home." I couldn't abandon Tinkie with Oscar so sick. What I was really worried about was telling Tinkie about Oscar.

"I'll call you when I land," I said to Coleman before I hung up.

As I stood on the steps of the plane, I saw Graf. I ran toward him and explained briefly, that Tinkie's husband was seriously ill.

"You're a good friend, Sarah Booth. Do you want me to come?"

I shook my head. Tinkie was going to require my undivided attention. And Graf's career was hanging in tatters. He needed to be where he could address a million issues.

"Stay here. As soon as Oscar stabilizes, I'll be back."

He kissed me. "Go. Call me when you get there. And be careful."

I kissed him with my heart tearing in two. But then Sweetie and I were on the plane, and in less than fifteen minutes, I'd ripped my friend's world apart and sat holding her as she cried.

We were headed back to Zinnia, but not as victors. Oscar's sudden illness could change our worlds forever. He was a fit and strong man, and it would take a serious illness to bring him down. But Coleman's tone of voice had frightened me. This wasn't just a case of the flu.

The truth was, I didn't know what we might find in Sunflower County. But one thing was for sure, I wasn't about to let Tinkie face it alone.

I sat on the steps of Dahlia House in the warm spring sun, my cell phone at my side, waiting for word. Tinkie was at the hospital. She wasn't allowed to see Oscar, except through a glass window, but she refused to leave her spot in the hall.

I'd spent most of the night beside my friend, but I'd come home to check on Sweetie Pie. She was fine, and the cotton planted around Dahlia House was a tender green, extending to the horizon in long rows.

I heard the squeak of rubber wheels, and I looked up to see who had a baby stroller at Dahlia House. But it wasn't a stroller. It was a wheelchair, and in it sat a chocolate rendition of Franklin D. Roosevelt.

"We have nothing to fear but fear itself." Jitty pushed up the small glasses that perched on her nose.

"What are you doing?" I asked. "Look, you can play Marilyn or Lana or Halle or just about anyone. But I don't think you can pull off FDR."

"I'm only going for the HBO movie, not a major feature release. Kenneth Branagh is hard to imitate. That man's got some moves."

I put my head in my hands. As glad as I was to see Jitty right back here on the front porch of Dahlia House, I was too worried about Tinkie and Oscar to enjoy her games.

The wheelchair creaked up to my side. "Did you know that polio victims were treated as if they had the plague? People were terrified of them. Sometimes no one would help them at all, and the high fevers killed them. Strange that it was a virus that could be controlled by a simple vaccine."

She was spoon-feeding me hope, and I mustered a smile for her. "Welcome home," I said.

"Right back at you." She pushed up the glasses that weren't meant for her smooth nose.

"What are we going to do?" I asked.

"Same as always, Sarah Booth. Fight. It's in your blood and in your bones. You fight for what you love and hold dear."

"Tinkie will die if Oscar doesn't make it."

"No, she won't. She may wish she died, but she won't keel over."

I swallowed back a lump. She was right. Loss made a person want to die, but it just wasn't that easy to lie down and quit.

"What am I going to do about Hollywood?"

"You know better than to ask me that question. Besides, you got to make the choice. Listen to your heart, Sarah Booth."

"I got my wish." I felt like crying. "For a few weeks, I was a movie star."

"Indeed you were. No doubt about that part."

I didn't even have the energy to make a drink. I just sat on the steps and watched the electric green leaves of the sycamore trees that lined the driveway dance in the spring breeze. This was the perfect time of year in Mississippi. This was the time of new birth and growth and high hopes and expectations.

But I was torn between two careers, two places, two men, and two times—the past and the future. But for this moment, I could pass the decision on all of them. I had only to stay and help my friend through the toughest time of her life. After that—well, I would worry about that tomorrow.

"Good decision," Jitty said. She was tired of the wheelchair, so she stood. "I think you need a drink."

"I thought you were worried I'd end up like Great-uncle Lyle Crabtree."

"It's in the blood, that cravin' for the drink. But somethin' tells me you gone need a whole lot of liquor before this is over."

"I hope you're wrong, Jitty." But as I closed the door of Dahlia House on the most perfect of spring days, my gut told me that she was right.

Here is an excerpt from

GREEDY BONES

**The next mystery in the Sarah Booth Delaney series,
now available from St. Martins / Minotaur Paperbacks!**

Dusk is a tricky time of day in the Mississippi Delta. Pinks,
mauves, and lavenders illuminate the western sky while
cobalt blue creeps forward in the east. Unlike dawn, dusk is
a time of ending, and I've never done well with good-byes.
Even with a lover at my side, or a friend, or my gallant horse
and hound, the close of a day carries a twinge of sadness.

Today, I wonder if I can find the strength to climb the
front steps of Dahlia House, home of the Delaney family for
nearly two hundred years.

Things are worse than even I imagined. Oscar Richmond,
the husband of my partner in the Delaney Detective Agency, is
dying. There seems to be nothing medical experts can do.
Now realtors Regina Campbell and her assistant Luann Bigley
are showing the same symptoms: a fever high enough to
cook a brain, chills, a rash that spreads by the minute and then
erupts in draining pustules, and, finally, coma.

There is no doubt that some terrible illness has settled upon
the land and the people I love. I am heartsick and scared.

"Bad times a'comin' to Zinnia, Sarah Booth."

Jitty's voice was soft and distinctly black, and I knew
Dahlia House's resident haint was with me.

"If I turn around and you're wearing a robe of many colors

and you say something like you're going to lead your people out of Egypt, *I'm* going to figure a way to exorcise you from this house," I warned her.

Though I would never, ever dare to let her know, I was so damn glad to hear her voice, I wanted to jump up and kiss her.

"You might consider revisitin' Sunday school. You're mixing your Bible stories. Moses led the people out of Egypt, not Joseph."

"And the walls came tumbling down." I shifted so I could take a gander at my ancestral ghost. Jitty had a tendency to skip through the decades to find costumes that flattered her latte skin and calendar-girl figure. What I saw shook me.

"Brother, can you spare a dime?" She wore tattered rags and held out a cardboard cigar box that I recognized had once held my collection of toy cowboys and horses. Dirt smudged her face, and there was a new gauntness to her high cheekbones.

"Are you sick?" Even asking caused me to leap to my feet and stride toward her. As far as I knew, ghosts didn't get sick, but my last adventure in Costa Rica had taught me that I knew almost nothing about the rules and guidelines of the Great Beyond.

"Soul-sick," she answered.

She was barefoot, her naked legs dusted with a haze of dirt. I'd honestly never seen her in such a condition. If I wore sweatpants to the corner gas station, she chewed my butt. Any slip of appearance and I put the future of the Delaney womb at risk. In other words, a potential stud might see me unadorned and be thrown off his desire to breed me on the spot.

"They run out of soap and hot water in the non-corporeal realm?" I asked, striving for a lighter note.

"I remember when the Confederate soldiers came through here, marchin' toward home after the war. Starvin', wounded, carried on by desperation. Same thing happened after the

Flood of 1927. Poor folks barely hangin' on. Then again, during the Great Depression. Hardship and hard times."

Hell, if I'd been depressed earlier, Jitty now had me two steps away from finding a cotton rope in the tack room.

"Stop it." I put my hands on my hips. "This isn't doing either of us any good. We're both worried about Oscar, Regina, and Luann. I'm terrified that if Oscar dies, Tinkie will give up, too. I can't have you out here looking like a ragamuffin from a Dickens novel, spouting doom and gloom." Tears blurred my vision, which only made me angry. "Stop it, damn it."

When I blinked away the tears, Jitty was staring at me. Though she was still dirty and wearing rags, her face was rounder. The corners of her full mouth slowly tilted upward. "You know, for one second, you looked exactly like your great-great granny. You got Alice's fightin' spirit. I knew it was under all that mopin' and self-pity. I just had to find the right button to push to rouse it up."

I had been played.

On the heels of my righteous anger, though, was relief. Jitty may have used foul means, but she'd managed to rattle me out of my maudlin mood. I was fighting mad, and that's exactly what she meant to accomplish.

"Oscar is going to be fine. Everyone is going to be fine." I swept my arm out to include the entire county. "Anything else is unacceptable."

"May I make a suggestion?"

Whenever Jitty asked permission to do anything, it always meant trouble. "No."

She grinned. "You know 'no' don't mean 'no' when you say it like that."

I leveled my gaze into hers. "If you say one word about my empty womb—"

She waved me to silence. "It's about Tinkie."

"Go ahead."

"She looks to you, Sarah Booth. You hold strong for her.

Through all the hard times, you stand steady. Folks got to have that strength when they can't see the next day."

"Sage advice. The problem is how to go about it when I'm as scared as she is."

"You might crack open some of those old magazines in the attic. Once upon a time there was a man with polio who taught a nation how to hold on." Her tone had softened, and I couldn't help but wonder what of her own memories she'd stirred.

"I'm not illiterate," I said. "I know about FDR." But my words were lost on a sudden breeze that swept across the newly planted cotton fields silhouetted black against the fiery gold-peach glory of a dying day. From behind me the sound of a car approached.

Graf! Somehow Graf Milieu, my handsome lover, had managed to escape his Hollywood duties and come to stand with me. But when I turned, it was to see the tan and brown colors of the Sunflower County sheriff's cruiser pulling up at the steps. In the front seat sat the tall figure of Sheriff Coleman Peters, the man who'd broken my heart—and falsely charged me with murder.

He got out and slowly came up the steps. In the near darkness I couldn't see his face, and I was glad he couldn't see mine. In the long and complicated years of our relationship—from high school adversaries, to the initial contentiousness of my first P.I. case and, finally, to the blossoming and acknowledgment of unrequited love—we fought a strong and powerful attraction that bound us. Only recently had we accepted that love wasn't enough to overcome the obstacles in our path. Through it all, I had never dreaded seeing Coleman. Now, I couldn't breathe. My lungs constricted. Because I knew that nothing less than tragic news would bring Coleman to Dahlia House. He'd come in person to tell me that Oscar was dead. I made a small sound, seal-like, and staggered.

"Oscar is still alive, Sarah Booth." Coleman was at my side, his familiar arms easing me into one of the rocking chairs on the front porch. "I didn't come to tell you anything bad. I tried to call, but no one answered. I left messages."

I held on to one fact—Oscar was alive. At last I drew in sweet oxygen. The strength returned to my limbs. "Thank you," I managed.

"I didn't mean to scare you."

I nodded. "I shouldn't jump to conclusions." Inhaling deeply again, I asked the logical question. "What are you doing here?"

"The illness is spreading."

A swallow worked down his throat, and again my brain seized. "Not Tinkie!" She'd been at the hospital since we got in from Los Angeles. But Oscar, Regina, and Luann were isolated. Tinkie hadn't been near them.

"No, not Tinkie." His voice was tired. "It's Gordon."

Gordon Walters was one of Coleman's two deputies. "But—how is he?"

"He's in the isolation ward with the others. Doc Sawyer is worried." He lifted his chin a fraction, a signal I'd learned to read as meaning he'd made a tough decision. "Sarah Booth, this could be serious. I'm going to call in the CDC and ask them for help."

The Centers for Disease Control was headquartered in Atlanta. If asked, they'd send in specially trained agents to try to find the source of the illness. "That's smart, I guess. Doc doesn't know what this is, but he isn't sure it's contagious. The isolation ward is a precaution."

"We have to determine what this is. The CDC is our best bet, I think."

Five months ago, the use of "we" would have made my heart sing. Now, though, I felt pain and sadness. My brief stint in Hollywood had changed me. Success had shown me my strengths as well as my limitations.

"Will you help?" Coleman asked.

"Don't ever doubt it. I'll do anything I can." In the gloaming of an April evening, I caught the hint of a sad smile on his face.

"I knew you would."

"I feel responsible for this. Tinkie was with me in Costa Rica and Hollywood because of my film career." When a killer destroyed all the footage of Federico Marquez's remake of *Body Heat*, my fledgling career was pretty much tanked. Tinkie would have been home in Mississippi taking care of Oscar if she hadn't been so worried about me.

"She made her own choice. It's the sixty-forty rule of life." He gazed out over the long stretch of cotton fields that were part of my land.

"Is this a Daddy's Girl rule?" Coleman was far removed from the pampered world of the DGs, but he'd grown up surrounded by them.

"Nowhere close." He was amused by my wary tone. "This is one that even you can use."

"So tell me."

"When you're a child, you make decisions that are totally, absolutely, irrevocably correct. The best an adult can hope for is sixty-forty. Sixty percent good and forty percent bad. In an adult world, it can never be one hundred percent right. Statistically impossible."

I considered this. My mind ran through my most recent actions—playing Maggie the Cat last January, going to Hollywood, sleeping with Graf. Damned if Coleman wasn't right. While my choices had been good ones, they'd all cost me something. Some had come at a high price.

"Okay, I give you the sixty-forty rule."

"Hollywood and a film career was what you needed to do. The right thing. Sure, it had a downside. But 'mostly good' is the best any of us can hope for. Sixty percent. You have that in spades, Sarah Booth."

"Thank you, Coleman." I wondered how he rated his decision not to dump his crazy, lying, conniving bitch of a
wife. Oddly enough, he told me.

"Connie was a one percent moment. I chose pride and
honor over love. That was one of the worst mistakes of my
life. I've filed for divorce, but that's not what I came to tell
you. Tinkie is still up at the hospital. She looks like she's going to drop. Doc Sawyer wants to sedate her, but she won't
let him. Maybe you could talk to her. Take your buddy Cece
along for muscle."

"I'll go now." But I didn't move out of the rocking chair.
My body was paralyzed by the revelation that Coleman fully
understood the depth of his choices. He knew. Too late, but
he knew.

"I'll call you tomorrow and fill you in on everything I've
discovered," he said. "I do need your help with this. The CDC
would be at the courthouse tomorrow morning."

"You can count on me." Funny how only ten minutes before, I was hoping that my white knight would ride up and I
would be able to rely on him.

Coleman got in the patrol car, the window down. The sweet
spring breeze, tainted now in the darkness with jasmine, that
saddest of all fragrances, filled the air.

"Good night, Sarah Booth," he said.

"Good night."

Tinkie stood in the hospital corridor watching her sick
husband. A clear glass window separated her from Oscar's
bed as effectively as an ocean. The impulse to rush forward
and catch her before she keeled over was hard on me.

Before I could act on my gut feeling, Cece Dee Falcon,
journalist and friend, blew by me and grabbed Tinkie's elbow.

"Tinkie, dahling, you look like caramelized shit. That
could be shit dressed in an exquisite sauce, but shit nonethe-
less." Cece gave Tinkie her sternest look.

I hurried forward and pinched Cece as hard as I could o
her taut, firm derriere. She had the unfair advantage of mal
molecular structure that gave her lean hips and sleek mus
cles. Cece, who had once been Cecil, was the society edito
of the local *Zinnia Dispatch*. Against the opinion of he
family, the town, and most of her friends, she had becom
the woman she was destined to be. I adored her.

"Don't fuss at me, Cece," Tinkie said. "I can't help it."

Never one to yield to badgering, Tinkie was at the end c
her tether. She was about to collapse. I gently took her othe
arm. "Let's get some coffee."

She pressed her palms to the glass. "I can't leave him. I'1
afraid if I do, he'll give up."

I glanced beyond her at Oscar, and my heart contractec
He lay in a bed, a ventilator pumping oxygen into his lung:
Tubes fed fluids and medication into his veins while othe
tubes drained things away. Sores covered his mouth and eye
lids. No telling what horrors were hidden beneath the sheet

At a slight angle were the beds of Regina Campbell an
Luann Bigley. They looked equally awful. Members of the
families were camped farther down the hallway.

Doc had created an isolation ward out of what had bee
the neonatal unit. A federal grant had built a new facility fc
Sunflower County babies, and this space, equipped to qua
antine patients, had been empty. Until now.

As I stood there, shocked into silence by Oscar's ap
pearance, several nurses, each wearing protective clothin;
wheeled in another bed. Deputy Gordon Walters lay upon
looking already dead. His condition, if it could be judged b
appearance, was more dire than Oscar's.

Tinkie stumbled, and Cece and I held her up as we battle
our fears.

"You need something to eat." Cece attempted to dra'
Tinkie away from the window. "We'll go to the hospit:
waiting room. That's not three minutes away."

Tinkie shook her head. "Oscar knows I'm here. He'll now if I'm gone."

I found my cell phone. "I'll call Millie and get her to fix a late." Millie ran the local café where we often met to discuss cases or simply to gossip. She was a big part of our close-knit group. I placed an order for chicken-fried steak, mashed potatoes and gravy, fresh green beans, and dewberry cobbler.

"Hold her up," Cece said, waving me to take Tinkie's arm. "I'll be right back." She disappeared down the hallway, her high heels efficiently smacking the linoleum tile.

"Is there any change?" I asked Tinkie.

"No. I saw Doc about four hours ago, before they found ordon. Doc doesn't know what it is or how to treat it, but it seems that all of the victims have visited one place. An old antation. Coleman is checking that out."

"What treatment is Doc using?"

"Oscar's on the most powerful antibiotic I.V. they have. hey've tried steroids." Her fingers brushed across the glass indow of the isolation ward. "Doc has consulted with ecialists at Johns Hopkins. They considered transferring m, but until they can figure out what this is and how it's ansmitted . . ."

I rubbed her arms. She felt cold to my touch. "Where's hablis?" Chablis was her dustmop of a dog that long ago as the source of our friendship—and partnership in the detective agency.

"At home. Can you keep her for a few days?"

"Sure. I'll get her when I pick up your food."

"Make way, dahlings." Cece returned carrying a chair and eposited it so that Tinkie could sit and monitor the window.

"Does anyone know what happened?" I asked.

Tinkie's blue eyes were glassy with fatigue and near ock. We'd been home twelve hours, and she hadn't left the spital hallway.

"Oscar and the bank manage the lease on the Carlisle es tate," Tinkie explained. "It's a thousand-acre plantation Eri Carlisle and her brother, Luther, own. Luther called Osca yesterday morning and told him he had a buyer. He wante Oscar to make sure the house and property were in good or der, so Oscar rode out there and looked around."

For a long moment there were only the sounds of tw nurses talking at a nearby desk. At last Tinkie spoke agair "He went back to the bank, ate lunch, and about two o'clock Margene went in to give him some papers. That's when sh found him on the floor, moaning, with those ghastly sore breaking out all over him. Doc said when Oscar got to th hospital, his temperature was . . . a hundred and five." Sh covered her mouth with her hand to hold back an anguishe rasp.

"When did Regina and Luann get sick?" Cece asked.

"That same day. Later in the evening."

"And Gordon?"

Tinkie looked so lost. "He went out to the Carlisle plac around six o'clock. From what I understand he checked th house, walked the area, then went home to change clothe He called in for medical help from there. He was nearly ur conscious by the time the paramedics got to him. The onl strange thing he said was that the cotton at the Carlisle plac was extremely high, like a late-August crop instead of new planted. Oscar had told Margene the same thing."

"And Regina and Luann? Were they at the Carlisle plar tation?"

"Coleman has confirmed that. They went out, hoping t list the property." Tinkie rubbed at her eyes.

"High cotton," I mused. "That would seem to be a goo thing. A farmer might get two crops a year instead of one there was a variety that developed this fast."

Tinkie fumbled in her pocket and brought out a tissu "As far as we know, neither Oscar nor Gordon saw anythi unusual except the cotton. Of course, they're not talking now."

I relayed the news about the CDC to both of them. Cece met it with a frown. "Are we positive that it's the Carlisle place that Oscar, Gordon, and the realtors have in common?"

That was an excellent question, and one that needed an immediate answer.

Cece picked up Tinkie's hand. "You're going to have to help us with this, Tink. We can't do it without you."

The blank look she gave Cece concerned me. "It doesn't matter where he got it, Cece. The only thing that matters is that he gets over it."

That wasn't my partner talking. That was exhaustion and desperation and fear. Tinkie loved Zinnia and the people of Sunflower County. She hadn't yet projected this illness to other residents. In her mind, it was contained within the walls of the hospital, within the room where her husband and three others lay dying.

"I'll get the food and Chablis," I told them.

"I'll stay here," Cece told me. "Just hurry."